REALITY

Daniel A. Liut

BQB
Virginia

A first version was published in 1995 in Argentina in Spanish, by author Daniel A. Liut, under the title Realidad, and name J. C. Ediciones. The 1995 version (ISBN 987-95472-0-9) is substantially different from this book's English version.

This is a work of fiction. All of the characters, names, incidents, organizations, and dialogue in this novel are either the products of the author's imagination or are used fictitiously.

Published in the United States by BQB Publishing
(Boutique of Quality Books Publishing Company)
www.bqbpublishing.com

Printed in the United States of America

978-1-939371-52-2 (p)
978-1-939371-53-9 (e)

Library of Congress Control Number: 2017939280

Book design by Robin Krauss, www.bookformatters.com

Cover art by Michael de Jong. Interior arts by Dan Brown, Ethan Thornsberry, Michael de Jong, and Jes Cole. Insignia logos and photo courtesy of the author.

First editor: Alex Padalka
Second editor: Jan Hall

To all who would not let reality die.

Acknowledgments

I am grateful for the advice and support of my wife, Joan. I want to recognize, very specially, for her hidden yet valuable immense contribution during the editing process of the book.

I also want to thank the BQB team for their commitment to excellence, especially to Terri Leidich, President of BQB, for making *Reality* possible and for her constant support; to Jan Hall, for her dedicated work and large contributions in her role as project manager; and to Alex Padalka, in his very valuable role as editor, which helped *Reality* take its final shape.

Foreword

The events related in this book took place in cultures and environments dissimilar to the cultures of Earth. Preserving the integrity of the accounts, while making the narrative accessible, has been a significant challenge. The language used by the characters, the descriptions of places, the customs, and the different technologies had to be adjusted to meet a common reference with the reader. A small but clear example is the type of units often used in the narrative: feet, Fahrenheit temperatures, twenty-four-hour days, etc. Many of the names that carry a meaning were translated into names that would suggest similar connotations—like Clara, for example, which means clear, bright. If the translation of a word would make it lose its intended musical beauty, the corresponding rendering was done with the aim of matching, or at least evoking, the original pronunciation.

The author wants to apologize for the inescapable inaccuracies involved in this adaptation.

Contents

CHAPTER 1

The Voyage

1.

Trying to stay up late to study was definitely not working that night. Most of the afternoon, Duncan had been too busy with matters not in line with his studies: reading a blog of a girl he had dated a couple of weeks before. He had been spending a lot of time doing that, and the resulting weariness was now overtaking his weakened concentration. Lying down on the floor, he flipped his shoes off and propped his feet on the lintel of a window in front of him. Beyond the pane, the moon was rising gently over a lonely silo. Isolated as it was from the small university town, this old house had its advantages beyond the relatively low rent.

Duncan's thoughts went back to the girl from his hometown. She was mature for her age and definitively attractive, facts that had not passed unnoticed by his friends. Although he had not developed a strong attachment to her, the one-date experience had set a standard of the type of female beauty he would seek in the future. But how realistic would that be? Looking vaguely at the stars, Duncan let his mind fly to the more plausible dreams of space exploration. Plausible, he thought, because a special space program for graduate students had recently started in his college. That was new, promising, but uncertain; yet it had been one of the main reasons for his applying there, despite the well-known demands and pressures, which he was now starting to face.

As Duncan pondered, he began to grow aware of some peculiar activity. For a while he dismissed it, thinking it was a byproduct of his late-night daydreaming. But now he began feeling, very clearly,

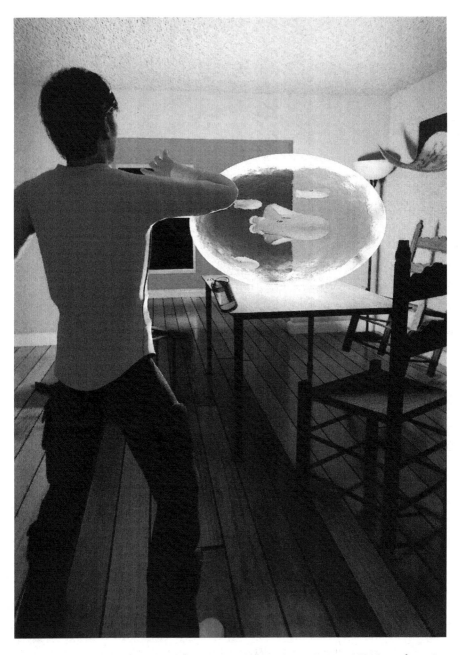

The objects were glowing with a surreal incandescence, mildly but sharply
heaving, pitching, and rolling in a way that struck
Duncan as menacing.

strange vibrations on the floor. Whatever it was, it was happening within the house. He looked at the doorway and noticed that the lights from the small corridor that connected to the living room were shimmering irregularly. He was not certain, but some low-pitched noises seemed to be coming from the same general area.

Standing up with caution, Duncan stepped into the corridor and edged closer to the living-room door. For a minute or so, he remained motionless in the gloomy aisle.

Hesitantly, Duncan stepped into the room. His first impression was that everything was normal, but immediately, the lights began flickering. Strange noises followed, apparently coming from literally everywhere inside the room. The whole situation was quickly reaching a disturbing paranormal status. Soon the noises began pounding with deafening strength, until they ceased brusquely, giving way to a high-pitched rasping beat.

Duncan ran to the door of the house, but it was stuck. Immediately, a dazzling blast flashed from behind him, followed by a battery of smaller flashes that flooded the room with a very intense light. Duncan squatted down, covering his eyes with his arms. Each flash was accompanied by a sonic boom, which was instantly reabsorbed by a buzzing-like pulsation. Elongated objects of different sizes, no more than a foot long, emerged from each burst of light, remaining in place, almost motionless.

As suddenly as they had begun, the flashes abruptly stopped, the sonic booms ceased, and the eerie noises and all light anomalies vanished. Only a humming sound emanating from the hovering objects could now be heard. Duncan remained motionless, kneeling on the floor against a corner. His arms, face, and body were damp with a cold sweat; his breathing was very intense.

One of the objects issued a series of glassy light beams toward the others, which began to move in response. The objects adopted a pyramidal formation and slowly drifted as one body toward a table in front of Duncan. Detaching from the center of the arrangement, the same object that had flashed the light beams began to descend slowly, eventually landing on the table. The others remained hovering, keeping their relative positions. They were glowing with a surreal incandescence, mildly but sharply heaving, pitching and rolling in a way that struck Duncan as menacing.

2.

After a few seconds of stillness, a thin flash came from a slit on the hull of the object lying on the table. The light fanned out and grew wider as the slit became an opening, exposing the shapes of two individuals. They seemed to be wearing suits with an energized texture. Very tense, and still squatting in a corner, Duncan thought he heard a voice.

"Dahncion . . . "

The name, pronounced by the larger of the two, somehow sounded like his name. Even stranger, he found the small visitors recognizable.

"Dahncion . . . "

Duncan nodded hesitantly.

The speaker grasped the hand of his companion, who was clearly female. She stared at Duncan with an intense gaze. Although humanoid in appearance, the faces of the two visitors evoked panda traits. The female was significantly smaller than the male, who now drew closer to Duncan. His name was O'sihn, and somehow, Duncan knew it. It was this strange, though vague, familiarity with the characters that kept his instinctive panic feebly at bay.

"Be not afraid," O'sihn said, waving a hand towards the objects that remained hovering behind him. "This is not fantasy, or insanity, or anything that you should fear."

Duncan grimaced uncomfortably.

"Our Universe is undergoing great strife," O'sihn continued in a calm cadence. "War is consuming Reality. We yearn for help, for a singular help. It's this hope that has brought us here."

"Help?"

"Yours, Dahncion," the female added.

"How?"

"We have developed a way to *transrealize* your body to our reality," O'sihn explained. "You could come with us, in one of our vessels."

There was an interval of silence.

"Time is running out," O'sihn continued. "The transition conditions that made this voyage possible are not going to hold much longer. The decision to accept our plea is yours alone."

Glancing at the small objects (which he realized were vessels) hovering above the table, Duncan shook his head awkwardly, waiting to wake from a dream that was not.

The visitors stared at Duncan, not certain of the meaning of his gesture. He was breathing fast, and his pupils were dilated. The mysterious subconscious familiarity he had with his unlikely guests, his natural curiosity, and his attraction to space exploration were pushing him to accept. At the same time, his apprehension of the bizarre situation poured an adrenaline cocktail of fear and numbing uncertainty into his bloodstream. Yet as if squeezed by the conflicting forces, Duncan was ejected abruptly out of his perplexity by a flash of insight into his own future. It contained the fulfillment—beyond any expectations—of all his dreams, including and surpassing those of space exploration. He was being offered the chance of becoming part of something larger than himself, and he could profoundly grasp his own destiny in it. It was a strong perception, with an unusual realism and a subtle sense of peace.

"You can count on me," he stammered.

"We are honored, Dahncion." The female spoke melodiously, with a brief bow. Her name was Laida. Duncan was also aware of that, although vaguely.

Several individuals came down a ramp that extended out of a

hatchway of the vessel stationed on the table. O'sihn joined them right away, as Duncan watched them unload equipment. All of them had traits similar to species that could be found on Earth. Some had a feline resemblance, others were more canine-like, others belonged to bird-like species of different types, and a few had bear-like traits—but each and every one bore clear human-like features, especially in their expressions. Yet there was something that made them look very different from any living creature familiar to Duncan. It was as if most of them had a metallic, yet very plastic and very flesh-like appearance. In addition to their small size—they were no taller than one inch—the characteristic sheen of their faces was replicated on their vessels, uniforms, and all their devices.

Laida approached Duncan. "Are you okay?"

As a side effect of the inter-*realitic* exchange, the temperature had dropped noticeably. Still, Duncan's face was sweating.

"Perhaps you feel somewhat strange, uncomfortable."

Duncan shook his head, almost imperceptibly, like a twitch.

"There will be time to explain," Laida said, reading Duncan's eyes. A signal began blinking on her communicator. "It's all set, Dahncion."

Duncan remained motionless, his mind drifting to personal concerns. What would happen to his rental? How long would it take for someone to notice his absence? What about his family? And how about his studies? It had been tough to get into that university . . .

Laida interrupted his thoughts. "We must increase the focal range of the RIBA[1] device. Please stand against the wall behind you."

Clumsily, Duncan stepped backwards, as Laida instructed him to relax.

3.

A translucent glowing curtain, which defined a boundary between two realities, was surrounding all the ships. It engulfed all hovering

---

1 Rilitian Integral Bio-Assimilator (R.I.B.A.)

vessels as well as the one stationed on the table, including the visitors and their equipment. It was like a seamless energy film with a feeble glimmering.

After some minor adjustments, O'sihn ordered the procedure started. A tenuous glassy beam flowed smoothly from the small artifact in front of Duncan. The beam made contact with the *realitic* boundary without piercing it: the boundary simply elongated, enveloping the beam, which quickly—but at a sufficiently slow speed for the naked eye to perceive its motion—touched Duncan's chest.

The energy surge widened into a cone, which immediately rearranged its shape to fit the human outline. Duncan lost consciousness right away. The initial gleaming radiation began to grow in intensity, and as it did, its yellow shade gradually shifted to a deep blue light. Soon, the only figure that could be discerned was the rather featureless contour of a human being. The beam's shade began to fluctuate between an emerald radiance and a strong blue glow; as it did, the *realitic* curtain expanded to engulf the beam and its human target. A battery of sharp streams flashed inside the glowing cone.

Duncan started shrinking in size, his body's center of gravity remaining stationary at all times. When his size had reached a proportion similar to the visitors', one ship detached from the formation and stabilized underneath his feet. At that point, the energy fan, now very narrow, began switching colors, gradually settling into a soft yellow luminescence that slowly faded out.

Still unconscious, Duncan fell on top of the vessel that had swiftly stationed itself underneath him. The ship started moving and landed quietly on the table alongside the RIBA device. Two vessels approached and stopped near it, hovering alongside.

O'sihn, Laida, and the working team immediately gathered around the ship on top of which Duncan lay.

As he regained consciousness, Duncan touched his arms. He felt different, yet perceived that nothing had changed within his innermost self. The peculiar metallic-plastic texture of the suit that now covered most of his body was similarly replicated in his face and hands, which were visible through a tenuous luminescence that somehow isolated his body from the environment. Still lying on the deck, Duncan looked around. The same room he had been in before was still there, only now, it looked like a huge cathedral, with a surreal appearance caused by his looking at it through the *transrealitic* boundary that enveloped all the vessels as a whole. He was soon being immersed into a state of amazement and anticipation. His fears had dwindled, mainly due to the different perception he had of his own feelings, with his newly reconfigured body. It was as if he had to learn how to feel all over again.

A ramp came forth off the starboard side of the ship, on which he was now standing, down to the table where it had just landed. As he stepped down, the captain of the expedition stepped forward to meet him. "We are honored to have the *Duhn-zaeon* among us," he said. The Rilik[2] expression, from which the name *Dahncion* stemmed, held the actual meaning of the name—the *Child Quickener*.

Duncan tried to respond, but found it difficult to communicate. He felt very strange, trying to adapt to the changes his body had undergone.

O'sihn nodded. "We have five minutes until *transrealitic* reentry."

Following Laida, Duncan headed towards the flagship. There was a luminescence, around their heads and hands, that looked like translucent helmets and gloves. It was produced by sealing energy fields generated by each suit, which allowed for independent gaseous mixes. The luminescence automatically ceased as each individual walked inside the ship through gates that emitted a similar glow.

As he walked through the corridors, Duncan had the odd

---

2 *Rilik* was the ancestral tongue from which the language spoken by the visitors had developed.

impression of recognizing one of the crewmembers he passed. Laida and Duncan soon reached the bridge. O'sihn was already there, sitting at his command post. As he looked around, Duncan again experienced déjà vu; some even smiled at him as if in recognition.

The reentry sequence started immediately, and all the ships began moving. Soon the fleet adopted a sharp conical arrangement, with the flagship in front. Onboard every vessel, all *transrealitic* systems were engaging sequentially, as transient meta-loci topological data were exchanged between navigational computers. The living-room lights started fluctuating again. For a fraction of a second, the room was saturated with a dazzling radiance.

On the navigational display, Duncan watched the actuality of the room dissipate, to be replaced immediately by a new Reality.

CHAPTER 2

First Mission

4.

High above the planet's surface, a city floated gently on the winds. Its base—resembling a gigantic uncut diamond—emitted a ruby luminescence,[3] which sparkled on the timid cloudiness that lay dormant underneath.

Except for thick cocoons of white and gray looming over the horizon, nothing else could be seen of the surface below. As the sun set between the clouds, the towers of Royal City glittered in the dusk. Gradually, the sky was acquiring a sapphire hue, which waned into reddish embers. Before long, a dense blackness dominated the scene, with a diaphanous curtain of stars of different colors, though predominantly white.

Looking through the wall-to-wall crystal pane that dominated the dining hall at the Memorial Palace, Duncan would now and then rest his eyes on the stars. He was the only human inside the hall,

---

3 The peculiar gleaming that radiated from the core rock was linked to the power source that held the hovering mountain high above the surface. The base of Royal City was a gigantic rock comprised of countless microscopically thin interconnected crystals. Cryna—the mineral that made up those crystals—is a highly conductive substance, which under high pressure and temperature conditions, crystallizes in strong hexagonal films with a beautifully complex three-dimensional snowflake type of structure. This mineral has a small density, and at very high temperatures, it becomes lighter than air, at Realitas' surface pressure.

A flat reactor in the lower regions of the city's mountainous base heated the rock, inducing a low-density air circulation in most of the countless inter-crystal receptacles. The result was a lighter-than-air massive structure capable of rising up to a few thousand feet above the surface.

On occasions, some volcanoes would release naturally formed overheated cryna rocks of different sizes, which could stay floating among the clouds for many weeks.

which was not unexpected in a universe where humanoid species were a small minority. But tonight, this was far from being Duncan's foremost preoccupation.

"If you, who do belong to this universe—and with this amazing technology—haven't been able to handle this . . . Establishment, how could . . . what could I do?"

As with many of Duncan's previous questions, Leonidas offered a short answer. "The present conflict has its roots in your universe, Dahncion. Our existence has a bond with the people of your world."

"If I only knew that what you expect from me is something I could do—" Duncan replied.

Leonidas reclined in his chair. "You have a rare gift."

Duncan shook his head slightly.

"Inclusive, boundless, quickening," Leonidas said slowly. He then looked frankly into Duncan's eyes. "We call it the gift of Childhood."

Duncan sipped a bit more from his cup, which contained an appealing yellow juice. "We are talking about war, about my helping you out, somehow."

The term *childhood* did not square well with his own idea of himself; to him it sounded childish, trivial, not in line with his college freshman status. Still immature, perhaps *not child enough*, as they would say in that culture, Duncan had not understood the real meaning of the word.

While fiddling uneasily with a circular object on the table, he mulled over his past goals and achievements, and the troubling thought of having left all his plans and life behind. And now, the new and strange expectations laid on him . . . Duncan resumed his objections, trying to convince his hosts that he was just not the person they thought he was.

Keethia, King Leonidas' wife, stared at Duncan with sympathy; from the glaze of his eyes, she understood he was not ready for more that night. So as a way to postpone the conversation for another occasion, the queen offered Duncan a simple thought: "Who dares have everything they wish? Who always reaches for what they dream? True strength and real greatness can only come from children, Dahncion, little children."

A total blackout interrupted the dinner. Red lights started blinking, and a loud alarm began blaring from outside the palace.

"Follow me," Leonidas said, leaving the table. Duncan looked at him without moving.

"It's an enemy incursion warning," the queen added.

Duncan got up immediately and ran after the royal couple.

Outside the palace, a shuttle was waiting. Leonidas, Keethia, and two people in military uniforms, followed by Duncan, stepped into the vehicle. It took off at once towards the south. Duncan was in the back seat, looking through a window on his right. Keethia was seated next to him. The queen smiled mildly with a serene gaze. Worried, Duncan smiled wanly back and turned to his window. He was concerned about the situation, but more so about the matters that had been discussed that evening. On top of that, and even if he would not consciously recognize it, the prospect of not being able to see his family again for a very long time, if ever, troubled him.

A dense traffic of orders and instructions was coming through a communicator carried by one of the two uniformed passengers. The short trip would otherwise be a very silent one. In contrast, Duncan's mind echoed with questions, doubts, and uncertainties that would play back and forth that night and for many nights to come.

5.

After the enemy incursion of the previous night, O'sihn's tactical team[4] was recalled immediately. The much-needed shore leave on Realitas had been quite brief, and before dawn, the whole team was once again back at work.

"Any questions?"

Lieutenant[5] Leepardian raised an arm. "How will we prevent enemy detection, sir?"

"We'll be discussing this right now, Lee." O'sihn switched to the next slide of his presentation, displayed on a large screen on the front wall. "As we all know, the Althean system has a significant Establishment presence. Although there are no military outposts in its neighboring space, the whole quadrant is under tight enemy surveillance. In view of this, we will not use conventional military vehicles for this mission." A diagram of a cargo vessel replaced the chart displayed. "The Althean system is a key spot within the peripheral systems of the Centhor quadrant. Freighters often cruise the region, which is patrolled regularly by the enemy. Recent rumors of arbitrary measures during Kervian cargo-inspections have tarnished the Establishment's image in the area."

---

4 The Realitas Royal Navy was organized into tactical teams trained to perform a wide range of operations. There was no such thing as the captain of a ship, or of a division, or of any military unit in the Royal Navy, but the captain of a team, or Team Captain, who might or might not have command of a ship. Someone holding a Team Captain rank was commonly referred to as *the Captain*, a rank that was independent of the actual commanding rank (such as major) the person would hold. On the other hand, a formal Captain rank could be a permanent assignment, like for example, the captain of a ship, or a temporary or in commission assignment, such as when someone was assigned to command a particular mission. A similar military organization was found on many worlds of the Realdom.

5 With respect to military ranks, although not always consistent among the different worlds and armed forces of the Realdom, they often were. That was the case between the Realitian and Veritian Navies, for example, including their Marine Corps, which were part of these Navies. We chose to render their officers' ranks as — junior officers: Spacer, Ensign, (2nd) Lieutenant, and 1st Lieutenant; —senior officers: Major, Lieutenant Commander or Sub Commander, Commander, Commodore, and different ranks of Admirals. Spacer was a rank assigned only to the fledgling graduates from a naval academy; they had an extra rank than those who joined the Navy through other programs, but they would ordinarily go faster through the rest of the junior ranks.

Kervians had never had a good reputation. They were allies of the Establishment, functioning politically as an autonomous concurrent state, independent although supportive of the Equity Conference. As such, they had authority as Establishment members. They were a strategic military factor in the war. Kervians had no qualms about performing certain tasks the Establishment would not be willing to engage in. However, the latter would never condemn such actions, wrong as they were, while quietly benefiting from them.

"As a result, such controls have been relaxed, and the enemy is currently putting up with some smuggling in an attempt to cool down the situation." A picture of a medium-sized ship appeared on the screen. "This is the *Angel Spark*. Her skipper, our friend Zor, will provide our transportation to the Althean system. He will jettison us in landing capsules for the final approach to our objective." Zor Foxso'l was well known within certain circles of the Royal Navy. His native star system had fallen to Establishment control early in the war. Since then, he had been assisting Realitas in different military operations with O'sihn's team.

"Captain, sir."

"Paninther."

"Regarding our weapons: we couldn't take down standard equipment in jettison capsules." Ovoid in shape, compact and versatile, the small single-pilot vehicles did not offer much room to spare.

"Althea 8 is the only inhabited planet of the system, and it's watched closely by the enemy. Its population is *loidean*—phenotypically similar to us—and it's distributed in clans that belong to young cultures,"[6] O'sihn explained. "Therefore, we won't be taking any equipment that could give us away to the Establishment, especially weapons."

O'sihn caught a disapproving grimace from someone sitting in the second row. "Cranehin?"

---

6 Non-technological and pre-industrialized cultures were referred to as young cultures.

"Sir, if the planet is under such tight surveillance, how are we to avoid detection? I mean, even if the landing capsules are small, we're going to be a large team."

"Trying to conceal fifty-six capsules through a well-developed atmosphere is not an easy task," O'sihn granted. "However, a celestial event will considerably increase our chances. The Centhor quadrant is rich in C.P.M.[7] clusters. The Althean system is beginning to cross through one such cluster. SERI's[8] laboratories have forecasted that a C.P.M. nodule will hit Althea 8's stratosphere at ten degrees from the zenith of our destination, at about 0130R,[9] fifteen days from today.

"The atmospheric characteristics of the planet will prevent most meteorites from reaching the surface. However, they will maintain a sufficiently large average size along their entry paths, which will allow us to mask our presence among them.

"Our plan of action consists in traveling on board the YSF[10] Cruiser *Stalwart* to the A7-9 quadrant, where we'll be jettisoned in reentry capsules at 0115R, fourteen days from today. We'll be drifting in space for about four hours, until 0500R, when the *Angel Spark* will be in position to pick us up. At 0130R, the following day, we'll be jettisoned again from the *Angel Spark* towards the reentry coordinates, within the meteorite cluster. Atmospheric contact will occur approximately one hour before dawn at our final destination.

"Upon landing, all capsules will disintegrate following standard procedure. Subsequently, we will converge on a local village of a tribe called Veridiawa. It is from there that we will organize and launch the rescue of Doctor Oyhtter.

"Captain Clara, along with Major Shoshuar and Lieutenant Saigtin, will be in the village waiting for us. Captain Clara and her

---

7 C.P.M., or Celestial Proto Material, is cosmic material related to a stellar nursery, in this case, of the star cluster to which Althea belongs.

8 SERI, the Space Exploration Realitarian Institute, was a branch of Realitas Royal Academy.

9 Realitas Standard Time.

10 Yik's Space Fleet. The term *Yik's* is a contraction from the old Realitarian language standing for *"Their Royal Majesties"*.

team were sent to the planet to make contact with the Veridiawan clan, which is located in a native war-sensitive area. They have been on the planet for more than two months already, and they have succeeded in earning the trust of the natives. Questions?"

Hostage retrieval was not one of the primary functions of O'sihn's team. The urgency to resolve the particular situation on Althea 8, plus the severe shortage of available forces, had resulted in the last-minute assignment. Doctor Oyhtter, the mission objective, had been working on a highly classified project on the planet when he was kidnapped by a group of locals. If the Establishment learned about the incident, it would try to get hold of the scientist, who was considered a threat. "Are we going to receive any preliminary training for the retrieval, sir?" Lieutenant Tygrum asked.

"I'm afraid not." O'sihn turned to the screen, which was now displaying an image of a large vessel. "Upon rescue completion, we are to be picked up by YSF *Freedom* retrievers. The carrier will penetrate into enemy space expecting to launch and receive the retrievers back within a constrained tactical window. Any comments?" The captain looked from side to side. "One last topic: Duhn-zaeon has decided to get actively involved in this war. His petition has been accepted and he's been assigned to our squad."

This came as a surprise. After having brought Duncan to Reality, no one in O'sihn's team had expected any further direct contact with the human from Earth.

O'sihn nodded. "This is it, *Erandie*.[11] We shall interact with him as with any other member of our team. Let's help him get used to the Realitian[12] way of life and to the Royal Navy."

---

11 Realitarian expression, neutral in gender, whose closest translation would be *ladies and gentlemen*.

12 a) *Realitarian* is a term used to denote something or someone belonging to Realitas, the planet where Duncan had first arrived, and from where his voyage from Earth

The time readings on the presentation screen started blinking, signaling the end of the period allotted to the meeting. "Departure is scheduled for today at 1400R. All personnel assigned to operation Shooting Star will gather on dock three at 1335R. For further instructions, I'll be in my quarters until 1315R."

"Ten-hut," Laida called.

As everybody stood up, O'sihn left the conference room. Duncan was already waiting outside.

6.

Immersed in a strict communications silence, the capsules had been drifting for more than five hours. The team had been due for pick up for an hour already. Through the glassy hull of his cockpit, Duncan glanced at the shimmering hulls of the other pods. He was striving to remain calm, but breathing was becoming increasingly difficult: the oxygen levels were dropping fast.

For the umpteenth time, Duncan looked at the digital dials and controls that were built inside the hull. "Just open the darned capsule. Everything's gonna be just fine outside." Duncan knew the thought was not at all rational, yet a moment later, he touched the active display of the cockpit with the flick of a wrist.

The life-support system immediately responded in bright red,

had been organized.

b) *Realitian* is a broader term referring to someone or something belonging to the alliance that was fighting against the Establishment. This alliance was commonly referred to as the *Realdom* (a term avoided in Establishment circles) of which Realitas was a founding member. Something or someone that was Realitarian would also be Realitian, but something or someone that was Realitian would not necessarily be Realitarian. For example, Veritians, those born in Veritas, are also Realitians, while not being Realitarians. Veritas and Realitas are two different planets of two different star systems, both of which belong to the Realdom. They will be referenced often in this narrative.

c) *Realitic* is another term that will occasionally surface in this account. This is a word used by the Realdom to refer to something that belongs to the Realdom's (and Establishment's) universe. It can also be used as referring to a particular universe or in relation to two or multiple universes, as in *interrealitic* or *transrealitic*. *Realitic* is close in meaning to the English word *universe* or *universal*, although *realitic* conveys a strong connotation of referring to a particular universal reality.

stylized letters: *Warning 4256: zero atmosphere outside. Will you carry on with requested procedure (Y/N)?*

For a moment, Duncan stayed immobile, staring at the message, panting and sweating, until he finally brushed a hand over option Y.

Fresh air rushed readily inside the opening cockpit, carrying a sense of relief. However, Duncan began breathing faster, with his mouth half open and his hands pressed onto his chest. The outside air was nothing but an unbreathable gaseous mix.

Gasping for air, Duncan opened his eyes. He looked around startled, clueless as to where he was. A dim red luminescence spread across the deck, reflected over the sleeping bags of the rest of the team. Of course, he was onboard the *Angel Spark*, in one of its hangars. Duncan sat up. The thought that he had leapt over to another dream crossed his mind. But he was fully awake.

"Is everything okay?"

Duncan turned around. "Yeah."

Despite the twilight, Laida could trace the tension on Duncan's face. "It's only 2307." She reclined on one arm as she checked her watch. "We still have more than two hours to the jettison coordinates."

Duncan grinned. "Some help I am; I'm not even able to help myself get some sleep." He was alluding to a comment O'sihn had made in his presence that night regarding Duncan's "newest help" to the team "to fight and win this war."

"It always feels like that the first time," Laida said in a whisper. "We don't get nerves of steel just by getting this job. It takes a lot of acclimation to many things."

"Too many things, I'm afraid," Duncan replied.

"You are no different from any of us before that first mission."

There was truth in Laida's comment, though it was lacking. For drifting in space for several hours, piercing through the atmosphere of an alien planet in an alien universe, meeting unknown and potentially deadly creatures, among many other things, was much more than what Duncan could process that night.

"What I feel doesn't make any sense," Duncan said.

"What we feel doesn't count, only what we do."

"That also worries me." Duncan smiled.

Laida made a gesture signaling him to remain quiet. Looking up at the hangar overhead[13], she reached quickly into her backpack for an L.F.C. (life-form classifier).

"O'sihn?" Laida said, nudging her husband. "O'sihn . . . "

"Hmm," he muttered from his sleeping bag next to her.

"We've got visitors, O."

7.

Barging into the cabin, a slender character—half-human, half-feline—flipped on the lights. "Skipper!"

Captain Foxso'l had gone to bed less than one hour before, after being up for more than twenty-seven hours. Sheltering under his thick sheets, he turned on the light of his watch and groaned. "Tora . . . what's the matter with you? I told ya not to call me up 'til one."

"I'm sorry, skipper, but there is a Kervian shi . . . battleship out there. They are asking all sorts of questions."

"Get back to the bridge." Foxso'l jumped out of his bed. "I'll meet you there. And wake up O'sihn and his guys," he added, hopping on one foot as he tried to get his other into a worn boot.

"Aye, skipper."

Shortly after, Foxso'l was on the bridge.

"They appeared suddenly in the quadrant and ordered us to decrease relative speed, Captain," First Officer Witts said with his usual composure. "As customary, they mentioned their weapons."

"Have we already identified ourselves?" Foxso'l asked.

---

13 Like ships, spaceships do not have ceilings or walls but overheads and bulkheads, respectively.

"I have only disclosed the fake name of our vessel," the *Crimson Star*. "I don't think they have us in their records, Captain."

A menacing figure materialized on an old-fashioned communications monitor. "Alien vessel, this is Kervian Cruiser *Vastitas*. Your identification is insuff—

"Zor Foxso'l, sir, captain of cargo vessel *Crimson Star*. May we be of any assistance, Commandant?"

"Get ready to be boarded," the Kervian replied in a coarse accent.

"Any emergency, Commandant?"

The alien sighed, with an expression that hardened his humanoid traits. "You're gonna have all sorts of emergencies, mister, if you don't brief us as to how to access your vessel right now."

"This is precisely what I'm trying to assess, Commandant," Foxso'l answered, trying to buy some extra time. "Are you bringing along any equipment that may require any special attention? I'm not positive about your environmental requirements."

"Mr. Foxso'l, I'm not in any particular mood for your technicalities this morning, and our plasma drill has already been energized . . ."

"At the moment, we are signaling access information to your network. We are ready to welcome you at the aft bay."

The Kervian bridge vanished from the monitor, as did Foxso'l from his own bridge. He was heading briskly for the aft hangar.

With his elliptical pupils wide open, Tora turned to Witts, who had taken over the conn.

"He will find some crazy way out of it," Witts said reassuringly, abandoning his customary reserve for a moment. "He always does."

8.

The emergency hatchway flung open, and ten soldiers—heavily armed, all wearing environment-independent combat suits—jumped into the aft hangar. As they adopted the standard boarding formation, Commandant Sorton came down on a small platform. Zor Foxso'l, escorted by two of the Kervian soldiers, approached him.

"It's an uncommon privilege to have an Establishment Commandant on board the *Crimson Star*." Foxso'l bowed reverently.

Sorton gazed around casually, ignoring the obsequious comments. "This vessel is not registered in the Bureau of Commerce records," he stated, refocusing his eyes firmly on Foxso'l.

"Odd, since it's been registered in GANSPAR."[14]

Sorton signaled to one of his men, who proceeded to check Foxso'l's claim in the cruiser database using a hand-held terminal.

"What is this old junk carrying at the moment, Captain?" Sorton asked, looking around distastefully.

Foxso'l's immediate impulse was far from friendly. But he swiftly relaxed his expression into an unconvincing smile. "This humble vessel is currently not transporting any cargo, Commandant."

"Hmm, I see. You and your crew just happened to pick this charming quadrant—mindless of its war status—for rest and relaxation . . ."

Zor Foxso'l laughed loudly. "We sure need rest, Commandant, but business comes first. Our present course is taking us to the Althean system. We expect to collect some cargo there, if we're not too late already. All those smuggling ships out there . . . " Foxso'l half shook his head and half nodded. "The natives can't tell them apart from us—registered merchants."

"Excuse me, Commandant."

Sorton turned around. "Lieutenant?"

"The vessel does have a PRERE,[15] sir," Lieutenant Brot added.

"Proceed with inspection."

"Aye-aye, Commandant."

Brot left the hangar followed by five soldiers.

Sorton stood up a few inches from the skipper and stared at him for a moment. "Captain, Captain," Sorton sighed. "How can you possibly expect me to believe that a . . . vessel like yours would spend a millisecond in deep space without carrying any cargo whatsoever?"

---

14 Galactic Navigational Space Register (Establishment regulations).
15 Preliminary Registration in the (Establishment) Bureau of Commerce.

Foxso'l's silence was interrupted by a signal beeping on the Kervian's communication device. "Sorton."

"Lieutenant Brot, sir. We've found forty-four capsules—correction, forty-eight . . ."

"What's your location, Brot?"

"Section A34, Commandant."

"On my way."

In no hurry, Sorton put away his communicator and turned to Foxso'l. "So, Captain," he gloated, "how about a little tour that includes section A34?"

9.

On reaching section A34, Sorton and his detail found Lieutenant Brot waiting at the entrance to the central hangar. "Fifty-six containers, Commandant, all sealed but one." That particular container was not only unsealed, but open.

Sorton stepped into the hangar, while Zor Foxso'l—closely watched by two Kervians—poked his head hesitantly through the hatchway. The sight was the complete opposite of the incriminating scene he expected to find: there was no trace of O'sihn's team.

Sorton drew near the open container. It was one of the landing pods to be used in the operation. At the last moment, O'sihn had ordered his team to get in the ejection capsules, or E.C.s, and sealed them for launch. This would make the pods both very difficult to probe with standard sensors and impenetrable for conventional weapons. Each capsule had its assigned occupant, except for the captain's, which Laida and O'sihn were forced to share. Unlike the rest, Laida's capsule had been left open, with fake cargo inside, to induce the Kervians to think (if they came across it, as they did) that the rest had the same content. Sorton picked up a handful of the powder from the open container and let it sift through his fingers.

"It's *thomellion* spice, Commandant, and there is more in those cadres." Lieutenant Brot pointed at some storage containers stowed in the back of the hangar.

"What about the sealed pods?"

Brot shook his head. "Neither our scanners nor our weapons could get through their hulls."

The commandant looked around intensely. He remained silent for a moment, until he finally sighed, with a contained chuckle. "Typical . . . "

A signal started beeping on Sorton's communicator again. "Sorton."

"Lieutenant Sobrumsom, sir. There is a large meteorite cluster twenty minutes C.R.S.[16] ahead of us. It seems to be an offshoot of a local C.P.M., sir."

"Plot a new course to our next patrolling zone. I'll be back momentarily."

"Aye, sir."

Sorton and his men began heading back to the aft hangar. Foxso'l followed them, flanked by the two soldiers.

"Regarding your E.C.s," Sorton said with a knowing smile. "They are not in compliance with chapter three, section thirty four of the *General Norms for Cargo Ships and Private Vessels*. You seem to have made some innovative use for the one you forgot to seal. A full *brosh* should be a good incentive to help you comply with regulations in the future." The fine was almost as expensive as the spice the rest of the pods would have allegedly contained.

"If I may explain—"

"Captain, we are short of time today, and you probably want to keep your cargo—I mean, your safety pods." Sorton walked a few more steps and turned back. "Though you do seem to be in need of rest, Captain. You may want to consider our penal colonies as an alternative to spending time and money in more bureaucracy and costly fines."

Foxso'l shook his head politely. "Work and duty first, Com-

---

16 Current Relative Speed.

mandant. We will gladly pay the required compensation for our carelessness."

"As you wish, Captain."

When they reached the aft hangar, a signal started beeping on Sorton's communicator again. "Sorton."

"Lieutenant Sobrumsom speaking."

"Yes?"

"The C.P.M. cluster is quite dense and widespread, Commandant." The comment implied a potential hazard for their ship and the safety of the boarding party, as long as it remained on Foxso'l's vessel.

"Make ready to receive us."

"Aye, Commandant."

Sorton made a sign with one arm, and his boarding squad started leaving the vessel. Escorted by three troopers, he stepped on the rising platform that would take him back to his ship through a hatchway in the overhead of the hangar.

"I may have been rather lenient today, Captain," Sorton added, as he ascended on the lift. "For your own sake, I trust you will be complying with all Establishment regulations on our next inspection. It will take place soon enough."

"It was an honor having you on board, Commandant," Foxso'l added, bowing mildly.

With the hatchway finally closed, Zor Foxso'l hurried up to the bridge. There, on the main display, Cruiser *Vastitas* covered most of the screen.

An abrupt bump made everybody on the bridge stumble. The *Angel Spark* had been released from the *gravitic* grip of the *Vastitas*. The Kervian ship dashed away along a standard hyperbolic course.

CHAPTER 3

Veridiawa

10.

That night, Seidy was covering the northern post, outside the village. He had always preferred night watches. That was not too surprising; after all, he was a *wuol*.[17] Seidy felt proud to be an all-Veridiawan *wuol*. Sometimes he wondered what would have become of him if he had been born a Creption. When he had little to do, during the long hours of patrols, he would explore the gloomy image of himself as a Creption citizen flying with his head bald for life—the Creption way. Seidy was on duty, but he was not alone. Veridiawan warriors were never posted alone. Close to him, more specifically, beneath him, was Boldowa—the *keiro*[18]—who did not like to be on duty during the day or during the night.

"How long is it before dawn?"

"Any moment now, Boldo."

"Seidy, you know, don't call me Boldo. My name is Boldowa."

"Yeah, yeah," said the *wuol*, shaking his head. "I've been thinking," he continued. "What good ones are the *newones*, aren't they?"

"Yes, they are very good *newones*," answered the *keiro* with his peculiar gravelly tone. "They've been here for but a crop, and they already go out with us to fight the Creptions."

---

17 Many of the inhabitants of Veridiawa have some resemblance to Earth's animal species. *Wuols*, in particular, are flying, intelligent individuals with owl-looking traits.

18 *Keiros* are massive individuals, with rhino-like features.

"Yeah, and the girl-Captain . . . " Seidy tilted his head to one side. "She has sort of magic powers, you know?"

The *keiro* frowned. "How do you mean?"

"Didn't you hear what happened to Citrina's daughter last week?"

"Oh . . . no, no," Boldowa said.

"Citrina's daughter—Aquiri—along with Soruri's daughters," Seidy continued. "They were playing at the flat cave, close to the river. All of a sudden, a *graspy*[19] bites Aquiri on her right leg. One of the kids runs to the village and tells her mother that Aquiri has been bitten by a *graspy*, and that she's very . . . very badly ill. People rush to the cave, and there they find her, still and gasping for air." The *wuol* paused and raised his eyebrows with an air of mystery. "And then, Boldo . . ." The *wuol* stared piercingly at his companion.

"But, but Seidy?" The *keiro* frowned. "You know, don't call me Boldo. My name . . . "

" . . . is *Boldowa*," Seidy completed the sentence. "D' ya wanna hear the rest of the story or not?"

"Oh, yes, Seidy, yes."

"The girl-Captain, she was coming from the riverbank. So she looks at the entrance to the cave, and she sees lots of people, and Soruri's daughters crying. She runs towards 'em and asks 'em what's goin' on. And Soruri's daughters tell her everything about the *graspy*. So the girl-Captain runs into the cave and kneels beside Aquiri and takes her right hand. Her face is all pale, and her right leg is very badly swollen. The girl-Captain uses a magic potion on Aquiri's leg, but still, Aquiri stops breathing."

Seidy jumped off Boldowa's back and flew to the top of a pole in front of the *keiro*.

"But then," the *wuol* continued, widening his eyes, "the girl-Captain opens a little box on her belt, and picks out a healing dart—a

---

19 *Graspies* are small, venomous animals native to Althea 8. They make their habitats in wet dark places.

heart-quickening-dart, she calls it. She pricks Aquiri's right arm with it and . . . foo! Aquiri starts breathing again.

"The girl-Captain then picks another healing-dart, but this one is different—all yellow—its point like a long needle. She pricks Aquiri's arm once more, and sooner than an arrow, Aquiri is talking and breathing like every day again. Her swelling is gone, and her face turns warm like the dawn." The *wuol* paused, staring at Boldowa with a mysterious gaze.

"Were those magic darts?" asked Boldowa.

"Of course, silly! That's how Aquiri could start breathing again and all."

"That was mighty good what the girl-Captain did to Aquiri. And, and, people say she fights like a mighty warrior, too."

"Sure she does. And this Major Shoshuar, and the lieutenant . . . "

"Lieutenant Saigtin," Boldowa said.

"Yeah, they make fine warriors themselves," Seidy asserted.

"They sure are good *newones*, but what I don't understand is where they come from. Do you, Seidy?"

"I sure do," the *wuol* stated with a self-confident expression. "The girl-Captain told me that personally. They come from one of the sky-lights, a sky-light so, so high up in the sky that it cannot be seen—not even from the top of the village tower."

"Gosh!" Boldowa uttered. "But how can that be? How can they live inside a light?"

"With the girl-Captain's magic powers," Seidy continued, with sharp, open eyes, "they sure can get themselves inside those tiny sky-lights—just like a sunray gets all the way into a tiny drop of water."

"You're so smart, Seidy."

"Boldo, I know that."

"But, Seidy, please, don't call me Boldo . . . "

"My name is Boldowa," the two said in unison.

There was not much talk for a while. They were very tired after the long night patrol. Seidy looked at the stars thoughtfully. How distant might those tiny lights up there really be? They most certainly were further away than the abandoned Creption village of the east. They might even be further away than the ancient creepy ruins of the south. Well, that would really be far, perhaps too far away . . .

A strange phenomenon suddenly woke Seidy from his thoughts. "Look at the sky!"

"What do you mean, Seidy?"

"Can't you see?"

In a dull voice, the *keiro* answered, "Oh, yes, it is a wonderful tiny-lighted night."

"You short-sighted *keiro*, can't you see what is goin' on up there?"

Boldowa looked up puzzled, squeezing his eyes towards the heavens to no avail.

"Wow . . . it's so beautiful!" the *wuol* exclaimed.

"What is beautiful, Seidy? What is going on?"

"It is fabulous, Boldo! It is the most beautiful shower of lights I've ever seen in my whole life."

11.

Making an atmospheric reentry inside a transparent[20] metallic capsule is the only way you can rightfully claim you understand the experience.

Within seconds, from floating freely inside the cockpit, one's weight begins pulling down strongly. All external skin temperature displays skyrocket as the vehicle plunges into the atmosphere. However, its hull remains unscathed, with a reddish-blue glow radiating from the external skin. At some point, a high-pitched chime—like a crystal glass vibration—reverberates all over the

---

20 Transparent from the inside but silver-looking from the outside, the hulls had a variable, outwards translucency, which was adequately opaque when exposed to highly intense sources of light, like that from a nearby star.

cockpit,[21] but only for a couple of seconds. As the air density increases, all vibrations vanish almost completely.

Capsule-reentry, or piercing, was a very popular sport in many cultures of the Realdom. But that night over Althea 8, it was not an occasion for recreation. Along with the squad of fifty-six tactical pods, thousands of meteorites were hurtling towards the surface of the planet, significantly increasing the risk of the operation. The spectacular beauty of the blazing trajectories was easing the tension of many a pilot, yet for Duncan, the experience was hardly pleasing. Even if he had dreamed of someday going into space, he had never imagined this could and would happen so soon, in such a vast expanse of space, and in another completely unknown universe.

Suddenly, a burst of light flashed from the back, signaling the start of the final deceleration stage. Each capsule, which had an ellipsoid of revolution design[22], had a small box built into the hull that would be positioned one hundred and eighty degrees with respect to the vehicle's reentry direction. For that particular mission, each vehicle's box had a device whose purpose was to cut a hole on the hull to allow for the release of a phase-parachute.[23]

Duncan was struggling in vain to see his parachute. It was as if

---

21 Technical note AGH120709, SERI's Stratospheric Laboratory: "[such] vibration takes place when the surrounding air reaches a specific value of density which, combined with the shape of the capsule, its drag distribution, and the peculiar crystallization that *spectro*-energized metals typically exhibit, meets the conditions for a pulsating turbulence, such that the frequency of shed vorticity coincides with the dominant natural frequency of the structure." For a moment, the entire capsule resonates with a pure tone.

22 Ellipsoid of revolution design: the surface that results from revolving an ellipsoidal line around a straight line.

23 Military capsules were versatile vehicles configured for the mission they were assigned. For Operation *Shooting Star*, discretion being the top priority, phase-parachutes alone were used for landing. These parachutes were designed to open in several stages, progressively reducing the speed of a capsule. Appropriate settings were selected for the unfolding process according to the atmospheric characteristics and the gravitational pull along the trajectory to the target. Many other features could also be adjusted, such as skin-friction properties consistent with altitude and the variable viscosity of the planet's atmosphere, which was a function of many variables.

it had detached from the capsule. The thought filled his eyes with panic. But almost immediately, he started feeling the sharp pulsating deceleration generated by the fast development of its opening stages. His pupils relaxed.

Suddenly, everything turned foggy as the capsule pierced through a few layers of clouds. The fog vanished, and very soon after that, the capsule hit the ground.

Duncan bumped against the front of the cockpit, tumbling out onto the planet's surface. The vehicle had automatically opened in two halves.[24] Within seconds, a disintegration process[25] began taking place. The two oval halves were rapidly defoliating into thousands of flakes, which were swiftly dispersed by a tender breeze.

It was a fair night, with a few slender and very tall clouds that conferred a solemn beauty to a sky populated with myriads of stars. Milky branches stemmed from a wide starry trunk, almost as brilliant as Earth's Moon. But beyond the spectacular beauty, it was the sheer number of stars that impressed Duncan—vastly more than he had ever seen on Earth. As he looked at the sky, his eyes gleamed. He suddenly experienced the intense realization of being on an alien planet, in an alien universe. The quiet loneliness and the surrounding beauty gave him, for the first time, the strong sense of having accomplished something he had always dreamed of.

An early morning glare was rising over the misty hills. Dawn was about to break. Except for an ache in his right knee and a piercing buzzing inside his head (probably due to the difference of pressures between the local atmosphere and the capsule's), Duncan was in fairly

---

24 This type of vehicle opened along an elliptical line coplanar with the capsule's main symmetry axis.

25 Disintegration process: a structural dissociation process known as energy *despectralization*.

good shape. The same could not be said of the compass he carried on his right wrist, which was producing nonsensical readings. Still, from the pre-combat briefing of the previous night, Duncan knew that the Veridiawan village should be somewhere towards the south, not very far from his position.

Looking down from the North Pole (north, according to Realdom conventions), Althea 8 rotated clockwise around its axis—the opposite of the Earth's direction. Unaware of that key factor, Duncan followed the orientation rules he had learned on Earth.[26] Using the looming light from the local sun as a reference, he started heading towards what he thought to be south, thus actually marching north, straight into hostile Creption territory.

12.

"Freeze! We got ya' surrounded, stranger. Put your hands behind your neck."

Duncan was stopped by an arrow hitting the ground right in front of him. In the early morning dimness, he looked around nervously, but he failed to see anybody.

"Don't make any funny movement or my warriors will pierce you, stranger," said the same voice coming out of the foliage.

Duncan was struck with fear thinking he had bumped into hostile natives, who, according to what he had heard, could be very dangerous.

A soldier came out of the vegetation, walking on four slender legs. He was wearing a metallic helmet and wooden armor on his back, carved all over with symbols. He had a resemblance to what on Earth would be recognized as a horse, although he had interesting

---

26 Duncan had been raised in a suburban town close to thick woods. His father had taught him basic orientation rules, including the recognition and relative position of some summer stars. Going back to those memories, Duncan realized that it was precisely when looking at those stars during warm summer nights that he had first dreamed of someday going into space.

differences. His legs, for instance, ended in paws he could use to handle objects.

The soldier strolled around Duncan, finally standing in front of him. "Don't you have anything to say, stranger? Have the Creptions cut your tongue?"

The comment gave Duncan some relief. "Are you a . . . Veridiawan?"

At this point, another soldier emerged from behind a bush, hopping on two long feet and holding a tense bow with an arrow ready to be released. "It looks like a Creption to me. Do we hitch him?"

The horse-like soldier remained quiet, studying the strange specimen. "The Creption people are just people. This is but a human," he pointed out.

"Yeah, but he might be a spy, too." The Veridiawan with the kangaroo-like feet narrowed his eyes. "Spying on us, ain't ya. *Ain't ya*?" he growled, waving his bow at Duncan's head while balancing on his broad feet.

The horse-like soldier resumed strolling around Duncan. "Maybe you are." He then looked straight into Duncan's eyes. "So, what do you have to say about yourself, stranger? How do you know we're from Veridiawa?"

"I'm a friend of Major Shoshuar, Lieutenant Saigtin and . . . and Captain Clara?"

The soldier looked at him skeptically. "So you are. And how did you get here?"

"In a landing capsule," Duncan blurted carelessly.

"Listen, stranger." The soldier with the carved armor hardened his already aggressive stance. "You just keep talking funny and you're gonna get it."

"I . . . I came down with the shower of lights in the sky; surely you saw it . . ." Duncan winced, realizing the answer had not been any wiser or safer.

However, it made some sense to the Veridiawan. "Hum! Well, the girl-Captain did tell us about friend-people coming from the sky, someday."

"Yeah, I'm one of them, one of these friend-people." Duncan smiled nervously.

The other soldier hopped forward, and stood up on his two feet in front of Duncan, always aiming his bow at him. "If you really are a friend of our friends, stranger, tell us something: Major Shoshuar, what breed-of-a-person is he?"

"Breed-of-a-person?"

"Yeah, *keiro*-breed? Human-breed? What sort-of-a-breed, stranger?"

Duncan looked at him with puzzled eyes.

"So, what-sort-of-a-breed, stranger?"

"I . . . I *am* a friend of theirs; they know me—they do know about me—though, we haven't met yet . . . "

"You don't even know what breed-of-a-person they are." The kangaroo-looking soldier shook his head. "How could you be a friend of someone you've never seen before, stranger? I say you are a spy, a spy spying on us."

"But I'm not!"

"The girl-Captain said that her friends would go right to Veridiawa, right after they had come from the sky," the equine soldier added, with a calm cadence and an intimidating expression. "But you were heading straight into Creption country."

Confused, Duncan did not know what to answer. "You must believe me! I am a friend, a friend of yours, and the girl-Captain's, and the others. Just give me a chance to prove it."

With a jerk of his head, the armored equine soldier tipped off his helmet, which now hung down from his neck. "You'd better prove it right now, stranger."

"I know the countersign, Captain's Clara countersign."

The Veridiawan lifted one eyebrow. Keeping the same tone, he grunted, "We are listening, stranger."

Very tense, yet trying to sound solemn, Duncan cleared his throat. "Reality only is."

The soldier in armor shook his head in disappointment and looked at his companion. "Put down your bow; he's just a friend."

"Human," he added, turning to Duncan. "Why didn't you say the countersign in the first place?"

"I . . . don't know."

"Hey, he's just a human," the other soldier said, hopping forward. "Nice to meet ya, human. My name is Taiteenidee."

"My name is Duncan, but people call me Dahncion."

"Greetings, Dahncion. My name is Raylayhiagus," the armored soldier said tersely. "I'm in charge of the northern platoon. This morning, we are only Taiteenidee and I."

"Nice to meet you."

Raylayhiagus nodded curtly but respectfully. "Our village is in Veridiawa. Where is yours?"

"Uh . . . Earth, the Earth village . . . "

"Earth?" inquired Taiteenidee, with squinted eyes. "That's a dirt's name."

"Please come with us," Raylayhiagus added. "We'll lead you to our village."

"Thank you."

"Why are you limping?" asked Taiteenidee.

"I bruised my knee when . . . when I entered Veridiawan country. Say, this is already Veridiawan country, isn't it?"

"All your eyes can see is Veridiawa," answered Raylayhiagus. "But there is a long way to the village. Come, get on my armor. I'll take you there."

Duncan glanced at the Veridiawan. Riding an *intelligent horse*, as he mostly perceived him, seemed strange. "I'd rather walk."

With puzzled eyes, Raylayhiagus hardened his stance again. "Is it anything wrong with my armor?"

"Oh, no, it's just that I don't want to, to burden you."

"You say words as if I were an old useless *whymeenidy*."

"Hey, my friend is the fastest *whymeenidy* of the whole Veridiawa, and a great warrior too," Taiteenidee remarked.

Duncan got the message and bowed respectfully. "I apologize. It will be an honor to ride with you."

"Humans sure talk funny," Taiteenidee added.

Raylayhiagus stared at him disapprovingly.

"I didn't mean nothing." Taiteenidee lifted his shoulders and extended his short forearms.

Duncan shrugged. "We do act a little funny, sometimes."

"You see, you see?" Taiteenidee said, pointing at Duncan. "By the way, where is this Earth-village you are from?"

13.

The people had gathered inside the Ivory Chamber, a semicircular stone building that was the traditional center of all major events in the village. Patriarch Coelious III was already there, holding his scepter, a clear sign that he was to exercise his patriarchal prerogatives. Behind him, the Council of the Forty Venerables was standing with customary solemnity.

When everything was ready, a scribe, holding a papyrus scroll, stepped inside, followed by three Veritians. Taking the papyrus, Coelious turned towards the Council. The Eldest Most stood up, and the Patriarch started to unroll the scroll. He rested his eyes on the Veritian soldiers—Captain Clara, Major Shoshuar, and Lieutenant Saigtin. They were standing on one side of the chamber, with an unassuming appearance.

"Since the first day they arrived to Veridiawa, the warriors from the sky-lights have given us strong tokens of valor, and strength, and wisdom. While still fledgling *newones*, they went to fight with us like the ancient heroes of yore. And like them, word hath come to us of the strong signs and the mighty deeds witnessed amongst Veridiawa."

That was the beginning of what was going to be a particularly long speech. In the end, the three Veritian soldiers would be pronounced Veridiawan Warriors.

For the previous two weeks, Clara and her two companions had been out in the country scouting the area where Doctor Oyhtter was held prisoner. They had not been in the village when O'sihn's squad arrived on the planet with the mission of rescuing the scientist, who had been captured by Creptions during a classified research expedition. However, Captain Clara had often referred to "the ones to come in the mighty flying stars." By then, the fifty-six Realitian visitors were already acknowledged as *newones*, for *"Any old friend of a newone, although an old one, is but a new one,"* as the old Veridiawan proverb went. Therefore, they were already accepted as part of the tribe, with the privileges and expectations this conveyed, like defending the village.

Like all the members of O'sihn's team, Duncan was in the Ivory Chamber. As the speech went on and Duncan's hopes for a short ceremony dissipated, his mind began to drift far above the events, wandering lazily from one topic to another without resting on any in particular. Now and then, his attention would fall on Clara, the "girl-Captain" he had been hearing about so much ever since he had gotten to the planet. She was the first human being he met since he had left his Earth. Clara was wearing metallic Veridiawan armor, and a purple tulle cape covered her back. Over it, her blond hair fell down to her hips.

Duncan perceived her as a particularly gifted person. She was young and had a singular mixture of valor and intelligence in her eyes. All that had captured his dispersed attention. To be sure, she was beautiful and yet, "That unrealistic touch . . . "

Duncan perceived her traits as straight, too well defined; maybe somewhat unreal, in a way, childish. There was something about her outline, as he sensed it, something too definite or delineated, perhaps simplistic, laconic, somehow stylized.

To Duncan, though beautiful, Clara looked, strangely, like a drawing.

14.

Both cultures use similar weapons, consistent with their rudimentary technology and aboriginal species. Bows and arrows, tomahawks and spears, are the standard weaponry for hominideans. Equus *sub-varieties often carry two pikes, one at each side of their wooden armors. Massive species are generally equipped with metallic boots with nails on their soles.* Proboscideans *also carry* arcteras, *cutting weapons consisting of a large pole with two circular blades, perpendicular to each other.* Canidis *are usually equipped with metallic fangs.* Felinnines *utilize similar weapons combined with silver claws. Metallic fangs are widely used by avis combatants, many of them often equipped with spears under their wings. Some* aviarian *species specialize in storming targets by dropping different types of projectiles. Many techniques and well-developed flying tactics have been observed for this purpose. [. . .]*

However, some interesting differences can be spotted between the two armies: so-called killing-suits, each one made of a long elastic fabric covered by protruding poisoned spikes, are very effective weapons only used by constrictor sub-species of Creption *soldiers.*

Excerpt from Captain O'sihn's personal log.

Swamp Valley was a muddy dale between two knolls, where two facing armies had been waiting all morning. On one side, long standards with intricate symbols around a horse-like skull hung wet from tall poles. On the other, white-and-blue flags were deployed despite the rain and the absence of wind. They carried an emblem standing for an old Veridiawan maxim: *"To conquer and win: though many, one will,"* which was symbolized by a yellow dot surrounded by a yellow wheel. In the Veridiawan tongue, the words for *will* and *wheel* sounded alike.

The hills, covered by dark thick foliage, were quickened by occasional lightning. A forest of green blazed with every flash.

A command rang out, and the armies started charging downhill towards each other. Duncan was among the Veridiawans. The high expectations he felt the Realdom had for him had triggered discomfort and anxiety. He sensed the need to bolster his own self-esteem—to prove himself, somehow. Thus, despite expressed instructions from O'sihn to remain in the village, Duncan had managed to get personally involved in the confrontation. However, he had yet to come face to face with the unforeseen trauma of close combat and the crude reality of war.

Running alongside Duncan was Antares, a Veridiawan soldier with a strong canine appearance. Yet, as a *leemow*, he had many feline features, especially in his legs and clawed hands. The Veridiawan overseers had assigned him to fight along the human, a fact that had considerably elevated Duncan's confidence. Antares was wearing a spiky collar around his neck and metallic claws, plus metallic fangs on his forelegs. However, he was not wearing metallic teeth like other native *canidis* warriors would. He considered them "too fancy and clumsy," as he would often say. Indeed, it was very easy to agree, judging from his well-developed set of natural teeth.

As the battle cry "*Veridiaweens Coelireques!*"[27] rang loudly from one side, it clashed with the roar of "*Death to Veridiawa!*" from the other. Both armies collided in the middle of the dale, exploding with howls of pain and the clanging of metal.

Cute impressions Duncan's Earth-bound mentality had concocted about the people of Althea 8 were rapidly dissolving with what he was witnessing in the muddy field.

A snake hiss froze Duncan in his tracks. Turning back, he saw a nine-foot reptilian, with a bear-trap-like device attached to its abdomen. The mechanism clasped, and the creature was hurled forward, displaying its metallic teeth. But while it was still in the air, another set of teeth intercepted its neck, bringing the aggressor down immediately.

Antares and the Creption fell in a tangle over Duncan, and the

---

27 For Veridiawa and Coelious.

three collapsed to the ground. Mud splattered in his eyes, Duncan was rendered half blind. After a rough wrestle, Antares managed to bite the neck of his opponent, only to be ripped off by the whip of his tail. Despite the paralyzing pain, the Veridiawan found the strength to dash forward and clamp his teeth into the Creption's tail.

Crawling out of the mud, Duncan stood up clumsily, stumbling a couple of times, abruptly running into a massive Veritian figure that was gazing at him.

"Are you all right?" Major Shoshuar said, extending one arm.

"We must help Antares," Duncan stammered, trying to get the stinging mud out of his eyes.

Shoshuar spotted the Creption struggling to rid himself of Antares's jaws. He noticed something else further ahead, but was suddenly knocked down to the ground. An enemy air squad had cast a heavy net, effectively immobilizing the Veridiawan.

"Not me, the captain!" Major Shoshuar barked, pointing at Clara when Duncan attempted to help him out. "Protect the captain."

Turning right, Duncan saw a Veritian woman, unarmed, with one of her legs stuck in a trap. A wolf-like creature was crouched in front of her on a large rock, ready to strike. Duncan was taken aback by the fearsome sight of the devilish-looking alien. But on seeing Clara completely powerless, he rushed quickly to her side. Stumbling on his knees, between the rock and the trapped female, he instinctively adopted a protective posture. Facing the Creption, Duncan put a trembling hand to his belt only to find an empty scabbard. He had inadvertently left his sword with Shoshuar during his attempt to release him.

Without warning, the Creption sprang forward. Duncan jumped towards Clara's sword, which was lying in the mud, and fell on its grip. The weapon sprung up like a catapult, ripping the rain in a fine spray of splitting droplets. Helplessly, the Creption spun on the propped blade and splashed down into the mud.

Duncan recoiled nervously from the inert body lying in front of him.

Without warning, the Creption sprang forward.

Still trapped by the metallic device, Clara raised her head and saw Shoshuar running towards her. He had just freed himself of the Creption net. Without saying anything, he clasped the trap and applied pressure against the sides. The mechanism snapped open, and Clara was released.

"How bad is it?" Shoshuar pointed at Clara's bleeding ankle.

"Not too bad."

"Can you walk?"

"Yes."

"I must go help Antares," Duncan said, rushing back to the battlefield.

"Hey!"

Duncan turned.

"Your sword." Shoshuar winked, tossing the weapon back to him.

Antares was about to strike a final blow on the reptilian's head, when the bulk of a heavy bear-like soldier knocked him to the ground.

"What do you think you're doing—bloody *leemow*? You'll never put your dirty paws on my friend again." The attacker smacked Antares on the face with one of his heavy arms, leaving him flattened on the ground. Brandishing his sword, the Creption thrust it towards Antares' neck. But the blade broke as it hit a rock buried in the mud two inches away from its intended target. Just in time, Duncan's sword had effectively averted the deadly strike.

The Creption turned around, holding the shattered grip in his hand, and abruptly hurled it at Duncan. Even as he eluded the missile, the soldier leaped at him. Duncan sprang to one side, and while still in the air, he thrust clumsily with his sword. Despite the sloppy jab, the blade sunk deep into the Creption's ankles, effectively hamstringing him.

To one side, the reptilian that had been fighting Antares lay dead in the mud. Attached to one of his legs was a metallic spike, still in its sheath. The hamstrung Creption grabbed the spike and started crawling towards Antares, who was struggling to regain consciousness. Duncan rushed towards the menacing soldier, wielding his sword ready to strike. But on reaching him, a strange impulse held him back. Something deep inside was suddenly halting Duncan from discharging the final blow.

"Stop! I'll spare your life."

His show of mercy did not have the intended effect.

"Don't you hear me? You've fought well enough, Creption. I'll spare your life—I will spare you!"

However, the Creption kept moving forward slowly, with a gory itch for the kill.

Desperately, Duncan jumped onto his enemy's back, and pressed the blade of his sword against the muscular throat beneath him. "Stop! Stop it, I say! I'll kill you, I will kill you!"

With that last thought, a stray projectile slammed into the back of his head. Like a rag doll, Duncan collapsed against the aggressor's ursine neck. Noticing that, the Creption thrust the human off his back into the mud. He immediately realized Duncan was merely unconscious.

"Hey, you! Bald one!" the Creption howled from the ground. "Go find someone to terminate that human."

"Aye-aye, sergeant," acknowledged a *wuol* flying in the fog.

Groggy, Antares lay a few feet ahead, totally exposed and unprotected. The injured Creption smirked and resumed dragging himself forward.

But he had lost too much blood. His paws looked unresponsive,

his muscles slack and his eyes unfocused. He was losing consciousness. The menacing spike he clutched in his hands would never reach
its intended victim.

Clara turned back and noticed Duncan a short way off, lying in the
mud. Smudged in blood, a dark green Creption with short legs and
a hyena appearance was sniffing at him. The *terminating trooper*[28]
cautiously bit one of Duncan's legs to check for any reaction; there
was none. Baring his combat teeth, he fixed his eyes on Duncan's
throat, slobbering.

Clara dashed towards him and slammed into his back. While the
Creption wrestled and jerked, Clara pushed her sword between his
shoulder and spine, killing him instantly.

After approaching Duncan, Clara lifted him gently by the torso.
She held him for a moment, keeping a protective hand under his
head. A streak of blood was running from beneath his right ear.

"How is he, girl-Captain?" said Antares, emerging from the fog.
He had some blood flowing from his nose.

"He's got a serious blow on his head. We must get him out at
once."

Shoshuar arrived. "What happened to the boy?"

"We must remove him from the battlefield." Clara wiped some
dirt off her nose. She turned to Antares. "Go get some help, Anty."
But the Veridiawan warrior stayed still, staring at her.

Clara gazed at Duncan. "Don't worry. Shoshuar and I will stay
here with him."

"I must stay with the boy-Dahncion during the whole battle, girl-
Captain."

Raylayhiagus—the same *whymeenidy* that had found Duncan the

---

28 The term was used for Creption soldiers whose only assignment was to kill
unconscious or seriously wounded enemy soldiers.

day he had arrived on the planet—now reached the spot. He looked weary, his wooden armor smudged with blood and mud. "'Got any trouble over here?"

"Rayly, we must take Dahncion out of this hell—now."

"Certainly, girl-Captain. You and bear-Shoshuar put the boy-Dahncion on my armor."

Clara nodded. "I will ride with you."

"If you just put the boy-Dahncion on my armor, I could run faster."

"Not a good idea," said Shoshuar, addressing Clara. "The Veridiawan warrior could get in big trouble if he's forced to defend himself and the boy. You'd better ride with him as well, Captain."

"An air-rescue squad is on its way, girl-Captain," a *wuol* yelled out, flying fast in their direction.

Clara looked up. "Right now, what we need is air coverage."

"Aye-aye, girl-Captain," said Seidy, disappearing into the fog.

"Let's get out of here," Shoshuar said, looking at Raylayhiagus. "Antares and I will be covering you."

The group departed immediately, trying to leave the battlefield in one piece. Duncan was lying on Raylayhiagus' armor, with his arms and head on one side and his legs dangling down the other. Clara was holding him firmly with her right arm, while clutching Raylayhiagus' mane with the other.

An enemy pack noticed the group moving across the field and started pursuit. It did not take long for the pack to catch up with the *whymeenidy*. Four Creption troopers were running readily along, exhibiting their copper fangs and metallic teeth. Shoshuar and Antares fought to protect Raylayhiagus, but the attackers were quickly overpowering them.

Just in time, a Veridiawan air squad emerged from the fog and began dropping stones over the Creption pack. Behind it, four sturdy *kerionteedos*, or flying snatchers, seized each Creption trooper, and after gaining lethal altitude, dropped them down to the ground.

The Veridiawan air defense had effectively saved the convoy from imminent danger.

Raylayhiagus was rapidly slowing down. The copper fangs had opened deep wounds on his legs. In addition to the bleeding, he was starting to feel weak and dizzy. However, they had not reached safety yet.

In the midst of a general weariness and despair, a fleeting image of the boy-Dahncion crossed the *whymeenidy*'s mind. Raylayhiagus did not know much about the human. However, he had heard a lot about him: he was supposed to be somebody very important, someone *who would save us all*—whatever that might mean. Even the girl-Captain herself was riding on his back to provide protection to such an important person.

Beyond his exhaustion, despite his open wounds, Raylayhiagus started regaining speed. The impression of having to protect Duncan's life above his very own was quickening his body and will unexpectedly. Out of the generalized depletion welling up from the searing pain, a powerful strength began to materialize. The Veridiawan spirit was now flooding Raylayhiagus' veins, outwardly crystallizing in a firm gallop. It was strange, unusual, something the warrior had never experienced before.

"This *boy-human* sure has magical powers," Raylayhiagus thought. "I have never felt better in my entire life."

15.

One female started yelling, and the other five, who were also washing at the pool, joined in the commotion. Yet they had not been the first to notice the smoke. The overseers were already summoning people for the emergency action parties to put the fire out. The task was proving problematic, since most of the male population was fighting in the

Swamp Valley. The sun had not yet set, but the dense clouds caused enough twilight to expose the approaching flames, fed by a dry wind from the south. A dozen straw shacks and stored wood, located in a rather isolated area within the city walls, seemed to be the epicenter of the conflagration.

Although a storm had pounded the Swamp Valley all day long, it had not rained over the city that day. But it was the season for heavy winds, which could spread the fire everywhere within the city walls. The old overseers looked concerned; they could not forget the big blaze of their younger days, which had consumed most of the village. Soon all the emergency parties were struggling to control the fire. As they worked, they wondered how it could have started. The winter had been a particularly rainy one.

But for Captain O'sihn, the smoky flames were the signal he was waiting for: three of his commandos had started the operation as planned. Aureerian—a Veridiawan flying warrior—was now about to reach the fortress' north-wing tower. At the top, there was a small window with sturdy bars across. Hovering in front of the window, Aureerian quickly rigged a rope around the bars.

From behind a thicket, about one hundred yards from the tower, three soldiers—two Veridiawans and one Realitian—were closing in rapidly on their target. Ivorai, Squirnoy, and Lieutenant Tygrum were racing against time. Although it might not have been too difficult for swift individuals like Squirnoy and Tygrum to remain unnoticed, that was far from the case for Ivorai, elephantine and slow as he was.

Upon reaching the target, Aureerian immediately dropped one end of the rope, the other end having already been attached to the bars on the window. Squirnoy picked it up and rapidly teased out five long wires at the end of the rope. Turning back, he fastened the wires onto the harness Ivorai was wearing for the operation.

"Apparel set," Squirnoy said, showing three fingers, the Veridiawan version of a thumbs-up.

Tygrum nodded and turned to Ivorai, who strained at the rope attached to his harness, the line shuddering in response. The rope stretched, twisted, and cracked noisily.

Suddenly, the stick Ivorai was holding in his teeth snapped as one of the five ends of the rope attached to his harness broke loose, opening a wound on one of his legs. But the rest of the rope held strong, still cracking and twisting, until a sudden slack on the harness made the Veridiawan stumble. The iron bars had finally yielded, shooting off stones and dust.

At once, Zainy—another flying Veridiawan warrior—dropped Commander Laida through the now unbarred window at the top of the tower. She landed inside on her feet, gripping a Veridiawan sword of jade.

"This is a rescue operation, Doctor. We'll get you out of here in no time. Hold this." Laida unhooked an extracting harness from her belt. Doctor Oyhtter stood passively, glancing at her. He looked sloppy, not very surprised, and somewhat annoyed. Wasting no time, Laida approached him and started attaching the harness onto his body.

"Once I have fixed this equipment, please stand in front of the window with your back against it." Laida passed a strap across the scientist's chest and fastened it tightly to his waist. "A flying Veridiawan soldier—Zeenthy—will lift you with this extraction-harness." Laida pulled on the already fastened apparel. "You will be retrieved by air."

Turning to Laida, Oyhtter finally spoke up: "And you call this a rescue operation . . ."

"Everything is well planned, Doctor," Laida asserted as she fastened a second strap.

"So, I figure you smart guys from the Navy have planned a way to carry my research material." Oyhtter pointed at a heap of thick yellow sheets with writing on both sides. He had manufactured the sheets from the coat of a dry fruit, the only food his captors had given him during his stay at the tower.

"Material?" added Laida, mainly focused on her work.

"Yes, Commander, all this material, my work of three months."

Laida kept working without paying much attention to him.

"This material is crucial for my project, which includes trying to stop this war of yours."

"I'll be covering you when you are retrieved," Laida continued. "After reaching the operational ceiling . . . "

"And believe me, I will not leave this place without it," Oyhtter reasserted, centered on his line of thought.

At that point, Laida stopped working on the harness, stood up in front of the scientist, and narrowed her eyes. "Doctor Oyhtter, I'm part of a team of ten, assigned to this high-risk rescue operation. Now that we have reached our objective—namely you—you can bet we're gonna get you out of here. We'll do this with or without your cooperation. And concerning your *material*: forget about it."

Oyhtter was about to reply when a door built into the floor, the only access to the tower chamber, opened abruptly upward. A remarkably large hominid popped inside, wielding a hatchet with both hands. He barged up on Laida, clumsily, but she spun around, chopping his head with a clean thrust of her sword.

"Now, Doctor, now!"

Oyhtter ran towards the window, where Zeenthy grabbed him at once. A moment later, Zainy, the same Veridiawan that had taken her there, dived by the tower and snatched Laida away.

Stress and fatigue could readily be traced on the eyes of the two flying Veridiawan warriors. Very different was the smug expression of Doctor Oyhtter: under his right arm, he was carrying his precious stack of yellow sheets.

Though it seemed an endless getaway, within seconds the team was beyond the fortress' moat. Along with the catapults that had started throwing projectiles, some archers on the city walls began shooting arrows. Even an improvised small *Creption* intercepting squad was now taking to the air. But the retrieving convoy was disappearing rapidly inside the lower clouds.

After a few minutes of flying inside the foggy ocean of freezing droplets, tension started to slack, and Laida began feeling very cold. She was now trying to make visual contact with Doctor Oyhtter, but he was far ahead, carried by Zeenthy.

The operation had been somewhat out of bounds. Many things could have gone wrong. For success, the enemy was assumed to behave "as expected" in too many instances, contravening standard military procedures.

Drifting away from her mission, Laida began to grow concerned about O'sihn and the rest of the team fighting in the valley. They only had rudimentary weapons and were still not fully acclimated to the conditions of the planet. And what about Tygrum and the others? Had they finally managed to get back into the tunnel the Veridiawans had been drilling for weeks? To involve someone like Ivorai in a job like that . . . It was true that no one else in the village had the strength to remove the bars, but to expect he would pass unnoticed still seemed insane to Laida. Yet, she had backed the idea at the war council. She felt uncomfortable about that.

Laida blew into her hands, trying to warm her fingers through the wet fabric of her Veridiawan gloves.

"Are you okay, bear-Commander?"[29] Zainy asked, laying his beak down on his chest.

"I am," Laida said, breathing through her gloves.

---

29 A better translation would have been "she-bear-Commander". However, in the current rendition, and in order to stay away from awkwardly long names, we chose to ignore the gender always used in Veridiawan titles, except for a few cases like "girl-Captain" or "boy-Dahncion".

"We still have some flying to do, but . . . I think we've made it, bear-Commander."

Laida looked up. The Veridiawan warrior looked definitively more at ease than a few minutes before.

"Yes," Laida added, "I hope we've all made it."

16.

Raylayhiagus stumbled and rolled to the ground, casting his two riders over his head. Clara fell on her back, all the time holding onto an unconscious Duncan and preventing him from further harm. It had been a painful fall. She felt disoriented for a moment. Laying Duncan down on the muddy grass, Clara ran towards Raylayhiagus, who was lying immobile but conscious.

"It was a hole, girl-Captain. I broke one leg."

Clara knelt by him and stroked his mane. "Don't worry, Rayly, everything will be all right."

"You go help the boy-Dahncion, girl-Captain. People say he is a very important one."

"Never mind. I can take care of you both."

Three Veridiawan soldiers had been escorting them from the air since the last Creption attack. Two of them, Daihyouleeby and Jasiris, now landed beside Duncan, while Jasindon, the third of the party, remained in the air scouting for enemy activity. The three Veridiawans were large flying individuals, similar to Zeenthy and Zainy, who had been working with O'sihn's team on the rescue operation.

"What do we do now?" asked Jasiris, stepping towards Clara.

"We are still far away from the village, but too close to the battle-field," Clara said, gazing at Duncan as she brushed a lock of his hair.

"Here come bear-Major Shoshuar and Antares, girl-Captain!" Jasindon yelled as he spotted the two soldiers approaching.

"What happened?" Shoshuar touched Duncan's forehead.

"Nothing new with Dahncion," Clara said, and gestured towards Raylayhiagus. "He has a broken leg."

"I'm fine, girl-Captain," said the *whymeenidy*, a statement belying his exposed fracture.

"You and Antares can stay here with Raylayhiagus," Shoshuar said. "I'll take Dahncion back to the village."

"What?" Clara argued.

"Antares will stay with you. We are too close to the battlefield," Shoshuar explained. "It would be dangerous for you to stay here alone."

"Never mind Antares or me. You can't carry the boy all the way back to the village."

"Girl-Captain, may I speak some words?" Daihyouleeby said.

"Uh-huh," Clara muttered, her eyes fixed on Shoshuar.

"The village is still far away, and the Swamp Valley is very too close. But the Pine Hills are very close by, and in the Pine Hills there are many caves—big and long caves. You can all hide inside one cave. And while you are hidden inside one cave, I can fly fast to the village to find help."

Clara gazed at the injured Veridiawan warrior.

"Don't worry about me, girl-Captain. Very soon people from the village will come for me and will rescue me."

"We can't leave you exposed to Creption terminating packs," Clara said.

"You take care of the boy-Dahncion, and I'll take care of myself," added Raylayhiagus. He was holding a broken spear in his teeth, to try to deal with the pain, somehow.

"We'll take care of both of you," Shoshuar added. "We'll put something together, and Antares and I will drag you out to those Pine caves."

"The caves of the Pine Hills," restated Daihyouleeby.

"Drag both Dahncion and Rayly to the caves?" Clara objected.

"Why drag? Why both? Better fly them to the caves," Jasiris stated. "The Pine Hills are very close by, and the boy-Dahncion is not very heavy. I can fly him there."

"And I can fly Raylayhiagus," Jasindon howled from the air.

"I am assigned to fight along and protect the boy-Dahncion," Antares contested.

Clara remained pensive, her long blond hair falling over her eyes. She felt she had to stay by Duncan, but she realized that would not help him. "As Girl-Captain Veridiawan Warrior, I am assigning you new orders," Clara said to Antares, invoking her new Veridiawan rank. "Jasiris, Jasindon: you two will carry Dahncion, but not Raylayhiagus. He is heavy and you are tired. You must get the boy-Dahncion to the caves at once without risking detection."

"We shall, girl-Captain," they acknowledged together.

"Daihyouleeby, go get some help from the village."

"Right away," he said, and took off.

"Anty—let's help Shoshuar to carry Raylayhiagus to the caves."

"Wait a minute." Shoshuar looked at Jasiris. "We don't know how to find the cave where you're taking the boy."

"Don't worry, bear-Major," said Jasiris. "Rayly knows the cave."

The *whymeenidy* lifted up his head. "Me?"

Jasiris grinned. "The cave we played in as kids, dummy."

"Oh . . . the curvy cave."

Without delay, Jasiris and Jasindon departed with their human cargo. Using the branches of a nearby tree torn down by the storm, Shoshuar and Antares began to improvise the stretcher for Raylayhiagus.

As they worked, Clara comforted the *whymeenidy*, but she began to notice he was ready to faint. That was something they could not afford, since he was the only one who knew the location of the cave. Taking a shot from her belt, Clara applied it to one of his legs. Raylayhiagus relaxed immediately, at the same time becoming very alert.

With the stretcher finally ready, the team departed, sheltered by a rolling silent fog.

17.

"Some dream . . . " Extending one arm to reach his bedside lamp in the pitch darkness, Duncan found his fingers brushing through something that resembled long hair.

"Everything is all right. We are safe in here."

Duncan sought a blanket he failed to find. "Who are you?"

"Clara . . . Captain Clara," she answered, not sure he could recognize her after the severe blow to his head.

"So . . . Captain Clara . . . " Duncan said, as he struggled to sit up. "I must be dreaming," he thought, and closed his eyes. But he was perfectly awake, somewhat scared, and had a nasty headache. "Where . . . what is this place?"

"We're inside a cave, not far from the village." The cave was long and had the shape of an S.

Duncan put his hand to his head. He felt dizzy. "What happened? The battle . . . "

"It was an air strike. A stone hit your head. Raylayhiagus, Antares, and Shoshuar removed you from the battlefield. On our way to the village, Raylayhiagus broke a leg; we had to seek refuge inside this cave."

"Raylayhiagus, the *whyny* . . . *whyneemidy*?"

"The *whymeenidy*, yes. He's inside this cave, too."

"How is he?"

"He suffered an exposed fracture, but Shoshuar managed to put the bones back together. It wasn't easy." She sighed. "I helped him splint the leg. He is sleeping now."

"What about Antares?"

"He's outside, doing his watch."

"Captain." A voice came from the entrance to the cave.

"Shoshuar?"

"Yes, Captain. We have visitors, from the village."

"Coming." Clara turned to Duncan. "I'll be back."

"Hey, wait for me." Duncan stood up, but a sudden surge of pain in his head pulled him back down.

At the entrance, Clara found a Veridiawan villager waiting for her.

"Girl-Captain, I am Inury."

Clara nodded gently.

"I convey an important message from His Majesty, Coelious III." As he talked, the small *skyer* moved his wings slightly. He was slim and had a sharp look. He was similar to a swallow, but the backs of his wings were bright blue. He had Veridiawan marks painted on his body, and a blue *V* mark on top of his head, as any messenger would wear.

"May *Waswillbe* preserve the Patriarch," Clara responded, following the native protocol.

"And may *Willbewas*[30] also give him wisdom and strength," the Veridiawan acknowledged. "Girl-Captain, thus speaketh Coelious: *Girl-Captain Clara, Iswillbe graciously granted victory to* Veridiawa. *The Creption army hath been defeated, and the* Wise Veridiawan Elder *hath finally been retrieved by Captain O'sihn's warriors.*" This was a reference to Doctor Oyhtter. "*At night, the bright flying houses from the sky landed in Veridiawa. All the* newones *entered the flying houses but for Captain O'sihn and Lieutenant Saigtin. They will stay in Veridiawa until they find the new* newone *Dahncion, and all the others who are with him. And then, the flying houses went up into the sky, from where they had come.*" This is His Majesty's message."

Messengers such as Inury had great powers of retention. They were capable of repeating what they were told, exactly as they had been told. "Captain O'sihn also has a message for you."

Clara waved a hand, inviting Inury to continue.

"*Wiri river has flooded the fields. That has momentarily kept us in the village. As soon as general weather conditions improve, we will head towards your current location. Your orders are to hold your position until*

---

30 *Waswillbe* and *Willbewas* are native terms that express exactly the same concept, with no distinction or differentiation in meaning. When in a conversation someone refers to God, the term *Waswillbe* is first used; the interlocutor or interlocutors acknowledge the reference with a sentence that contains the equivalent term *Willbewas*. When no exchange is used, *Iswillbe* is used, the neutral term for God.

we arrive. We will keep you posted on a daily basis. If after two days you cease receiving any communication from us, present instructions will expire and you will proceed according to your best judgment. This is Captain O'sihn's message, girl-Captain."

"Thank you," Clara said. "Would you stay here and have some rest?"

"My orders are to find the girl-Captain, to give her the two messages, and to fly back to the village, right away."

Clara nodded. "I have a couple of messages I'd like you to carry back to the village."

"Copying."

Clara smiled. "Please tell His Majesty Coelious III: *Thy Majesty, we are all well—including Raylayhiagus—and we are all much honored that thou hast sent a Veridiawan messenger to see to our safety.*" Clara paused, looking into the fog.

"Is that all?" asked Inury.

"Please deliver this message to Captain O'sihn: *Don't worry about us, Captain. We are okay and reasonably safe inside these caves. Dahncion has recovered consciousness and he seems to be all right.* Oh, tell him also not to take unnecessary risks. Let him wait until the river folds back."

"We are glad to see you well, girl-Captain," said Inury, speaking in the name of Veridiawa.

"May *Waswillbe* send you speedy winds."

"*Willbewas* may He." Inury immediately took off. Clara watched him disappear in the thin morning haze. At the horizon, a shivering sun disk was starting to warm the surrounding rainforest.

18.

"Boy, this smells really good," Duncan said enthusiastically. The smell from the firewood reminded him of the cookouts that he and his friends would occasionally have in the woods near his hometown.

"You're just really hungry." Clara chuckled as she stirred up the contents of a huge pot they had received by Veridiawan "air" delivery.

"That has nothing to do with it. And by the way, what is it?"

"I'm trying to cook some *reiba* soup," Clara said, pointing at the smoky pot. "And to barbecue a couple of *wedias*," she added, gesturing her head at some embers.

Not very enlightened by the clarification, Duncan smiled politely.

Clara brushed aside the lock of hair that had just dropped in front of her eyes. "*Reiba* is the root of a *litic* that grows almost entirely under the ground. The only parts of it that come out are its fruits, the *wedias*."

"*Litic?*"

"Uh-huh . . . animals that grow like plants?[31] Have you ever heard of them?" Clara added.

"I'm afraid you will have to lecture me on *litology*."

"*Lotanics*." Clara grinned. "But only if you bring me those twigs, over there."

Duncan smiled. As he picked up some small branches, Clara rearranged her blond hair into a long tail, tying it up with a blue ribbon.

Duncan was soon back with enough firewood. "So, what about your lotanics class?" he asked, holding a dry curly stick by the *reiba* soup pot.

"Well, *litics—animalitics—are livoids*[32] that look like vegetables, though they belong to the animal kingdom. They are similar to tuber roots and typically grow around vegetal roots from which they feed."

"Interesting."

"Yep, and some species of *litics* are even carnivorous."

"You mean they eat . . . animals?" Duncan asked, peering suspiciously at the surroundings.

---

31 The meat of edible *litics* is similar to what we would recognize as beef. *Litics'* roots are always covered with a thick skin very much akin to hide. Note that even when *litics* are rooted, like plants, the parts that surface from the ground move significantly during the day. These motions are generated by the muscular structure of their "bodies." Although they are very slow, they can have a large influence in the shape of a *litic*. The way a *litic* looks in the evening can be very different from how it looked in the morning.

32 Living entities.

Clara giggled. "Only in old horror stories. They just feed on other *litic* roots."[33]

Duncan threw the stick he was holding into the fire. "And what about those . . . *wedas?*"

"*Wedias*. They are the fruit of the *reiba*. They have very tender meat, and their *flidias* are cute." Clara took some spicy dry leaves and sprinkled them in the soup, rubbing them to powder with her fingers. "*Flidias* are the flowers of the *litics*. They are beautiful—most of them—though they have no scent. But you seldom use *flidias* as ornaments; they decay very fast—and with a nasty smell." Clara wrinkled her nose and shook her head with a very feminine gesture.

"The meaty turnips that I ate in the village and in Realitas . . . I guess this is what it was," Duncan said. "I wonder what the white creamy stuff was that they served at the palace, in Royal City."

"That might've been *wada* cream," Clara nodded. "It's prepared from the fruit of the *brental*. Would you keep stirring the soup while I keep an eye on the *wedias?*"

"Sure."

Clara took out a knife and started slicing the *litics* finely. "Are there many humans on your planet?"

"No. Actually, I wouldn't be surprised if I were the only one," Clara said.

"I thought you had been born there."

Clara shook her head. "I most likely came from a very different place, perhaps a planet called Kriggis, in the Kalept system. The people of Kriggis are mostly humans—tori humans—whereas the people of Veritas are *ossians*."[34]

"*Tori?*"

"Uh-huh. My ancestors clearly had *tori* traits."

---

33 This statement is a rough generalization. We will leave the special cases for another occasion.

34 Genetic phenotype with bear-like features.

Clara looked noticeably different from any woman Duncan had seen on Earth. To him, the texture of her skin was reminiscent of a drawing or a cartoon. The same distinctive traits were present in O'sihn's wife, Laida, even if she was an *ossian* and not a human, like Clara. Actually, Laida had been born in *Veritas*, although she had lived most of her life in Realitas, O'sihn's home planet.

On the other hand, Duncan himself did not look like any human being from Earth. After the *transrealization* procedure, his body had acquired a *rilitian* morphology. His appearance was now like that of the people of Realitas who had brought him to their universe. The texture of his skin had changed; it was more defined, more resilient, and it had a distinctive brilliance, like that of a smooth plastic, with traces of a metallic gleam.

"The people from Veridiawa, like the Creptions, are *rilitian*," Clara continued. "But other peoples live in other parts of this planet—even humans like us—who are *tori*."

"So people in this universe are either *tori* or *rilitian*," Duncan added.

"Oh, no, there are many other strains."

"Have you been to Kriggis lately?" Duncan asked.

"No, and I don't actually know whether I'm from Kriggis or not." It was during the Klymbom Wars,"[35] Clara continued. "Veritas and Kriggis were allies, as they had always been. One day there was a full-scale attack on Veritas. Many people died. Veritian soldiers found me close to a Kriggian wreck. I was unconscious, badly wounded. I was dying. They took me to Veritatis Verius, a close-by city—or rather, what was left of it. There, they healed my wounds and took care of me.

"The war went on for one more year. A young couple—Maercus and Mirtiam—adopted me as their daughter. They were scientists— they are—like most people of their world." Veritas was literally a scientists' planet, with an ancestral high regard for wisdom.

---

35 "The Klymbom crisis" was an early stage of the larger conflict with the Establishment.

"I learned to love them like my own parents, whom I can't remember." Clara paused for a moment. Her eyes were peaceful, with a subtle trace of sadness. "The people of Veritas managed to heal my body, but they could not restore my memory—my past memory. I only have fuzzy images, like flashes of old recollections.

"When the war was over, Maercus and Mirtiam helped me to try to locate my relatives, but to no avail. Most likely, my family died, either in the wreckage where I was found, or on Kriggis itself. Ninety-five percent of the Kriggian population was obliterated in a direct attack shortly after I was rescued."

Duncan was staring at Clara in silence. "I . . . I am very sorry to hear all this."

Clara looked at him with a tenuous smile.

"How long ago did all that happen?"

"About eight years."

"So it took you only eight years to become a Marine Corps Lieutenant Commander?" Duncan said, seeking to change the topic of the conversation.

"I'm a sub[36] commander because of the war. I joined Veritas Naval Academy about six years ago, shortly after the war started. The huge mobilization led to a shortage of officers, which pushed me up the ranks very fast."

Duncan smiled, "This war may have helped a little, but I've seen plenty of other reasons for you to have become a Marine Lieutenant Commander."

Clara laughed unassumingly. "And what about you? What about your Earth, your universe?"

"My life on Earth hasn't been as exciting as yours, I'm afraid."

Clara rested her eyes on the steaming pot. "What about your folks?"

---

36 *Sub Commander*, instead of *Lieutenant Commander*, was only used by senior officers referring to a junior officer of that rank, as for example, a Commander addressing a Lieutenant Commander as Sub Commander. It was also used when referring to one's personal rank, like here in the case of Clara.

"Nice. I had many friends where I grew up, and I was starting to make new ones at college. But I sort of miss my old friends. My hometown is relatively small, and most of us knew each other since we were kids. We grew up together, all attending the same school. When I was younger, my family and I—"

Clara made a brisk signal, bidding Duncan to be silent. Very quietly, she laid down the branch she was holding, and crouched down. Her attention was focused on the dense foliage in front of them. With silent dexterity, Clara began to unsheathe her Veridiawan sword.

"So, that's the way you meet your rescuers . . ." said a voice coming from the forest.

Clara put down her sword, relieved.

"I'm very glad to see you well," O'sihn added, stepping out from behind a long, dark green leaf. Lieutenant Saigtin emerged simultaneously from a different angle.

"How is Raylayhiagus?" the captain asked.

"He's fine." Clara nodded and looked to her left. "He's inside a cave, behind those trees."

"I'm happy to hear that," O'sihn said, patting Duncan's right shoulder. "Some people from Veridiawa are on their way. Once they reach us—later, this afternoon, if everything goes well—we will start making preparations to carry Raylayhiagus back to the village." As he talked, O'sihn glanced at the bubbling pot of soup. "You guys could even find time for a picnic, huh?"

"Aye, Captain," said Clara, raising an eyebrow.

"Hey, take it easy, girl. Saigtin and I would like to join you."

"In that case, you're just in time for grilled *wedias* and *reiba* soup."

"They certainly helped us locate your position." Saigtin chuckled.

"Your cooking does smell good," O'sihn said, "though I'm not too fond of *litics*."

"With the captain's permission," Saigtin added. "Is it too long before dinner?"

"It's almost ready. You just wait here while I go get Antares and Shoshuar."

"We won't move from this spot," O'sihn remarked, gazing at the humid green leaves behind which Clara disappeared. "Wonderful girl, isn't she?"

"Sure she is," Duncan agreed with a subtle excess of emphasis. In his eyes, a furtive impression became palpable, perceptible. It conveyed a lack of interest, a veiled disappointment, an unfulfilled desire flowing from a lacking, or perhaps, oversimplified reality. As the thought materialized in his mind, Duncan shook his head in silence: "Only, she's just a drawing."

CHAPTER 4

A Far-Off Clue

19.

The first day of shore leave back in Royal City did not seem to promise much fun. It was a working day, in difficult times, with everybody constantly busy. Duncan was in no particular mood for having fun with his comrades, much less meeting new people. He wanted his distance that morning, and the Sky Prairies seemed a very good choice for that. It was a quiet place with hills, woods, and meadows, which extended to the outskirts of the city.

After spending a couple of hours walking through the plains, Duncan lay down in a field of wildflowers. He rested his eyes on the city, which loomed behind the foliage, crowned by its castle. Duncan had the impression of having had left his Earth many years in the past. The reasons for his unlikely trip remained obscure to him. After the initial excitement, fear, longing, and a strong sensation of worthlessness were settling in. For the first time in his life, Duncan had been exposed to war and had even watched death pass close by. He had seen suffering, bloodshed, killing—he had witnessed the crudeness and cruelty of war. His experience in Veridiawa had made him realize how real things could get to be in Reality, and how different from what he thought certain realities could actually be. Only a few weeks had passed since his arrival in this universe, but he had already been forced to adjust very rapidly, to many things.

After half an hour in the field, Duncan resumed his walk. He eventually reached the Sky Shore, where the Sky Prairies and the sky literally met. Ten thousand feet below, a splendid continental

Ten thousand feet below, a splendid continental landscape slumbered
beneath the hovering island. The endless Breezian Sea
appeared through a misty summer haze.

landscape slumbered beneath the hovering island, with pine forests and hills showing no signs of civilization. Lakes and rivers, and beyond them, the endless Breezian Sea, appeared through a misty summer haze. Above, Realia—Realitas' splendid satellite—shone with its dark blue brightness, crossed by vivid crimson bands. The satellite was truly impressive, even if that night, only a portion of its indigo, emerald, and golden triad of rings was visible, since it was in its first quarter. Its disk, the size of many moons, was starting to set off under the warm blanket of the rosy clouds below.

Dusk was spreading quietly. The first stars began to emerge in the crystal-clear sky. Duncan gazed at the brightest star without getting much comfort. He had been thinking a lot after the battle in the Swamp Valley, and now he had doubts and questions, but not many answers. In his perception, his first actions to help the Realdom had been disappointing, to say the least. What was so special about him that many should have such great expectations for him? How was he supposed to make any difference at all? And there was still something else. The alternative of going back to Earth having not accomplished anything of value in this universe was depressing. However strong his longing for home was, he did not want to consider this possibility.

The same sensation of worthlessness he had experienced during the past week was intensifying as the night drew in. Duncan finally started making his way back towards the city. The lonely evening had not been of any particular help to him.

20.

"May I talk with you for moment? It won't take long." Captain O'sihn was coming from headquarters, still wearing his uniform. He looked fresh and sharp, even though he had started his day very early.

"Sure."

O'sihn sat down by a wall-sized window in the main lounge, which had a glimmering view of Royal City. They were at the top of the tall building where Duncan was living.

"So, how is Realitas treating you?"

"Very kindly." Duncan nodded and turned to the window. "So far."

O'sihn looked at him with a raised eyebrow.

"Don't get me wrong," Duncan said. "I know you all mean well, but I also know who I really am."

O'sihn listened with an unchanged expression.

"Surely you don't think, still, that I am 'the one' you've been waiting for," Duncan added.

"I think you're an essential factor to win this war."

Duncan sighed. "I've been nothing but a nuisance so far."

"I disagree."

"In Althea 8, I was rendered unconscious in battle. Because of that, many had to risk their necks for me. You and Saigtin had to stay on the planet, a Veridiawan warrior broke a leg trying to save me, and I caused trouble for Major Shoshuar and Captain Clara. And all because I didn't stay in the village as you instructed me."

They had already gone over the issue of Duncan's involvement in the battle against directives, and for O'sihn, it was a closed matter. "Getting hit by a medium-sized rock on the back of one's head can be inconvenient," the captain commented, with a gentle smile.

Duncan snorted. "I suppose you're right, but this inconvenience forced you and the others to stay on the planet."

"We do things of the sort when any of us gets in trouble. And in real operations—particularly during external missions[37]—some of us get in trouble once in a while."

Duncan shook his head. "The purpose of my being here is not yet clear to me. Everybody seems to believe that I'm about to save the entire universe—my own Earth included as some sort of a bonus." Duncan forced an uneasy smile. "If my performance against those Creptions—who belong to a primitive culture—was deplorable, how

---

[37] External missions were operations that unfolded in real battlefields, like the battle at the Swamp Valley in Veridiawa. Internal missions, on the other hand, took place within close quarters, such as battleships or headquarter-monitored operations.

am I supposed to be of any help against the Establishment?"

Duncan paused and looked at O'sihn, who glanced back calmly. It was not the first time the captain had heard such arguments from him.

"I don't know," Duncan continued. "I just don't know. The whole thing doesn't make much sense to me. I feel I am out of place, giving false hopes to many who expect from me something I just cannot give."

"I think I understand some of your concerns, Dahncion, although I have a very different perspective. First of all, I wouldn't rate your performance in battle as *deplorable*. Your inexperience causes you to come up with such a limited evaluation. The facts are clear. Your attitude towards Antares was commendable, and you saved Clara's life. For all her experience and professional qualifications, Captain Clara had been rendered out of combat and caught in a dead-end situation. Yet, risking your life, you saved hers."

"That was luck," Duncan said. "I was trying to get her sword when that . . . alien got himself killed by falling on it accidentally."

"Perhaps, but before that, you ran towards Clara, placing yourself between her and the Creption. Upon discovering you were unarmed, you were caught in a dead-end situation yourself. However, you successfully found a way out by locating and reaching that sword."

"I didn't realize I was unarmed until I was there."

"Because you didn't think of yourself first, but of Captain Clara's safety," O'sihn responded.

"My having saved her doesn't mean I am anything," Duncan retorted. "We're talking about the Establishment, here, which by now holds a vast empire. And it seems like it already outmatches the combined forces of the entire Realdom." Duncan's evaluation was somewhat negative and premature, but still not too far from the truth.[38]

---

38 During the previous days, Duncan had been researching the history of the conflict and the current situation. He had done it mainly from his room, utilizing the standard media and information system. This had given him a good overview of the

"It would take a giant to defeat such power."

O'sihn gave Duncan a pointed look. "Perhaps, only a boy."

"I guess I mentioned I was going to be brief." O'sihn reclined on his chair.

"No . . . this is good. It's good talk."

"I'd rather not take much more of your resting time tonight. Tomorrow, we're leaving for Cerendal, a nearby asteroid in our local inner belt. We need to pick up some strategic procedures,[39] and possibly give Doctor Oyhtter some feedback. His laboratory is on Cerendal, in one of SERI's facilities. He has been looking forward to talking to you since he was rescued in Veridiawa. It's a short trip, but we might stay there for a week or so."

"When would we be leaving?"

"We should be ready by 500R."

"Sounds early."

"There is a regular red-eye shuttle at 545 we must not miss if we don't want to spend a whole day just traveling. We would be arriving at Cerendal by 900R. Up there, they hold the same time convention as here."

"Is Laida coming along?"

"Yes, and also Lieutenant Commander Clara."

"Clara?" Duncan said with surprise. He expected she would be back in Veritas, by then.

---

general situation in a very short time, but all according to what he was searching for. This, combined with his interpretation of events from Earth's standards, gave him a skewed understanding of the status of the conflict. Still, it was true that the situation was looking more favorable for the Establishment than for the Realdom, which was starting to cause great concern.

39 Cerendal was a research facility, specializing in many fields. This included procedure development in *Logical Dynamics*, some of which were generated for military operations. The incoming mission was going to demand specific training and special procedures, both of which O'sihn was planning to obtain during the trip to the asteroid. We will revisit the *Logical Dynamics* subject later in this chapter.

"She volunteered to be assigned with us, and Veritas Headquarters approved her request. So I think we'll have her valuable help for quite some time."

"It sounds good."

"It certainly does."

O'sihn put a firm hand on Duncan's shoulder. "See you in the morning."

21.

"Dahncion, Captain O'sihn, Commander Laida . . . " Doctor Danal stopped at the young human female, a quizzical expression on his face.

"Doctor, let me introduce you to Lieutenant Commander Clara, Veritas Marine Corps," O'sihn said.

"We've heard about you, Lieutenant Commander. We are honored to have you here."

"Doctor." Clara nodded, flushing slightly.

The group was standing on the platform where the shuttle had just landed. Cerendal was a rather large asteroid, though still devoid of any atmosphere. Accordingly, all its facilities were pressurized. Life on such research centers was fairly similar. But Cerendal had a few peculiarities, including the Realdom's highest density of scientists, ninety-one percent.

"At this moment, Doctor Oyhtter is chairing a working session. He and his team have been devoted full time to the project that brings you here since he came back a few days ago—something we owe to all of you." Danal bowed respectfully.

"We don't want to distract Doctor Oyhtter or any of his collaborators unnecessarily," O'sihn remarked. "This team is entirely at his convenience."

"Oh, no, no, no, Captain. Doctor Oyhtter's expressed desire is for all of you to get involved immediately upon arrival. He's aware of your short stay here, so he intends to take advantage of your presence on Cerendal as much as would be convenient to you. The working session he's chairing at the moment started a few minutes ago, and it involves a subject that concerns all of us." Danal paused, staring at his guests. "You may be tired from the trip, though."

"We are here to give full cooperation," O'sihn said. "Yet we may disturb this meeting with our late arrival."

"Absolutely not, Captain."

"In that case, let's get to work, Doctor."

Danal nodded. "Your luggage is presently being carried to your quarters. We hope you'll find them comfortable. Now, if you'd follow me, *Erandie*."

The Realitian team reached the conference room quickly. O'sihn, Laida, Clara, and Duncan slipped quietly through one of the side entrances. There were few seats left, so they scattered among the attendants and sat down wherever they could find a spot.

The room was semicircular in shape, and sloped gently to a wide platform located in its center. Oyhtter stood in front of an adjacent wall that functioned as a large screen, along with three other scientists. Each had a c-card[40] behind their ears. Doctor Oyhtter had the unpleasant habit of storming screens with several simultaneous pages. He would then switch from one to another at the speed of his mind. Despite the impression of sloppiness that could give, his thoughts would always follow a relentless, though often elusive, logic.

But what caught Duncan's attention in particular was not so much the procedure, or the strange notation on the screen, but the eerie conclusions the scientists were drawing from it all. In the culture in which Duncan had been raised, the possibility of conceiving such analysis would have seemed farfetched at best. Fascinated, Duncan

---

40 C-cards, that is, *control cards*, were brain-activated terminals used to write on the screen.

gazed intently at the screen. The symbols written on it were grouped much like formulas or equations, although arranged in a fashion wholly unfamiliar to him. He could recognize only a few abstract words, scattered through the expressions between bracket-like symbols. Doctor Oyhtter and the other three scientists were at the center of the discussion.

"After three years, we're still stuck here," Oyhtter said.

"Well, we *have* isolated this HCQ system, finally," Doctor Giriana pointed out. She was a young scientist, younger than usual for someone working on Oyhtter's team.

"Even if solving this system may pose some particular challenge, we should be able to produce some useful preliminary results from its present formulation," Doctor Sealing added, trying to relieve some of Oyhtter's tension.

"This *particular* challenge is what *particularly* worries me, Doctor," Oyhtter complained, his eyes boring through the screen. "Time is running short. The team from Realitas is about ready to collect the strategic mode of action for the next phase, and what is it going to get?" Doctor Oyhtter looked at Giriana, who glanced back in silence. "An unsolved system of hyper-causal *logai*—that's all it's gonna get. We ought to find something far more practical than this, some explicit procedure."

"Maybe . . . " Sealing added, and paused.

"Go ahead." Oyhtter waved a hand and squinted.

Doctor Sealing started working on the screen through his c-card. Some characters switched from the blue color of the general text to a fluorescent scarlet. They were part of a specific set of symbols that seemed to be replicated only in a few *logai*.

"In my opinion," Sealing continued, "the key to solving this problem lies in replacing the terms in red with a fitting particular solution."

Oyhtter stared at the screen with a finger on his lips. "Interesting."

"May I, Doctor?" asked Giriana.

"Mm."

"The *logoid* system seems to exhibit a self-determined, self-adjoined structure. If that's the case, the particular solution Doctor Sealing suggests would be a unique solution."

"Never mind," Oyhtter objected. "This system cannot reach a *para-excelsus* structure. The generalized strength is non-symmetric. We would only get degenerate solutions this way."

"Still," Tigurst said, "I think Doctor Giriana may have a point. True, there is an inherent strength-truth asymmetry in the way the problem is posed. However, if we replace this term by initial condition thirty-five—" Tigurst pointed at the upper right corner of the screen—"we may still reach a *para-excelsus* structure, though in a Plinidas form. Thus we would have a full C.T.G."[41]

Oyhtter remained absorbed in the screen for a moment. "And since the solution to any C.T.G. is unique," he commented, "that would constitute a general solution to the system." He kept staring at the screen, nodding repeatedly with an optimistic gleam, as he grew more confident with Tigurst's approach every time he looked at it.

"Hm. So, what should we do?" Oyhtter sighed, tilting his head towards Giriana without removing his sight from the notation.

"A candidate solution search?"

"Precisely." Oyhtter turned to the scientific community present. "I would appreciate everybody's input now." He looked from side to side. "So, who is willing to cast the first dart?"

Professor Elefborg raised the base of his trunk, letting the rest hang in a dignified manner. "From the form of the third *logoid*, I would propose the {*Deolibior*} set." The *logum*[42] was related to the concept of intelligence.

---

41 Continuous Transcendental Group.

42 *Logum*: logical abstract operator, with definite properties and qualities, used in and defined within the discipline known as *Logical Dynamics*. This science was widely used in strategic planning to help predict certain actions, to produce plans designed to generate specific events with controlled effects, or to try to change or

"Doctor Giriana, would you please help us out?"

Giriana entered the corresponding *logum*-set into her QD, a device used to solve *logum* systems. "It does not satisfy the system, Doctor."

Oyhtter lifted his eyes to the audience. "Yes, Doctor Kahn-inne Dee?"

"Based on the topology of the natural boundary conditions, I would try {Loyalty}."[43]

Oyhtter turned back to Giriana, who was already feeding her QD with the new candidate *logum*. "It does not satisfy."

From the first row, someone slightly waved a colorful feathery tail. "Doctor Peacordk?"

"I'd propose {Beauty}."

Giriana tried the *logum*, along with two other possible solutions of the same family. "It doesn't satisfy either."

"Yes, Doctor Foxroxina?" Oyhtter continued.

"{Sagacity}?"

The QD's answer was not different.

"Professor Lia Kollumba, please."

"{Peace}, and its first five *q*-derivatives." But it produced dysfunctional solutions.

"Doctor Hyens?"

"The {Bliss} family, in its compact form."

The QD took a few seconds to process the solution, but eventually Giriana looked up and shook her head.

"Please, Doctor," Oyhtter said, fixing his eyes on a conspicuous figure.

"I propose {Fortitude}," Dr. Oxington said.

It did not work either. Oyhtter's uneasiness was plain to see. His eyebrows were furrowed with tension, and he was starting to pace hastily back and forth.

---

prevent certain outcomes. Warfare was one of many fields where *Logical Dynamics* was utilized.

43 All subsequent *logai* will be spelled with related English terms to try to minimize awkwardness in the text.

"Yes, Doctor Sheeplova?"

"The {Bounty} Kareman *logum*," Sheeplova postulated, in her distinctive accent.

The *logum* did not yield any positive results.

"Let's try {Wisdom}," Oyhtter said with confidence.

Giriana's swift reply thwarted his expectations.

Oyhtter remained thoughtful for a moment. "All right, all right," he continued, shaking his head. "Let's see, who else? Doctor Von Beavern, please."

"{Assiduity}?"

It also failed.

"Doctor Kang-Urha . . ."

"{Aegis}, and all {Alacrity} group inferences."

Giriana tried these *logai* and all their modal combinations, but to no avail.

"Doctor Eaglstein?"

"I guess we haven't tried {Freedom} yet."

They had not, but the QD's answer was not different.

They went on exploring many other *logum* sets, including combinations of *logum* sets that had been tried and failed. They attempted several algorithms and abstractor solvers, various *logicalizers* and *transcendectors*, and all types of *logoi* inference strategies. However, one after another, each proposed solution utterly failed to satisfy the elusive logical system.

Since he had entered the auditorium, Duncan had been struggling to make some sense out of the strange notation on the screen. One particular symbol had made a subtle impression on him—a cryptic, yet graspable, impression. It was as if in that symbol, somehow, lay the essence of the solution to the problem.[44]

---

44 The symbols used were ideograms, analogous to Chinese symbols, although

"Mmm . . . " Duncan muttered, at a moment of silence, as he puzzled over the symbol, nodding.

"Yes, young man."

Looking up, Duncan found himself looking at Doctor Oyhtter's intense eyes.

"Your candidate solution, young man. What's your solution?"

Duncan looked around swiftly, suddenly worried. Never in his life had he had the perception of so many waiting eagerly for him to express his thoughts. His first impulse was to explain in basic terms his intuition about the symbol, yet he realized he could not even explain it to himself.

Having no clue what to do or say, Duncan stood up hesitantly and started reading aloud the first word of a long expression next to the symbol that had evoked the odd impression. "*Stern . . . essence?*"

Giriana hurried to check the new candidate solution. Her QD seemed to have some trouble solving the logical system, so she tried an alternative *q*-solver algorithm. For a moment, it seemed as if the solution was about to diverge, but then, a series of statements flashed on her display.

"Conservation of reality, preserved; historicity threading, circumscribed; structural logicality, super-orthogonal; physical compatibility, satisfied; transcendental scope, comprehensive." Giriana turned to Oyhtter, handing over her QD. "It does exhibit inclusivity with the entire system."

A general mumbling filled the conference room. It was an indistinct loud whispering marked by a definite name—*Dahncion*. But Oyhtter was totally disconnected from the environment. He just kept looking at the solution while making snappy checks and double checks with the QD.

Oyhtter finally nodded, without detaching his attention from the display. "*Erandie*, it seems we have something pretty hot right here.

---

different in style and shape. They were associated with perceptions, and sometimes images, that would evoke the concept they symbolized.

We must start tree-correlation check immediately. Let's get back to our labs to initiate I.C.P.[45] Doctor Petrel, if you and your team would remain here for a moment, please?"

As everybody began leaving the conference room, Duncan approached Oyhtter and stood behind him. O'sihn motioned to Laida and Clara to wait for Duncan outside.

Oyhtter was now briefing Petrel's team concerning a prospective model based on the auspicious candidate solution. Noticing the young human waiting—utterly unseen by the intently absorbed Oyhtter—Giriana approached the scientist and tried to attract his attention.

"Not now, not now," Oyhtter grumbled, before she had a chance to say anything.

"Doctor—"

But Oyhtter kept giving instructions, heedless of anything else. Duncan decided it was not the right time to talk with the scientist, so he left the auditorium discreetly.

"No, no, no," Oyhtter continued. "Let's stay away from Lionel's substitution. It can generate coupled non-linearities, which would take too much effort to correlate. Remember, we have very limited time. The final model must be as straightforward and robust as possible. Let's try to optimize the discerner supervisor for any co-substantial substructure we may get. Do you think you could take care of this, Doctor Bulldwing?"

"Certainly."

"Good, good. So, I think we have a fine strategy to start working with; good. Any other questions?"

There were none.

"Fantastic. So we can meet back together, at, let's say . . . 1900R?"

Everybody agreed.

As Petrel's team left the room, Oyhtter remained standing in front of the screen, checking the system of *logai* still displayed there. "Hum, oh, Doctor Giriana?" Oyhtter said, as she was about to leave.

---

45 Interactive Correlation Procedure.

She turned around. "Doctor?"

"Well, you wanted to say something, didn't you?"

"Oh." She walked briskly up to him, nodding. "You may have not noticed him, Doctor, but when you dismissed the meeting . . . " Giriana paused. "Dahncion stayed behind for a couple of minutes," she added, in a discreet tone.

"Dahncion, Dahncion . . . *Duhn-zaeon* was here?"

"Well, yes."

"You mean Dahncion from Earth?"

Giriana looked at Oyhtter with surprise. "He was the one who gave the answer."

"Answer . . . what answer?"

"*Sternessence*, the stereo solution, Doctor . . ."

Oyhtter blinked his bright eyes as if emerging from a torpid slumber. "*Groka!*"[46]

22.

Back from Cerendal, Duncan went out to the Sky Prairies, seeking solitude and solace. Solitude he did find, but the peace of mind he was looking for seemed very distant and elusive. The view of the castle beyond the foliage was becoming a familiar companion: the same views, the same flowers, and the same rays of Realia filtering through the treetops.

But Duncan began to grow aware of something else, a subtle presence he could not grasp. He turned around and noticed a blue luminescence behind him. In the midst of it, a human form was clearly discernible. Everything around him had become very quiet, with a breeze barely ruffling the surrounding foliage.

The visitor made a peaceful gesture with his hands. "Don't be afraid, Duncan." The luminescence around him had dwindled, but a gentle glow remained.

"How do you know my name?" Duncan gasped.

---

46 No English translation.

The visitor gazed at him in a manner that implied he knew Duncan very well. "Don't waste energy fighting your discouragement," he continued. "Focus on your mission. This is what is worth fighting for."

Duncan disliked the implications of the words. "My mission? What do you know about my *mission?*"

"What do you know?" the visitor replied.

"I have serious doubts about having any mission at all."

"And yet your mission is as real as you are real."

The visitor talked with a gentle strength. Trusting him felt natural. His face was firm and stern—as if marked by war—though at the same time, brilliant and peaceful, with a gleam of wisdom emanating from his intense eyes. He looked like a man in his fifties, with abundant hair. Yet there was something beyond his human appearance, something that transcended the manly features.

"And how am I supposed to carry out such a mission?"

"That, you already know."

Duncan shook his head, but the visitor looked deep into his eyes.

"*Sternessence,*" Duncan heard distinctly within himself.

"*Sternessence . . .* " Duncan sighed. "I don't even know the meaning of the word. Not even that Doctor Oyhtter could figure out what to do with it. He and the others are still working on some . . . *way of action.*" Duncan smiled with a touch of pessimism. "They've got nothing yet."

"Yes, and it will take them too long to find the right path. And by then, it might as well be too late. It depends on you," the visitor added with a deep look, "and on the other people of good will who are fighting with you."

"Why does everybody insist that I should or could do anything? I'm an ordinary guy. I don't see how I could be of any help at all."

"The day you grasp the meaning of *sternessence* even the size of a blade of grass, you may begin to understand. But first, you ought to accept your mission. The decision is yours alone."

Duncan remained quiet for a moment, his mind trying to go back to the meeting at Cerendal. But he could only vaguely remember it. "What's the true meaning of the word?"

"*Sternessence* is the essence of love, which is above feelings, beyond our very selves. That is where, up to this point, the Realdom has been failing. That is why the Establishment cannot yet be stopped." As the visitor spoke, his face began to change. His voice became stronger, and from the blade of the sword he carried on his back, a glowing crystal blue glare sent forth an incomprehensible music. The visitor's whole body was now emanating a bright white light.

It was the pain caused by the intense radiance that woke Duncan up. Disoriented, he turned on the lights, his mind still half submerged in his dream. It had felt so real. He had actually spent a couple of afternoons in a field like that at the Sky Prairies more than a week in the past, when he had returned from Cerendal. But above all, it was the lucidity of the dialogue that impressed him, especially about the veiled question of *sternessence*. He felt as if he had been conscious while still sleeping.

While pondering, Duncan was startled by the emergency panels in his quarters. The sudden red flashing and blaring battle signal yanked him back to the reality of being on board the *Intrepid*, a Realitian destroyer.

"*All personnel to battle stations. This is not a drill, this is not a drill. All personnel to battle stations.*"

CHAPTER 5

Practical Assignment No. 5

23.

"Intercepting time?"

"Twenty minutes, thirty-three seconds at present acceleration, Captain," Leepardian reported.

"Anything new, Mac?"

McAwian, the communications officer, checked all distress channels once more. "Negative, captain."

"Keep trying."

"Aye, sir."

"This quadrant is far away from enemy outposts," Laida added. "We might be dealing with a scout ship."

Today, only O'sihn and Laida were on the bridge. Through multipurpose stations, duty officers could operate from there as well, but they would usually work from their own department posts through virtual consoles, or VCs. Only the captain and the X.O. had permanent posts on the bridge, although the tactical officer, or T.O., would often be present there as well.

"Captain," McAwian said. "I've reached a channel. It's coming through with distortion."

"On TD," O'sihn said, as he verified the *Intrepid*'s position on his console. The slightly curved image of a blank tactical display, or TD, immediately materialized in front of him. Multiple TDs[47] could be

---

47 Multiple areas of the neighboring space were typically displayed on different TDs, with the appropriate magnification scales.

engaged simultaneously to monitor different activities. Like any other virtual display, including any VC (which linked with the different departments), TDs could materialize anywhere, with no hardware image-supporting background.[48]

"Research Vessel *Plinidas*, we have you on visual," O'sihn said.

The shape of a vessel's bridge began to form on the TD opened by McAwian. The image looked distorted, but it was sufficiently clear to convey the general situation. A crewmember from *Plinidas* came into view. "Commander Maxis, captain of the expedition."

"This is Commodore O'sihn, Commanding Officer of the YSF *Intrepid*. What's your current status, Captain?"

"We were collecting data from the Menikalian star, when we were unexpectedly hit by some form of energy vector."

"Any positive identification of the aggressor?"

"No. We tried to communicate with them, but they would not respond."

"Perhaps they thought—"

Maxis shook his head. "We told them we were just a scientific vessel—through all channels we tried. We insisted we were unarmed. Then we were hit again." Maxis paused. He looked distressed, and his words were faltering. "The engine room is smashed. All life support systems are failing, and five people are dead. The Research Commander . . . she is also dead." Captain Maxis paused, trying to regain control of himself. His wife's body could clearly be seen by his side. A third eye was painted on her forehead, as was customary for all Veritian female research officers with a commanding rank.

"We are expeditiously closing distances to assist you, Captain," O'sihn said. A 3D image of the surrounding space materialized in and beyond the bridge, as if it had no bulkheads. That was the

---

48 There was mutual visual contact between the bridge and the different officers of the watch, and among the officers themselves through their VCs. However, the captain could disconnect the bridge from particular virtual consoles, or keep a private link with some of them. Multiple independent groups could also be set and were often set to optimize the flow of information.

3D-SIS,[49] or the "3D" for short. When activated, a three-dimensional view of the surrounding space was projected inside the bridge. Objects, instruments, and even persons on the bridge would become partially or completely invisible with the 3D on. The projection gave the impression of literally flying in space.

Maxis stood up, strengthening his expression.

"Please, try to lock us onto your navigational computer, Captain," O'sihn said.

"Impossible. It's out of line and short-circuited."

"We have the attacking ship on our scanners," Leepardian interjected.

"Command her to identify herself," O'sihn ordered, looking up at the image of McAwian on the TD.

"I'm trying, sir, but she won't acknowledge."

"We have a missile locked onto us!" Captain Maxis stated.

"Sensors picking up one missile closing distances on *Plinidas*, Captain," Leepardian confirmed. "E.I.T. (Estimated Intercepting Time): thirteen seconds, sir."

"Tango (Tactical Computer) indicates out of range," Laida added, referring to the *Intrepid*'s weapons systems.

"The unidentified vessel is closing on us fast," Maxis stressed, his eyes fixed on his own TD.

"Illuminate the aggressor with tactical scanners," O'sihn commanded Leepardian. That was a standard intimidation procedure intended to divert the enemy's attention, in this case, forcing it to protect itself from a possible imminent attack and thus abandon its guided missile.[50]

But at that point, the image of *Plinidas'* bridge vanished.

---

49 Three-Dimensional Stereo Imaging System.

50 Focusing tactical scanners on a target implied an accurate assessment of its position and kinematic pattern.

For a moment, the background noise coming through the virtual consoles was the only noticeable presence on the bridge. Recovering quickly from the shock, O'sihn proceeded to verify status. "C.I.C.[51]/conn."

The image of Lieutenant Deehra appeared on the C.I.C.'s virtual console. "Yes, Captain?"

"Status of *Plinidas.*"

Deehra lowered her eyes. "TD, Captain." That meant *Total Destruction,* which implied no significant remains of the vessel and no survivors possible.

O'sihn was silent for a couple of seconds. "Thank you, Deehra."

"Picking up a Doppler positive contact astern," Leepardian reported. "It's gaining on us fast, Captain."

"Interception time?"

"Five minutes, four seconds, sir."

O'sihn set condition one on his console. All combat stations immediately acknowledged the command. "Tango on line with the rudder. Engage evasive pattern Alpha-Charlie-Eight."

"Tango rudder on line, Alpha-Charlie-Eight engaged, sir," Foxin, the navigational officer, confirmed.

"Maximum evasive acceleration."

"Maximum *A* aye, Captain."

"Tango is providing preliminary enemy I.D.: frigate type, about ten thousand tons,[52] conventional tactical weapons . . . she's a *Strages* class warship." Laida raised her eyes from her display and looked at O'sihn. "So much for any doubt about dealing with the Establishment."

"Combat engagement evaluation, X.O."

---

51 Combat Information Center.

52 The translation "tons" is a scaled adaptation to units we are familiar with.

Laida shook her head. "We'll stand a small chance against a modern *Strages*-class ship."

O'sihn looked at the Tactical Officer's virtual console. "Recommended way of action, T.O.?"

Tygrum linked his system with the captain's console. "On bearing zero-four-three dash zero-three-zero we have ionic nebula Solis." The nebula appeared on O'sihn's display. "I recommend hiding inside it, turning off engines and non-vital equipment, and waiting there in electronic silence. In case of engagement, I'd advise using plasma cannons. Missiles would not be effective or fast enough within a dense and highly ionized environment."

O'sihn nodded. "Course of action accepted."

"Down-starboard rudder. New course setting: zero-four-three dash zero-three-zero, maximum evasive acceleration."

"Course zero-four-three dash zero-three-zero, maximum evasive acceleration, aye, sir," Lieutenant Foxin confirmed.

"Time estimates?"

"Three minutes to nebula," Leepardian said. "Seventeen for enemy overtaking."

"Copied."

The *Intrepid* was soon piercing through the edge of the gaseous formation. Immediately, the ionization equalizers were turned on to hide the path of the ship. Ten minutes later, it stopped its engines deep inside an ionized ocean with no shores.

"All non-vital systems in standby, Captain," the X.O. reported. The crew was working fast to adjust the vessel's instruments to the new tactical situation.

The Chief Engineer, Lin Beaver, now came through, overriding all other virtual consoles for a private communication with the bridge.

"What's up, Lin?"

"Sir, high external radiation and ionization levels. Keeping our radiation neutralizers down can damage vital equipment."

"Understood, Chief, but we will have to maintain this condition for a while."

"They're above us!" Leepardian's clipped comment broke through.

"Enemy status?"

"Not clear, Captain. But it's stopped about fifteen hundred kilometers above our position."

"We are nothing but sitting ducks in here," Laida said. "I strongly recommend that we abandon this area immediately."

O'sihn nodded. "Foxin, ahead point one, standard escape velocity."

"Ahead point one, standard escape, aye, sir."

"Steady as she goes."

"Steady as, sir."

A crimson frame, edging the engine room's virtual console, popped up on the bridge. O'sihn set all other consoles in standby, except for the T.O.'s. The stand-by consoles dimmed their luminescence by seventy percent.

"Yes, C.E.?"[53]

"Hull outer temperature, seven thousand KGs.[54] The ionized environment will . . . will fry us up if we maintain present speed, Captain."

"I do understand the situation, C.E." O'sihn checked the hull temperature gauge on his console as he released all consoles from their stand-by condition. "Foxin, down to point zero, eight, five standard escape speed." The fine-tuned speed adjustment (from 0.1 to 0.085) only served to aggravate Beaver's anxiety.

"Point zero, eight, five standard escape speed, aye, sir," Foxin acknowledged.

The *Intrepid* was opening a burning trail through the *Solis* nebula.[55]

---

53 Chief Engineer.

54 Kilo-*gradients*.

55 Ionization equalizers were ineffective at that speed.

She had been responding well despite the harsh radiation, but as the result of an overload, the weapon's network suddenly went down. It needed to be reinitialized, a procedure that would take about an hour. As Beaver briefed the captain about the problem, the ship reached open space, adopting standard acceleration automatically.

After a few minutes of relative peace, O'sihn ordered a new course to the A57 quadrant. He was about to demote the tactical alert condition to a lower status when an emergency warning popped up on his console.

Two simultaneous shots slammed into the ship, leaving it mostly without power for a second or two.

"Damage control/conn, report."

"Damage control, Captain." Lieutenant Deehra's voice came through the D.C.'s[56] virtual console, as alert one was reinstated on all decks. "Sir, bow missile launchers and bow bay exposed to radiation. Pressure leak in compartment B-57 under control. Total decompression in compartments F-56 and Y-34. Additional damage of lesser significance."

"Effect bow-area evacuation, Lieutenant."

"Acknowledged."

"C.E./conn here."

"What's our current status with the weapon system, Chief?"

"We are doing all we can." Beaver's voice came through amidst a flurry of technical jargon from the engineering team.

"Enemy activity ahead. Range within yellow zone," Leepardian said. "It seems to be the same ship, sir."

"Full astern, maximum escape acceleration."

"Full astern, maximum escape A, aye, Captain," Foxin acknowledged.

---

56 Damage Control.

"I have another contact off the down-starboard beam," Laida added. "It seems to be following us on a parallel course."

O'sihn was quiet for a moment. "Odd. Keep an eye on it."

"Three *dart-wolves* locked on us," Leepardian called. "Bearing zero flat relative." That meant three incoming missiles straight ahead.

"One hundred-and-eighty degrees hard about, maximum escape acceleration."

"All hard about, max. escape A, aye, sir," Foxin said.

"Overtaking time?"

"Twelve minutes, thirty-three seconds P.K.P.,[57] captain," Leepardian said.

"Procedure twenty-four." That was an anti-missile electronic-counter-measure routine.

"Twenty-four engaged, Captain," McAwian acknowledged.

Despite the imminent threat, O'sihn kept pondering on the contact Laida had detected a moment before. "Is the missiles' point of origin correlated to the second contact?"

"Negative," Laida replied. "Second contact moves on a parallel course. It might as well be an echo from the nebula."

"Or some trap," added Tygrum.

Shaking his head slightly, O'sihn opened his all-decks channel. "Dahncion to the bridge, Dahncion to the bridge. Engine room/conn."

Lin Beaver's console came on again. "C.E., Captain."

"Estimated time for weapons operational?"

"No less than thirty minutes, Captain."

"Lin, we have three *dart-wolves* locked on us. They will reach lethal range in less than twelve minutes."

"It's impossible to have the network reinitialized in less than thirty minutes, Captain! It's . . . it's just impossible."

"We could try activating one missile manually," Laida added.

"That would also take about half an hour, ma'am," Beaver added

---

57 Present Kinematics Pattern.

hurriedly. "Plus, it would divert key personnel from the main weapon controller."

"Never mind, C.E.," O'sihn said. "Concentrate all hands on resetting the main system."

"Aye-aye, captain."

"Dahncion to the bridge, Dahncion to the bridge." O'sihn's voice came up on all decks once more.

"Ten minutes for overtake," added Leepardian.

The captain stood up, slowly stepping forward. Three bright objects were displayed in front of him on the space projection surrounding the whole bridge. They were heading relentlessly towards the ship. The captain stood for about a minute, immersed in the 3D, striving to come up with some way out. But there was not much he could do.

"Summon a security squad to the bridge."

Laida turned towards O'sihn, but he did not divert his attention from his console. Still looking at him, the X.O. activated the internal security alarm.

Fifteen seconds later, an officer with taut canine features was standing at the entrance to the bridge with four security personnel. "Security squad reporting as ordered, Captain."

"Axas, locate Dahncion and take him to recon vessel *Sagacious*. Do whatever you judge necessary to get the boy on that vessel. Am I sufficiently clear?"

"Yes, sir."

"Dismissed." O'sihn tipped his head to the X.O. console. "Find Lieutenant Commander Clara and instruct her to stand by to assume command of the *Sagacious* immediately."

Laida held her response for a second. "Acknowledged."

"Reentering Solis nebula," Leepardian reported.

"Stabilize speed at point zero eight standard."

"Point zero eight standard, aye, sir," Foxin confirmed.

"Keep adjusting velocity to maintain external hull temperature below seven thousand KG."

"Aye."

As O'sihn checked the data on his tactical console, a window popped up showing the *Sagacious'* bridge. Axas' team was already entering the recon vessel with Dahncion.

"McAwian, tie me in on all decks, but make sure I don't reach the *Sagacious.*"

Immediately, O'sihn's voice began echoing everywhere in the ship. "This is the captain. Three enemy missiles are locked tightly on us. Estimated overtaking time, seven minutes. Our weapon system is off-line. As I speak, we are penetrating an ionic nebula at maximum allowable thermal speed." That meant everybody was trapped inside the vessel. Escape capsules could not withstand ejection inside a nebula at tactical velocities. Only the Sagacious would be able to survive a jettison procedure.

"Lieutenant Lin Beaver's team is currently engaged in restoring our weapons system." O'sihn paused. "*Erandie,* the Realdom cannot afford the luxury of further loss of personnel or material. We must and will complete this mission. All stations stand by for tactical orders."

O'sihn switched to an internal channel. "Conn/*Sagacious?*"

"Lieutenant Commander Clara in command. I've got an all-systems-go, Captain."

"What's goin' on?" Duncan's voice came over O'sihn's console. "Have this lady release me, Captain."

Duncan was handcuffed, the security team having followed O'sihn's instructions to the letter. He had correctly surmised that O'sihn had decided to have him abandon ship due to the tactical situation, and he had resisted.

"T minus fifteen seconds," O'sihn added, looking at the main TD now displaying a new console with the *Sagacious'* bridge.

"Copied," Clara acknowledged.

The final sequence was displayed both on the bridge and the recon vessel.

"Wait!" Duncan protested, barely raising his handcuffed arms.

"Five, four, three . . . "

"Stern strength . . . " O'sihn muttered, invoking the beginning of the Veritas Marine Corps traditional salute.

Clara nodded at the TD with a strained smile.

The *Sagacious* was immediately jettisoned towards an uncertain fate.

24.

The three bright spots on the main TD remained peaceful and steady, but the figures on the scale display kept changing at an ever-faster rate. Despite O'sihn's determination to resolve the crisis, the main weapons system had not come back yet. Without it, there was not much he could do. The captain understood there was no point in bothering Beaver about it again.

"Leepardian, launch record logs." Consisting of very thin solid cards (less than ten thousandths of an inch thick and about one hundredth of an inch in length and width), the logs contained detailed encrypted data of the previous three hundred and sixty operational hours.[58]

"Record logs away, Captain."

"Thirty seconds for overtake," Laida added.

O'sihn stood up in deep silence. Then he felt a warm touch on his right hand. He smiled briefly, turning to his wife.

" . . . *Twelve, eleven, ten, nine, eight* . . . " The final countdown drowned out the constant background noise of the instruments. For O'sihn, each second was like an hour, each spent looking for options with a disciplined barren optimism. But when the sequence reached

---

58 The cards were virtually undetectable. Only when activated by a special code through a particular communications channel, would they become visible to instruments. The information inside was meant to provide the causes of the catastrophic events that would have destroyed a ship.

three, the 3D and all TDs became blindingly white. Instinctively, Laida covered her eyes.

" . . . *one, zero.*"

The background sounds continued on the bridge without change. A noisy ionized environment was the only visible activity on the main tactical window. The missiles were not there anymore, whereas the ship remained untouched.

"Full stop."

"Full stop, Captain," Foxin acknowledged.

"C.E./conn. Estimated time for weapons operational?"

"Less than ten minutes, sir."

"Let's expedite this, C.E."

"Aye, sir."

"Full stop effected, Captain," Foxin confirmed.

"It seems we've detonated one of the incoming missiles," the X.O. reported. "The other two were destroyed by the same event."

"*We*'ve detonated?"

"A torpedo was fired from the emergency bow launcher," Laida explained, staring at the captain.

O'sihn shook his head in disbelief. "Let's have this one checked." Laida nodded. "Should we try rendezvousing with the *Sagacious*?"

"Not yet. It wouldn't be prudent to leave our job inconclusive this time. Let's terminate the attacker first."

"Aye-aye, Captain," Laida said approvingly. "Searching pattern?" O'sihn shook his head slightly.

"Searching pattern, Captain?" Laida repeated, raising her eyes from her console.

"Staying right here will be our best move," O'sihn said. "The enemy most likely picked up the detonation, but nothing else. They know that our weapons system is damaged, and after the explosion, they might presume our condition is precarious. However, they will have to penetrate the nebula to find out whether they destroyed us or not. Should they proceed accordingly, we will be ready to pay back all their attentions."

"What if . . . " Laida started.

"We will adapt our course of action according to their movements, X.O." O'sihn looked up to a VC on his left. "Leepardian, launch four tactical probes one hundred thousand kilometers ahead of us, and link onto them via N.B.L."[59]

"Tactical probes away, Captain."

"X.O."

Laida turned to O'sihn, raising her eyebrows.

"Let's make ready to welcome our guests, my dear."

25.

After half an hour of silence, Duncan decided he had had enough.

"With all this poking, testing, and checking around every instrument on board, has it crossed the captain's mind to remove these . . . these things?" Duncan raised his handcuffed wrists at the woman standing in front of him. She could not help but chortle.

"This is not a joke," Duncan said harshly.

"Take it easy." Clara grabbed a card from one of her pockets and put one corner into a small slot on one of Duncan's handcuffs. They should have opened on contact, but they did not. Clara tried again—on both wrists—but the handcuffs refused to yield.

"So?"

"They won't open." Clara held the card between her thumb and forefinger, staring at it.

"Stop playing games, Captain, and get these things off me!"

"They just won't open, and I don't know why."

"Well, try it over until they *do* open!"

Clara tried again and again, but to no avail.

"There has to be something wrong with the code." She stood up and nodded. "Don't worry, it's about nine hours to Soledad." Soledad was a small scientific outpost assigned to study different types of cosmic radiation. "It may take a bit longer, though. We will have

---

59 *Neutrinion* Beam Linkage

to wait a couple of hours to be beyond enemy sensor range before restarting the engines."

"I'm not interested in your touring schedule or your tactical analysis. Use your gun, your brains, use *anything*, but get these things off me."

"Nothing in this modest bridge would be of any use, Dahncion— including my gun."

Duncan bit his lip and gave a curt nod. "I'm not sure I like this attitude of yours, Captain."

Clara's expression hardened. "My *attitude* is trying to keep you alive, mister."

"I should be onboard the *Intrepid*," Duncan retorted. "And I have the feeling that you are an accessory to my being here today— handcuffs included."

"Neither you nor I know exactly why O'sihn ordered us onto this vessel," Clara replied. "But the fact that he decided on this course of action, handcuffs included, makes it very clear that he had a very good reason. And by the way, I think it's good for you to be acquainted with the fact that I'm here strictly by captain's orders, definitely not by any personal interest in the matter."

"Really? Lately, you've been poking around into everything I do. It's becoming annoying."

Clara fixed her intense blue eyes on Duncan. "I see. It would seem I'm nothing but a nuisance to you. Some kind of a *drawing-woman*, I suppose."

Duncan was flabbergasted by her comment. Somehow, Clara had managed to expose a very deep and obscure feeling he had been trying to conceal for weeks, even from himself.[60] Clara's expression might not have been deliberate, though. In the Realitarian language, a *drawing-woman* could also mean a busybody. However, it seemed

---

60 Due to the delineated *tori* features in her appearance, Duncan's perception of Clara tended to minimize her womanhood. But that was probably not something that only Duncan would experience. To people from Earth, *tori* features could likely suggest drawing-like traits.

that Clara did mean more than what the common expression conveyed. Her formerly positive mood had changed noticeably, and a trace of sadness, not present in her eyes before, had become visible.

Duncan wanted to say something, to apologize in some way, but he could not find the words. The captain was now sitting in front of the tactical screen, fiddling with some instruments, with her back to him.

The tension did not last long. Within minutes, a familiar voice broke over the communications console.

26.

Most of the *Intrepid*'s instruments were of little, if any, help within the ionized environment. Four short-range, high-resolution sensors had been deployed about one hundred thousand kilometers ahead of the ship—quite close from a tactical standpoint. They were linked to the ship through the N.B.L. system.[61]

"Conn/engine room." Beaver's virtual console came back up on a TD.

"C.E.?"

"Weapons system eighty-eight percent operational, Captain."

"Good job, Chief."

"Class two contact,"[62] Leepardian said. "Bearing zero-one-zero flat relative, range one hundred and twenty thousand kilometers."

"Right off the bow?" O'sihn asked.

---

61 The N.B.L. system (Neutrinion Beam System) was the least conspicuous and most effective data linkage that could be used in the ionized environment of the nebula. The system would minimize the likelihood of giving away the *Intrepid*'s presence to the enemy while providing a large data transfer rate, with minimal loss of information.

62 Unconfirmed contacts were classified into three categories according to the estimated probability of dealing with a real enemy vessel. A class one contact was the closest to a confirmed-contact classification. The evidence for it, though not yet conclusive, would be strongly consistent with that of a hostile ship. A class two status meant there was strong evidence for the presence of an enemy vessel in the tactical theater, albeit with some ambiguity involved. A class three contact meant there was reliable data partially consistent with the presence of an enemy vessel in the area.

"Yes, sir, and it's moving towards us at a very slow speed, about one hundred kilometers per second."

"They may be following our gravitational trail," Laida commented.

O'sihn nodded. "I very much doubt they could pick us up otherwise inside this nebula, and at this distance."

"We have a very good *tetragonalization* of the contact, Captain," Tygrum added from his virtual console. "The *gravitic* signature is consistent with a *Strages* class ship. Updating to class one."

"Copied." O'sihn set alert one on his console, and the all-hands-to-battle-stations drill started blaring on all decks.

"Picking up modulated *neutrinion* radiation," Tygrum said. "Updating contact to confirmed status, Captain."

"Weapons system locked on target and in stand-by," Laida reported.

"Fire all weapons."

"Vectors in the ether," Laida confirmed, as a multicolored display of lights pierced the ionized environment with an unintentional beauty.

"Cease fire."

"Fire ceased," Laida confirmed.

"Hard-down starboard rudder, mean escape velocity."

"Hard-down star, mean escape, aye, sir," Foxin acknowledged.

"Seventy percent direct hits," Tygrum informed. An icon on his virtual console, displaying the number 69.97, confirmed his statement. "Tango's still computing—"

"The enemy is starting to move," Leepardian interrupted. "Speeding up at a high rate. Course heading three-one-three dash three-four-five."

"New course three-one-three dash three-four-five. Match kinematic pattern with the enemy's," O'sihn said.

"Engage energy bursts on target, highest hit probability pattern," he added, patting Laida's hand.

"Acknowledged."

"Heat absorbers are starting to saturate," Laida added with concern.

"Are we gaining on target?"

"Negative, Captain," Leepardian answered.

"Engine room / conn."

"C.E., Captain."

"Link auxiliary power to engines."

"Hull temperature is reaching twelve thousand KGs. We should've blown up already."

"Engage auxiliary power to engines, Lin."

"Captain, we're being tracked by three missiles," Leepardian reported.

"Lock onto them and neutralize with energy vectors," O'sihn said, unconcerned about the threat.

"Aye, Captain," Laida acknowledged.

"Strong indication that their energy weapons are out of service," added Tygrum. The tactical judgment was based on the fact that missile effectiveness .was seriously compromised within densely ionized environments, unless a missile were firmly locked on target.

O'sihn nodded.

"Missiles neutralized, Captain," Laida reported.

"Conn / engine room."

"Yes Chief."

"Sir, hull temperature twelve thousand, eight hundred KGs . . . " Lin Beaver's troubled tone was immediately muffled by a violent crack that shuddered the whole ship.

"Losing speed fast." Foxin nodded tensely.

"It seems we've hit a gravitational mine," Tygrum added.

"Captain, the enemy is also halting!" Leepardian reported.

"Which weapons remain operational?"

"I'm afraid missiles alone, Captain," Tygrum said.

"Full stop," Foxin confirmed. O'sihn raised his eyes to Foxin's console in silence.

"So has the enemy," Leepardian added.

The ship was in serious danger. A long list of unknowns was troubling O'sihn, although he was quickly identifying them and establishing priorities of what had to be done next. "T.O., what are the chances they've also stumbled upon a mine?"

"Unlikely, Captain. We would have detected the explosion."

"Their sustained high speed might have crippled their vessel, at least partially," Laida commented.

"If so," O'sihn said, "everything would now depend on who fixes their technical difficulties first."

"The enemy is starting to move again," Leepardian said.

"R.S.C.,[63] Lieutenant."

"Range, two thousand kilometers. Collision course, Captain, and gaining speed fast."

"C.E./conn." Beaver's console became active once more. "The enemy is closing on us very rapidly, Lin. We must try anything possible to bring back the engines. Anything."

"Captain! We are being illuminated by tactical scanners." As the words left his mouth, Tygrum knew he might well have uttered the *Intrepid*'s final epitaph.

O'sihn stood up, his eyes fixed on the red spot that glowed brightly in the center of the main TD. It was checkmate, and O'sihn's expression reflected that. The enemy was closing in at a fast rate, and as it did, every countermeasure alarm in the *Intrepid*'s bridge was activated, one after the other.[64]

Now the captain was about to try a desperate missile counterattack, knowing that the odds of success were extremely low. He had not started working on the activation sequence yet when the hostile red spot on the main screen burst into a bright small sun.

---

63 Range, speed, and course heading. Speed would typically include acceleration patterns.

64 The bridge had alarms to alert about different threats coming from enemy attack operations. For example, there were alarms to warn about tactical weapons targeting systems, alarms about long-range scanners, alarms about gravitational perturbation waves used to pinpoint the position of the ship, alarms about scanners that tried to tie in on the ship's communications, etc. As the enemy vessel approached, virtually all systems from the attacking ship were homing in on the *Intrepid*. As a result, almost every alarm on the bridge was going off.

27.

The virtual space image on the 3D immediately returned to the natural darkness of space. "I hope I've not spoiled your party, guys." A voice came through a non-military channel onto every tactical console, including the bridge.

"Captain Foxso'l," O'sihn said tartly, suppressing a smile.

"What the hell is the *Intrepid* doing in this quadrant?" An image of Foxso'l materialized on a virtual monitor. "You respectable people are not supposed to hang around these neighborhoods. By the way, we have a couple of presents for you."

"Presents?"

Foxso'l looked to his left, where Clara stood. A handcuffed Duncan appeared from behind. "It seems the boy caused you some trouble."

At that point, the medical department chief, Doctor Raikun, entered the bridge. He approached O'sihn discreetly, in a rather casual manner. "Captain, we need you in sickbay."

"I'll be down there right away, Ray."

"You'd better come now."

The exchange had been obscured by continuing remarks from Foxso'l. O'sihn turned back. Something was unusual about Raikun's expression. "X.O., take Lieutenant Commander Clara and Dahncion on board. I'll be back shortly."

"Aye, Captain."

"Captain Foxso'l," O'sihn said, addressing the communications screen. "I must attend to some matters at the moment. You and your crew are very much welcome on board."

"I sure appreciate that, Captain, but I understand you are short of time. We'd rather leave your invitation for some other day."

"Think it over, Fox'. I'll be back momentarily."

"The X.O. has the conn," Tygrum said, as the captain left the bridge.

O'sihn and Raikun headed towards sickbay, which was three decks below.

"Any casualties, Doctor?" O'sihn asked.

"No."

"How many injured?"

"Ten, one female in critical condition." Raikun's expression was grave.

O'sihn did not speak for a few seconds. "Who's she, Rai?"

"Spacer Aleia, O."

There was a brief silence between them. "What happened, doc?"

"Early this morning, she had been given a training assignment: manually arming and programming the firing sequence of a torpedo at the bow section. During the tactical engagement, some of the bow radiation neutralizers[65] yielded, right before the enemy launched the three missiles against us, about half an hour ago. Aleia stayed at her post,[66] and after completing the programming sequence, she managed to load her torpedo manually into one of the emergency shafts and launch it. The enemy missiles were intercepted and destroyed by the torpedo, but at a very close range. The bow area was bathed with lethal radiation."

O'sihn and Raikun reached sickbay. The captain walked in first and stood before a seriously wounded *ossian*. She was covered with blankets, which did not hide the severe radiation burns on her face. The young female was in agony. There was no point in asking the doctor whether she would recover.

"Spacer Aleia, the captain is here," said Raikun in a gentle tone.

Aleia smiled, without changing her pained expression. O'sihn approached her bed and stood in front of her.

---

65 Radiation neutralizers: energy shields that prevent radiation from reaching exposed areas of the ship, protecting the crew and vital equipment.

66 In battle, Spacers, which had the status of students, were instructed to move to well-protected sections of the ship, with easy access to escape pods. Knowing that the *Intrepid* was fighting against bad odds, Aleia decided to remain in the bow area and complete the assignment she had been given: manually arming a torpedo. While she was working, the radiation neutralizers yielded, but she continued with her task while aware of the consequences, not only from a potential attack (as did happen) but from the surrounding radiation coming from the nebula where the ship was navigating.

Looking into space (she was blind), Aleia spoke in a feeble voice. "T.A.[67] five, completed. Nothing to report, Captain."

"We all know this, Spacer. You did an excellent job." O'sihn's tone was low and exceptionally tender.

Aleia extended one burnt hand towards the captain. She smiled once more, though now with a last timeless but peaceful expression.

O'sihn's face sunk into bitter sadness. The captain of the *Intrepid* knelt to grasp the young sailor's hands. Only one other onboard could share his searing grief. For on that day, O'sihn's and Laida's eldest daughter had fulfilled her last daily task. In that simple act, she had saved one hundred and thirty-seven lives.

---

67 T.A.: training assignment

CHAPTER 6

A Dose of Common Sense

28.

Enticing to the eyes and alluring to the heart, there she was. Glittering pink attire covered her body completely. Although the splendid gown concealed most of her female features, her charm was overpowering, as if possessing an irresistible witchcraft.

She was standing barefoot on a cold lake covered in a silky ethereal haze. Floating over the surface, clouds of fog spread to the horizon.

Her hands and arms were covered with seductive glossy gloves, which concealed everything within them. Her hair, glimmering like strings of emeralds, fell abundantly over her back down to her hips. Her neck radiated a crystal mistiness that adorned her face with the beauty of a goddess. Yet, it was in her eyes that her power resided. But her eyes were closed. She did not appear to be sleeping; she was standing on the lake. Occasionally, her eyes would move slightly while remaining closed, as if she were staring intensely into herself.

As he approached, Duncan reached cautiously for his sword. But the glamour of the female vision turned his fear into curiosity, and curiosity into desire. Soon, he had reached the edge of the hazy shore. The woman standing on the lake was close, about twenty paces away.

Abruptly, she opened her eyes. They were narrow and yellow, their gleam enhanced by the thick silver powder sprinkled over her cheeks.

Duncan was enthralled by the light in her eyes, which now looked deep into his own. A strong impulse to give in to her and let her be his only guide and reason poured lustily through his blood.

The woman smiled. It was a ravishing smile. Her lips were moist and red, but Duncan could not see her teeth. The young man's passion had been captured by the woman's eyes. "Duncan, if you give me your love, I will be your only guide and your only love. And in loving me, I will love you, and no other, forever."

"I would also love you forever," Duncan said, carried away by her beauty.

Smiling, the woman lifted up one arm, and one of the clouds that hovered over the hazy sea became translucent. Six men were revealed looking at her, possessed by passion.

"Who are they?" Duncan asked.

"They are the others whom I love, only each one of them, and no other single one, forever."

Duncan's exuberant expression faded. "You said you would love me . . . only me . . . "

"To be and not to be, so there it be. Don't think of this, and let our passion also be."

The clouds became gray and dense again, and again the woman closed her eyes. Duncan kept staring at her face until she opened her eyes once more. Their color had faded. They had turned glassy, transparent, as glassy and transparent as her new smile. "Duncan, if you give me your love, I will be your only guide and your only love. And in loving me, I will love you, and no other, forever."

"Only me . . . " he muttered.

She nodded and lifted up one arm. Six more clouds became diaphanous. Sixty-six men were there, beholding her in rapture. They seemed to be aware of her and only but her, not of each other, or of themselves.

"Who are these men?"

"They are the others whom I all love, to only each one of them I gave my heart, and no other but only one of them I love."

The painful fear of having to share her love with other men made

Duncan fall to his knees. "What do you mean, you love each one of them and only one of them?"

"To be and not to be, so there it be. Don't think of this, and let our passion also be." The woman closed her eyes, and the clouds rapidly recovered their dense pattern again.

Duncan was baffled by the creature. Her beauty seemed to have cast an irresistible spell on his soul. He stayed motionless, contemplating the female in awe.

Now, she opened her eyes. They were completely white. Her face was empty, but still irresistibly seductive. "Duncan, what's holding you up? I've told you, I'd love you and you'd be my slave—you and no other, forever. Why don't you do like the others and relinquish to me your heart and your mind, so that my mystery can always be your guide? It's only you, and the others, but only also you, I will love all together, forever."

At that point, all the clouds disappeared, and myriads of people stood there beholding the woman. Both males and females, human and nonhuman, were watching her ecstatically with very different, yet very strong passions.

"What's your name?" Duncan asked.

"I have no name. Just give me your heart, and I will be the light of your mind."

A strong impulse compelled Duncan to surrender his mind, his heart, his very self. His sight started to blur. His soul, craving for the possession of the woman, was already suffering from the crowded emptiness of loving her.

"No!" he finally cried out, covering his eyes.

Duncan awoke exhausted. It took him all morning to put away the feelings he had experienced, and to disregard the anguish he had suffered.

29.

O'sihn looked pensive, facing the stars through the transparent bulkheads of the observation bay. The *Intrepid* was making a stealth navigation towards her next assignment with minimum systems on. The mission had some unresolved uncertainties, but at that particular moment, they were not occupying the captain's thoughts.

"I don't know," Duncan said. "It was a strange dream. It doesn't have to have a meaning."

"It reminds me of the *Equel*," O'sihn commented, his eyes still perusing the stars.

"*Equel?*"

O'sihn nodded. "It is the prevalent belief among the officials of the Establishment, and was the unanimous belief of its founders." The captain sat down on a comfortable glassy chair. He took a *twees* from one pocket, a small cane similar to a sugar cane but the size of a pen. "It's a mystery-belief system based on the premise that everything is ruled by some entity, or rather some kind of *something* whose existence consists in equalizing every existence until existence and non-existence—or as they say, being and non-being—become one living idea that transcends all being."

Duncan grinned. "Does this . . . *something* have a name?"

"The godless-goddess-self, the naked *pleroma*," O'sihn sighed mildly. "The ethereal-everlasting-equalizer."

"Ethereal-everlasting-equalizer . . . " Duncan muttered.

O'sihn tapped one end of his *twees* on one knee. "It is the mystery of nothingness, which cannot be understood, but from where everything flows, because it's eternal and eternity itself. Everything has to resemble nothingness, if anybody or anything is to achieve completion. Pure equality, in removing all differences, leaves sameness, which is the living image of Nothingness—the utmost uniformity, the root of all peace, the never-ending rest, the source of ultimate happiness."

Duncan shook his head. "Nothingness . . . is just, nothing."

"*Nothingness does persist because it can never perish,* they would insist. The very fact that we can talk about it would show that, even for us, there is something comprehensible about it."

Duncan grimaced. "You said only a few follow these beliefs."

"No, I said it's the prevalent belief among the officials of the Establishment. And they are doing a very good job of spreading it. It's the ideological foundation of the Establishment, and the philosophical basis of the Equity, written almost two hundred years ago by Em-Rasinka."

Duncan had first heard about the Equity while staying in Realitas, after his mission in Veridiawa. It was the Magna Carta of the Establishment, but it was not a mere constitutional document. It went far beyond, reaching the status of a cultic emblem for many.

"Nonsense."

"Agreed. Now tell me, where is the nonsense?" O'sihn said, raising an eyebrow.

Duncan looked at the stars from his own glassy seat. "I don't know," he said, with a half-smile. "How to tackle such an idea?"

"With Reality." O'sihn paused. "And a dose of common sense."

30.

After making a *starfall*[68] with Gama-Algenib, the *Intrepid* left the pulsar off its down-port board, assuming a course that would take her to the rendezvous point. Three hours later, the ship joined with space carrier *Freedom*, which was escorted by the YSF *Perseverance*. The *Intrepid* maneuvered swiftly into formation position.

Two light-hours[69] ahead, nine small patrols joined the task force to provide a screen protection. All ships were traveling along inertial trajectories under strict silence procedures, which implied no engine activity.

At long last, contact was made with an old space buoy close to

---

68 After many days of navigating an uncharted area, a *starfall* was the procedure of identifying charted nearby stars and establishing the ship's position using them as a reference.

69 Light-hours (equivalent inter-universal units): equivalent distance an Earth-universe-like photon would travel during an Earth-like hour in the *Realitic* universe. Between universes, there are large differences in light speed, and in what we would understand as Relativist and Quantum physics, in general. We will not address these subjects in this book.

the destination. The five main gates of space carrier *Freedom* yawned open, and four attack squads and a small division of landing vessels slipped into space. Within ten minutes, they would start their chemical engines to avoid detection, thus initiating the final approach to the mission target.

31.

Sternessence. After the battle onboard the *Intrepid*, when he'd finally found some free time, Duncan had checked the etymology of the word. He did find abundant references to it in the ship's electronic library. The word was rooted in an ancient term that alluded to the essence of love. How could he have guessed the meaning of the word in the dream he had had before the battle? He did not remember having ever had any contact with the term before the scientific meeting at Cerendal, and after that, he had not thought much about its meaning. The strange insight and its relation to his presence in this alternate universe cast shadows on his thoughts. The sense of having a role in the tapestry of the war would, at times, shed rays of reassuring hope. But more often, Duncan would be under the impression that his uncanny vocation was but a mirage, a will-o'-the-wisp, a time-bomb fantasy that sooner or later would explode, exposing the shameful reality of his being nothing.

"Initiating phase Z. Atmospheric reentry in T minus thirty seconds."

The intercom announcement brought Duncan back to more tangible matters. Red lights started blinking inside the tactical compartment of the assault shuttle. Nobody was talking. A loud signal whirled, and all helmets started clicking closed automatically. As the shuttle decelerated and the soldiers regained their own weights, the ship began to vibrate sharply. The vibrations waned, replaced by a hissing hum.

Without further warning, the ship decelerated violently as it struck the surface. The landing hatchway hit the ground, and all forty-two soldiers popped out of the shuttle, deploying rapidly according to the prescribed assault configuration.

The final destination was going to be a colorful planet with thick forests and a rich variety of vegetation—or so they had been told in the last briefing on board the *Intrepid*. However, a colorless, uniform landscape of grayish tones was what Duncan and the others encountered. The local atmosphere had suffered major changes connected to the environmental reconfiguration the Establishment military had performed to render the habitat suitable for their own leading species. The local fauna and flora had been adjusted to survive and even thrive under the new conditions. The forest was still lush, although stripped of any colors. However, the atmosphere was no longer breathable for the Realitian soldiers, who had to wear pressurized combat uniforms for the mission.

Far ahead, in a valley, a construction was visible. It was noticeable amidst the abundant gray foliage. That construction was the mission target.

Careful in their deployment, the soldiers started closing distances with no delay. Behind them, the landing ship waited over a hill, concealed by a large willow-like tree. Sensors did not register anything out of the ordinary. The only detectable source of energy was a dim grayish gleam emanating from the local sun.

Everything was transpiring with absolute precision—too much precision. So far, it seemed like another exercise, at least for most of the team. Not as much to Duncan. For him, the stillness of the dark landscape created a sense of anxiety and distress.

Suddenly everybody's eyes were riveted to the ground. In the blink of an eye, the situation had turned chaotic and even desperate.

"What was that?" someone yelled over the tactical network.

"I didn't see anything," another voice replied.

"Wait—"

"Ah!"

Most of the soldiers were suddenly shooting almost randomly, and the tactical channels were quickly saturated with orders and counter-orders. An army of very swift slippery small gray creatures of different species—not native to that world—was popping up from everywhere. Dark and small, they were coming from under the ground.

As soon as they surfaced, they shot and then literally dove under the ground again. This tactic, combined with the surprise factor and the appearance of the attackers—some rodent-like, others reptilian—was causing panic. In all his years of service, O'sihn had never faced a situation like it. The enemy had clearly been waiting in ambush.

"Emergency orders, fall back, I repeat, emergency orders, fall back to the landing ship immediately." The instructions were simple, and everybody in O'sihn's team wanted to comply. However, proceeding accordingly was proving extremely difficult.

All the soldiers were striving to converge onto the assault ship, which had already started its engines. But the parched foliage had turned into a deadly trap. Patches of fire started by the gun blasts were rapidly merging into one another all over the foliage, helped by a breeze that was rapidly turning into a heavy, dry wind.

"Follow me!" O'sihn yelled at Duncan.

No sooner had they started running than a constrictor-like alien entangled the captain's legs. Using its fangs, the attacker opened a rent on the pressurized uniform. Duncan stood frozen for an instant. Overcoming his shock, he activated an energy blade and cut the aggressor into four whirling pieces, which fell from O'sihn's leg.

Another creature stood up on its back legs and fixed its eyes on Duncan. It was small and very agile. It resembled a miniature kangaroo, with bear-like claws and the head of a rodent. It had two sets of fangs on each side, each fang dripping a substance that Duncan perceived as poison. A small device emerged on its right shoulder.

A fraction of second later, a tree behind Duncan was cut in half as he rolled to the ground, successfully eluding the lethal blast. As he sat up on the grass, a glowing red spot materialized on his forehead. Duncan desperately crawled back, trying unsuccessfully to get on his feet. But at that moment, a silver arrow darted from the foliage, ripped through the attacker, and landed on a tree trunk.

The enemy trooper was hanging dead on the arrow.

Following the captain's homing system, Duncan found O'sihn. He was lying on the ground, unable to move, his uniform hissing as air escaped through the rent in one of his trouser legs. Soon the hissing would stop and the caustic reconfigured atmosphere would rush inside the uniform, killing the captain in a matter of seconds.

"Run. . . ., to the shuttle!" O'sihn yelled.

Duncan looked at the captain reluctantly.

"Run, boy, run!"

Kneeling down, Duncan reached for an emergency patch from O'sihn's combat belt. But the belt receptacle was stuck.

Pulling out the arrow that had just saved his life (and shaking off the corpse that hung from it), Duncan began to force the receptacle's lid using the arrow's point. Abruptly, the lid flung open, and he hastily managed to get the leak to stop.

Helped by Duncan, O'sihn got on his feet again, and both resumed their march. But they were not falling back with the rest. It was part of the plan that if the platoon were to find resistance, as it had, the team would lure the defenders towards the landing vessel, while Duncan and O'sihn would proceed on to the target. Through intelligence, they knew the potential resistance would be relatively small. If the platoon managed to distract them away from the mission target, few would remain to defend it during a critical time window. The one thing that intelligence had not predicted was the type of resistance they had encountered. Despite the element of surprise and the confusion caused by the very aggressive and unconventional attack—and the aversion associated with the external appearance and movements of the attackers—the operation was proceeding according to plan, and the rest of the platoon was safely back in the assault vessel.

Duncan and O'sihn were now trying to make visual contact with the building that was supposed to be ahead. However, the thick smoke coming from the burning vegetation around them had drastically reduced visibility.

On O'sihn's and Duncan's visors, a blinking yellow marker popped up, display-ing the bearing along which the target lay.

"This way!" The captain raised one hand, showing the direction to follow. He was pointing straight to a sea of fire.

Instinctively, Duncan lifted up one hand to shield his eyes. "What do you mean?"

"Trust me." O'sihn took Duncan by the elbow.

Within seconds, Duncan was experiencing hell. The temperature inside his uniform climbed brutally. After covering what felt like many yards through the flames, the only thing Duncan could still see was more fire and dense smoke everywhere. Fear began to numb his senses, but he kept moving in he direction shown by the yellow marker.

Suddenly, as if waking up from a nightmare, he found himself in the open. Right in front of him, a large solid building stood unscathed in the midst of the flames.

32.

Although control of the air space had finally been achieved, so far the landing forces had failed to establish any secured *landhead.*[70] Nevertheless, the operation was still moving forward within the planned parameters.

Commander Laida had been following all these events with growing concern, monitoring them over one of the tactical channels. She was closing distances to her target. About five hundred yards ahead, she spotted a high-tech Establishment construction, mostly concealed by the surrounding foliage.

Laida and her team stopped and began scanning for potential enemy activity. She instructed her team to go around the target following a particular reckoning pattern. Fifteen minutes later, the platoon met back behind the construction. There were no signs of enemy presence, but a sudden electronic blackout reignited the platoon's tension. They had lost contact with mission control and the rest of the platoons.

The team maintained its position, waiting for directives from any element of the tactical operation. About half an hour later, having received no instructions, Laida judged they had waited long enough and decided to proceed with the last phase of her mission.

After planting explosives in carefully selected spots around the target, Laida blasted the entrance to the building open with her gun. She led her team underground through a pitch-black corridor, guided by visualization systems on each soldier's visor. About fifty yards below, the group met the target: a chamber containing a row of three-foot-tall crystals that glowed with a grayish intensity. Using a super-conductive wire, the team proceeded to link the crystals to a device designed to short-circuit them.

Other teams were simultaneously attacking similar targets. The success of the operation depended on neutralizing more than eighty percent of such buildings, in which resided the power sources for

---

70 A *landhead* was the first objective of a military force after landing on an enemy planet, consisting of securing an initial position that could be used for subsequent landings. That position would function as the preliminary headquarters of the operation.

maintaining the reconfigured environment in that area. Laida's target was of particular relevance for the completion of O'sihn's assignment.

Laida made a sign with one fist, and the team began evacuating the chamber at once, moving in a fast and orderly fashion. However, on reaching the entrance, they met a drastic change in their tactical situation.

33.

Duncan raised his head. Dark walls, smudged with dust and mold, rose up into the discolored clouds. The building and the whole area around it looked calm, desolate, cold. Panting, Duncan bent forward with his hands on his knees. The wind was blowing against the fire behind him, keeping the area safe and clear of smoke.

Suddenly, O'sihn emerged from the flames. "Watch out, we may be under surveillance."

Duncan turned around.

"This way," O'sihn said, moving stealthily towards the entrance. He motioned to Duncan, and both flung themselves against the walls, holding their guns to their chests.

"Now!" O'sihn called.

Throwing themselves to the ground, they rolled over in front of the entrance with their guns pointing ahead. They could see a long corridor. O'sihn aimed his *biodetector* into the building.

At that point, someone shot at them. They returned fire, and each ran to a side of the entrance. A rapid exchange of blasts followed, until O'sihn threw a grenade inside.

"Take cover!"

Following the captain, Duncan plunged back inside the sea of fire, seeking shelter behind a rock. A smoldering blast of heat, followed by a tide of black smoke, bathed Duncan's suit.

"It's getting too hot!"

"Hold on," O'sihn called through his speaker, checking his *biodetector*. Duncan began to cough. "To the target."

Muffled by the intense crackling of the burning forest, O'sihn's command did not reach Duncan. Suddenly, he saw O'sihn's right arm emerge from the flames and grab his own. He let himself be dragged, until he and the captain emerged back into the open.

Running towards the entrance, Duncan squinted, trying to see inside the corridor. His sight was somewhat impaired, like most of his senses.

"The corridor is clear." O'sihn waved Duncan in; he followed with an awkward stride. Following the readings from O'sihn's scanner, they crossed three more corridors until finding the elevator they were looking for. On reaching the upper level, they threw themselves to the floor, guns pointing ahead.

"Sensor registers three individuals on target level," O'sihn muttered. "Be prudent. They may be part of the technical crew."

Duncan nodded, and the doors opened.

Three blasts hit the back panels of the elevator. O'sihn fired back with precision, disabling the gun that had opened fire, without harming the shooter or anybody else. "Put your hands behind your necks— behind your necks, I said!" he yelled.

Sluggishly, the three individuals complied with the command. Bipedal and tall, they bore similar traits to humans. The clothes they used were typical of Kervian technicians, although they themselves were not Kervian. O'sihn checked them from his spot using a scanner. They were unarmed.

"There! The master terminal." Duncan moved towards it.

O'sihn nodded as he quickly checked his watch.

Without wasting time, Duncan began working on the terminal. He typed loudly and persistently, filling the room with the clicking of an old-fashioned keyboard.[71]

---

71 Duncan had been trained for the operation on board the *Intrepid*, using a simulated terminal very much like the one they found there. He was familiar with the basic instructions to operate the system. He had also learned how to initialize the required

"What's wrong?" O'sihn asked.

"I don't know. I can't get through."

The captain moved cautiously towards Duncan, keeping his gun aimed at their captives. "It is locked, all right," O'sihn complained, looking briefly at the monitor. "Unlock the system," he ordered, walking towards the prisoners.

One of them smiled.

"The game is over," O'sihn said, aiming his gun at him.

"The game is over, indeed," the technician replied, and chuckled.

Duncan rushed towards the man and put a gun to his head. "This is not a game, pal. You unlock the system now . . . and I mean *now!*" He bit his lip as he pressed his gun against the man.

"Enough." O'sihn looked at Duncan with a grave expression.

Duncan turned around, confused.

"This is not our way. Strap them," the captain said, keeping his eyes on the three men.

"But—"

"Don't waste time."

Grudgingly, Duncan took some strapping tape from his backpack and proceeded to immobilize the technicians' wrists and ankles.

"You will not get away with this," one of the aliens said, as Duncan strapped him up.

"You'll be *equalized*," added the man who had first shot at them. "All of you."

Duncan looked at him silently.

"Okay, inside there," O'sihn ordered, pointing his gun at the three men. Leaping on their tied-up feet, the technicians moved into an adjacent room. "I will seal the room to preserve your environmental conditions, so that you will not suffer any harm when the atmosphere is reset to its native state."

"And I suppose, Captain," said the same technician that had first

procedures to complete the mission. O'sihn was much more familiar with these types of systems, which were pretty standard in Establishment usage.

spoken, "that you—and your assistant—will accomplish that feat all by yourselves."

"The atmosphere will be reconfigured," O'sihn said.

"Captain," the same man continued, "you will never manage to unlock the master computer, especially with the very limited time that you have. This building will be secured in a matter of minutes. You know all this. It is better for you—"

O'sihn locked the room and sealed it. Patting Duncan's shoulder, he ran towards the master terminal.

34.

"Drop your weapons," said a soldier holding a gun. He had humanoid traits, blended with not quite human ones. He was wider than a man, especially around his chest, although very thin around his waist. His eyes, which had no eyelids, were entirely blue.

Using the bio-scanner she carried on one of her wrists, Laida assessed the extent of the ambush. About a hundred enemy troopers were waiting hidden in the foliage.

"To the ground!" Laida yelled through her speaker, and activated the explosives planted around the building.

Only five out of the forty devices detonated, moderately damaging the edifice but setting fire to the vegetation around it. Soon, the surrounding forest turned into a crested sea of uncontrolled fire.[72] Evidently, the enemy had detected and deactivated most of their explosives.

Taking advantage of the confusion, four of the Realitian commandos escaped, but Laida had been too close to one of the detonations. Dizzy and sick, she was now struggling to get back on her feet.

As she did, three soldiers rushed from the jungle and seized her

---

[72] One side effect of the biotransformation was that it made the vegetation much more susceptible to catching fires. There was a system of drones designed to control such events. At that particular moment, half a dozen drones had made it to the scene, not enough to control the fire.

before she could run away. Out of the smoke, a fourth humanoid emerged, and behind him another, both of them males.

"Well, well, well, what do we have here?" said the fourth soldier, standing in front of Laida.

Laida recognized the uniforms. She was dealing with Kervian forces.

"Let's tie her up and throw her to the fire," someone else said.

The commanding officer turned and glared. "How am I gonna teach you manners?" Shaking his head, he turned to Laida, and started strolling around her. "Throwing a living animal to the fire . . . " Brusquely, the officer drew a gun from his combat armor and aimed it directly at Laida. He kept the weapon steady for a couple of seconds. Then he withdrew it, holding it against his chest with both hands.

"What's wrong, honey, don't you like us?" The officer laughed sarcastically and fired a shot at Laida.

He had deliberately avoided harming her, but had chosen to destroy the gas regulator on her belt. Instinctively, she grasped her smashed regulator. It was beyond repair. Before long, Laida was holding her chest, gripping the lower portion of her helmet.

"Come on, babe, take it off and give us a kiss, uh?" One of the troopers leered.

"Yeah, and your space suit too!" yelled another.

The soldiers laughed uproariously as they watched Laida fall down on her knees, coughing.

"Ah . . . that's fresh air. You oughta try it," said a soldier, taking a deep breath.

Soon the last remnants of breathable air inside Laida's combat suit had been consumed. Her instinct to take off her helmet was becoming overpowering. She was now on the ground, coughing and gasping helplessly, surrounded by fire.

At that point, a noiseless tremor started shattering the area.

35.

"The nothing nothingness that is forever.

"The nothing nothingness that is forever.

"The nothing nothingness that is forever.

"The nothing nothingness that is forever.

"The nothing nothingness that is forever.

"The nothing nothingness that is forever.

"The nothing nothingness that is forever." The phrase was repeated over and over in bright green letters on a black display. O'sihn and Duncan had been trained to operate the master environmental computer for the mission. They had also brought along a password sorter, but the instrument was unable to disengage a program like the one that was locking the system.

"What the heck is that supposed to mean, anyway?" Duncan scowled, after trying and retrying some prescribed procedures through the keyboard.

"Nothing," O'sihn said.

"What?" Duncan turned around, irritated.

"It's an *Equel* formula, one of their beliefs." O'sihn stared at the screen, his mind struggling to find some way around the enigma.

"Beliefs?" Duncan asked.

"The computer has been fed with its *logum*," O'sihn said. "And has been set to solve it."

"How do you know that?"

O'sihn pointed at the upper right corner of the screen. The words "Recursive L-solver[73] active" were displayed in small red letters. "It's attempting to solve the *logum* recursively, but it will proceed *ad infinitum*, trying to find a solution that, I'm afraid, does not exist."

"Let's try to unlock it activating some other procedure," Duncan suggested, "like an environmental emergency check. We know how to do that."

---

73 L-solver: *logum*-solver.

O'sihn shook his head. "The computer has deliberately been locked on by having it use all its processing power to solve the *logum*."

"So . . . we can do nothing?"

O'sihn brought his right hand towards his forehead, unintentionally striking his helmet, and closed his eyes. "I will stay here trying to find a way to unlock this contraption. In the meantime, you will leave the building, fall back with the main group, and alert control of what has happened."

Duncan hesitated. "The main group is more than three miles away."

"This is not a recommendation, Dahncion."

"I can't abandon you here."

"The chances of unlocking this computer are extremely slim. It's not rational to gamble two lives to attempt the impossible."

"If it's impossible, it's not rational to risk *any* life," Duncan retorted. "Let's get out of here."

O'sihn walked to the elevator door and pushed the down button. "You are leaving this building." But after three more tries, he realized that the situation was worse than he had thought. He ran to the main panels and started working frantically on the building controls.

"What's going on?" Duncan asked.

"I'm afraid neither of us is going anywhere. The whole building is locked, and we are running out of time."

"Let's get the technicians and force them to unlock the computer," Duncan blurted.

"I sealed the door to the room where we put them." O'sihn explained. "We won't be able to open it."

Duncan closed his eyes. "Let's . . . let's try unlocking the computer, then, somehow."

"I am fully open to suggestions," O'sihn muttered.

Duncan sighed, with clenched fists. "You should've let me have them unlock the computer."

O'sihn shook his head. "They would have died rather than unlock the system."

"Huh! I don't know about that. They looked pretty panicky to me."

"Do you think your approach was compatible with what we talked about last night?" They had gone through the Royal Navy Officer's Credo, in particular, the part that read: "With the conviction that the dignity of any person is as high a priority as the success of any mission."

"Kervians don't take prisoners, Captain!" Duncan stated, raising his voice.

"What you had in mind is not our way, the way of Reality."

Duncan looked back with a disapproving stance. "So why don't we try reasoning with the freakin' machine, then?"

"Reasoning?"

"Yeah, some of that Realitian common-sense philosophy of yours," Duncan said acidly.

O'sihn looked at him and laid his hands over the old keyboard. "You tell me what you want to try."

Duncan raised his eyes to the barren sky beyond the window in front of him. "Nothingness . . . well. Let's try emptiness."

O'sihn clasped his fingers and entered the corresponding logum. The computer replied on the spot:

"The emptiness that is forever."

"The nothing nothingness that is emptiness."

"Nothingness is emptiness."

"The proposed *logum* is a redundant solution."

O'sihn gave a terse smile while shaking his head. "What if we tried something silly, something trivial?"

"A pebble?"

"Like a pebble." O'sihn turned back to the keyboard and entered a logum containing the concept.

The computer responded:

"The pebble that is forever."

"The nothing nothingness that is a pebble is forever."

"A pebble is something."

"The proposed *logum* does not satisfy the *logoid*."

"I know!" Duncan snapped his fingers. "*Sternessence*."

O'sihn nodded and typed its *logum*.

The solver began to blink, indication that, at least, they had peeled off some logical layer.

"I'm sure this is it," Duncan said. "This is what Oyhtter gave us. It oughta be it."

After a full minute of a black screen, the computer was not giving any signs of life.

"We really don't have time for these games, Dahncion. We should start preparing our defense."

"Wait." Duncan pointed at a cursor that began to blink on the left bottom corner. The screen became alive again. "Yes!"

The computer responded:

"*Sternessence* is love."

"Love is forever."

"The nothing nothingness that is love."

"Love is everything."

"The proposed *logum* contradicts the *logoid*."

O'sihn sighed. He looked at his watch, and then at his bio-scanner. It was not clear what was transpiring outside the building, but his instrument registered growing activity. This could mean that enemy forces were encircling the compound. On the other hand, it was clear that Laida had failed in her mission to destroy the nearby power station. Had she succeeded, a major power loss would have ensued in the area. In response, the building energy fence would have automatically been activated, thus keeping enemy troops from regaining control of the facility too soon.

Duncan looked at O'sihn working in silence, trying *logoid* after *logoid.* But none of his attempts were shedding any light on how to unlock the system. The spark of optimism that had animated Duncan's spirit just moments before was rapidly dissipating. In a few more minutes, the enemy would secure the whole area. In dealing with Kervian forces, their lives would most likely end right there, and quite likely with cruelty.

Duncan reflected on all that and found it hard to believe. He looked back on his life, and he was afraid. A sense of emptiness, of having done nothing of relevance so far, was his dominant feeling. This, combined with the type of death that awaited him, was making Duncan fall into a cold state of depression that made him wonder about, and even regret, his decision to accept his mission to Reality.

O'sihn kept staring at the screen with an intense stance, until he finally nodded.

"Let's give more serious thought to this nothingness nonsense."

"Checkmate nonsense," added Duncan with defeated sarcasm.

O'sihn had his eyes fixed on the monitor, with a serene expression. "Nothingness. If I remember something from the philosophy courses required at the Naval Academy, there is no such thing as a substantial nothing. There is no essential nothing. Nothingness must always be referred to something that is, or rather, to a lack of that something."

"How about *lack of something?*" Duncan muttered, looking at the terminal.

"We must nail down the idea to one concept," O'sihn replied.

"Well, *lack of something* is just *nothing.*"

"We can't feed the computer with *nothing.* It would give us a tautological error."

Duncan sighed, checking his watch nervously without actually looking at it. He sat down on a chair by the console, stretching his legs forward, until he let them sag loose without purpose. There was a clear sense of surrender in his posture, but there was a remnant in him, now mostly fed by the fear of the events to come, that moved him not to give up yet.

"As you said yesterday, the way to fight all this nonsense is with some 'common sense and reality'," Duncan said, his arms dangling. "Well, common sense tells me that nothing is something that doesn't exist, something that is not real—and that's the only reality I can see." Duncan paused. "So why don't we go ahead and try unreality?"

O'sihn raised an eyebrow and immediately entered the corresponding *logum*.

The reply was instantaneous:

"The unreality that is forever."

"The nothing nothingness that is unreality."

"Unreality is nothing."

"Unreality is nothingness."

"The nothing nothingness that is forever is unreal."

"The proposed *logum* satisfies the *logoid*."

36.

One of the men pointed up to the northern sky, and the rest stopped their mockery of Laida abruptly. An incandescent blue shock wave, extending from east to west, was sweeping the forest from the ground all the way up to the grayish sky.

All but one of the Kervians ran away, desperately seeking some shelter. Fully aware of the implications of the lethal shock wave, the commandant chose to spend his final moments kicking Laida, trying to open a rent in her suit. But he was soon blown away by the rushing wind.

The helmet Laida was wearing was torn off, and she smashed into a large bush, which providentially cushioned her fall. Immediately, a gust of fresh air rushed into Laida's choked lungs as the dim surrounding landscape started recovering its original multicolored splendor.

Laida was soon on her feet. The threatening fire around her had completely vanished. She turned around and gazed with astonishment at the marvelous vision of growing colors sprouting all around her.

Worn out by the ordeal she had just gone through, Laida fell down on her knees, weeping and raising her eyes to the sky. From the speakers on her helmet lying on the ground, she readily recognized her husband's voice on the main tactical channel.

" . . . complete. I repeat, bioconversion system disengaged. Reconfiguration wave expanding as expected. Mission complete."

37.

It was impressive how the once grayish world had turned, so quickly, into a paradise of color and light. Trees with green, blue, and phosphorescent branches; yellow ferns whose leaves were nibbled by all-transparent tiny hummingbird-like creatures; sapphire patches of grass covering a wet ground graced with hues of emerald. Iluminia was a world of exotic beauty. Even if storms never developed in its atmosphere, its skies were speckled with small dense clouds, which constantly bathed the ubiquitous forests below with a warm drizzle.

Rainbows crystallized continually above the dense foliage, even after sunset. Father Rainbow provided enough light for their formation most days of the month. Irisiom, as the natives called it, was a large satellite with a surface that reflected much more light from the local sun than Earth's moon does. Yet nights were clearly differentiated from days, and not only because the night rainbows were dimmer and lacking in color compared to the day rainbows. Every evening, after the local sun had set, the Earth-like blue sky turned into a glowing emerald green, mostly from the light reflected by Mother Rainbow, or Irisia—a well-developed ring of clean ice in equatorial orbit. Its resplendent spectrum prevented darkness from ever reaching the poles.

A woman from a distant world was savoring the unique beauty.

She was tired. It had been a particularly long day, and not merely because it took thirty-six hours for the planet to complete one sidereal revolution.

Night was rapidly taking over, and thousands of tiny lights started flaring everywhere. Irisiom was in its new "moon" phase, and Irisia's tender light let numerous stars[74] show their glare in the firmament. As if in a mirror, myriads of uniquely bright glowworms—or jungle stars, as the locals called them—would gradually begin to display their nightly flickering love-calls throughout the woods.

Clara was pondering the day's operation, the war, and some personal matters. She had picked a lonely spot.

Stepping out from the woods, Duncan walked up, holding a silver arrow in a hesitant hand. Clara noticed his presence, but her instincts kept her eyes focused on the stars above the horizon.

"I hope I'm not intruding," Duncan said, holding the arrow with both hands.

Clara was sitting on a tree trunk that lay on the ground. She was still wearing her combat suit, her long blond hair falling delicately over her shoulders.

"I . . . I just came to return this," Duncan added, holding the gleaming needle-like weapon which had saved his life earlier that day.

"You are not intruding." Clara gazed at some flowers alongside the tree trunk where she was sitting. "Not at all."

"Would you like to walk a little bit?" Duncan asked.

"I'd like that."

Clara and Duncan started strolling across the dappled field. It was a peaceful evening, filled with the twilight calls of local animals.

"How beautiful," Duncan said gently, pointing at the sky.

"Yes," Clara muttered, raising her eyes to the magnificent rings of light. "They call her Irisia."

"Yes . . . so beautiful." Duncan found himself somewhat at a

---

74 That planet was close to the center of its galaxy, where the star density was very high. Many of the neighboring stars were just a few light-weeks away, measured in the speed of light of our universe.

loss for words that evening. The attractive presence of the woman walking beside him was making him feel tense. It was the first time Duncan became aware of Clara's personal beauty. Indeed, it was the first time he noticed her womanhood.

Plucking a long grass-like reed, Duncan started peeling off its thin, soft layers. "You looked absorbed a moment ago."

"Irisia, the stars, the little flying lights here and there." Clara shrugged. "Everything is so beautiful."

"I haven't seen lightning bugs in a long time."

"So you also have glowworms on Earth?"

"Uh-huh. I remember, when I was a kid, we liked to play who'd catch more."

"That must've been fun."

"A silly game."

"I wish I could remember any childhood game." Clara sighed.

"We can play it now."

"Do you really mean it?"

Duncan tossed away what was left of his reed. "If we only had a couple of jars for the bugs we catch."

Smiling, Clara produced a small vial from a pocket. She emptied out the nutrition tablets it contained and put them back inside the same pocket.

"We still have only one vial," Duncan pointed out with a smirk.

"I'll keep the vial," Clara said, "and you keep the count, for each of us."

"Fair enough."

With that, they split up. Soon the vial started to glow vividly, and Clara's bug-catching score was way below her opponent's. Then Duncan laughed softly. She was trying to trap a bright flying light with one hand above and the other below it.

Clara smiled broadly, shaking the vial full of lights.

"It's not fair," Clara objected. "I'm competing against an expert."

"I don't intend to be very helpful, you know? But you'll hardly catch any bugs while they are flying."

Clara smiled as a glowworm slipped through her fingers.

"Come on, over here," Duncan added, taking her by the hand. Surprised, Clara followed him to a bush full of tiny lights.

"Look, the secret to this business is that you catch 'em when they are crawling." Duncan extended one arm slowly towards a bush. "You see?" he added, a whirling little creature struggling to get off his fingers.

Clara nodded and touched her hand, the one Duncan had just reached for.

"So, now show me you've learned something, Captain."

Clara slipped quietly towards the same bush, capturing her prey easily.

"You learn fast," said Duncan. "But don't expect any further help for the night." Spotting a large blinking light on top of a tree, he climbed up to catch the insect. Back on the ground, he stood in front of Clara and looked at her hesitantly. "I think I should've said this before."

Clara smiled broadly, shaking the vial full of lights.

"I mean . . . I'm sorry, Clara."

"Why?" she asked, with a faint smile. The apology did not seem to fit the statement she expected.

"The *Sagacious*. I didn't mean the things I said that day."

Clara shook her head gently. "Never mind. We were dealing with a very complicated situation that day."

"Maybe, but I know I hurt you, and I didn't mean to do that."

Clara grinned. There was a steady trace of sadness in her expression, associated with her tragic past and her lack of contact with human beings. But being with the man she was in love with— her first love—gifted her eyes with a special joy. "I don't recall your saying anything wrong."

Duncan shook his head. "You're too good to me."

"Watch out." Clara turned around. "I'm gonna beat ya after all. What's the score?"

Duncan shrugged.

"You were supposed to keep count, mister."

"Perhaps we have already disturbed enough glowworms for the night," Duncan said, looking into her eyes.

Removing the lid of the vial, Clara proceeded to empty it out on the spot.

"Why don't we just . . . walk a bit more?" Duncan added.

Clara nodded.

After a short hike, they were back to the spot where Clara had been resting before sunset. They sat down side by side, on the tree trunk that lay on the grass. Clara gazed towards the horizon, Irisia's light shining mildly upon her gleaming blue eyes. A wandering glowworm landed by her right ear. That gave Duncan the perfect excuse to brush softly at her hair. The twinkling light was sent away into the night to resume his loving call, somewhere else, not far away from that very spot.

38.

Duncan opened his eyes, disoriented. Even though there were still more than three hours left in the resting period, everybody was up, working hectically.

"Get up, boy, we have no time."

Duncan turned around and found Captain Foxso'l standing in front of him. "No time?" Duncan said from inside his sleeping bag. "No time for what?"

"We are gettin' outta here."

"Wha—Where?"

"I don't know about the others, but you're coming with us." Foxso'l tilted his head towards a shuttle, in which he had landed less than an hour before.

Duncan sat up. "What are you talking about?"

"New royal orders. You are coming along with us to the Aquarius quadrant. You'll meet O'sihn and the others later on, on Aquaelight—some planet up there," Foxso'l said, casually waving up a hand.

At that point, O'sihn stepped in. "Flash orders from headquarters, Dahncion. Captain Foxso'l will explain everything. Follow his instructions."

Duncan stood up right away.

"Captain," somebody called out.

"Coming." O'sihn turned to Duncan. "I really need to go."

"Where is Clara?"

"She's already been picked up. Don't worry." O'sihn put a hand on Duncan's right shoulder. "We'll all meet again in a few days. Good luck."

Duncan kept staring at O'sihn as he disappeared into the busy crowd.

"Don't try to understand the military." Foxso'l rolled his eyes. "It's the stupidest thing there is."

"But . . . "

Foxso'l's communicator started to beep. "Cruise engines energized and standing-by, Captain." That was Witts, the *Angel Spark*'s first officer. The ship was orbiting the planet, waiting for Foxso'l and Duncan.

"Copied," Foxso'l acknowledged.

"May I—" Duncan said, but broke his questions off. Foxso'l was looking at him with impatience.

A couple of minutes later, Foxso'l's shuttle restarted her engines. She lifted off in a rather unconventional manner, leaving a trail of light. The glare of her engines swiftly waned, merging in the majestic disk of a rising *Irisiom*.

CHAPTER 7

The Encounter

39.

"Confirmed, Captain." Witts lifted his head from the aft scanner visor. "It's an Ultoris class frigate, and it seems to be chasing the first contact."

"And unless we change course, we'll pass way too close by her," added Tora.

Foxso'l nodded. "Changing our course would make us look more suspicious."

"What's going on out there?" Duncan asked.

Nothing good, you can bet," Tora responded.

"They are opening fire on the unidentified vessel," Witts called, and smacked the long-range passive scanner, seemingly the only way to have it work properly.

"Any signal from the attacked vessel?"

"No, Captain. It's following a complex evasive trajectory."

"They might be unarmed," Duncan suggested.

"Uh-huh," Foxso'l muttered, his eyes glued to the navigational display.

"And we aren't gonna do anything?"

"This ain't the *Intrepid*, son."

"What? We oughta help those guys." Duncan fixed his eyes on Foxso'l. The skipper's expression remained unchanged, constantly reassessing the situation.

"The chased vessel is veering to port," Witts said. "Present mean course: three-three-zero dash two-eight-five. Nebula Gabot ahead vessel's mean trajectory, Captain."

"Contact time?" that meant, for the vessel to enter the nebula.

"Approximately one minute, Captain."

"Maybe we can still please Dahncion, skipper," Tora said. "The moment the Establishees get inside the nebula, their scanners will lose our position."[75]

Foxso'l listened, watching the main scanner.

"Inside that thing they will have to travel T.L.S.,"[76] Tora continued. "And it's a long, narrow, nebula, skipper."

Foxso'l turned back to a virtual monitor located on the port side of the bridge, where a chart of the quadrant was displayed with some additional data. "All right. Plot a parabolic course to the other side of the nebula. Final incidence angle: three degrees tangent to nebula's maximum curvature coordinates."

"Aye-aye, skipper."

"We're gonna be waiting on the Blishees'[77] ship to come out," Foxso'l added, turning to Duncan. "Then we'll kick its a—"

"Blips penetrating nebula, sir," Witts interrupted.

Foxso'l turned to Tora. "Is our trajectory computed yet?"

"Affirmative, skipper. I've already passed it to the navigational computer."

"Full ahead along computed trajectory."

"Full ahead aye, skipper."

"Effect full stop when reaching ten thousand kilometers from the nebula."

"Got it."

The *Angel Spark* began to accelerate. A large, starless dark blotch—the dark nebula—appeared on the main display. The ship

---

75 Sensors experience a significant loss of accuracy when moving at high speeds in ionized environments.

76 Thermally Limited Speed, which implies slow speeds.

77 *Blishee* was a contraction of *Establishee*, both being derogative terms referring to the Establishment.

started going around the self-constrained ocean of gas, leaving it off the upper starboard side. Gradually, the nebula's outline became more rounded, until acquiring a nearly perfect circular shape. At that point, the ship stopped.

"Ten thousand kilometers to the gas-nebula's max. curvature azimuth, and standing by, Captain," Witts added.

"Good. Download the attacking routine[78] from the bow cargo-bay computer," Foxso'l said, addressing Tora. "Set parameters for one missile to lock on the second target that comes out of the nebula. We'll launch the missile right after the first ship emerges."

"Got ya, skipper."

"What if the only ship to come out is the Establishment's?" Duncan asked. "I mean, what if it has destroyed the ship it's chasing inside the nebula?"

Foxso'l shrugged. "We would hide ourselves inside the cloud."

"Yeah, we do this sort of thing all the time," Tora said. "Never mind about that."

Duncan did not show any reassurance.

"One vessel emerging from Gabot's nebula," Witts said, and marked a pin in his electronic chart.

Foxso'l glanced at the data on screen and tapped twice with a forefinger in the air.

Tora nodded. "Missile away and in searching mode, skipper."

The missile was not intended for the first vessel, whose signature did not correspond with an enemy ship, but for the Establishment battleship that was expected to come out after it.

"Vessel one exhibits signs of severe damage," said Witts, adjusting his ear-speaker. "And . . . yes, it's transmitting an emergency distress

---

78 The attacking routine software was scrambled and spread over the cargo software in order to conceal it from the Establishment's constant inspections.

signal. All readings confirm it's definitely not the enemy battleship, Captain."

Foxso'l listened to Witts while keeping his attention on the main display.

"Our missile is five thousand kilometers from the nebula, skipper, and still no contact with any emerging ship." Tora paused for a moment. "Forty-five hundred klicks, forty hundred, thirty-five hundred . . . "

The missile suddenly began accelerating at an extreme rate.

"A second blip is emerging now . . . "

"—pact on target," Witts' composed voice confirmed simultaneously.

"Woohaaaa!" Tora yelled, clapping hands with Duncan.

"Estimated damage?" Foxso'l inquired.

"Enemy ship destroyed, Captain," Witts confirmed.

Foxso'l's tension slackened. "Any distress signal?"

"No communications detected from any source, Captain."

"I'm not one hundred percent sure, skipper," Tora added, "but I don't detect any engine activity from the first vessel. It seems to be following an inertial trajectory."

"Tie us in with it, Witts."

"I'm trying, Captain, yet . . . picking up some form of communications, sir. It's coming low and with distortion."

"Let's listen to it."

"It's not a conference message, Captain. It's some code. I've engaged the cryptosystem to attempt to decode it."

"Code? What kind of a code?"

Witts was very focused, trying to make sense of the strange signal. "Aha. It's a K43 Karindian code, Captain: *Five thousand kilometers. Ejecting escape capsules. Imminent propulsion plant collapse. Lethal area: five thousand kilometers.* It starts all over again."

"What's our distance?"

"One hundred thousand klicks, skipper," Tora said.

Foxso'l nodded, and as he did, an energy surge flashed white on the main display.

"Wow!" Tora quickly gauged the extent of the electromagnetic discharge now registering in his sensors. "That thing has blown up like a *meganova*," he added, referring to the ship that had first e-merged from the nebula.

"Distress signal interrupted, Captain," Witts added.

"Picking up some weird, old fashioned radio signal," Tora continued. "Bearing one-six-three dash one-five-zero relative. This sure is a funny signal, in a funny frequency, skipper."

"Confirmed, Captain," Witts said, looking up from his station. "Its point of origin seems to be a small metallic object. Range ninety-four thousand kilometers."

Foxso'l rubbed his chin. "Let's start closing distances, but *really* carefully. Ahead point zero, zero, one relative; interception course factor three."

"Ahead point zero, zero, one relative; interception course factor three, Captain," Witts acknowledged.

"Go take care of the port battery,[79] and stand by there for instructions."

"Aye-aye, skipper." Tora left the bridge.

Foxso'l turned to Witts. "Give me some ranges."

"Eighty thousand kilometers . . . seventy thousand . . . sixty thousand . . . "

"Cannons activated and in stand-by, skipper," Tora's voice sounded through the captain's console.

---

79 The port battery contained a standard plasma cannon. The battery was concealed and totally disconnected from the ship's network, like any other weapon onboard, to hide it from Establishment inspections. The only link with the network (or any weapons system) was through an encoded channel that could be accessed through any standard communication system, but whose signals were shielded from leaking into space.

"Good. Keep the target tracked, but don't open fire unless I tell you."

"You've got it, skipper."

"Forty thousand kilometers . . . thirty thousand . . . "

"Slow down," Foxso'l instructed.

"Picking up a life form inside the object," Witts reported.

"Estimated size of the object?"

"Three meters average, Captain," Witts answered. "It looks like an escape capsule of some sort, but I'm not detecting any others in the area."

"And it doesn't look like any conventional escape capsule, does it?" added Foxso'l. "Any sign of activity?"

"Nothing other than the life form, Captain."

Foxso'l swung slightly on his chair. "New speed setting, point zero, zero, zero two relative."

"Point zero, zero, zero two relative, Captain. Present range seventy-four hundred kilometers, sir."

"Let's get the object in through the bow bay main gate."

Witts nodded. "Capture sequence engaged. Bow bay main gate opening, sir. Zero relative speed."

The unidentified object was right above the bow bay main gate.

"H.R. scanners,"[80] Foxso'l said.

"H.Rs engaged and probing, sir. *Megalium* alloy metal, thickness ranges between one and three inches. No propulsion system detected. No dangerous instruments for unknown purposes scanned. No chemical explosives detected. Internal atmosphere with high contents of *bioxyn* and *catalyon*.[81] Traces of inert gases. No radioactive materials detected. No perilous free sub-particles identified. One water canister. Organic material registers as possible food. No toxic

---

80 High-Resolution, close-range scanners used to examine the inner structure and constituents of any object or device.

81 *Bioxyn* and *catalyon* are gases comparable to oxygen and nitrogen, respectively, in our universe.

gases or liquids. Abundant additional data of lesser relevance. Safety classification one: no threat detected, Captain."

"What about the life form?"

"Humanoid."

"Tora, are you still there?"

"Affirmative, skipper."

"Watch out for any sign of activity."

"Aye, skipper."

"You stay here. I'm gonna take a closer look at that thing," Foxso'l said to Witts.

"Acknowledged, Captain."

"I'm going with you," added Duncan.

Foxso'l and Duncan now stood waiting in front of the hatchway that connected to the bow bay. Once the repressurization sequence was completed, a whirling electronic sound rang, and the hatchway began to open.

In the middle of the hangar, a dark gray object—conical in shape—stood alone in silence. Tenuous vapors were emanating from the capsule's skin. Foxso'l stepped into the bay, followed by Duncan. They stopped about three feet from the object and watched.

"Don't touch it!" Foxso'l yanked Duncan's arm, holding him back. "It's still extremely cold."

Duncan stepped back from a small lever that had just sprung out from the capsule's hull. Above the lever, a smashed yellow arrow pointed down.

After adjusting his gun, Foxso'l began irradiating the lever with an amber-colored ray. Duncan gave him a curious glance. "Just heating it up so that we can handle it," Foxso'l explained.

Shutting down his gun, the skipper approached the lever, his nose almost touching it. He could not perceive any heat. Using his fingers, Foxso'l carefully made a final check. "That's much better," he said, and waved to Duncan to go ahead.

Duncan grabbed the lever and pulled it down. An equalization-of-pressures hiss issued from the hatchway as it opened.

The capsule's only passenger looked first at Foxso'l, with apprehension, and next at Duncan. "Where am I?"

"You are on board the *Angel Spark*, ma'am," Foxso'l said.

The passenger looked around cautiously.

"I am Foxso'l, captain of this vessel, and this gentleman is Dahncion." The skipper waved a hand casually. "One of my assistants."

Duncan drank in the Earth-looking woman—a perfectly Earth-looking woman. She did not exhibit any of the traits of the different creatures he had met so far in that universe—*rilitian, tori,* or any other. She looked fully human and was definitely most attractive.

"Would you help our guest out, Dahncion?"

Eyes fixed on the female presence, Duncan delayed his reply for about a second. "Sure, yes." He stepped forward clumsily, extending his right hand inside the capsule. Leaning on his arm, the woman stepped down onto the bay deck. Her attire, practical though it seemed, enhanced her beauty.

"Welcome on board the *Angel Spark*," Foxso'l added courteously.

"Thank you, Captain."

"My pleasure, ma'am." Foxso'l inclined his eyes gallantly. "Could you tell us something about yourself?"

The woman smiled kindly. "My name is Erina Brikana, and I come from planet Earth."

40.

It was about 2100R when Erina was rescued. She was exhausted and did not feel like having any food. She did not feel very well either. Erina looked and talked as if she had not slept in days. The *Angel Spark* was far from being a pleasure cruiser, but her captain kindly granted his own quarters to the new passenger.

While Foxso'l showed her his cabin, accompanied by Witts, Erina shared a few comments about her trip and immediately retired. She said very little, mainly that she did not belong to that universe, even if she was familiar with some aspects of it.

After she went to bed, Foxso'l, helped by Duncan, ran several tests on her capsule. He could not find anything threatening or anything that would link it, or Erina, to the Establishment. Her claim could not be verified yet, but there was nothing that would contradict it, either. Eventually, Duncan retired, but Foxso'l stayed on the bridge two more hours scanning for any activity in the area. He found nothing.

41.

In the morning, Duncan headed to the commissary for breakfast. It was too early for Foxso'l to be there, who had gone to bed much later than Duncan, and too early for Tora, who had covered the early morning watch and would be in his resting period. As for Witts, he was covering his watch on the bridge. Yet Duncan would not have his breakfast alone.

"Good morning," Erina said, as Duncan walked toward the food machine. She was sitting at a corner table, behind the entrance.

Surprised, Duncan turned around. "I thought you would still be sleeping."

"I had enough sleep." Erina's tired eyes did not seem to agree with that statement.

After pouring some *amis*[82] and picking up a couple of *klets*,[83] Duncan approached the table. "May I?"

"Please."

Duncan sat down and started breaking his *klets* in halves. They were hot and steaming. "You must've had quite a day yesterday," he said, stirring his *amis*.

---

82 Effervescent, transparent beverage reminiscent of coffee in flavor. In a dark room, a phosphorescent blue radiance sparkling from its small bubbles could be observed.

83 Toast-like tablets with a tile-like texture that melts in one's mouth with a sweet and satisfying flavor.

The capsule's only passenger looked around cautiously.

"I sure did." Erina pushed her hair to one side and sighed. "But we finally made it. I'm the first woman ever to get to this universe."

"No doubt you're the first woman, but certainly not the first human," Duncan said, with a grin.

"As far as we know, the other team had not been able to make it."

"I don't know about this." Duncan wrinkled his forehead. "But I did get here without anyone's help—anyone from Earth, that is."

"I guess many travels to my universe may have already taken place," Erina commented. "This would clarify a number of unexplained sightings people claim once in a while."

"I am from Earth," Duncan declared, with a strong emphasis.

"No doubt." Erina smiled kindly. "Though not from *my* Earth, the Earth from my universe."

"That is precisely where I'm from," Duncan asserted. "From our universe, from our same old Earth."

The woman looked at him and sipped more of her *amis*.

"I am a human being, like you," Duncan added, with a touch of discomfort.

Erina moved her chair closer to him and looked into his eyes. Immediately Duncan could detect an attractive scent emanating from her body, though nearly imperceptible. It had been some time since he had been in the presence of a woman from his own world. Perhaps this was enhancing his perception of her femininity.

"Take my hand," Erina said, her palms up and a wrist gently bent. Clumsily, Duncan touched her hand.

"You see? I'm different. I wasn't born in this universe," Erina explained.

"Neither was I," Duncan said, putting his other hand on top of hers. "This is not my true appearance. I mean, I look pretty much like this, but I had to be changed—my body, that is—to be brought here, to this universe. They call it bio-assimilation."

Erina took her hands away and stared at him. "I'm not sure I understand."

"People from this universe brought me here through a *transrealitic* jump."

"Do you mean that one fine day, some people over here teleported you into this universe?"

Duncan chuckled anxiously. "It was not quite like that. They came to our universe in some *transrealitic* vessels, reconfigured my body with a . . . a RIBA device, and took me to one of their planets—Realitas—in this universe."

"They . . . forced you—"

"No, no, no, nobody forced me into anything."

"Incredible."

"I know, but that's how it happened. You might've gotten here in a similar fashion, I mean, even when using Earth technology."

Erina raised an eyebrow, moving her head slightly to one side. "The *transrealitic* procedure you've mentioned seems . . . different from the technology that brought me here."

Erina's story was quite different, indeed.

"So, how did all this happen?" Duncan asked.

Erina put her cup on the table and crossed her legs. "I guess everything started when a group of scientists, rather accidentally, discovered the existence of this universe, while working for a military project. Right from the start, they found strong evidence for intelligent life. Some people in the government decided to keep the discovery a secret. The repercussions would have been unpredictable. They wanted to collect the maximum amount of information before making it public, especially about the advanced technologies they had picked up. They were also concerned that some other countries could use the discovery against us."

As she went on with her story, Duncan looked at the woman with fascination. Her uniform, which covered her whole body, did not hide any of her beauty. Beyond the external appeal, her intelligence made her even more appealing to him. Erina had a magnetism that energized Duncan's senses.

Erina continued. "Two years later, the first version of a system called T.D.C.—Trans-Dimensional Connector—was completed. A quasi-trans-dimensional door, or Q.T.D., could now be generated. That meant a physical link between universes.

"In the beginning, Q.T.Ds were opened for just a few microseconds. Within a few months, the microseconds had turned into milliseconds, and soon the time threshold needed to send massive objects, and reconfigure their physical structure, was achieved. But even before that, different types of radiation emitted through open Q.T.Ds had been detected and processed, indicating possible intelligent origins.

"Finally, we were able to send large objects. We started by injecting three probes that sent back very valuable data. We tried to open Q.T.Ds as close as possible to some of the sources of the signals. The third probe landed on a planet, close to what appeared to be a city. It was a very small device. Passing natives never noticed it. It sent many images of different people, some of them quite similar to us, some looking more like you do now."

Duncan tapped on the table with his fingers and nodded. "So, how were you selected for the trip?"

"I was involved in the space program. A couple of years ago, somebody asked me if I would be willing to take part in a new project. It was a highly classified program, so if I accepted, I wouldn't be able to back out for a number of years. I knew the person who was proposing this unexpected deal, and she was somebody I could trust.

"She said the project was much more exciting than the entire space program put together, and reassured me of my personal qualifications. Her proposal sounded truly exciting, and the mystery surrounding it added a good share of fascination to it, though it was a leap in the dark.

"It didn't take me long to make up my mind. I soon got deeply involved in the new program and was glad to be there in spite of the risk. I remember very well the day the first images were sent back by the third probe from what we came to call planet *Alpha-u1*. It was amazing. None of us had ever thought that in the course of our lifespans, we would make contact with an alien civilization—from a different universe."

Erina sipped more of her *amis* and leaned back in her chair, holding her cup with both hands.

"How did you finally make it here?" Duncan asked.

"A team of *univnauts*—that's the fancy name they found for us, which soon evolved into just *u-nauts*. I was one of them. Then, one got ill, two showed a negative sensitivity to the Q.T.D. system, the physiology of two others rejected the bio-reconfiguration necessary to live in this universe. In the end, I was the one chosen for the job."

"It must've been a tough process."

"Quite," Erina said. "Soon the day—yesterday—came for me to step into the transition-capsule, the same capsule that you found me in. After a three-hour countdown, a Q.T.D. was opened—the largest Q.T.D. ever—and I was projected through it. The transition was made to a position close to *Alpha-u1*, although something apparently went wrong."

"How does it feel?"

"The projection?"

Duncan nodded.

Erina sighed mildly. "The Q.T.D. opens, and suddenly you are here, in this universe. You don't feel much of a change."

"Sounds similar to my trip," Duncan said.

Erina grinned. "Anyway, I found myself inside some ionized environment, and immediately a ship appeared and captured my capsule. In the process, many of the external instruments and sensors were damaged; from that moment on, I lost contact with most of what was transpiring around me.

"The atmospheric sensors were still operative, and soon I was picking up readings of a breathable atmosphere surrounding the capsule. I decided to open the hatchway, but the locking system was stuck. I tried again, but it wouldn't open. I hoped that someone would activate the emergency exit latch from the outside, but that was not happening either. After a while, I was starting to get worried.

"Half an hour or so later, the capsule shuddered violently, and I experienced a strong jolt. I was very fortunate to be in my commanding console at that moment.

"Now all external atmospheric readings were gone, and I was floating in the capsule again. The disturbing idea of being a derelict in space hit me. But not long after that, I started hearing noises on the hull. Almost immediately, I fell down to the capsule's deck. Breathable atmospheric readings reappeared in my console display." Erina rested her chin on one hand, leaning her elbow on the table. "I didn't have to wait long until you and Captain Foxso'l triggered the emergency opening system."

Duncan was impressed with Erina's story, but had mixed feelings about the implications. All of a sudden, he was not the only human being that had ever traveled from his Earth to that universe, and Erina's trip suggested that many would follow. Thus, the exclusivity aspect of his being there was no longer true. The notion of his having a unique and potentially important role in resolving the universal conflict, as he had been told, had just been undermined by this revelation, and his doubts about his alleged role began to haunt him again. On the other hand, Erina had been able to make the trip without having to change her perfectly human appearance—from Earth's standards—whereas his seemed alien to her, which bothered him.

"The ship that first picked your capsule up was probably a Realdom vessel, which was being chased by an Establishment battleship," Duncan explained. "The one we destroyed, as the captain told you yesterday."

"Establishment?"

"It seems the Establishment's ship badly damaged the one that recovered your capsule. You were probably jettisoned right before it exploded."

"Establishment?"

Duncan nodded. "As we speak, the Establishment keeps adding worlds to its Equity."

Erina nodded slightly, stroking a lock of her hair.

"This Equity can be very persuasive, invasive," Duncan hurried to explain, "and very difficult to question." He had learned a lot about the conflict while staying in Realitas, after his first mission in Veridiawa, mostly through Realitas public network.[84] He would hear very little about the Establishment, and the conflict in general, from his comrades, although Foxso'l, and in particular Tora, were much more outspoken about the whole thing.

"So people resent the Equity?" Erina asked.

"Not all. For many, it's like a holy book. It was written by Em-Rasinka, about two hundred years ago. She is considered the founder of the Establishment. Moving from planet to planet, Em-Rasinka spread the Equity with amazing speed—and success. There is not one single world where she preached her Equity that has not been converted, if I may use the expression. Not that everyone falls for it, but once installed, no one dares to oppose it."

Erina sighed. "So an actual war is waging right now."

"Unfortunately. Some time ago, a coalition of many worlds known as the Realdom elected a General Council and declared its autonomy from the Establishment. The General Council began to issue regulations related to foreign commerce and other activities on Realdom worlds. The Establishment took that as a violation of principles of their Equity." Duncan pushed away from the table a little, holding up his cup of *amis*. "They asked the Realdom to dissolve the

---

84 Both in Realitas and on the *Intrepid*, he had spent several hours watching history *scienscenes*, which are a type of documentary.

General Council in favor of a Universal Council constituted by both parties but based on Equity principles. The Realdom didn't accept that, and that's how the war got started."

Erina was listening to Duncan with attention, but she was not asking too many questions. She seemed more interested in Duncan's personal story. "How long have you been living in this universe?" Duncan blinked. "Mm . . . five months, I think."

"And what have you been doing all this time?"

"Well, it's a long story, but . . . I'm involved in the war, on the Realdom's side."

"We belong to a different reality." Erina raised an eyebrow.

"I know, but there's more to this. Some people think there is a connection between things that happen here and on our Earth."

"How so?"

"I don't know yet, but they think I could be of some help to end this war, and perhaps even help our own Earth." Uncomfortable, Duncan rubbed his temples. "That's why they invited me over to this universe in the first place."

Duncan's attempt to tell his story without implying his being someone of relevance had just derailed. From his first day in Reality, he had been reluctant to accept his given role in the universal conflict. He found it hard to believe and had a feeling of incapacity in its regard. Yet at the same time, a sense of discovery and attraction to the unknown often made him flirt with the idea of putting his doubts aside. And always in the background, there was a strong perception of purpose for his alleged role, of a very fulfilling purpose.

"I know it sounds . . . weird," he continued. "It's not been easy for me to accept any of this, but certain things tell me there may be some truth in it." Duncan sighed, shaking his head again. "I don't know."

Erina listened without making any comments.

"By the way, are you staying here long, I mean, in this universe?" Duncan asked.

"I wish I knew. The capsule's tracking system is completely smashed. Unless someone figures out a way to pinpoint my position back on Earth, I'm afraid I'm pretty much stuck here." Erina frowned, and took both her own and Duncan's cup. "Do you want some more?"

"Please."

Erina was back soon with two refills.

"Thanks."

"I don't have any particular directives of what to do under these circumstances." Erina sipped some of her *amis*. "The main purpose of my voyage was, and still is, to study any culture I may come into contact with. So here I am, in the middle of a conflict in which you are deeply involved. And you're traveling quite a lot, meeting different peoples and cultures."

Duncan nodded, his attention drifting to the perfectly human-looking woman in front of him.

"Perhaps I could accompany you on your travels, Dahncion."

Duncan quickly tuned in to what she was saying. The prospect of traveling around with a woman from his own world—with a particularly *attractive* woman from his own world—was alluring. Erina looked young, although she was older than he. But it was precisely the age difference, combined with Erina's wits, which conveyed a special appeal. Her beauty and maturity worked like a magnet to his fledgling manhood.

"I'm positive O'sihn will like this. He is my commanding officer, and a very good friend."

"I may not fit in with the people you are working with," Erina cautioned.

"I'm sure you'll like it here. The Royal Navy is like a family. You'll see. I have met lots of people already—made many good friends."

Erina put a hand on top of Duncan's. "Well, you've just made yourself another good friend."

CHAPTER 8

Tribulation and Trial

42.

It took Captain Foxso'l ten days to reach the rendezvous point. Once he arrived, he had to resort to all his experience and skills to keep his ship undetected. The track had been computed as meticulously as the situation allowed, in a quadrant where all navigational aids had been cut off or interfered with. As usual, Mr. Witts had been in charge of the track computations, and by then, he had completed the calculations of the last phase of their journey.

With an E.P.E. (Estimated Position Error) of only ten kilometers, Witt's fix correlated very well with the estimated track—much better than what would be expected from classical dead-reckoning calculations.[85]

For a moment, Foxso'l thought of having the fix double-checked, but he simply nodded, turning back to the main display again. It would have been pointless to question Witts' ten kilometers of conceivable error. At any rate, it was evident that the only ship in the sector was the *Angel Spark*. There was no sign at all of the *Intrepid*, which was supposed to have arrived earlier than they had.

After a couple of hours of silent waiting, Foxso'l decided to carry

---

85 This included taking into consideration the influence (mainly estimated gravitational effects) of the uncharted nearby stars met during the navigation.

Positioning computations, on the other hand, were conducted by means of at least three well-known charted stars, with sufficiently large angular separation. A minimum of four stars was typically used to minimize measuring errors and uncertainties. The principles of the positioning technique were the same used as in the good old days of tall ships.

on with the alternative plan. But even that had to suffer modifications. The piercing capsule that was to be used had to be reconditioned for two travelers. The vehicle had originally featured two compartments, one for its passenger and the other for equipment and supplies. However, for this mission, two humans had to be accommodated in one single capsule—one in each compartment—significantly restricting the assigned payload for the mission.

More than five hours had gone by since the capsule had been launched into space. Before leaving, Witts had shown Duncan images of Aquaelight as seen from space. Its appearance, a bright blue sphere with crisp white threads spread all over its surface, and two polar caps, was very reminiscent of Earth. According to the navigational time-schedule, the capsule should, by then, be not far from the planet. But the only features Duncan could make out were two igloo-like bodies, which seemed to be orbiting around a point between the two. As the capsule closed distances, it became apparent that the portion of space between the two "igloos" was a dark, flat, starless circular blotch. The Establishment's environmental reconfiguration of the biosphere had turned the vast blue oceans that extended from pole to pole into a lightless, monotonous sea.

Duncan started the deceleration stage. With it, his mind began drifting towards the woman from his own world, physically very close but seemingly as distant as the *Angel Spark* due to the capsule's compartment division. Erina had never been in a military piercing capsule, or been exposed to a seven-hour, launch-to-landing, tactical approximation to a military target in space. Once more, Duncan knocked on the opaque division panel, and again no answer came back from the adjacent compartment. He did not expect any response, though; he was aware that the panel's material should absorb any vibration he produced.

A couple of hours later, Aquaelight could be seen with a wide angular scope. As Duncan initialized the reentry sequence, the vehicle stopped decelerating, and started to travel along a trajectory that would take it to one of the poles. On the white surface below, geographical features were becoming discernible. The capsule finally made contact with the upper atmospheric layers, and as it did, its serene inertial trajectory rapidly shifted to a vibrating deceleration.

After a few hours of weightlessness, Duncan gradually began to perceive the compartment division of his cockpit facing up, with the other end of the compartment facing down. A reddish-blue induced incandescence, always present in a capsule reentry, encircled the entire vehicle. For a couple of seconds, Duncan experienced the already familiar high-pitched landing chime resounding inside the cockpit. He looked at the altimeter display. Only two hundred thousand feet separated the capsule from the surface. At that point, the thermo-induced booster engine was automatically activated to prevent the vehicle from losing momentum. The temperature display began to reach ever-rising levels, as the external reddish-blue radiance shifted to a white incandescent glow. Duncan moved an arm towards his face, partially covering his eyes. Then the external over-hitter was also energized, since the hull had not reached critical plasma temperature yet. A moment later, the engine booster engaged the over-thrust, and with that, the incandescence surrounding the vehicle flashed, rapidly dissipating after that.

Although the planet's surface was in a bright morning of a dawning spring, total darkness had suddenly enveloped the landing pod, which was now making its way under the ice.[86] Immediately, the over-thrust disengaged, and the engine started decreasing its thrust.

---

86 Upon contact with the planet's surface, and now sheltered from detection, the capsule had automatically turned on a specially designed compact gravitational compensation system. Maintaining a constant 0.8Gs inside the cockpit, this system would protect its occupant(s) from the subsequent abrupt and violent deceleration. The planet's acceleration of gravity at sea level was 0.8Gs.

The vehicle decelerated rapidly until finally stopping several hundred feet below the planet's surface, inside the core of an ancient glacier.

The frozen walls of the icy tunnel drilled by the incandescent capsule trembled and cracked, but held firm.

Once more, the external over-hitter energized, and large amounts of melted water started flowing between the hull and the glacier. The capsule was significantly lighter than the weight of the equivalent volume of liquid occupied by it, so it started to make its way up swiftly through the gelid water. During the reentry, the vehicle was expected to mimic an iron meteorite collapsing into the surface, in an attempt to conceal the pod's true nature from enemy detection systems. That had been the first time such technology had been put into use, and so far, it seemed to have worked quite well.

Before starting the emerging phase, the capsule had turned one hundred and eighty degrees about, so that now Duncan was sitting on the compartment division, facing upwards. The entire navigation had gone through without a glitch. Despite the circumstances, the contact with the planet's surface had been much milder than Duncan's previous experience in Althea 8, much to his relief.

The capsule rapidly reached an area where the tunnel, drilled by the piercing vehicle a few minutes before, was clear from ice. Duncan kept looking upwards. The dark environment was gradually picking up the light of the polar morning above. As the external hitting system went off, the external hull temperature rapidly stabilized at about thirty-five degrees Fahrenheit.

Breaking through a thin icy film that covered the small crater lake, the capsule emerged with an elegant swish.

The first thing Duncan did was to check the environmental data. Everything seemed within reason, even though the temperature outside was about ten degrees below zero. Neither he nor Erina had brought along combat suits. However, they were wearing appropriate insulated clothing, which could be adjusted to handle extreme temperatures.

When everything was ready, Duncan activated the opening system, and the top, bow quarter of the hull was jettisoned. A white, barren, flat landscape appeared, stretching to the horizon.

Duncan extended a retractable paddle and started rowing towards the bank of the freezing pond. Reaching shore, he popped off the capsule and anchored it to the ice. He picked up some basic equipment from the cockpit (a few supplies and some handy instruments) and anxiously threw a switch. The pod's circular divider was jettisoned into the polar air.

Erina appeared on the other half of the cockpit. She looked perfectly well.

"Are you okay?" Duncan asked.

"I guess so." Erina looked around, very much in control of herself.

The local sun was very close to the horizon. The sky was clear, and an icy breeze was whispering. After helping Erina out of the pod, a much more relaxed Duncan proceeded to activate the bio-scanner he had picked up from the cockpit. He walked a hundred yards or so from the landing spot and placed the instrument on the frozen ground. Erina walked by him.

Suddenly, the bio-scanner began beeping.

"What's the meaning of that?" Erina asked.

"Life-forms nearby." Duncan did not hide his concern.

"What kind of life-forms?"

"I hope this will tell us." Duncan knelt on the ice, exchanging data and instructions with the sensor. "Well, at least they are *loids*," he added, standing up in front of the bio-scanner, eyes focused on it.

Erina looked at him and squinted.

"Earth-looking life forms, for the most part," Duncan explained.

Abruptly, Erina slammed into Duncan. Instinctively, he threw himself down to the ground, pulling her along.

The landing capsule, along with the supplies and instruments it carried, had been pulverized by a big explosion. Duncan reacted quickly, getting back on his feet. In front of him, seven white Earth-like military tanks were approaching fast, their gun turrets aimed towards him and Erina.

"These are not Establishment forces."

"So they aren't—" Erina said sarcastically.

"Those insignias aren't Establishment's marks."

Erina stepped back with apprehension.

The tanks did appear to be native machines. Foxso'l had told them about the indigenous technology, which had similarities to that of Duncan's Earth. The characteristic sound of the diesel-cycle engines, plus the way the landing capsule had just been destroyed, agreed with Foxso'l's briefing.

The heavy vehicles stopped about thirty feet from Erina and Duncan, adopting a V configuration. The turret of the tank in the center lifted up, and an individual appeared on top. It had polar-bear-like features, though it still had a human resemblance in many ways. It was wearing a white beret and something similar to dark glasses concealing its eyes.

"Drop your guns!" he shouted.

The soldier definitively looked and sounded like a male. His physical appearance matched what Foxso'l had anticipated about the natives. Besides, nothing on him or in the tanks seemed to be under the Establishment environmental reconfiguration.

Duncan carefully took the gun he carried on the side of a boot and dropped it to the icy ground. "Sir, we come to join forces—"

Keeping his dark glasses fixed on the horizon, the soldier made a movement with one arm that clearly indicated that he did not want to hear any more.

Skimming the ground, a helicopter rushed through from behind the tank formation, landing near an armored vehicle. The strong draft produced by the aircraft dragged the two extra-Aquaelitians against the caterpillars of one of the tanks. The roaring blades promptly spun down, giving way to the high-pitched revving of the turbo-engines.

On one side of the helicopter, a hatch opened up. Two soldiers in thick white uniforms popped out. They carried weapons Duncan could not identify. Seizing him and Erina, they handcuffed them and forced them into the vehicle.

The aircraft took off, stirring up a dense cloud of sparkling white dust, which lingered over the field with a smell evocative of kerosene.

43.

In the middle of the room, there was a table, and in front of it, a chair, where the only person present was seated. It was a comfortable chair, a fact reluctantly welcomed by Duncan, who by then, had already been seated on it for more than three hours.

Before being put into the room, Duncan had had his handcuffs removed. Nothing in particular prevented him from walking around the place. Yet that did not seem prudent, since he had been strongly advised to remain seated, and since the surveillance camera, constantly watching him, seemed to follow even the movement of his eyes.

Except for the table, the camera, and the chair, there was nothing notable inside the room, not even a window. The light came from the whole ceiling, which was a uniform glowing plate. The technology did not seem very advanced, since the lights dissipated lots of heat.

A good-sized individual barged in through the door to the room, slamming it shut behind him. He was carrying a chair with his left hand and a pile of papers under his right arm. He approached the table and remained standing in front of Duncan for a moment.

"Very well, Mr. Dahncion," he said, placing the chair in front of him. "I hope you're ready to tell us the whole story, thereby sparing yourself further unnecessary nuisances."

"Where is Erina?" Duncan demanded.

"Mr. Dahncion," the Aquaelitian said, with a heavy cadence. "You've been treated very kindly, so far. The least we expect from you is a few good manners." He tapped on the table with one side of the stack of papers he had brought along. "Besides, I'm here for the sole purpose of getting some answers from you." Taking a device from a pocket, he put it on the table and pushed a button on it. A red light went on. "The young lady . . . " The Aquaelitian fixed his eyes on Duncan's. "She has some significance to you, doesn't she?"

Duncan nodded slightly, trying to conceal his emotions.

"Well, I can tell you that she is perfectly all right and safe, and as long as you exhibit a cooperative disposition, you have absolutely nothing to worry about. Do you understand this, Mr. Dahncion?"

Duncan nodded, looking at the device right in front of him. Its red light blipped with every word said.

"Do you understand what I am saying, Mr. Dahncion?"

"Yes."

"*Yes, sir*, is what we expect from you, Mr. Dahncion."

"Yes, sir."

"I'm glad we're starting to communicate smoothly. Now, Mr. Dahncion, would you kindly explain to us the real purpose behind yours—and Miss Erina's—intrusion into our territory?"

"We represent a large force of resistance against the Establishment. We are your friends, and—"

"Friends, Mr. Dahncion?"

"Yes, sir, and—"

"I'm afraid your surreptitious landing in an area well within our borders doesn't appear to be a friendly action."

"We were trying to avoid detection."

The interrogator stared impassively at Duncan for a moment. "Let me read to you a brief excerpt I happened to come across, of the preliminary report about your and your companion's incursion."

The Aquaelitian put on some narrow glasses. "*Apparently performing a stealth incursion into Aquaelight's territorial space, with no indication of any intent of adopting and/or following any identification procedure and subsequent request for landing. It goes on . . . aha, their presence having been detected in a widely uninhabited area of our polar continent.* Do you confirm these reports, Mr. Dahncion?"

"Sir, I think I should—"

"No, no, no, no, no, Mr. Dahncion. You must not forget that you are under a strict interrogatory procedure. Therefore, you will strive to limit your answers exclusively to the scope of my questions. Do I make myself clear?"

Duncan did not answer. Resistance could be read in his eyes. Yet he knew he was dealing with potentially important allies for the Realdom. Their nation was at war with another that was known to receive Establishment aid. Impossible as it seemed, Duncan had to do his best to try to communicate with his interrogator.

"Do I make myself clear, Mr. Dahncion?"

"Yes, sir."

"Excellent. So now, I will make things easy for you. I will reformulate my last questions addressing the details. Mr. Dahncion, have you and Miss Erina performed a stealth penetration into Aquaelight territorial space?"

"Yes, sir."

"Have you, at any moment, tried to identify yourself or your vessel?"

"No, sir."

"Did you follow any procedure for requesting landing in our territory?"

"No, sir."

"Did you pick a highly uninhabited area of our polar continent to avoid detection of any kind?"

"Yes, sir."

"Very good, Mr. Dahncion. Very good. Now, tell us, are you aware of the extra-Aquaelitian aggression we are presently undergoing?"

"Yes, sir."

"Were you acquainted with the fact that the area you landed in was not under control of the enemy of our planet?"

"Yes, sir."

"Did you have any information about the people who live in this hemisphere and our present status?"

"Yes, sir."

"So you must know we are at war."

"I do, sir."

"And I'm sure you will agree with us that if entering a territory under conflict is not to be interpreted as a hostile action, above anything else, identification and expected procedures should be rigorously adopted."

Duncan delayed his answer.

"Do we agree on this, Mr. Dahncion?"

"Well . . . yes—"

"So again, Mr. Dahncion, did you try to contact us before landing on our territory?"

Duncan closed his eyes, as if trying to find some way to get the course of the interrogatory changed.

"I'm still awaiting your answer, Mr. Dahncion." The Aquaelitian raised his voice.

"Well, I didn't, but—"

"No excuses required, Mr. Dahncion. You've already answered my question, *I did not!*"

"Yeah, I didn't!" Duncan repeated hotly. "But you aren't giving me a chance to explain the whole thing!"

The Aquaelitian hit the table with one of his white, bearish fists. Fixing his eyes on Duncan's, he resumed his grave low tone. "Mr. Dahncion, please don't make me lose my temper. I believe I've been very specific about what is expected from you. Therefore, you must strive to confine your answers to the interrogatory procedure hereby implemented.

"Now, Mr. Dahncion," the Aquaelitian continued, leaning threateningly towards the human, "listen very carefully to the next two questions, and please, give me a straight, clean answer to each one of them. Do you, or Miss Erina, have any connection with the so-called Establishment? For your own good, and your friend's, I strongly recommend that you do not depart from the facts concerning this matter."

"No, sir," Duncan replied with confidence.

"Mr. Dahncion, are you part of the invading forces?"

"No, sir."

"You are lying!"

"I'm not lying, sir."

With a more relaxed tone, the Aquaelitian continued. "Let us be reasonable, Mr. Dahncion. You intruded into Aquaelight's territory, landing stealthily in a carefully selected, widely uninhabited area of our country, having done all that without attempting to make any contact with us, and being perfectly aware of the current war status—facts that you have just corroborated," he added pointing at the red light on the device he had placed in front of Duncan.

"Now, Mr. Dahncion, I will give you just one more chance, so for your own sake, and that of your friend's, I advise you to restrict your answers to the actual facts. Do you confess to being part of the invading force to Aquaelight or having cooperated with the enemy at any point?"

"No, sir, absolutely not. We are not part of any invasion, quite the contrary—"

The Aquaelitian suddenly thrust the table to one side. The papers he had brought were now fluttering to the floor, leaf after leaf. Leaving his chair, the interrogator kicked it aside and started walking towards Duncan, cornering him against a wall.

"You have already proven yourself a remarkable fool, Mr. Dahncion. You're deliberately attempting to twist the facts in the

"You're deliberately attempting to twist the facts in the face of
all the blatant transgressions that you have committed!"

face of all the blatant transgressions that you and your friend have committed! But I can assure you that your foolishness will not interfere with our work." The Aquaelitian shook his head, a shaking that quickly shifted into an asserting nod. "I'm positive Miss Erina will be more reasonable, much more reasonable."

The Aquaelitian placed his reading spectacles carefully in a narrow tin case, and put on some dark glasses. "I hope I'm right—for her own sake." Stepping towards the door, he opened it calmly. "We will meet soon enough, Mr. Dahncion."

44.

Duncan stood still in one corner, leaning against the wall. The shattered table lay crippled, with one of its legs on the opposite side of the room. Having suffered a similar fate, a chair lay by the table, upside-down.

After a while, Duncan started pacing, restlessly, until he stumbled over the broken chair. He put it upright on its cracked legs, and resumed his nervous walking. He was startled by the chair falling back down behind him.

The camera in one corner buzzed and buzzed, with an obsessive automatism, rotating back and forth, following each of Duncan's movements.

But Duncan did not care anymore. He was immersed within himself, delving into the episode he had just gone through and dwelling on the way he had been dealt with. The last words the Aquaelitian had said about Erina were a constant theme in the background of his thoughts. Her presence in this universe had been quite brief; her knowledge of it, very limited. The complex circumstances of the war and the different cultures involved, the peculiarities and diversity of all the different intelligent species, and so many other things, would be beyond her current understanding, he reasoned. Duncan pictured the Aquaelitian yelling at her as he had done to him. The thought triggered hate, and hate, despair.

And to think that *sternessence*—love—was the key. That seemed too lofty, ethereal, alien to reality, if not obnoxious under the circumstances. Depression followed, with the reenergized perception of being of no account, already defeated. Reflecting on his distressed state of mind, Duncan recognized that the feeling of hate had triggered it. He decided to put away the subject, at least temporarily, and focus back on the mission. That did not work entirely, but still gave him some serenity. With it, a much needed sleep overpowered his tired mind and immersed his body in a relaxing slumber.

45.

Duncan woke up. He had lost track of time and wondered whether it was night or day. Even the fact of being immersed in a long polar daylight season now escaped his mind. He was very thirsty and still tired. After a while, he began daydreaming of an outdoors landscape much cooler than the overheated, stifling room in which he was locked.

Eventually the door opened again, and someone new, a female, stepped inside. Smiling at Duncan, she raised a hand. "I'm glad to meet you, Mr. Dahncion. My name is Kaletectla." Her movements were feminine and graceful. She had traits reminiscent of a polar feline, though sharply humanoid. She was larger than Duncan.

"I don't know whether to say good morning or good evening, Ms. Kaletectla," Duncan said in an upset tone.

"I understand." The female looked at her wristwatch. "It's three o'clock in the afternoon."

Duncan had thought it was much later, though he was not sure about the time convention used by the natives, either.

"Mr. Dahncion, I anticipate that after your exposure to Mr. Moglontl's complete lack of courtesy, you may not be in the best of moods. Fortunately, I have quite different manners and—I believe— a much different perspective."

"Does that mean that after one hell of a day, somebody is finally gonna listen to me?"

"I'd like to apologize for any inconvenience. Of course, I'm here to listen to you, and to try to help you in any capacity within our reach. By the way, you can just call me Kaletectla. May I call you Dahncion?"

Duncan was upset but still focused. He was there to make contact with the local authorities, if possible. He had to maintain a positive disposition above anything else. "Of course, Kale . . . tec-tla?"

"That's a very good pronunciation."

Duncan's next question was predictable. "Excuse me if I start by asking about my companion, Erina."

"Erina?"

"Yes, the woman—the female—that came along with me."

"I'm afraid I don't know about her."

Duncan gazed at her skeptically, but he decided not to challenge her claim of ignorance. "So, how can I help you, Kaletectla?"

"As I've just told you, I'm here to help you, and to try to make up for any lack of understanding you may have experienced."

"I hope this is not just another form of interrogation."

"I don't think that would help anybody," Kaletectla said, with a dismissive smile. "Although . . . yes, a better insight of the circumstances that brought you here—to our planet—could be mutually beneficial. You can talk freely; you are safe here. A positive disposition will make it easier for us to help you in every way possible."

The sudden change in his captors' approach was not making a positive impression on Duncan. "My mission is about helping you. I can't explain this in a few words, Kaletectla. If you'd let me explain all the facts, you will see that I bring a new hope of freedom to your people."

"I'd be very glad to listen to anything you want to share with us. And, please, don't have any time misgivings. You'll have all the time you need."

Duncan smiled politely. "So, I guess—"

"Excuse me, Dahncion, would you like something to eat or drink? Please, don't hesitate to ask for anything that would make you feel more comfortable."

Duncan smiled uneasily. "I don't know much about your customs, but . . . is it possible that I go to . . . a rest room . . . for a moment?"

"Of course. I'll have someone show you there. In the meantime, I'll have some food brought over."

Kaletectla gave some instructions through a communicator, and a security guard appeared at the door. "Molotkl, show Dahncion to the hygiene aisle, please."

"Yes, ma'am."

Duncan looked at the trooper and back again.

"Please, take all the time you need, Dahncion," added Kaletectla.

"I appreciate this." Duncan got up and left the room, escorted by the hostile-looking guard.

They were back within minutes. A table had now been set with dishes full of what looked like broiled *litics*. There was a jar with water, and another with a dark bubbling juice. Duncan picked a small *litic* and started his story.

A few minutes later, Kaletectla asked her first question.

"So you come from a world different from the Establishment's," Kaletectla said.

"That's right."

"You seem to suggest there are many other worlds inhabited by intelligent species."

"Haven't you been in contact with people from other worlds before?" Duncan asked.

"Our actual enemy is extra-Aquaelitian."

"Right, but in this universe there are probably millions of different civilizations, about thirty thousand in this galaxy alone," Duncan nodded. "Most star systems are teeming with life—I mean, in this universe."

"Why do you stress *this universe* so much?"

"Because this is not the only universe that there is."

"Oh."

"Yes, as a matter of fact, I actually come from a different universe."

As he said that, Duncan realized he was already stretching the limits of what he should be discussing in his first conversation with the Aquaelitian. "And so does Erina—the woman that came along with me to this world."

Kaletectla pressed her lips together, inclining her head to one side. The gesture distressed Duncan. Perhaps having actually seen Erina already, he thought, she found it hard to believe that both Erina and he had come from the same world or universe. Duncan's *rilitian* traits looked very different from Erina's, and rather similar to those of many people who lived in Aquaelight.

"Yes, it's a long story. We got to this universe in different ways— we're not even from the same country. I was actually brought by a people from this universe. They sort of adjusted the way I look. That's why my complexion looks somewhat similar to yours, while Erina's—if you'd seen her, you could tell the difference." Duncan paused, trying to stress confidence with a positive gesture.

"It's a fascinating story, but how did you—and Erina—manage to come to our world alone?"

"We were traveling in a rather small ship, the *Angel Spark*, that was supposed to rendezvous with a battleship at some point in space near the boundaries of this star system. But something went wrong. So instead of coming with the *Intrepid*'s team —the battleship's team— Erina and I had to come alone, following an alternative plan."

"Why didn't you let us know of your coming? Your entering our airspace had the appearance of an enemy incursion."

"That was the best way we could find to get here without raising suspicions on the Establishment detection systems."

"But we both know that the enemy has technology far superior to our nation's." Kaletectla paused and looked into Duncan's eyes. "It was very easy for our modest technology to detect and plot your trajectory, Dahncion."

Duncan nodded. "We intended to simulate a meteorite trajectory. The vehicle that brought us here was specially designed to act as a meteorite would when piercing through the atmosphere."

"But when a meteorite hits the ground—if it manages to get there—it does so at a very high speed," Kaletectla objected. "The final deceleration your vehicle would have required to avoid crashing against the surface would have been something very easy to spot, something that would have given away the real nature of your vessel to the extra-Aquaelitian forces."

"Right! But our vehicle was specially designed to penetrate and decelerate within the ice. That's why we picked a thick glacier to land in."

Duncan's story, which would have sounded odd to an average Realitian citizen, was clearly reaching levels of unconvincing extravagance in the Aquaelitian's perception. "I don't mean to contradict your facts, Dahncion, but it's hard to picture a vehicle hitting the surface at hundreds, if not thousands, of miles per hour without being destroyed—or, at the very least, without killing its occupants."

"I know it sounds incredible, but that's the way we got here, hoping to pass unnoticed by the enemy."

Kaletectla stared at Duncan. "I certainly want to help you, Dahncion. But for that to be possible, we must have an environment of mutual reliance. You have to trust me—to trust us."

"And I do trust you, and I am trying to cooperate with you—with all of you."

Kaletectla sighed. "Let me describe our situation from our perspective. We are currently at war with an alien force that is supporting, with technology and intelligence, our old enemy, the Krytiff Islanders. We are living in critical times. Many of my people have died in a very short time, while many others have been taken prisoner. My country is shocked, yet still committed to a *personalitarian* disposition with prisoners of war. We know that being a POW is a traumatic experience; soldiers typically have precise instructions about what they can't say and what they are supposed to say. I guess that's pretty much the same in any side of a conflict. We understand this well. The only thing we expect is a reasonable amount of honesty, that's all."

"Honesty?" Duncan shook his head with frustration. "So I'm not being honest?"

"We are not saying that, Dahncion, but your story does have unclear spots."

"Ms. Kaletectla," Duncan said, standing up. "You must believe me."

The interviewer smiled politely and checked her watch.

With a beaten expression, Duncan sat down again. His complex story, regardless of its veracity, had been anything but convincing.

46.

Events transpired rather quickly. After the interview with Kaletectla, Mr. Moglontl came back and bluntly demanded that Duncan confess to being part of the invading task force. Seeing that he was not getting anywhere, the Aquaelitian summoned a soldier who seized Duncan and escorted him out of the complex.

Outside, the powerful engines of a gargantuan aircraft were already revving. The vehicle was basically a big cargo bay with a cockpit on its bow. Several smaller compartments stuck out around the fuselage, creating an ugly, bulky appearance. The helicopter looked truly imposing, much bigger than any other Duncan had seen on his native Earth.

Moglontl led Duncan inside the aircraft. As the Aquaelitian talked with the pilots, Duncan thought he heard something about a concentration camp. A male soldier, with a feline appearance similar to Kaletectla's, ordered Duncan to sit down in a corner on deck, in the back of the bay. A moment later, another soldier hustled Erina into the aircraft and pushed her onto her knees towards Duncan.

Duncan looked at her with a reassuring grin. "Everything will be all right."

"Prisoners will not talk during the flight!" yelled the soldier in front of them.

Both Erina and Duncan stared at him. "Is that clear?"

"Yes, sir."

The trooper stumbled as the helicopter took off.

The phrase *concentration camp* came through again amidst the general noise. Mr. Moglontl's lack of subtlety sounded quite intentional.

Erina looked up, stunned.

47.

The trip gradually turned into a long, dull episode, complete with continuous droning turbo engines and little sunlight. Duncan and Erina were under constant surveillance by at least one soldier. Most of the others passed the time with loud, coarse conversation. Studying a chart off to the side, Mr. Moglontl seemed indifferent to the scene.

The dullness was interrupted when a brusque bump made the aircraft slide sharply to one side. An explosion followed, and with it, a big hole opened on one of the bay bulkheads, close to the flight deck.

Immediately, fifteen soldiers boarded the main cargo cabin through the opening. Behind the helmets of their airtight Establishment-type combat suits, bear-like features were clearly discernible. Faces and uniforms bore a uniformly gray appearance.

The foes opened fire, and two soldiers fell down. The feline-featured Aquaelitian who had been watching over the two prisoners jumped on the back of one of the intruders, driving his combat teeth through the trooper's uniform. But he was thrown onto the deck by a gunshot. Two more Aquaelitians were quickly dispatched. At that point, three of the attackers ran to the flight deck; from there, another shot rang out. The enemy seemed to have gained control of the aircraft.

The remaining six members of the crew were forced to stand facing a bulkhead, their hands on their heads. Moglontl lay on deck, very close to Duncan. Between him and the Aquaelitian, a machine gun was lying on the deck. Surreptitiously, Duncan moved to pick it up.

He was still trying to reach it when Moglontl popped up and jumped over the two soldiers who were aiming their guns at the prisoners. One of the enemy troopers reacted quickly. Using a device he was carrying on one leg, he completely immobilized the Aquaelitian with a sticky net. Another trooper pushed himself forward and placed a knife at Moglontl's throat.

"Finish him off!" somebody yelled, and immediately someone opened fire with a machine gun. The enemy trooper dropped his knife, falling motionless on top of Moglontl.

Throwing himself down onto the deck, Duncan held on tightly to his smoking machine gun. He then rolled over three times and opened fire repeatedly at the intruders. Paradoxically, Duncan had never used a firearm before, even though on his Earth, these weapons were still widely in use. It was lighter than he had thought it would be, and it did not recoil as he had expected.

In the confusion, two Aquaelitians recovered their guns. The situation had turned chaotic: shots from both sides, mixed up with yelling and moaning.

Picking up the knife that had just been used against Moglontl, Duncan began ripping off the net that kept the Aquaelitian immobilized. Erina remained in shock in one corner.

"All right, drop your guns." One of the crewmembers seemed to have regained control of the situation. "Drop your guns, I said! Everybody, put your hands on that bulkhead. Now!"

Two enemy soldiers were pushed against a bulkhead. Surreptitiously, one of them tried to open fire with a hidden gun he carried close to his knee, but Duncan shot it out of his hand, or so he thought.

As the crew checked the enemy soldiers for weapons, Duncan looked through the hole opened on one side of the bay. It was too dark for him to grasp any detail. Perhaps it was the compartment of another vessel. It was as if the enemy incursion had come from a different aircraft, which had somehow docked onto the port side of the helicopter.

"Okay, who's coming with me?" Duncan said, jerking his head towards the hole. The invitation did not resonate with the crew. "Never mind, I'll do it myself!"

"There's no need for that."

Duncan turned around.

"There's no need for that, Mr. Dahncion. You've done more than enough already." The Aquaelitian's change of tone made Duncan hesitate.

"There's still work to be done, Mr. Moglontl. Enemy soldiers may still be waiting for us behind this bulkhead."

Moglontl smiled kindly. "There is nothing special behind that bulkhead, Mr. Dahncion. It's just another bay of this helicopter."

Duncan looked at him and shook his head. A female Aquaelitian, casually stepping in through the opening, startled Duncan. She glanced around swiftly, and approached him with a confident gait. Erina drew near to Duncan's side.

"Mr. Dahncion, Miss Erina, let me introduce myself again." She raised her head and inclined it slightly. "I am Pan-Kaletectla, President of the United Republics of the Austral Continent.[87] In the name of my people, and in my own, I welcome you to our country. I hope you'll find the good will to overlook the grievances caused to both of you.

"As I told you, Mr. Dahncion, we are living in critical times. We had to be sure about your identity. Before your arrival, your people had made contact with us, promising they would be sending a full tactical team shortly. Your two-person alternative plan did cause quite a headache to our Intel agencies. Your true nature was not at all clear, but not any longer."

As Kaletectla spoke, the Aquaelitian pseudo-prisoners standing in one corner removed their helmets, while the "casualties" from both would-be factions got back on their feet.

---

87 A shorter and more common name was the Austral Union.

CHAPTER 9

Long Shadows

48.

After a particularly hectic day, Duncan had had little trouble falling asleep. He had been living in Austral City for more than two weeks already, and during that time, he had learned how to adapt to the local culture—including his extra-large, extra-comfortable bed. Living in a twenty-fourth floor apartment on Crystal Springs Avenue was truly living in style.

Austral City was reminiscent of many big metropolises of Duncan's contemporary Earth, although somewhat older. The noise from the street below was loud, even on the twenty-fourth floor. The street vehicles were considerably larger and more powerful than those familiar to Duncan. However, it was not their noise that was stirring him from his sleep, but the stubborn ringing of a bell.

After deciding he had had enough of the buzzing aggravation, Duncan got up. Now, he had to face the dilemma of trying to remember where he had left his bathrobe. The bell kept ringing and the dressing gown remained elusive. Finally, Duncan took a coat and put it on. It fell heavily all the way down to his knees.

Opening the door, he saw Erina standing there, perfectly dressed and with a backpack on. She was staying in an apartment right above his. Erina gave Duncan an uneasy look. He tried in vain to compose his disheveled appearance by some uncoordinated movements of his hands.

"Hurry up! We must get out of here!" she said before Duncan could think of anything to say.

"Why . . . wha . . . what's going on?"

"Don't you know? We are under missile attack! We must go to a shelter at once!"

Duncan's eyes opened fully. "I'll be back." He rushed back to his bedroom.

A couple of minutes later, fully dressed, he and Erina were on the elevator.

"They said the missiles could be carrying lethal gases," Erina stated, as she pushed the first-floor button.

"Who said that?"

"Someone from the military, on TV."

"Well, in that case, we don't have much to worry about." Duncan shrugged. "The anti-gas masks they gave us are safe. Let me help you put yours on."

Erina nodded and pulled her mask from her bag. Standing behind her, Duncan helped her strap it on.

At that point, an eerie siren started blaring all over the city. They were still at the fifth-story level. The elevator was going down with a quiet floor-by-floor unnerving cadence. Slamming of doors and loud talking was echoing through the entire building. Finally, the door slid open, and Duncan and Erina plunged out into the street.

"We're lucky you were watching TV," Duncan said. "Otherwise, we'd be struggling down the stairs right now."

The closest shelter was about six Australitian blocks away, equivalent to twelve regular blocks on Earth. They had not finished their first block when Erina and Duncan were forced to stop. A caravan of cars going down a wide avenue crossing Crystal Springs was blocking their way.

"Put your mask on!" Erina yelled.

"Hmm." Duncan looked at the sky, trying to make out any sign of the incoming attack.

"What do you mean, *hmm*?"

"I forgot it in my apartment."

"What?" Erina said looking at the mask he was holding on one hand.

"The filter! I don't have the filter."

Erina sighed with irritation. "We must go back and get it."

Duncan shook his head. "We're only five blocks away from the shelter."

"We are still too far away," Erina objected. "We must—"

An explosion interrupted her. A large truck, about one hundred yards from them, had blown up. People started running away in terror. Duncan held Erina and dragged her to the sidewalk. The street had become dangerous and chaotic, filled with panic-stricken citizens running for their lives.[88]

"We must go back to your apartment!" Erina insisted. "We gotta grab the filter for your mask." Both Erina and Duncan had seen several TV news programs with gruesome scenes of people coughing and jerking on the ground from the effect of the lethal gases released by missiles.

Duncan looked at the fire ahead and checked his watch.

"We must go back, Dahncion." Erina took his hand. Although Duncan was finally letting himself be led by her, the crowd was making it hard to make headway in any direction.

49.

"You just wait for me here—"

Duncan had not finished the sentence when the door to the elevator slid open and ten people dashed out desperately. As soon as it was clear, he jumped inside, and Erina followed him.

"At least wait for me as I run to my apartment," Duncan said curtly as the elevator went up. "We don't want to miss our ride."

---

88 Both Duncan and Erina looked very different from the natives, since there were no humans on that planet. However, Australitians were familiar with occasional representatives from the Realdom, who would be wearing distinctive clothes provided by the Austral Union government. As a result, Duncan and Erina were not bothered by the Australitians, beyond curious looks and occasional polite questions that would often give way to friendly conversations.

On reaching the twenty-eighth floor, Duncan rushed to his place. Within seconds, he was back, holding his mask with its filter on.

The lazy trip down began right away, but between the fifteenth and fourteenth floor, the electrical power shut down and the elevator froze in its tracks. An emergency light automatically turned on. Duncan tried to force the elevator's doors open, but to no avail. They were two-paned sturdy plates, with no place to clutch. He looked around trying to find some way out, but he failed to see any opening or hatch.

"We're stuck in here," Erina muttered.

Duncan looked at the ceiling, thinking of some way to get it open.

"What're we going to do?"

"Just relax, and wait until it's all over."

"This is hardly a shelter."

Duncan sat down on the floor. "You heard it yourself. It's just a chemical-weapons attack. The only thing to fear is toxic gases, and our masks can take care of them."

"What if a missile hits the building?"

"Unlikely. We saw the truck explosion. It was hit by a missile, all right. That was about two blocks from here. From what I've learned about these attacks, missiles are relatively few and well spread out, launched mostly to cause panic." Duncan rested his mask on the floor to display confidence. Unstrapping hers, Erina sat down by him. "I hope I'm not making your life unnecessarily difficult," she added, grasping her knees.

"Why?" Duncan said.

"You're a soldier here, and I am not."

"A soldier . . . " Duncan rested his head against the wall behind him. "It's good for a soldier to have someone strong around. The people who chose you for your transuniversal trip sure knew what they were doing."

"Don't tell me you're afraid." Erina cuffed him lightly, with a joking smile.

"*In fear, defiance.* O'sihn said once to me, as I discussed my fears with him." Duncan paused.

"You often talk of him—almost as a brother," Erina said.

Duncan chuckled. "He could be my father, in a way. He had a daughter about my age. She died in the war."

Erina extended her legs and leaned her head on the wall. "What does he look like?"

Duncan sank one hand inside a pocket. "Here he is, this big guy in uniform." The picture had been taken moments before boarding the vessel that would land on the surface of Iluminia. Duncan was standing by the captain, wearing an uneasy smile. "Last night I came across this picture card. I had forgotten I had been carrying it all the time."

"He looks like someone special," Erina said.

Duncan pressed on the side of the card, and a new picture materialized. "Yep, and here are O'sihn and Laida." Duncan was holding Clara in that last scene. He kept on pressing the card, and Clara kept appearing in many of the ensuing images. He finally reached a picture in which Clara was putting a helmet on his head. That picture, the last one of the set, would remain despite Duncan's pointless pressing to jump to a non-existent next.

"I guess this is the last one."

"And it's a very good one," Erina said approvingly.

"Clara . . . " Duncan shrugged slightly. "She's a very valuable member of our team."

"Don't be unfair. She's also been the only human being in your life since you came to this universe."

"True," Duncan said. "But, we belong to different worlds—different universes."

"Is there anything wrong with that?"

"No. She is a very talented woman, but . . . " Duncan turned towards Erina. "But there is nothing like a woman from your own world, a woman who is strong, intelligent, and . . . " he sighed slightly, with a half-smile, "and, beautiful . . . "

Erina took one of Duncan's hands. Putting the other on top of hers, Duncan looked into her eyes.

At that point, the lights of the tubes on the elevator's panel ceiling started twinkling back on. The power had been fully restored, and with a jolt, the elevator began moving down again.

The enemy attack was over.

50.

Changing positions, adding and subtracting blankets, even counting the blue blinks from her desk-side communicator, nothing seemed to work. Clara started to wonder if it would not be better to give up her exhausting attempt at getting some rest. But there was still some time before her next watch on the bridge, and there was a long day ahead. She had to try to get some sleep.

As she gradually relaxed, her breathing was becoming deeper and quieter, until someone knocked at the door. Clara looked at her watch and slid nimbly off her bed.

"Open door," she thought, and sighed, standing disheveled in front of it. The opening system immediately complied with her mind instruction.

"I'm afraid I woke you up." Laida grinned.

"No, I was in bed, but not sleeping. Please, come on in, commander."

Laida hesitated but stepped in.

Clara offered the only chair in her small quarters. The X.O. took the seat as her friend reclined on her bed.

"What brings you here, Commander?"

"Neither of us is on duty right now, so I thought it was a good time to pay a visit to an old friend."

"Thank you, Commander."

"Like I said, we're not on duty now," Laida insisted, raising a friendly eyebrow.

Clara smiled. "Would you like a cup of *seeb*?"[89]

"Only if you are frank and tell me if you weren't planning to do something else before your watch."[90]

"My only plan was trying to catch some sleep, but it wasn't working. Your visit is quite welcome."

Laida inclined her head graciously. "We haven't had much of a chance to talk since our last mission."

"I know."

"I've got some good news," Laida continued. "Task force thirty-three has finally managed to gain control of quadrant AC27."

"Hey, that's really good news. How did you learn that?"

"We docked with a dingy[91] a couple of hours ago. From it, we got an encrypted message from Admiral Pardo giving us the green light[92] for the last phase of our mission."

Clara sighed and passed a steaming aromatic cup to her friend.

"It smells good."

"At last, some breathing room," Clara added.

"Well, yes, though this also means we'll have to be more careful now. The enemy may turn more unpredictable."

"*Tweesser*?"[93] Clara offered a pot, which had a feminine touch.

"Hmm, yes." Laida dropped two spoonfuls in her cup.

"Anything new about Dahncion?" Clara added casually.

"Not much. He seems to be doing well in Aquaelight, winning the trust of the natives, according to Intel. That's pretty much all I've heard about him."

"Haven't we been able to make contact with Foxso'l yet?" Clara asked.

---

89 Aromatic beverage prepared with the leaves of a tree native to Veritas.

90 Clara had recently been included in the list of qualified officers for chief of the watch assignments. Note that in times of war, watches would be covered by any qualified officer except for the T.O., the X.O., and the Captain.

91 Small spy cargo ship.

92 She actually said "white light," which would not make much sense in our culture.

93 Light blue sugar-like substance refined from *twees* canes.

Laida sipped her *seeb*. "As far as I know, we haven't. The last we heard from him was that short message he sent a couple of weeks ago."

"*Mission completed according to alternative plan,*" Clara recited.

"The same. Nobody has heard from him since. But you know how he is. He likes to disappear, as if he didn't exist."

"Right." Clara smiled.

"He was reporting from the Aggar section," Laida added.

Clara tilted her head quizzically.

"You know, the Zwilitian Star Fields."

"So, Aggar section; this must be the new normalized nomenclature. I guess I'll have to bring myself up to speed with it. I'll get a file with the new classification from the comm station today."

"Hasn't Victor brought one up to you yet?"

Clara delayed her answer. "I guess it's in that card, over there." She pointed at the small desk by her bed.

Laida smiled. "You shouldn't postpone checking your mail."

Clara grinned.

"I wouldn't want to intrude in your personal life—"

"Please, Laida."

"It is about Lieutenant Commander Victor."

"What about him?" Clara blushed.

"Well, in Armonia[94] you were assigned together on the same mission. Later, during the navigation between Armonia and Karisol, I noticed that Victor liked to spend time with you. But lately I haven't seen you talking much to each other." Laida sipped some of her *seeb*. "Besides, to be frank, Victor doesn't seem to be quite the same."

"I don't think you should worry about that."

"I am the X.O., responsible for the morale of my crew, and one of my officers is not behaving as usual."

Clara filled her cup and Laida's with more *seeb*. "True, after the

---

94 A planet that, for a long time, had been under the Establishment's control.

mission on planet Armonia, Victor started showing interest. In the beginning, I didn't pay much attention.

"A couple of weeks ago, he invited me over to the officer's mess for a cup of *amis*. I was not in the mood, but he's always been such a gentleman that I felt obliged. At some point of our rather casual conversation, he suddenly confessed his feelings and said he'd like to have a special friendship with me." Clara paused. "I didn't know what to say."

"Surely Victor is a handsome man, and a true gentleman," Laida commented.

"He took me by surprise. That's why I really didn't know what to say. His feelings had been evident before; I knew I had to talk to him, to sort of make things clear? But I didn't want to hurt him. I wanted to wait until finding the right occasion. That was a mistake."

"What did you say to him?"

"That I already loved another man, and that I already had a special friendship with him."

Laida nodded. "How did he react to that?"

"He asked me if that man was Dahncion."

"He doesn't know him personally, does he?" Laida inquired.

Clara shook her head.[95] "He said he could imagine the feelings that I may have for someone like Dahncion, yet we belonged to very different realities, different universes." Clara sighed. "You can guess my answer."

Laida moved her knees together from side to side, holding them with her hands. "Knowing you, I guess you said something along the lines of how you already loved Dahncion, and that was that."

Clara chuckled. "I said I appreciated his words, the nobility of his intentions, but that my affection for Dahncion is something deeper than my feelings, something very real I can't explain. I also told

---

95 Lieutenant Commander Victor had been temporarily assigned to the *Intrepid* after Duncan had left with Foxso'l. Clara and Victor had served together in a previous mission, two years prior.

him that I had considered many things very carefully—especially the fact of our being from different universes."

There was a moment of silence, partially filled with the sound of the old-fashioned *seebpot* brewer. Clara's surrogate mother had given it to her adopted daughter before her embarking in the war. The *seebpot* had been in the Veritian family for many generations.

"Your love for Dahncion is strong, and pure . . . " Laida paused and reclined on her chair. "But it could be premature to take it beyond friendship."

"I don't think so," Clara replied harshly. "I fell in love with Dahncion soon after meeting him. At first, I knew he didn't feel what I felt for him." Clara shrugged. "I knew he was adapting to a new life, to a whole new universe. It was not the time for romance yet.

"The last night we were together, in Iluminia, we spent time walking around the campground,[96] talking about many things. He said he liked me and that he was very thankful for everything I had done for him; that he would never forget I had saved his life, twice." Clara lowered her eyes. "He said he knew I loved him, that he was still adapting to his new life, here—that his feelings towards me were growing stronger every day.

"I asked him how he regarded our friendship already. He said that he didn't believe in uneven loves, that whoever is not loved with the intensity he or she loves suffers for it, that he needed more time to be sure he could love me the way he said I deserved to be loved.

"I wanted to say that I didn't care about suffering for him, if I had to. But I just kept looking into his eyes." Clara paused with a thoughtful stance.

"I understand. We are quite alike in many ways." Laida nodded slightly. "But I think there are certain things you might have to consider more carefully and—I know it's not easy—objectively."

"I've been thinking a lot," Clara said.

---

96 After their lightning-bug collection "contest".

"Like you said, Dahncion needed to adapt. And yet, regardless of how much he may adapt, he still comes from a different universe." Laida raised an eyebrow. "Someday, he might want, or even need, to go back to his world. Even if he liked to take you along, that might just not be possible. The bio-assimilation is non-symmetrical. Assuming your size and body functions could be adjusted to that of a human being from Earth—which is a big assumption with our current technology—you would still retain your *tori* complexion. And it might not even be possible for you to be exposed to the new environment without harm.

"If Dahncion—hypothetically—would someday want to marry you, it would be he who would most likely have to stay here, and that might not be the best for him. His being among us is mostly due to an immense conflict. But eventually this will come to an end, and Dahncion may very well have to leave us."

Laida paused and gazed into her friend's eyes; Clara lowered hers. "His feelings towards you are still not clear, Clara. He is right: it is not truly love yet. Love meets in one truth, not two.

"You have a deep . . . profound . . . capacity for love." Laida opened her arms. "And to fall in love. I would not like to see you suffer for trying to be part of a love—a mutual love—that just wasn't there yet."

The time for Clara's watch was getting closer, and Laida had yet to discuss a few details about the upcoming mission. So she decided to set aside personal matters for a moment. "O'sihn still has to confirm this, but you—along with nine of us—have been included in the landing team for Aquaelight. Non-conventional pods will be used for reentry. The operation is scheduled five days from today."

"Acknowledged, Commander."

"I thought you'd have some special reasons to get down to this particular planet, so I put your name down in the list of recommended officers."

Clara smiled. "I can hardly wait."

"Well." Laida put her cup on Clara's desk. "I guess you need to start getting ready for your watch."

"I needed this conversation—with a friend," Clara said, taking Laida's hand.

"We can talk more about this later," Laida added, and headed to the door.

"I don't want to take more of your time," Clara said. "But there is something I'd like to share with you—short, but important to me."

Laida turned back from the door.

"I understand your concern. I appreciate it so much." Clara nodded. "But I do love Dahncion. That's just the way it is. I will always love him."

In humans, such statements, even when honest and full of ideals, are often the product of a temporary, though sometimes prolonged, emotional state. But Clara's last words sounded like a stream of pure light, the type that could not be ignored.

51.

As Laida walked towards the bridge, her mind went over the conversation she had just had with her friend. Had she used the right words? Had she said all the things she had to say, or perhaps she had said too much? Had it been the right moment for such a talk?

As she pondered Clara's last statement, a visible concern crystallized in her expression. It brought back to her mind the last words a Veritian admiral had said to Clara a few weeks before, after a brief inspection on board the *Intrepid*. Laida slowed down, reflecting on the traditional salute the admiral had used, customary among Veritian marines. As she thought of that, a hidden jewel within the phrase lit up her eyes: "Yes, my friend, *stern strength, if at war*."

The X.O. stepped onto the bridge. Her last thought was left alone in space where it had materialized, perhaps as a beacon of things that were meant to be, the way they were given to be.

Yes, since in Veritas, in the vast and marvelously far-reaching culture of Veritas, everybody knew that in the original ancient tongue, *at war* and *in love* were pronounced just the same.

52.

The elevator was going up with the characteristic slow cadence of any Australitian elevator, its destination the eighteenth floor. Right above it, a large heliport crowned the building. Nobody was there.

An official had told Duncan, in a short telephone conversation, that his unexpected, upcoming trip was closely related to other unexpected, upcoming events he could not yet reveal. For a moment, Duncan had thought of calling Erina on the phone, but he changed his mind. He had just asked the building manager to tell her about his trip after he had left, and that he would contact her as soon as he could.

Now, as he waited at the heliport, Duncan wondered if he had done the right thing. During the past few days, he had noticed his own tendency to overprotect Erina. Though she had been living in the current universe for about two months, it was too soon yet to expect her to be adjusted either to the new cultures, or to the universal war. Duncan would often think that the course of events—constant attacks, meetings with Aquaelitian officials, training for potential enemy incursions—was applying more pressure than she, or anybody else, could take. But, then again, perhaps his growing feelings were starting to influence his objectivity. Erina was an intelligent woman, very independent, and she did seem to be adapting very well and very fast. Duncan would find enticing new facets of her personality every day.

"If only Clara . . ." Duncan thought, and shook his head slightly. "Every person is different," he redirected his mind. "We must accept people the way they are."

The woman from Veritas was still present in Duncan's heart. Her spontaneous faithfulness and simplicity, the pure, almost naïve love she had showed towards him had inspired in Duncan a special affection for her. And yet, her external appearance, her childish drawing-like features . . . Duncan rejected the perception once again, and once again he felt the same strange sense of embarrassment, plus a new dose of conflicting feelings.

Looking at the skyline with its tall and predominantly bluish buildings, Duncan let his mind drift back to Erina. He did seem to share many things in common with her. Both coming from the same old Earth, they were apparently the first to have traveled to a different universe outside their own. There was common ground even in apparently trivial matters, Duncan realized. All that, combined with Erina's noticeable external appeal, made it desirable for him to have a much closer friendship with her.

Yes, that was very enticing, much as it would crush Clara's heart. Why did it worry him that much? He did not seem to have a good answer. But certainly the woman from Veritas still managed to touch his feelings in a mysterious way.

Skyscrapers loomed above, boasting twice as many floors as those back on Earth. The imposing view of Austral City met Duncan's homesick gaze. The city's engineering standards were multiplied by a factor of two or even four, consistent with the size of its citizens. There was no pavement on the streets: instead, a smooth and compact ice was constantly kept in shape by an army of ice groomers. Street vehicles had many similarities with those familiar to Duncan on Earth. Private cars would typically carry four to six occupants, and they usually had four doors. All of them had radios, stereos, and even lighters mostly used for some cigar-like canes or *sweektoclots*, which produced a sweet innocuous substance in one's mouth[97]. The smell reminded Duncan of spruce trees, very abundant in his hometown.

In addition to the ice groomers and private automobiles, there were public transportation buses, police vehicles, and ambulances. Besides their size and robustness, the main distinctive feature was that, instead of wheels, they had synchronized articulated skates that moved to provide propulsion and direction. There were no tire problems in Austral City, or any other city of the Austral Union.

From behind a tall building, about ten blocks away, a massive helicopter appeared, rapidly approaching the heliport. The aircraft looked heavily armed, with military marks on its sides. Duncan hurried up inside a small shelter beneath the level of the landing platform. Except for the shelter, he would have been easily blown away by the powerful drafts stirred by the spinning blades.

The helicopter landed on top of the building, idling its engines rapidly. An aft hatch opened, and a bear-like soldier with a blue beret—somehow fixed to his head —jumped out right away. Leaving the shelter, Duncan approached the vehicle with caution. The Australitian hurried to meet him.

"Mister Dahncion?"

"Yes, sir."

The soldier saluted politely. "Colonel Ber-Meglacontl."

"Good morning, Colonel." Duncan's words were obscured by the sound of the engines and the blades.

"Ready?"

Duncan nodded, squinting his eyes.

"You may board the aircraft!" the Australitian shouted through the very loud sound of the idling engines.

"I'll try!" Duncan yelled, looking up at the massively powerful

---

97 They emit a pleasing smell, not producing smoke, only a tenuous vapor. *Sweektoclots* were popular mainly among individuals of bear-type species. They came in many brands, for males, females, and even for children, although they were much more popular among adults.

sluggish blades whirring twenty feet above the platform. With no further ado, he lowered his head and ran inside the vehicle.

53.

Once again, Captain O'sihn checked the coordinates on his G.G.F.[98] Three minutes had passed since the first capsule should have hit the ice. There was no reason to be worried yet; everything was still within the expected time margins. But there were many unknowns about the Establishment's activity in the quadrant, which increased the risk of an operation that was not standard to begin with.

Colonel Meglacontl had been assigned to the reception of the incoming Realitian team. One day before, he had picked up O'sihn, the first to arrive in a landing capsule. Today they had flown back to a widely uninhabited area where the landing of the rest of the team was scheduled to take place.

O'sihn looked to the sky once more. It was a clear evening, with the local sun hovering close steadily above the horizon. The tangential path of the sunrays through the thick polar atmosphere turned the star's dazzling brilliance into a muted icy glow. The light was still capable of projecting long and wavy shadows across the frozen wilderness, which extended over an endless plain to the pristine horizon.

As Captain O'sihn checked his G.G.F. for the umpteenth time, a tapping on one shoulder made him turn around. He looked back at Colonel Meglacontl, and immediately to the sky.

A smile of relief spread over the captain's face.

54.

It was her twenty-fifth military capsule reentry, but this one was

---

98 A Gravitational Geo Fixer was a device designed to compute the position of the user on the surface of any planet or planetoid, or in its interior, based on the gravitational waves generated by the motions of nearby stars of known trajectories. These trajectories would have to be pre-computed by the mother (space) ship and passed to the G.G.F. when users were exploring unknown areas of space.

going to be different. Its landing phase was designed to end several hundred feet beneath the surface of a planet. Although Clara[99] had spent many hours in the simulator rehearsing the new procedure, it was still not as second nature as other standard routines. In any case, if everything went as expected, the onboard computer would take care of almost everything.

A display went on and a synthetic voice announced the next phase: "Ten seconds to solid immersion."

As Clara focused all her attention on the instrument panel, the capsule hit the ice, stopping moments later deep inside a thick polar glacier. Spinning over, it was finally ready to initiate the emerging phase according to plan.

The vehicles[100] had proven quite successful. Yet when Doctor Caricia Castor had first discussed the project with Doctor Oyhtter, his reaction had not been very encouraging. After listening to her, his only comment had been that she should not spend time and effort researching "fancy methods of preparing scrambled *yems*."[101] Humor and tact were clearly not among Oyhtter's talents.

A few weeks after the exchange, Oyhtter learned that Caricia had already finished and tested a computer model of the vehicle, with very promising results. Oyhtter apologized and assigned an official status with high priority to Doctor Castor's project.

Clara's capsule was now engaged in a slow trip towards the surface, and her thoughts drifted towards the rest of the team. All nine capsules would complete their reentry trajectories during a thirty-hour period, hitting the surface—one at a time—over a widespread area in an uninhabited region of the planet's south polar continent,

---

99 All members of the *Intrepid* assigned to landing operations, including Duncan, had received landing training for weeks on board the ship's simulators for this type of vehicle.

100 Vehicles that landed inside the ice had never been used (in a real mission) before Duncan's landing in Aquaelight.

101 With a thin, solid external layer rich in protein, *yems* are peculiar fruits produced by some litics.

according to the native convention. The night previous to the first launch, O'sihn had given her a card with a list of numbers from one to nine, arranged in a column. The first line had O'sihn's name. Clara took the card without any need for the captain to explain anything else.

She had first checked with her good friend, the X.O. Not surprisingly, Clara's name already appeared second after O'sihn's, which had caused some squabbling with Laida. Eventually, Laida yielded, accepting a third place. It was not easy to have the rest of the team agree in which order each one was to be launched. Everyone seemed to prefer being ahead; waiting for one's turn only increased anxiety. Clara felt reluctant to resort to her seniority to resolve the matter, and sooner than expected, O'sihn asked for the list. Only three names were still on it. It had been a long day for the captain. With an uneasy glance, he took the card and put together the final sequence right there.

"Am I forgetting something?" O'sihn inquired, after instructing Clara to pass the landing precedence to each member of the landing team.

"No, Captain."

"Carry on, then."

Clara was now last in the list, right after Laida. She turned around, keeping her eyes out of O'sihn's censuring sight, and walked away. Her anxiety to see Duncan had worked against her. O'sihn was always pressing his team to leave personal interests behind, in the service. Putting herself down second in the list—even before the X.O.—had given the captain sufficient evidence of her strong emotional motivations.

A tenuous external glow made Clara focus back on her instruments. The sunlight was becoming visible, exposing narrow icy walls. Above, the water surface appeared undisturbed. Clara was even able to spot some clouds beyond it. Soon afterwards, the capsule emerged in the middle of a liquid crater, sending forth short-crested ripples in every direction. The icy shore was gradually reflecting the incoming wavelets, transforming the circularly un-dulated surface into a shimmering crystal of random beauty.

The top of the capsule was immediately jettisoned. Clara squinted at the glistening scenery. Deploying a small retractable paddle, she began rowing towards one side of the pond, cutting through the thin film of ice that had already began to crystallize here and there.

About two hundred yards away, a huge helicopter was already waiting, its engines revving. The cargo ramp opened down to the ice, and a soldier jumped out of the vehicle. After scouting the landing site with his binoculars, he turned his head confidently towards the landing party inside the aircraft. Five more troopers stepped out.

Clara looked at them, hoping to identify somebody from the Realitian team, but she could not. A few seconds later, two other individuals stepped out. One of them looked around and waved at her. It was O'sihn, and Duncan was standing beside him.

Clara started running towards the helicopter when the Australitian soldier and his five troopers began to walk out to meet her. She immediately slowed down, trying to look composed. "Lieutenant Commander Clara, Veritas Marine Corps in commission for Realitas Royal Navy, sir," she said, and saluted.[102]

"Colonel Ber-Meglacontl from the United Republics of the Austral Continent. Welcome to Aquaelight, Lieutenant Commander."

"Colonel."

O'sihn stepped forward.

"Lieutenant Commander Clara, reporting for duty, Captain." Clara saluted again. "Trajectory and landing as planned; nothing to report, sir."

---

102 The Realdom's military salute for bipedal and some other species consisted of placing the right palm on the chest for about half a second, keeping the hand in a straight line with the arm and perpendicular to the uniform.

"As you were, Sub Commander."

"Sir."

"Lieutenant Dahncion," O'sihn said, "would you please help the Lieutenant Commander with her equipment?"

"Most certainly, Captain."

Duncan approached Clara, and they started walking towards the capsule. After a few steps, Duncan looked back. Nobody seemed particularly interested in them.

"May I still call you Clara, Lieutenant Commander?"

Clara smiled blissfully. "I'll always be Clara to you, Dahncion. How have you been all this time?"

"Good, but tell me about yourself."

"I missed you."

"I'm so glad you are here," Duncan said, his eyes drifting towards the landing pod ahead.

"So, what about these?" Clara asked, pointing at Duncan's fledgling lieutenant stripes.

"Well, the first thing O'sihn told me when he arrived yesterday was that a dispatch from headquarters had been received last week, whereby the Royal Council had promoted me to the rank of Lieutenant—in commission. When I get back to Realitas, I can get a regular status by taking the officer training program at the Realitas Naval Academy."[103]

"Congratulations, Dahncion. I'm really happy for you." By then, they had reached the capsule.

"How can I help you?" Duncan asked.

"I have very few things. I think I can carry them all. I guess O'sihn sent you along so that we could talk a bit," Clara said, and smiled.

Right at that moment, a violent burst of white light, coming from behind the horizon, shot two crisp human silhouettes over the icy ground. It lasted a fraction of a second, but it was bright enough to

---

103 In times of war, an officer with a commission status could still be promoted. That was the case in the Realitas Royal Navy, although not in all Realdom navies.

make Clara and Duncan instinctively cover their eyes—after the flash had vanished.

"What was that?" Clara stammered.

"I don't know." Duncan headed back towards the helicopter. Clara quickly picked up her equipment and started running after him.

Back at the aircraft, Clara and Duncan found everybody gathered on the flight deck.

"I can't make contact with headquarters," Lieutenant Lyn-Tretl said.

A bear-like figure, with colonel stripes, stood by the communications officer. "Keep trying."

Only static came through the speakers.

"Forget about Austral City," the colonel grumbled with growing impatience. "Try Base Admiral Li-Poteklatl."

"What channel, sir?"

"Any channel."

Tretl moved the dial from one end to the other, unable to tune in on any frequency. An eerie white noise was all that would come through the speakers.

"Something's very wrong out there," Tretl blurted. "I can't pick up any frequency at all."

"Excuse me, Colonel."

Colonel Ber-Meglacontl turned back. "Sergeant?"

"I've finished checking what you asked for, sir," Sergeant Pecotl said discreetly.

The colonel looked at O'sihn confidently, implying the foreign military team could be trusted.

"It was a nuclear discharge, sir."

Meglacontl kept his eyes on the sergeant for a second or two. "Magnitude?"

"Still undetermined, sir. But no less than ten megatons."

"Coordinates?"

"The computer is working on that right now."

"Give me what you already have, Sergeant."

Pecotl rushed to his panel and started tapping on his keyboard. A set of figures popped up in luminous green letters on a black screen. "We should wait a few more minutes for a more accurate fix on the emission, sir."

The colonel leaned on the table in front of the display. The co-ordinate readings were flashing in sharp square figures.

"This is just a preliminary estimate, sir," Pecotl insisted.

Meglacontl put on his dark glasses and turned to a porthole. He stood there in silence. The slow revving of the engines became the dominant sound in the cockpit.

Discreetly, Duncan approached the sergeant and pointed at the monitor, with an inquiring look.

"Austral City," Pecotl whispered, with a nervous twitch of his head.

Meglacontl kept his eyes fixed on the horizon, immersed in silence.

Clara watched Meglacontl as he left the flight deck. She turned to Duncan, but he did not pay any attention to her. Clara understood very well the devastating implications of what had just taken place. The odds of anybody in the city having survived such an attack were practically non-existent.

Duncan finally gasped a single word: "Erina . . . "

Clara turned to him, but he did not see her at all. She had never heard that word before. However, in her heart, Clara clearly perceived that the word was more than that. It was a name, the name of a woman, and not just any woman—at least not for Duncan.

55.

"A soda, ma'am?"

"No, thank you."

"You, sir?"

Duncan shook his head politely.

"Enjoy the flight." The flight attendant smiled briefly and turned to another row of seats.

Duncan had been gazing through the window on his left from the moment the airplane had taken off. Peeping over his shoulder, Clara was now doing the same, though Duncan did not seem much aware of her.

Since Clara had arrived at Aquaelight two days before, she had found a quite different Dahncion from the one she thought she knew. He was absent-minded and barely talked.

"This is the first time I've ever flown this way," Clara commented. "I've flown in many vehicles, but never in an airplane."

Duncan blinked his eyes, and turned slightly to her. "Hum . . . yes, I expected some long weary trip by helicopter."

Clara nodded. "In a way, we are lucky that Base Pan-Togletetl is more than two thousand miles away."

"I guess so," Duncan answered, his gaze wandering somewhere outside, through the window.

All the members of the Realitian team were at that moment flying towards the same naval base, from where they would depart for their next mission. For security reasons, they had been assigned in pairs to different flights.

"This first-class flight was a nice gesture from Madam President," Clara said.

"Uh-huh," Duncan muttered, keeping his attention outside the airplane.

Clara's endeavor to start a conversation had not been successful so far. Still, she felt it was time to try to do something about Duncan's strange behavior and obvious depression. "I'm very sorry about Erina, Dahncion," she said, with a compassionate expression.

Duncan turned to Clara with haunted eyes. "How do you—?"

"We've all heard about Erina from Earth," Clara explained.[104] "Everybody who met her agrees she was a very intelligent and attractive person."

"I should've mentioned her from the very beginning. I mean . . . " Duncan shook his head.

"Never mind," Clara said gently. "What happened was terrible. You don't have to talk about her."

Duncan leaned back in his seat and sighed, glancing upwards. "Erina was a wonderful woman. I learned to respect her greatly. We shared many views and many things, even though we came from very different places."

"I'm truly sorry, Dahncion. I am sure I would've had a lot to learn from her myself." Clara's true empathy was reflected in the beauty of her simple eyes.

Putting one hand on top of Clara's, Duncan gave her a small but warm smile.

A sign above the cockpit door went on. Duncan turned to his window and beckoned Clara to do the same. A handsome display of intermittent lights, from Admiral Pan-Togletetl airport[105], was signaling the airplane its landing track.

56.

Clara and Duncan were among the last to leave the airplane. Through a window of the jetway that connected to the airport, Clara glimpsed snowflakes being carried away by a light icy wind. As soon as they

---

104 She, and the rest of the team, had heard about Erina from O'sihn and from the Australitian intelligence officers. O'sihn had arrived to the planet one day before the rest. During that time, Duncan had explained to him in detail all the events associated with Erina.

105 The military airport had a large civilian section.

stepped off the jetway, a woman emerged from a large group of people waiting to board another airplane.

"Dahncion!" She threw herself into his arms.

Duncan's face was suddenly filled with a strange mixture of blissfulness and astonishment. The woman gazed up at him while still holding onto him.

"How ... I mean ... " Duncan stuttered, shaking his head.

"I left the city as soon as I'd learned about your sudden trip." Erina grasped Duncan again. She looked tired and distressed. "That horrible flash ... "

"It's okay, Erina, it's all over now." Duncan gently brushed her hair from her eyes.

"You have no idea how difficult it was to track you down. The whole country is upside down."

As they continued talking, Clara discreetly immersed herself into the crowd. She had to struggle through it until reaching one end of a long corridor. She glimpsed a sign and went on quickly to an elevator that went down to the luggage area. It was very spacious, with Clara as its only occupant. The luggage bay was ten levels below.[106]

During the descent, Clara kept her gaze down, her hair gradually sliding forward over her face. She closed her eyes with a subtle moan. Clara felt very lonely, her feelings somehow magnified by the large empty space. She was suddenly coping with warring emotions. On one hand, the woman, whose death had so much changed Duncan's character, was alive. On the other hand, Clara had just witnessed a very visible and intense exchange of emotions between Duncan and Erina, which had gone way beyond the circumstances, however extraordinary. The scene had darkened many of her dreams, and her heart was now tainted with a perception of betrayal and the notion that she had only herself to blame for all she was feeling.

---

106 The airport was on top of a hill, but the luggage area was far below, allowing for an easy access to public transportation, which included a metro station.

CHAPTER 10

Aquaelight

57.

It was not that the room was more comfortable than anywhere else onboard the submarine, rather that it was the most private spot on the vessel. Captain Ber-Gueelmietl had kindly offered his own quarters as a conference room. The meeting had started a few minutes before. "By then, the submarine will have closed distances to about six lonamies[107] from Blue Cliffs." O'sihn marked the spot with a pointer on an Australitian chart neatly stuck on a bulkhead with classical Australitian adhesive tape. "Three hours later, the third and last group will be launched.

"It is at this point that Lieutenant Commander Clara's platoon number three will start its seal-navigation. On reaching the beach, the team will proceed to climb the cliff by means of basic training equipment alone." O'sihn looked at Clara and continued. "Your first landmark: this stream course," O'sihn strained to make out the tiny characters on the chart, printed with Realitian characters by Australitian Intel, "Keteketl river, which falls into the sea over this ridge, right here.

"Over here," O'sihn pointed at a different site, "on top of," he paused to try to get the right pronunciation, "Cieventetl mount, you'll reach the birth of the Keteketl, the selected location where Lieutenant

---

107 Local nautical mile. Arc subtended by a degree of a maximum (average) circle on the surface of the planet. A circle subtended 20,736 degrees in the Australitian standard units of those days. If the same units were used on Earth, an Earth nautical mile would be about four percent larger than a *lonamy*.

Dahncion will launch the environmental restoration." The captain looked at Duncan, who nodded in agreement.

"Your assignment, Lieutenant Commander Clara, is to make sure that Lieutenant Dahncion and his equipment are there before you receive the target-destroyed signal from platoon number two. That would indicate that a key target, the telecommunications complex by the temple construction that is behind Lake Huatepetl, has been destroyed."

"What are my time margins, captain?" Clara asked.

"Once you receive the signal," O'sihn continued, "platoon number two will have less than ten minutes of estimated safety, whereas platoon number one, only eight more. If the restoration is not initialized within eight minutes after receiving the signal, platoons one and two will be exposed to heavy enemy forces. Should that happen, our chances of returning back to this submarine would drastically decline. We must carry out this operation right on schedule."

"It will be so, Captain," Clara asserted with confidence.

Duncan subtly rolled his eyes (annoyed with Clara's optimism).

"I want all of you to know," O'sihn continued, "that this operation has been a very controversial and thoroughly reassessed tactical sub-procedure at Realitas Headquarters. We all know what we are getting ourselves into. Still, this course of action seems to have the best chances of success.

"I also want to disclose a piece of classified information. The operational performance of this team has been ranked as *top excellence*. I'm sure this is the main reason for our having been picked for this job. High Command would not have hesitated to assign this mission to any other team, had any out-ranked our competence. We just happen to be the best, *erandie*, and we will show that once more tomorrow."

O'sihn paused, looking at his audience. "And keep in mind: we can't afford the luxury of failure. There is much more than our lives at stake in here. If we lose this planet, we will most certainly lose the entire quadrant, which would further compromise our situation in this war."

The room was getting very hot, and the air quite stuffy. It was becoming uncomfortable for everybody, and O'sihn was aware of it. But he still had important matters to discuss.

"I don't want to lose anybody in the field tomorrow," O'sihn continued, holding his wooden pointer with both hands. "We are to resolve unexpected situations with our brains, not our guts. I don't want fits of corny heroism. The Realdom can't afford dead heroes nowadays, only reusable winners. Questions?" O'sihn drummed his fingers on Captain Gueelmietl's desk. "Very well, let's move on to our last topic.

"Though ten of us are to be launched on this mission, we will be eleven fighting together. I intend to make a new addition to our group, and this is the main reason I asked Erina to attend this meeting.

"Over the past two days, I've been delving into the possibility of Erina's joining us in the field tomorrow.[108] As some of you are aware, I've been discussing the issue with members of this team."

O'sihn paused. He seemed uncomfortable with the decision he had made. "I'd rather have you here on board this submarine tomorrow, Erina, monitoring our deployment."

Erina pushed her hair back with one hand. "I didn't expect this decision, Captain."

"And I am not fond of it myself," O'sihn said. "But you are a very valuable element of a team that is about to get involved in a complex

---

108 Erina had volunteered to join the Royal Navy under the condition of always being assigned with Duncan. As a commodore, O'sihn had the prerogative to recruit new members under special circumstances, so he incorporated her under an *in commission* status, which implied that to make the incorporation regular, the new recruit should complete the required courses and training when circumstances allowed. In O'sihn's judgment, although Erina had virtually had no exposure to the Royal Navy yet, the thorough training she had received on Earth to become, first, an astronaut, and then, a *u-naut*, were more than sufficient credentials to incorporate her into the team, with the rank of private, promotable to a junior officer rank.

operation. It's neither reasonable nor fair that you should engage your first mission under such circumstances."

"So my first assignment will be to wait onboard this submarine, while Dahncion and everybody else are out there exposed to all kinds of trouble." Erina scowled. "The least I can say is that I am not fond of this either, Captain."

"I understand." O'sihn wrinkled his forehead.

The name—Dahncion—stung Clara's ears each time Erina pronounced it. Clara tried to hide her feelings behind her hair, though not very successfully.

A hand went up. "Yes, X.O."

"I regret we haven't had the chance to discuss this before, Captain, but this course of action will probably not help anybody, particularly Erina."

Everybody turned towards Laida with surprise. It was very out of the ordinary that she would openly question the captain's decisions.

"Certainly, X.O.," O'sihn said, without showing disapproval. "I guess we have all been pretty busy during the past few days. But we are here to discuss all alternatives, so please go ahead."

"Thank you, Captain. It is true that Erina has no combat experience, but she has displayed very promising qualities. On the other hand, I don't think she's going to be safer on board this submarine than on the island. If we fail, this ship will most likely be detected and immediately destroyed. The enemy has a very good antisubmarine capability—enhanced by Establishment technology, of course. But if we succeed, she would have had the chance to engage in her first mission, which will be a tough one. This would give her a great deal of confidence for future assignments." Laida's tone was firm, though respectful. O'sihn remained pensive as the X.O. continued. "Besides, I don't think there is going to be any major operational complication if we were to include her in platoon number three." That was Clara's and Dahncion's team.

O'sihn nodded. "The X.O. may have a point here." Leaving his pointer on the desk, the captain turned to Erina. "Very well. Any objections to being assigned to Lieutenant Commander Clara's team?"

"None, Captain."

Almost simultaneously, Duncan raised his hand.

"Yes, Lieutenant?"

"I think we're overlooking something," Duncan said, frowning. He was clearly upset. It would have been improper for him to question the captain outright, but he could try pointing out obstacles. "Erina has no battle suit, and without a battle suit, none of us can survive in a reconfigured environment."

"She could use mine," Clara said from behind him. "We don't have large physical differences. And I could wear one of the Australitian battle suits available on board. These uniforms are cruder than ours, but still safe and pretty functional."

"Unfortunately, they don't have suits for human beings," Duncan objected. "Not even uniforms for humanoids," he added, fixing his eyes on Clara for a couple of seconds.

"First Lieutenant Ber-Pli' Petlakan's uniform will suit me fine," Clara replied, referring to one of the Australitian officers assigned to the submarine. "I'd have to make some adjustments to it. Nothing that couldn't be done on board, though."

"Pli' Petlakan is an *ursidean*!" Duncan snapped.

"An *ursidean* of a small size. I've lived in Veritas for some years, which is mostly inhabited by *ursideans*, and during that time, I had to adapt myself to many of their ordinary things—including their clothing." Clara kept her eyes on O'sihn, evading Duncan's censuring eyes.

"Very well. Try on First Lieutenant Pli' Petlakan's uniform, make all adjustments you judge necessary, and when you're done, please come see me," O'sihn said. "I'll make a final decision on this matter only at that time."

However, Duncan was not giving up yet. "We may be rushing into a decision which may not be the best for Erina." His comment and tone lacked the deference that Duncan's junior officer status demanded.

"Indeed? You need not worry about that, Lieutenant," O'sihn remarked calmly. "No hasty decisions will be made under my command. And, of course, Erina has always the final word. She will have our total respect in whatever decision she makes."

"And my decision is to go along on this mission, Captain," Erina added, taking Duncan's arm. She and Duncan had been sitting side by side during the meeting. "I just couldn't stand being left onboard without knowing what is going on out there. Besides, being with Dahncion—and under Lieutenant Commander Clara's command—I have nothing to worry about."

58.

"Make sure to double-check the procedure with—"

"Excuse me, Captain."

Turning around, O'sihn was somewhat taken aback by the unfamiliar costume, but recognition quickly dawned. "That suits you well," he said, muffling a chuckle.

Clara took off her helmet. Her expression was tense.

"Though it doesn't seem to allow much mobility," O'sihn pointed out.

"It's not like ours, but it's acceptable, Captain."

"Good, good. Now I wonder how your uniform suits Erina."

"I've already taken care of that. It suits her almost as well as me."

"So, I guess it's all set, then."

O'sihn turned back. "I'll meet you in a few minutes."

"Aye, sir." Lieutenant Jartung saluted and left.

O'sihn stared at Clara for a moment. "All right, we'll carry on with the mission according to the X.O.'s recommendation. Erina will be assigned under your command, in addition to Lieutenant Dahncion. Watch out for the boy. He has learned a lot—he's a good soldier already—but he's still inexperienced. Keep an eye on him."

"I certainly will, sir."

"Very well. And, concerning Erina, this will be her first mission. She's totally inexperienced." O'sihn pursed his lips slightly. "I am still concerned about letting her go. Regardless of what's been said so far, if you concur with me about her staying onboard, it would settle the matter. She'd stay."

"I think I can handle the situation, Captain."

"So be it, then. During the navigation from the submarine to the beach, I doubt you will encounter any difficulty. You will be using active vectors,[109] so it won't be physically demanding. But climbing the cliffs won't be an easy task, especially with inexperienced personnel." O'sihn looked intently at Clara.

"Anything else, Captain?"

"Yes. Remember what I stressed during the meeting. Be objective." O'sihn raised one eyebrow.

"I sure will," Clara blushed slightly. "Like in any other mission."

"Certainly, but unlike any previous mission, somebody special to you will be your direct subordinate."

"Sir?"

"I mean Dahncion," O'sihn replied slowly.

"I . . . how do you know, sir?"

The captain smiled and nodded. "But during this operation, he's just another soldier, like Erina." O'sihn kept his eyes on Clara, who lowered hers slightly.

"*Platoon number three, to the bridge. Platoon number three, to the bridge.*" The message came through with a soft blinking of lights, with the pattern of a Realitian code.[110]

"I guess the X.O. is summoning you," O'sihn said. "Tell Private Erina about her being confirmed in your team. I also want you to double-check the breathing system of your uniform thoroughly. You

---

109 Small electric propellers for personal use.

110 In order to improve the stealth characteristics of the submarine (thus minimizing its chances of detection), the internal communications system worked with light codes rather than sounds, as in all Australitian submarines.

won't leave this ship without giving me a satisfactory report regarding the operational status of all your equipment. Any questions?"

"No, sir."

"Carry on, Sub Commander."

Clara saluted and turned back. She looked clumsy walking through the narrow submarine corridor in her modified Australitian uniform. O'sihn stared at her for a moment, and shook his head slightly.

59.

Having been released into the partially reconfigured[111] cold waters of the Fire Seas, Clara was immediately exposed to the freezing environment. Lieutenant Pli' Petlakan's uniform protected her from everything, except from the pervading cold. Her body had gradually grown numb, to the point that she could neither feel her feet nor her hands. It took her team more than one and a half hours to complete the navigation to the beach.

Once on shore, Clara, Duncan, and Erina started towards the mouth of the Keteketl, which belched out a slimy waterfall into the Fire Seas below. The first step was to climb up the sheer walls of the ridge in front of them. Though not very high, negotiating that obstacle demanded a considerable effort. A local storm was not making matters any easier. The intense wind produced drafts that made the ropes they were using for the climb oscillate and vibrate menacingly. It was difficult for Erina, but excruciating for Clara. Her Aquaelitian uniform was heavy, and as Captain O'sihn had pointed out, not very functional. As a matter of fact, it was very dysfunctional. Every time Clara moved a hand up on her rope, she felt a juncture scraping her wrist.

---

111 As we saw in Iluminia, Establishment occupational forces, such as Kervian's, would typically reconfigure the areas under their control to suit the environmental demands of their leading species. The reconfiguration affected the environment and the native species, to preserve them and adapt them to live under the new conditions. The reconfiguration of the area where O'sihn's team was about to land had started a few weeks before and was still incomplete. The low temperatures and the constant storms on the area were a consequence of the still on-going reconfiguration process.

As she came across the initials *P. P.*[112] on Pli' Petlakan's gloves, Sergeant P. P. Kloph's "prophecies" came back to her mind with a sense of fulfillment. Kloph—Clara's drill sergeant in boot camp back in Veritas—had truly been the Prophet of Pain that he liked to boast he was.[113]

Despite the pain and the exertion, Clara reached the top of the cliffs right after Duncan and Erina. The next phase, the ascension of the Cieventetl, had started. The mountain was not very steep, but it was still a long way to the spot from where the Keteketl sprang. As Clara and the members of her team reached higher altitudes, the temperature dropped. A thick layer of clouds covered the sky completely; it was much colder than what was to be expected for near-equatorial latitudes on the planet.

The *Realitian* suits Erina and Duncan were using provided them with a comfortable seventy-degree[114] atmosphere. The only indication they had of the outside thermal conditions came from their suits' sensors, which displayed readings on one corner of their visors. The situation was quite different for Clara. Although she was somewhat warmed by the physical demands of the climb, she could still not feel her frozen toes and her fingers. Her heavy and uncomfortable Australitian uniform was wearing her out very fast. All this, plus a very intense thirst she could not dismiss, was starting to affect her blood pressure and her concentration.

---

112 The initials were written in the relatively simple Australitian alphabet. Clara had gotten familiar with it when studying the maps for the landing. Only the most relevant elements in them had been translated by Australitian Intel, which forced her to learn the basics of the local alphabet to extract important information from them.

113 During the very intense physical and psychological instruction, Kloph would often give "prophecies" such as "The civilians out there . . . the poor devils: they are missing the real fun right here, a foretaste of the good days to come."

114 Seventy degrees Fahrenheit or twenty-one degrees Celsius. That was the default temperature generated by the suits, which could be adjusted to the user's needs.

The team had started toward the mouth of the Keteketl, which belched
out a slimy waterfall into the Fire Seas below.

A persistent drizzle had started, which was paving the trail they were following with mud. This slowed down the platoon, which had already used more time than expected to climb the cliff. Late as it was, Clara realized she was pushing her team to its limits. For a moment, she thought of leaving one exhausted member waiting there until after the target had been reached. But Clara rejected the idea immediately. Were her feelings starting to interfere with her mission? The thought crossed her mind.

"Keep going. We haven't reached our target yet." Gathering strength from her own exhaustion, Clara supported Erina around her hips to help her walk.

"You look tired," Duncan said to the captain.

"Focus on the mission, Lieutenant." Clara's tone sounded grim, though weak. Erina stumbled and fell to the ground. Duncan hurried to help her up.

"Let's stop, just for a minute," Erina muttered.

"We can't stop," Clara replied. "We must reach the target with no delays. We have no choice."

"Hey Clara, it's just a minute. This is her first mission," Duncan said.

"I'm well aware of the details, Lieutenant. We're already running behind schedule, and we just can't afford to be late. The whole operation—the lives of everybody—depends on our being on schedule. Come on, Erina," Clara added. "One last effort and our part of this operation will be over."

Duncan helped Erina up and supported her as she walked.

Twenty minutes later, they made visual contact with their target, a bubbling spring of thick water on top of the mountain. The three started moving faster. A hundred yards from the spring, Clara's communicator started beeping. That was the signal they expected from platoon number two.[115] Clara's platoon had very little time left to complete its mission.

---

115 As O'sihn had explained in the briefing on board the submarine, this was the target-destroyed signal expected from platoon number two, indicating that a critical telecommunications complex had been destroyed.

It was at that point that a disk appeared in the sky, on top of the mountain.

Moving along a soundless trajectory, the disk headed swiftly for platoon number three. Clara grabbed the heavy-particle howitzer she carried on her back, threw herself to the muddy soil, and clicked on the power magazine. A high-density plasma vector struck the approaching disk on one side, and a dumb flare of light flashed off its surface. For a moment, the vehicle remained hovering in its position, oscillating and vibrating in an unstable manner, until an object was ejected, right before the disk exploded.

The three Realitians kept their positions, their bodies on the ground, anxiously watching the descent of the jettisoned object. War regulations forbade shooting down ejecting capsules or parachutes.

Soon it touched down, and three heavily armed humanoid figures jumped out. They immediately adopted a searching pattern and opened fire in the direction of the platoon. Captain Clara returned the fire with her handgun, but the aliens evaded her gunfire.

"Hurry up, behind that rock!" Clara yelled, gesturing for Erina and Duncan to take cover.

"Look out!" Duncan shouted. Immediately, Clara threw herself to the ground behind a tree trunk. A shot pierced clear through the trunk, barely missing the captain.

Duncan returned the fire, killing one of the attackers. Having found cover behind a rock a few yards ahead, he was now trying to locate the remaining two soldiers.

"Drop your weapon," an unexpected gravelly voice came from behind. One of the aliens had taken hold of Erina and was pointing a sharp cutting tool into one of the seams of her battle suit.

Duncan was confronted with a critical decision: give in to the enemy, rendering the whole mission wasted and facing an uncertain future, or open fire, risking taking Erina's life in the process. Captain O'sihn's pre-combat briefing played back in his mind. Objectivity had been the major point. However, Duncan's feelings towards Erina seemed too strong for him to overcome.

Unexpectedly, Clara appeared from behind the alien and cracked a large rock over his head, rendering him unconscious. The remaining soldier, who had been covering his comrade from a distance, opened fire. In an attempt to protect Erina, the captain instinctively jumped in front of her.

Duncan returned the fire at once. Waiting for a reply, he immediately heard a subtle hissing noise. He turned around and saw a foggy gas gushing out of a rent on Clara's uniform, above her right knee.

The alien had been mortally wounded, but even so, his last shot had struck the captain, rendering her suit useless.

Clara was lying on the ground struggling against a caustic pain. Although the shot had only damaged her uniform without injuring her, the lethal reconfigured air was penetrating rapidly into the suit, causing serious burns on her skin. Clara was gasping with the searing pain. Duncan tried to fix the rent, but the rustic cloth pattern of the Australitian uniform was making the task very difficult. No standard procedure seemed to work. Not knowing what to do, he looked back at Erina.

"He may have something we can use," Erina said, pointing at one of the soldiers lying dead on the ground.

Duncan searched the body without any success. Finally, stripping off its jacket, he rushed towards Clara and started working on a coarse patch for her uniform.

"Never mind me, go reach the objective," Clara said. But Duncan kept working on a double tourniquet using the alien's jacket.

"I gave you an order, Lieutenant!"

"Stop moving, Captain," Duncan said, putting a hand on her right shoulder and pinning her down onto the ground.

A few seconds later, both the hissing sound and the foggy emanation coming from Clara's uniform had stopped. Duncan's improvised effort had been successful. Carrying Clara over his shoulder, Duncan began moving towards the target.

"Stop it! Leave me alone. The target, run to the target."

An emergency signal from platoon number two began ringing on Clara's communicator. The platoon had made contact with enemy forces. Exhausted, Duncan stumbled and fell to the ground.

"Dahncion, listen, you must listen to me, please," Clara said from the muddy ground. "We just won't make it this way—any of us. Leave me here and run to the target. There is no enemy activity around. I'll be fine."

Duncan tried to see her face behind her fogged visor. A red light began flashing on the tactical communicator the captain carried on her belt. There was no time left.

Placing Clara carefully on a flat rock, Duncan rushed towards the top of the mountain. Erina ran after him. As Duncan approached the target, he began unloading the large device he carried on his back.

Clara lay motionless, moaning from pain, but still striving to follow the events beyond the watery curtain of the raging storm. Visibility was very poor, so she soon lost visual contact with Erina and Duncan. As she kept her sight ahead, a bolt of lightning pierced a nearby tree. For an instant, the scene became as bright as a thousand flares.

Behind the visor of Clara's helmet, the pervasive flash captured a smile of relief, stung with suffering.

60.

Duncan was standing on the highest spot of the island. He looked around, but he could not see very much; the rain was too heavy. He quickly turned back to the E.R.G.[116] he had just placed on a flat, mud-spattered rock. After adjusting some settings, he turned the device on.

Duncan checked his chronometer as the countdown sequence was initiated. Grabbing Erina by the arm, he started to run, looking for cover behind a large boulder a short distance down the hill.

The storm was growing worse, with violent lightning continually illuminating the eerie twilight. Duncan remained focused on his chronometer, his visor flashing along with every lightning bolt.

"Now!" Duncan barked, holding Erina protectively.

A dense white ray shot from the E.R.G., straight up towards the local zenith. As it flowed from its source, the complex energy vector grew continually in definition. Suddenly, a fast-expanding silver umbrella of light materialized in the sky. The energy surge was impinging on the local ionosphere; in response, a gigantic shockwave bounced down to the ground, fired from the silver umbrella above.

As striking as the scene was, Erina was even more stunned by something else.

Duncan was kneeling on the ground, beside her, staring at the sky. He had not moved in the last minute or so. But his eyes glowed with an intense blue incandescence, as his body did.

61.

The evening of the same day, small landing ships from the Australitian Cruiser *Admiral Ber-Osclotetl* picked up the whole Realitian team. As the boats approached the battleship, sailors started gathering on the port side. By the time the small ships had docked alongside, all personnel free from duty were watching over the main deck.

A ladder was lowered, and the members of the Realitian team started getting on board, one at a time. Each was received with full military honors—naval whistles included. Certain things seemed to be truly *transuniversal* constants. Special care was taken in raising a stretcher carrying Lieutenant Commander Clara.

---

116 Environmental Restoration Generator.

That night a banquet was held with all the officers of the *Osclotetl*, presided over by Commodore Lyn-Enroblotep, the captain of the cruiser. Afterwards, Laida hurried to sickbay to check on her friend's condition. Clara seemed to be out of danger, thanks to Doctor Raikun's proficiency in administering some basic, but effective, Realitian medicines.

While her chances of survival were promising, Clara was far from safe. Serum was being administered through her right arm, and two plastic tubes stuck out of her nostrils, according to rudimentary Australitian procedures.[117] Her right leg was virtually a single bleeding wound. All over her body—including her face—severe burns complicated her very delicate condition.

Despite the tranquilizers, getting some sleep seemed unattainable. Pain was patent in her expression. But now, she smiled as Laida, followed by Duncan, entered her room. Clara lifted an arm, with serum ducts hanging from it. Gently intercepting it, Duncan put it back on her chest.

"How do you feel?"

"I'll be fine . . . pretty soon."

"Of course you will." Duncan remained standing by her bed.

"I must look . . . awful . . . " Clara added, with difficulty.

"In your case, that's impossible, Captain," Duncan said, and smiled. It was clear Clara wanted to talk some more, but her pain was making it very difficult.

"You need to rest now," Laida said. "We'll come back tomorrow, in the morning." She turned to Duncan, who nodded back.

Before leaving, Duncan stood by the bed and kissed Clara's forehead. "I'll see you in the morning, Clara."

Laida's eyes gleamed with surprise.

A few minutes later, O'sihn also arrived. Nobody but Clara was

---

117 Raikun had brought along a medical kit from the *Intrepid* that had been very helpful in treating Clara. But what he had was not enough, and however coarse, he had no choice but to use medical procedures available on board the Australitian cruiser.

in the room. Despite the injuries, her expression looked bright and calm. The captain stayed for just a moment; everything seemed better than expected.

Clara was immersed in a restoring peaceful sleep.

62.

Duncan was standing in front of a wide river that ended in a large bay about one mile ahead. It was a starry night, warm, with no wind. Very far away, ahead of him, a large cloud trailed above the horizon. Its base was about one thousand feet from the ground, and its top was thirty thousand feet above or more.

The cloud was vibrating with an intermittent light irregularly covering its surface. Every five or ten seconds, powerful bolts of lightning crossed the cloud from side to side, from bottom to top, and from top to bottom. It was largely a quiet spectacle, although occasionally, a distant yet powerful thunder came from the cloud.

From behind Duncan, another cloud came in, moving towards the first. In the beginning, it was dark and small, but as it moved towards the horizon, it started to glow with a reddish color as it took the shape of a massive and sturdy giant. A strong wind coming from the cloud began to blow.

The trees began to growl with the force of the wind. Some branches began to fall, one landing very close to Duncan. The words *cloud giant, cloud giant* could be heard, as if pronounced by the roaring wind. The cloud looked defiant and unstoppable. It was as if it wanted to tear the forest apart. The river, though shallow, began to develop waves that broke on shore with an ever-increasing strength.

"Someone has to stop it!" Duncan cried.

At that point, a new cloud appeared from behind. It looked like a warrior, all covered in armor also made out of clouds. The armored cloud had a real sword made out of iron. The giant cloud growled at him. But the warrior cloud charged at the cloud giant with his metallic sword.

Once in front of it, the warrior cloud pierced the cloud giant with his sword. But the cloud giant began to rain a very heavy rain inside itself. The rain was thick and warm, and it was too much for the sword. The iron started to rust, until the metal peeled off in reddish scales that were washed out by the wind. The same happened to the armor of the warrior cloud. Bereft of its armor, the warrior cloud could not survive, and it dissipated.

Another cloud appeared from behind, which turned out to be two clouds joined together. One looked like a horse of war; the other, like a knight, riding on top of the first. The knight was not human, but Duncan did not recognize its lineage. Like the warrior cloud, the rider cloud also had a real sword. It was made out of ice, but it was very sharp and deadly; fire and lightning had no power over it.

The knight cloud and its horse charged towards the cloud giant. As the rider passed the giant, it wielded its sword to chop off the cloud giant's head. The cloud giant laughed with derision. It was still raining its warm thick rain, but the rain got thicker until turning into enormous balls of hail. The rider cloud hit the cloud giant on its breast. But as it did so, the hail began pelting the sword, which immediately broke into a thousand pieces. The rider kept on galloping until disappearing behind the horizon.

Then another warrior cloud appeared. It looked like a bear, dark, but with green eyes made out of stars. He also had a real sword, but this one was made out of fire. With each star in his eyes bright as an emerald sun, he charged towards the cloud giant.

Turning to the approaching warrior, the cloud giant changed its hail into a freezing snow. When the warrior tried to pierce it through with the sword, the snow, which was stronger than fire, drove into the flames. The fire vanished immediately, and so did the bear-warrior cloud.

The cloud giant was getting stronger. Its winds began to spawn tornadoes. Trees were flying through the air, as well as people and creatures of all kinds, and even stones, rocks, and ponds.

Two new clouds appeared. They looked like a panther riding on an eagle. The panther like cloud was white, and beautiful; her eyes were glowing with yellowish bolts of lightning. And she also had a sword—a real sword—made out of diamond. Seeing it, Duncan thought: "This sword will never be broken."

The panther cloud, riding on her eagle cloud, charged towards the cloud giant with a battle roar, but the cloud giant replied with thunder. The panther rider hit the cloud giant on its breast. Its sword was strong indeed, but too stiff to withstand the rumblings of the thunders. The diamond sword began to vibrate and resonate like a delicate crystal cup until breaking into ten thousand pieces of remarkable beauty. Each piece fell into the bay ahead, causing massive waves. The panther cloud and its eagle were quickly dissolved by the infuriated wind.

The cloud giant was unstoppable, and now it looked as if it wanted to wash Duncan away. But then the first cloud—the cloud that was shimmering with lightning above the horizon, with powerful bolts and deep distant thunders—took the shape of a man. It looked like a man in his fifties, very dignified and wise. Duncan immediately recognized him and smiled.

The giant cloud heard the new cloud approaching from behind and turned around. In its wrath, it began raging with grayish-white lightning and thunderbolts. The words *cloud giant, cloud giant* coming from its thunders were eerie and deafening.

The man cloud took a sword from his back. It was a real sword like the others, but its essence was different, for it was pervasive and stern. He did not know exactly how, but Duncan noticed that immediately. The sword became a beam of blue energy, and with it, the man cloud pierced the giant through its heart. All lightning inside the cloud giant gathered at that very spot to meet the blow.

Yet in doing so, the energy surge from the man's sword penetrated the cloud giant's lightning bolts, and from them, the most recondite parts of the cloud giant. Although the cloud giant doubled the strength of its lightning bolts, it could not stop the light from the sword of the man cloud. For how to stop a ray of light with another ray of light? The best it could do was to overwhelm the incoming blue ray with the light of its own lightning bolts. But they were not constant. They flashed on and off, whereas the light from the man-cloud's sword was steady, and therefore, stronger. It was piercing each and every bolt of lightning, turning them into blue light from within themselves.

After a short fight, the cloud giant began to shine with the dazzling blue intensity coming from the light beam of the sword of the man cloud. There was no way to fight that light or its energy, for it was true light, and so, it could pierce and reach anything that is. The cloud giant began to evaporate in rivulets of darkness, and soon only the man cloud remained.

Everything had become calm and peaceful. The forest had recovered its gentleness, and the waters of the river, their kindness and serenity. The man cloud stared at Duncan. "Victory belongs to *sternessence alone.*"

"What is your name?" Duncan asked.

The man cloud stared at Duncan again, and Duncan immediately heard the man's name within himself.

Startled, he woke up.

63.

Green, blue, purple, ocher, yellow, silver, and even splendid white: the stars were the sole rulers of the heavens that night, like any other summer night, above the restored ocean. Aquaelight had no satellites and no rings, and at those low latitudes, aurora borealis never developed. The brightest body that could ever be seen was She-sun, a dazzling star not visible at that time of the year. Yet, after sunset, a special clarity always quickened the oceans, especially in the tropical latitudes; a bluish phosphorescence glowing in the waters completed the twilight of the stars above.

"Someone has to stop it!" Duncan cried.

Leaning on the railing board, on the roundhouse area, Duncan was contemplating it all. He had awoken from a brief light sleep he had fallen into while reclining on his bed with his uniform still on. Now, as he sought some fresh air, he was comforted by the surrounding beauty as he rested his eyes on the wake left behind by the battleship. Its two propellers were tracing bluish trails on the sea, their blades constantly splattering streams of gleaming water over the sides.[118]

Despite the relief of successfully completing an especially difficult mission, Duncan was visited again by uneasy thoughts. The general situation of the Realdom was precarious, and he still failed to see how the military machine could be stopped.

To Duncan, winning the war remained something distant, uncertain, theoretical. The *sternessence* issue was back to haunt his thoughts, floating over the dark waters of the widespread conflict. If there was to be a victory—a final victory—that very word, or rather its implications, was supposed to play a key role in the whole scheme of events.

Duncan had just had a dream, where the same character of other dreams—Lan Leakim was the name he had revealed today—had reappeared to remind him of the significance of *sternessence*, and the relevance of committing to it. Yet, although those dreams recurred, their consistent message was not gaining strength in Duncan's heart.

---

118 The tropical waters were very rich in bioluminescent microorganisms.

CHAPTER 11

A Good-Bye and a Hope

64.

"Commander Laida said you wanted to see me."

O'sihn raised his eyes from his terminal. "Dahncion, come on in, please."

Duncan stood in front of O'sihn's desk.

"Please sit down." O'sihn gave an uneasy glance to the clock on one corner of his display. "I have a special duty for you this morning. I know you are quite busy with the ammunition inventory, but today I would prefer that you give me a hand with Sub Commander Clara's transfer to the YSF *Temperance*."

"Transfer?"

O'sihn nodded. "Doctor Raikun's post-battle report clearly indicates the need for sending her to a specialized medical center at the earliest possible convenience. She will be all right," he added, anticipating Duncan's next question. "She's out of danger, but we don't have all the equipment required for her rehabilitation on board. Sending her to Realitas right now is the best way to get her back with the shortest delay."

As reasonable as it was to expect such a transfer, considering the injuries Clara had suffered, Duncan had been unconsciously avoiding the matter. Now he realized—despite what O'sihn had just said—that he might never see her again. After her treatment, she did not necessarily have to be transferred back under O'sihn's command, especially since she belonged to Veritas' Navy, which was regulated by its own statutes.

"I apologize for the short notice, but we ran into the *Temperance* less than an hour ago. It was only then that we learned she was heading for Realitas."

Duncan stood quietly, staring at O'sihn with gloomy eyes.

"You'd better hurry to the port bay, Dahncion," O'sihn added, as he checked the time once more. "The shuttle assigned for the transfer will be taking off at 1000R. Clara is already on board."

Duncan looked at the clock. He certainly had very little time left.

"Permission to proceed, Captain."

"Granted."

65.

Duncan headed for the *globular*, a spherical vehicle that moved through different sections and decks.[119] It was on the *globular* that he first realized that, since the last battle, things had changed within himself. Even if he experienced a strong attraction towards Erina, Clara reached his heart with a singular peace and freedom, like a warm breeze he could not ignore, especially when being close to her. The prospect, or at least the possibility, of not seeing her again saddened him.

Soon, the door opened at the port bay. Blinking lights were already denying access to the shuttle, which was ready to take off. The depressurization gates were about to seal the vessel from the rest of the bay. A crewmember hurriedly waved Duncan in from the gate to the vehicle, and he ran inside.

During the short trip, nobody would experience any acceleration

---

119 The ship was honeycombed with a network of tube-like tunnels, through which a *globular* could reach any part of the ship. There could be up to fifty *globulars* operating at the same time, although it was very rare to have that many running simultaneously. The *globular* operation was very simple: a magnetic field generated inside the tunnels induced the motions for these vehicles and kept them from ever touching the tunnel-walls. Of course, the system was fully automated: the user only needed to voice the destination, although there were specific instructions for priority and speed typically used in combat.

or sensation of motion. The gravitational equalizer system, used in most spaceships, would provide an inertial environment at all times.

"Lieutenant Commander Clara is at the end of this corridor." Lieutenant Sadeer, the officer who had waved Duncan in at the bay, indicated the direction with a tilt of her head.

"Thank you."

Hurrying up to the cabin, Duncan found Clara sitting on a medical chair.[120] A blue mantle, with the Royal Navy's emblem on it, covered her body. Her long hair was made up into a neat plait that Laida had hastily, but skillfully, arranged minutes before Clara had been sent to the shuttle. Duncan noticed her hair and the beauty behind it. Despite her evident facial injuries, Clara still looked attractive.

"I'm so glad you could make it," Clara said, after a brief silence. Her voice, though clear, lacked her peculiar elegant determination.

"How long is that treatment of yours gonna take?" asked Duncan.

"The doctor said that I should be completely recovered in three months."

"Three months?"

"That's shorter than the time we were apart during your previous assignment."

Duncan nodded. "I'll miss you."

Clara smiled gently.

"*Now hear this . . .*" A voice came through 1-MC.[121] "*This is Lieutenant Kaitting. We've initiated the docking sequence with the YSF Temperance. Lieutenant Dahncion, stand-by for Lieutenant Commander Clara's transfer at the docking gate.*"

Keeping his eyes on Clara, Duncan stepped back to a communicator built in on one bulkhead and laid a finger on a glassy slot. "On my way, sir." He looked at Clara sadly; she smiled.

---

120 Medical chairs were mounted on a gravitational base that kept them about one foot above the floor. The system was designed to absorb sudden accelerations and to prevent the chairs from capsizing.

121 Main circuit for internal communications used to transmit orders and information reaching all decks. For the current English account, we adopted the same term used in the U.S. Navy, to avoid coining a new word.

The doors to the cabin opened. "We need to go," Sadeer said, standing in front of them.

Duncan started pushing Clara's chair towards the transferring section. On reaching it, Sadeer knelt down to rearrange the mantle that covered Clara's body as they waited at the docking gate. It immediately opened like the pupil of an eye, with a sharp metallic sound.

A long, narrow cylindrical passage, which belonged to the *Temperance*, appeared in front of them. Duncan carefully moved Clara's chair inside the docking corridor. He had to bend his head when stepping into it. "Maybe you can wait here," he said, turning back to Sadeer. "It's a narrow corridor."

"Certainly," Sadeer said. "I wish you the best, Lieutenant Commander," she added, looking at Clara over Duncan's shoulders.

"Good-bye, Sadeer."

Duncan moved Clara down the corridor as slowly as possible. An unexpected grief welled up deep inside him. Too soon, he and Clara had reached the other end. A second gate then opened as harshly as the first.

Duncan saluted the officer from the other ship. "Lieutenant Dahncion transferring Lieutenant Commander Clara, sir."

"Welcome on board, Lieutenant Commander," the medical officer of the *Temperance* responded.

Duncan helped to transfer the chair to the docked ship. A nurse moved forward to transport the injured officer to sickbay.

"Just a moment, please." Clara turned towards Duncan, who was looking at her from the docking corridor. She looked at him in silence. Then she offered him her hand. In it was the medallion she always carried. Clara had been wearing that medallion when she had been first found alone in a wreck on Veritas, all those years before. It conveyed a special meaning to her, as it was the only link she had with the past she could not remember. "I don't know if I'll ever see you again. Probably not."

Duncan took the medallion, looked at it, and turned his gaze back to Clara, hesitant as to if he should accept it.

"But, no matter what happens," Clara continued, "no matter where we are—remember that I love you, and I always will."

Clara's salute lacked the persuasion to check the tears she wanted to contain. Duncan saluted back, holding his arm up until Clara lowered her own.

"I also love you, Clara," he replied.

But the gate had already closed.

CHAPTER 12

Alishar

66.

"Time for reentry?"

Lieutenant Leepardian's virtual console came on, together with that of McAwian, the communications officer of the watch. "Shuttle's E.T.R.[122] three minutes, Captain."

"T.T. mag.[123] by four."

"T.T. by four, sir."

The bright ocher surface of Serena, spotted with downy bluish clouds, filled the whole tactical screen. Duncan and Erina had been assigned to a routine reconnaissance mission to one of the most beautiful charted planets of the quadrant. The area had not yet suffered the stings of the universal war. Though its strategic potential was growing, the territory was not formally claimed by any of the warring parties yet.

"Here goes Ensign Erina's first mission," O'sihn commented.

"Uh-huh," Laida mumbled, her eyes focused on the screen.

"It doesn't look like a tough one, anyhow," O'sihn added.

Laida sighed. "I would feel much better now if we had sent a couple of interceptors[124] as an escort."

O'sihn nodded. "We don't want to overprotect the boy—or Erina."

122 Estimated Time for atmospheric Reentry.

123 Tactical Theater magnification. Scale magnification was computed as T.T. scale = $2^{(\text{magnification factor})}$. Thus *T.T. by four* would mean a scale magnification of sixteen.

124 Although the *Intrepid* was not a carrier, it had a small squadron of nine interceptors.

Laida kept her eyes on the main TD.

A female voice came through O'sihn's console communicator. "Wide and short range scanners show all clear, Captain."

"Copied, C.I.C."[125]

"Shuttlecraft entering planet's atmosphere," Leepardian reported.

"Chart of the landing area on L.B."

"Aye, Captain," McAwian acknowledged.

A detailed picture appeared on the left bottom (L.B.) section of the tactical screen.

"I like this place," O'sihn said. "We could set aside some time for shore leave . . . "

"There seems to be something wrong with the shuttle's communications," Leepardian interjected.

"Reentries have never been good for communications," O'sihn commented, "no matter how hard engineers keep trying to change this."

"I don't know, sir. This seems different. I have something like a complete echo blackout."

O'sihn straightened up in his chair. "C.I.C./conn."

"Yes, Captain?"

"Deehra, do you detect any unusual activity close to the shuttle's position—anything?"

"Mm . . . no, sir."

"Engage high radiation scanners."

"Aye, sir."

"Anything new?" O'sihn asked, looking at the virtual console of the chief of the watch.

"I really don't know," Leepardian replied, "but the blackout is very intense."

"I don't like this," Laida muttered. "I don't like it at all." She focused her attention on some digital noise that had just materialized

---

125 C.I.C.: combat information center.

on the main screen.

Almost at once, the ship was rocked in a vicious fashion.

"Conn / C.I.C.," Deehra's agitated voice came through on the captain's console.

"X.O., signal alert one on all decks. What was that?" O'sihn asked Deehra, who was waiting on the intercom line.

"Now hear this, all personnel to battle stations . . . "

"Plasma impact on port side, sir," Deehra reported.

" . . . alert condition one . . . "

"Point of origin?" O'sihn asked.

" . . . all personnel to battle stations . . . "

"From the shuttle's estimated position, Captain."

" . . . this is not a drill."

"What about that ultra-radiation scan?" O'sihn continued.

" . . . I repeat, all personnel to battle stations . . . "

"We're picking up some weak unusual bands, but nothing out of standard spectrum."

" . . . Alert condition one . . . "

"Aim every scanner we've got onto the shuttle's last bearing."

"Aye, Captain."

The lights faded down, and a 3-D image of the surrounding space was projected, enclosing the entire bridge. Laida, who was very focused on her console, suddenly raised her head and startled with vertigo. She found herself as if floating in space right above the impressive view of the planet below and moving at an incredible speed over its surface.

"Damage control reports minor damages on port sub-level bay. DAS[126] absorbed 99.98 percent of impact energy."

"Copied, X.O."

"Permission to assume T.O., Captain," said Tygrum, who had just arrived at the bridge.

"Permission granted. Bring yourself up to speed with current situation, T.O."

"Aye, Captain."

"Conn / C.I.C."

"Deehra?"

"Sir, we have identified a gravitational disturbance near the shuttle's estimated position."

"What kind of disturbance?"

"We're still working on that, but it could come from a medium-size ship."

"Captain!" Leepardian called.

O'sihn raised his eyes and looked at the tactical screen. On one side of Serena's globe, a target acquisition marker popped up on the display.

"Unidentified object emerging from the planet's atmosphere," Leepardian said.

"Unidentified vessel registers as a *Corregum* class destroyer," Deehra confirmed.

"What about the shuttle?" added O'sihn.

"The only reading is from the unidentified vessel, Captain," Deehra said.

---

126 DAS: Dynamic Armor System. Spaceship hulls had a network system designed to neutralize, automatically, extreme loads due to weapons attacks or to collisions with meteorites or other types of derelict objects in space. Such systems were designed to increase the molecular cohesion around the impact area almost instantaneously, though for very short time spans.

DAS systems were used in both civilian and military vessels, although the latter had more sophisticated and powerful units designed to withstand attacks and quasi catastrophic collisions.

"A destroyer emerging from the atmosphere?" Laida said with a skeptical tone.

Once again, O'sihn checked the tactical data on his console. "Try to locate the shuttle, Deehra."

"We are trying, Captain."

"Unidentified contact has assumed a parallel course to ours," Tygrum added, "as if trying to escape."

"C.I.C./conn, anything about the shuttle?"

"No readings from it, Captain."

"Any signs of debris along estimated trajectory?"

"We only register the atmosphere spectrum, plus a limestone, salty surface with rich traces of organic material below," Deehra explained. "That's all I've got, Captain."

"Keep on scanning."

"Aye, sir."

"Permission to dispatch a searching probe to the landing site," Laida added, referring to the area selected for the shuttle's landing, as she switched bands on the bow tactical scanner.

"Permission granted."

"Unidentified vessel is leaving us behind rapidly," added Tygrum.

O'sihn clasped his hands together and leaned his chin on them. "Full ahead, Leepardian. Let's try to catch up with it."

"What about Dahncion?" Laida asked.

"Full acceleration ahead, Captain," Leepardian acknowledged.

"I have a pretty bad hunch that Erina and Dahncion are on board that vessel," O'sihn replied.

"It doesn't seem very likely the vessel could've captured the shuttle so rapidly," Laida commented.

"It wasn't likely at all to find a *Corregum* class destroyer immersed in a well-developed atmosphere either, but that's exactly what's happened, X.O."

"But . . . "

"The S.P.[127] you've launched will be able to detect the shuttle or any vital signs from Erina and Dahncion, if they are down there on Serena."

"They may be injured."

"They may have been captured by the unidentified vessel," O'sihn retorted."

Laida turned to the tactical screen. A small yellow dot, surrounded by stars, was marked out by a red locking cross.

"I guess you're right, Captain," the X.O. conceded. "But, if we find out we can't close distances with that ship—" Laida pointed at the yellow dot—"I'd strongly recommend abandoning pursuit and returning to Serena immediately. If anyone is injured, we'd be there to help."

"Fair enough," O'sihn concurred. "If, after one hour of pursuit, we fail to close distances onto target—"

"—Or we do it poorly," interjected Laida.

"—Or we do it poorly, X.O., we'll follow your recommendation."

67.

The prisoners were at the entrance of two contiguous cabins, standing in a dim corridor. As the doors in front of them opened, a character— with human traits—wearing a pressurized uniform commanded Erina to step inside one of the rooms, pushing her mildly on the shoulder. Duncan was still gazing at her when another individual, much bigger than the other and wearing a similar uniform, ordered him, not as mildly, to enter an adjacent cabin through an antechamber. The entrance door to the cabin closed immediately, and so did a second door to an antechamber that separated the cabin from the entrance door. Having entered with Duncan, the alien declared that the environment was suitable for life, and directed him to remove his suit. He did not specify what type of life, but with a gun aimed at him, Duncan had little choice. He complied with the order and found

---

127 Searching Probe.

the atmosphere to be safe. The alien left the cabin, taking along the Realitian suit.

One hour later, Duncan received a peculiar visit. An individual was now standing at the doorway in the antechamber[128] to Duncan's quarters. He was wearing a suit that covered his entire body. The alien had distinctive human features with masculine traits. Although his head seemed to be exposed to the environment, a very tenuous aura emanated from the collar around his neck. Some form of energetic capsule enveloped his head, providing for an independent gaseous environment different from the one in which Duncan was immersed. The visitor stepped in and stood in front of Duncan, who was sitting on a couch.

"Lieutenant Dahncion, my name is Alishar. I'm honored to meet you." The alien extended his right hand towards Duncan, who stared at him without moving.

"I understand the people of Earth greet friends in this manner." The visitor pulled back his fist with a refined movement. Picking up a chair behind him, he placed it in front of Duncan.

"You might be concerned about Miss Erina," he added, and paused as if measuring Duncan's reaction. "She is perfectly safe, assigned to quite adequate quarters, not too different from this cabin." There was a distinctive look in Alishar's eyes that inspired trust.

"You might be wondering about many other things: the events of the last couple of hours, the reason of your being here, the war . . . " Alishar sighed. "First, and in a quite unexpected manner, you and your fellow officer are captured by an enemy ship; next, you are treated rather cordially—something you may not have antici-pated."

---

128 The air mix of the ship was different from that of the cabin in order to accom-modate an environment in which Duncan could live. The antechamber with the two-door system enabled access between the two different environments. When someone came in from the ship, the air inside the antechamber would be that of the ship. Then, with the two doors closed, the air in the antechamber was replaced with the air in the cabin, at which point the door to the cabin would open. The inverse process took place when someone left the cabin.

"What do you want from us, Mr. Alishar?" Duncan said, breaking his silence.

"We know your origins," Alishar responded with an affable expression, "and the way each of you reached our universe—and the way each of you got involved in this war." Alishar nodded and paused for a moment. "I'm sure you have met different cultures, already, even if mainly within the context of the Coalition."

"Coalition?"

"*Realdom* is a term you may be more familiar with," Alishar asserted, gently stroking his beard. It was carefully trimmed, like his sideburns, which ended in a dignified gray. "All this time you have been hearing about this conflict—and this universe—from one single source." He paused and laid one arm along the quilted side of his chair. "We would like to take the opportunity to give you a broader perspective."

"I'm not particularly interested in your *perspective*, sir." Duncan's words were intended to convey conviction, but Alishar perceived hesitation, or at least a trace of curiosity in his tone.

"I don't think a closed-minded disposition will do any good. And it is not precisely a frivolous matter what is at stake here. You and Miss Erina represent an entire civilization, an entire race—the *Terran* race. The responsibility that comes with it is remarkably important and not unlikely crucial." Alishar stared into Duncan's eyes intensely, but with a cordial expression. "Lieutenant Dahncion, we are only asking for an open disposition today. This, however small, could constitute the starting point to ending this dreadful conflict."

Duncan looked at the man, barely narrowing his eyes. He did not trust him, but what he had said so far made sense.

"We don't expect you to understand our perspective with just a simple talk," Alishar continued, with a collected posture. "These things do take time. But after much consideration, the people I endeavor to represent have a proposition for you, a proposition that conveys a promise and a new hope for ending this war and bloodshed."

Duncan's eyes widened with anticipation. "What kind of proposition, Mr. Alishar?"

"We would like to appoint you and Miss Erina Ambassadors of Peace between the Coalition and the Establishment."

68.

"They will kill the hostages unless we abandon pursuit," was Tygrum's immediate objection to the captain's intention to persist with the chase of the hijacking ship. The threat, issued through a standard communications channel, had been heard on the bridge and all its virtual stations. With it, all their fears of what had happened at Serena had been confirmed.

"I don't think so," O'sihn said from his seat at the head of a long table in the *Intrepid*'s main conference room. "All of us are quite familiar with Em-Rasinka's esoteric beliefs, and how initially Dahncion was considered a serious threat to the Establishment." O'sihn sipped from a glass of water he was holding in one hand, merely to wet his throat. "However, Intel reports indicate that the First Equitarian has lately been obsessed with making contact with Dahncion." Em-Rasinka had coined her own title, First Equitarian, shortly after the Establishment was founded.

"True," Laida said. "But ever since she concealed herself behind the walls of the Milenia,[129] it has become practically impossible to gather any information about her." The Milenia was the neuralgic center of the Establishment's government.

"The reports I've just mentioned are recent," O'sihn clarified.

"The threats we have just received from the enemy ship indicate their hostility towards Dahncion has not changed," Tygrum pointed out. "Getting rid of Dahncion, they would get rid of a big risk."

"Many think this way," O'sihn conceded. "But there is more to it. Em-Rasinka and her followers seem to believe that if Dahncion or

---

129 The Milenia was a vast complex that extended over thousands of square miles on one of the planets of the Establishment's Capital stellar system.

Erina were won over to the Establishment's side, they could become a key factor in winning the Realdom over."

"You gotta be kidding," Tygrum growled. "Sorry about my outburst, Captain, but even if these reports are mostly accurate, it would still seem safer for the Establishment to just get rid of Dahncion and Erina without taking chances."

O'sihn shook his head. "Some in the Establishment believe that with Dahncion in their ranks, they could effectively reach the Realdom, favoring an easy and peaceful equalization of it, and its subsequent assimilation into the Equity."

Tygrum sighed in disbelief.

"However strange," Lin Beaver, the Chief engineer, interjected, clearing his throat. "However strange, there is an intriguing parallel between the First Equitarian's alleged beliefs and our own beliefs about Dahncion."

"I don't know," Raikun objected, with a twitch of his head.

"Yes, doc?" O'sihn asked.

"What about the rumors about Em-Rasinka's death, apparently from natural causes? Hasn't the Establishment tried to conceal it?"

"We can dismiss all that. The notion has most likely been generated by Establishment's Counter Intelligence."

"For what purpose?"

"To have us believe that the future of this war has turned in our favor."

Tygrum grinned. "And for what purpose?"

"Bait." O'sihn clasped his fingers. "To lure us into taking more aggressive actions according to some painstakingly planned counter procedures. It could also be an elaborate strategy of psychological warfare."

"Probably both," Laida commented. "The enemy seems to believe that we see the First Equitarian as a deadly threat."

"*Isn't* she a deadly threat?" Tygrum leaned back in his chair. "In the last months, she has managed to anticipate and neutralize several key initiatives of the Realdom."

O'sihn nodded. "Yet, as a consequence, the Realdom has become more careful in its moves, which is having the effect of prolonging the war beyond the Establishment's expectations. Therefore, if we thought her dead, our morale would go up considerably, spurring us into taking more aggressive steps that could potentially make us fall into—"

The intercom rang with a call from the C.I.C. announced on its display.

"Yes, C.I.C.?"

"Captain, we've lost contact with the target."

"What?"

"It . . . it's just disappeared, sir. Apparently some form of sophisticated invisibility field. The ship does not register at all, not even in the gravitational bands."

"I'll be there in a moment."

"Aye, Captain."

With frustration, O'sihn looked at the X.O., who was sitting in front of him. Laida sighed. "I'm afraid we will not have to worry about our hot pursuit any longer."

69.

Ambassadors of Peace between the Coalition and the Establishment. . . The statement, and the proposition, made a strong impression on Duncan, who stared at Alishar, dumbfounded for a moment. Could that be true? Could he be, indeed, a decisive factor to end the war? His fears over his very uncertain situation as a prisoner had dropped with the unexpected proposal. Even the constant anxiety and misgivings about his role in Reality had slackened. But suspicion immediately kicked in.

"Why do you think any of us could have any influence in the Coalition, as you call it?"

"Because some key elements within the Coalition believe that you may have a decisive role to play to end this war," Alishar answered.

Duncan sighed. "What makes you believe that?"

"It doesn't take a great intelligence effort to be acquainted with these facts, Dahncion. Peace is why you are here today, a new hope for peace."

Duncan rubbed his neck uneasily. "So what are we to tell the Realdom? That you don't want to force your Equity on it anymore?"

"Certainly there is always room for dialogue and mutual understanding—for trying to repair mistakes, where they have been made. But perhaps a blurred picture of us is making you believe we'd have an awful lot to change before peace can truly be achieved. You may eventually find out, Dahncion, that reality is somewhat different from how you perceive it today."

"Perhaps, but . . . would this peace deal include the Realdom's unconditional acceptance of your Equity?"

Alishar smiled briefly, shaking his head. "You are inclined to refer to the Equity as if it were some instrument of oppression."

Duncan smirked. "And what is it?"

"It constitutes a powerful means for universal peace and harmony between very different peoples, with diverse species, and dissimilar cultures and behaviors," Alishar stated with pride.

"Having one equalized culture, you can surely have a very convenient, uniform, one-colored, strange-to-diversity civilization. But I wouldn't call that *harmony*, Mr. Alishar."

Alishar reclined on his chair and stretched out his legs. "Dahncion, isn't the prospect for peace, the hope for stopping all this bloodshed and useless destruction, motivation enough for you to reconsider your position? Won't you allow for the possibility of the facts not being exactly as you think they are?"

"I think I have a pretty good idea of reality already, just by looking at the facts, Mr. Alishar."

Alishar smiled. "Whose reality, Dahncion? The Realdom's?"

A light began blinking on a device Alishar carried on his wrist. He touched the top of it gently, and the blinking ceased.

"I suppose you must be very tired," Alishar added. "Please consider this commission of peace we are offering you and Miss

Erina. We can talk more about this later. Now, if you'd excuse me, I have some pressing matters to attend to."

Alishar stood up and stepped back into the antechamber. There he typed a code on a transparent display and turned back to Duncan. "If you need anything, please use the intercom by your bed."

Duncan nodded briefly, with a polite but cautious stare.

70.

Many hours had passed since Mr. Alishar's visit, a long enough time for pondering about many things. Duncan was reclining on his couch. Through what seemed to be a general purpose exchange-channel built into a bulkhead, some food had been sent to him, but he had not touched it.

While he was thinking, Duncan absentmindedly raised his eyes. Above the terminal from where he had received his dinner, a rectangular panel, previously unnoticed by him, was blinking. A moment later, the lights of his room flickered for a fraction of a second, immediately followed by an up-and-down fluctuation in the gravitational field.

Duncan stood up and started looking around. Other than the blinking light, nothing else seemed to be happening. But he knew the perception was likely not true. All those signs were indication of the ship having engaged in battle. At first, he felt some relief, thinking the Realdom had finally come to his rescue. But that hope rapidly yielded to the fear that, whatever engagement the vessel might be getting into, Realdom forces would not necessarily have to be aware of his or Erina's presence on board, in which case they would be trying to destroy the ship.

The power went off abruptly and came back again. This happened four times, until the lights literally blew up.

The ship shrieked and groaned like a wounded whale, and a deadly darkness ensued. In the midst of the deep silence, Duncan suddenly started hearing a hissing sound, which made his ears pop.

Running to the door, Duncan tripped over an object and knocked his head against a bulkhead. Poking his way out in the darkness, he finally found the door. He tried to pry it open by pushing the panes sidewise with his hands, but to no avail. With a clack, an emergency-light panel turned on, and a door slid open on one bulkhead.

A locker was revealed, with three suits inside. They appeared to be abandon-ship suits. A pressure leak was taking place, and in response, the automatic system had opened the emergency locker.

Duncan looked at the suits. They were in three different sizes. He picked the one in the middle and put it on quickly. It fit him almost perfectly. The final step was sealing the headpiece around his neck. Duncan zipped it without much reflection, and immediately, its life-support system activated.

"Argh!" Dashing his hand to the zipper, Duncan almost ripped the headpiece off. The life support system of the suit was adequate for the alien crew, but lethal for humans. The caustic air and the icy gas mix had produced a rash on Duncan's neck, but it was only a superficial wound.

Frustrated, Duncan threw the other two suits to the floor. In doing that, he noticed that each one had a canister on its back. He stared at them for a few seconds and finally stepped onto the biggest suit. Grabbing its canister, Duncan managed to rip it off without damaging the suit. He immediately took off the medium-size suit he was still wearing and put on the large—or rather, super extra-large—one. Duncan hoped that the size of the suit would help it engulf enough air to give him some extra minutes, once the air in his cabin was gone. But what to do with those extra minutes?

With the new suit on, Duncan carefully zipped the headpiece, squeezing his eyes shut. The system clicked on, and much to his relief, nothing else happened. The suit was perfectly sealed from the environment, but it had no more air than what was engulfed in the loose folds of fabric hanging everywhere around his body. However, there was still plenty of air in the cabin. Trying to keep the limited air of his suit fresh as long as possible, Duncan opened the headpiece again.

Nevertheless, the critical question remained: what was he going to do once he was forced to seal the headpiece definitively before the air pressure in his cabin dropped too far? Before he had the chance to start truly worrying, a sudden hissing noise from the pressurizing antechamber to his room made him turn around. Duncan slowly moved back, his face dripping with a cold sweat.

Almost as a reflex, Duncan sealed his headpiece again. He did not know what to expect. He could feel his heartbeat going berserk.

Immediately the door to his cabin was activated, and Erina appeared standing in the twilight. Behind her, the entrance to the antechamber from the external corridor was wide open. On seeing the unsuspected individual in the bizarre suit, she hesitated. Erina was carrying a gun, and now she pointed it at Duncan.

"Don't shoot, it's me, don't shoot!" Duncan cried out without removing his headpiece. His cabin was already filled with the lethal atmosphere of the vessel.

Suddenly, the ship groaned and wailed with twice as much intensity as it had before. Duncan smashed into a bulkhead, hit his head against the cabin's overhead, and fell to the floor. Disoriented, he struggled to his feet.

Erina was lying on the floor by his bed. He rushed to help her and soon realized she was not wearing a helmet. Two tubes ran from her nostrils down to some apparatus hanging from her neck, inside an alien suit. Though obviously she could not breathe the ship's air, the human-like complexion of her body (quite different from Duncan's reconfigured complexion) seemed to have no problem coping with the alien atmosphere. Still, a yellowish, gelid sweat was starting to exude from her skin.

Erina was unconscious, and Duncan quickly realized that his attempts to revive her were not having any effect. He also knew he had little air left in his own suit. If they were to survive, he had to act quickly. At that point, the shuttle in which they had been captured flashed back into his mind. The hangar where it had been docked was not far, and he thought he could find his way back to it. However, would the shuttle still be there? Maybe not, but there seemed to be no other hope.

Becoming aware of the ZB_2[130] accumulating in his suit, Duncan darted forward into the quiet hallway.

The ship's gravitational field, maintained by the artificial-gravity system, was weak, similar to twenty-five percent of the equivalent Earth's pull. Carrying Erina in his arms was relatively easy and not terribly exhausting. As Duncan crossed different corridors, he could see bodies of aliens strewn all over the place. They looked very different from Alishar or the two soldiers that had carried him and Erina to their cabins. They were rather short, very thin, and had large, bald heads. Many had orange streaks of blood coming from their mouths and ears. Fostered by the sub-freezing environment in which they lived,[131] the bodies had already acquired the stiffness of death. Clearly, the aliens' physiology was less resilient than Duncan's or Erina's in absorbing violent accelerations.[132]

Emergency lights were on everywhere, with depressurization warnings flashing at several spots. However, the ship was not dead yet. Twice, Duncan noticed blinking lights on panels connected to the main system, hinting that the ship's plasma weapons were still being used. Besides, the gravitational system was still fully operational. The

---

130 Zaoohn di-bioxyn. This gas was analogous to the carbon dioxide—CO_2—exhaled by our lungs.

131 The temperature in the vessel was about thirty degrees Fahrenheit, unlike the comfortable seventy-three degrees that Duncan had experienced in his cabin.

132 During the battle, the explosions had induced very brief but large accelerations inside the ship.

contrary would have meant instant death for both Duncan and Erina, since the ship's acceleration[133] would have squashed them against a bulkhead.

Sooner than expected, Duncan reached the hangar area. Everything had gone smoothly so far, but trying to get the gate to the hangar to open was now proving problematic. Feeling that he was about to faint, Duncan knelt down.

In doing so, he saw a red button close to the floor. He pushed it several times, but it was stuck. Standing up, he kicked it with all his strength. The large panes that formed the gate suddenly slid open. Ahead, the shuttle was standing proudly on deck.

Exhausted by the effort and the lack of air, his body totally numbed by the cold, Duncan stumbled towards the vessel, virtually dragging Erina along. His vision blurred, Duncan could only hope that he would not have to deal with the vessel's opening system. Fortunately, it responded at the first try.

Duncan placed Erina on the copilot seat and checked the control panel. Everything seemed to be in order. As a first step, he activated the life support system. He had to wait one very long minute until the cabin was cleansed of the alien gaseous mix.

A blue light on the panel finally came on. Duncan snapped his headpiece open and threw it to the deck. He immediately turned towards Erina and looked at her. She was still unconscious. After a moment of doubt, he snatched the tubes from her nostrils.

Coughing and gasping, Erina responded rapidly to the cabin's warm air. Without delay, Duncan turned back to the control panel and initiated the takeoff sequence.

While Duncan was working on the trajectory the ship was to follow,[134] a lateral gate to the hangar opened up, and five armed

---

133 A standard artificial gravitational system not only generates gravity inside a ship immersed in the vacuum of space, but it keeps a constant gravity environment at all times despite the very large accelerations a ship can generate, especially in battle.

134 He was setting a trajectory to move the shuttle away from the alien ship in the fastest and safest possible manner.

troopers began firing on the shuttle. Time had run out. Only two alternatives seemed to be left: aborting the escape attempt and surrendering to the enemy, or trying something crazy.

Reason did not prevail, and Duncan opened fire against a bulkhead. The shuttle cracked miserably, but its gravitational system compensated for the ensuing brusque acceleration pattern as it moved out through the hole it had opened, pushed by the difference of pressures between the ship and space.

Far away from the enemy vessel, the small craft was suddenly drifting alone, resting peacefully in a star-filled expanse of serenity and solitude.

71.

Duncan had had no luck in getting the engines started. He had tried for several minutes, following all kinds of emergency procedures, with no results. Except for the gravitational system, the auxiliary life-support system, and a few more devices, everything seemed dead onboard.

Erina was now starting to come around. "What happened?" she finally asked, with a faint voice, but fully awake.

"We are free, drifting in space. I'm turning on the emergency homing system."[135]

Nodding, Erina sighed. They looked into each other's eyes, and finally, Duncan burst into a nervous laugh.

Erina gazed at him. "Dahncion . . . "

Duncan stroked a lock of her hair and smiled. "Duncan . . . you call me Duncan."

---

135 The emergency homing system was an autonomous system designed to work even if the ship suffered serious damage.

CHAPTER 13

When *All Things* Does Mean Everything

72.

"Let's face it, we are stuck here." Erina stretched back on her chair, putting her hands behind her neck.

"We've been here for only three days. The *Intrepid* will pick us up any time now." After escaping from the Establishment's ship, they had been rescued by a vessel from a large deep-space complex, and the event had been reported to Realitas.

"Besides, a little vacation here at Nereida's[136] station is hardly going to harm us," Duncan said smoothly, circling the rim of his glass with one of his fingers.

"Yes, and after this, the *Intrepid*, and next another mission, and then another one . . . but the people that brought you here can't send you back home—unless some next-to-impossible, inter-universal conditions unexpectedly arise." Erina pushed her lush hair to one side, over her shoulder. "And those who sent me here haven't shown any signs of being able to retrieve me back. They might think I'm dead."

"They would eventually send someone else," Duncan commented.

"Highly unlikely. They were not aware of the special conditions

---

136 Nereida was a space station of the Fouchè Principality. Its planetary systems had not been involved in the war so far, though their sympathy for the Realdom was palpable. This space station was a huge deep-space complex of about one cubic mile in size.

that had to take place for these sorts of trips. They were very lucky in sending me here."

However negative the comment, it had an unconscious positive effect on Duncan. The unlikelihood of further trips from Earth would increase the chances of the alleged unique role that he would have to resolve the conflict, reinforcing the validity of the reasons for his trip to Reality.

Duncan poured some more of the silver-gleaming beverage he had ordered and started sipping it quietly. "I'd prefer to think of the whole thing as a temporary situation."

"Maybe, but we should probably discuss this with O'sihn when we have the chance. He might be able to send a hint to someone back in Realitas."

"Someone like whom?"

"Someone from SERI, for example."

"I think the people at SERI have hardly time for breathing these days," Duncan stated.

"This may not be the best time to ask for personal favors," Erina said. "And I am aware of the expectations that some may have about your fighting in this war. But I think that we owe it to ourselves to be clear about our desires of going back home."

Duncan kept staring at his drink, tilting it from side to side. "I've started having second thoughts again about fighting this war. Even when I've never liked the Establishment or its Equity, I must admit that some of the things Mr. Alishar said made sense to me."

"I know what you mean." Erina had related to him her own experience and the talk Alishar had also had with her.

"Could we be certain of their intentions?" Duncan continued. "And even if they wanted to use us for their political scheme, what if some—or many—of them were well-intentioned about us? What if some of them truly have a hope of peace with us? After all—and even if I find this questionable—some in the Realdom do believe I would be a key element to end this conflict. So what if we—you and I—could truly help put together the hopes for peace for both sides?"

Erina listened to Duncan, nodding.

"I wish I knew the right thing to do," Duncan added, holding his glass with both hands while looking into it.

"Well, like you said before, you perceive that there are some in the Realdom who expect something special from you—extraordinary perhaps. Why think now that you might be someone special for the *Establishment,* or for any side?" Erina put a hand on Duncan's. "I wouldn't worry too much about the expectations people may have about us. What matters is what we do today. If, in the future, any of us happened to play some role in the course of events, it would come out naturally, and it would be beyond ourselves."

Duncan laughed. "You've got the most common sense of any woman I've ever met."

"I hope this doesn't take any from the rest of womankind."

"No, no." Duncan smiled. "But you are very special, in many ways."

Erina acknowledged the compliment with a slight bow. "By the way, who is that woman on screen?"

Duncan turned to look at a monitor close to the bar. "Mmm . . . yeah, she's the First Equitarian—and she's not a woman, she's a *tilian*, a female *tilian*."

"You mean, Em-Rasinka?"

"The same."

Duncan and Erina started listening to Em-Rasinka's speech. She was talking about her early years, when she had begun spreading the Equity from planet to planet, before the Establishment was founded. There was strength in her words, and an evident charisma in her personality. Her greenish skin was brilliant and smooth, and her movements were somewhat different from those of a human. She had long, thick blue hair, though pronounced receding temples clearly exposed the front of her head. That was a sign of middle age in *tilian* females, a period that went well past their reproductive years.

"It looks like a recent recording," Erina said, keeping her gaze on the screen.

Duncan shook his head. "It's an old speech, ten years old, at least."

"Does she have a . . . mate?"

"She was married, more than a century ago. *Tilian* males don't live more than fifty years."

"Quite an intriguing race," Erina commented.

"*Tilian* females can live up to four hundred years," Duncan continued. "Sometimes they can even reach five hundred."

"I wonder what the reason is for such life-span asymmetry between sexes."

"I learned from a *scienscene* that it has to do with the ZB_2 cycle of their mother planet," Duncan explained. "It is a very cold place, with no plants to release *bioxyn*[137] from the ZB_2 produced by animals. Their own animals do this job, more specifically, all the female animals, after their reproductive stage is over. That's the reason females of any type live very long on their planet, including *tilian* females, of course."

"Intriguing. This may be related to the color of her skin." Erina looked at the monitor, which was exaggerating the green[138] brilliance of Em-Rasinka's skin.

Duncan nodded. "They process energy directly from light, like plants do. As a matter of fact, middle-aged and old *tilian* females need eat only once or twice a year, depending on how much light exposure their skins have."

---

137 *Bioxyn*: B_2.

138 The green color was produced by a chlorophyll-type substance present in the skin of mature female *tilians*.

" . . . *the equalization of all peoples into one people, of all cultures in the* Culture, *of all freedoms into the* Our Freedom." Erina nudged Duncan to keep listening to Em-Rasinka's speech. However much one might disagree with the content, the First Equitarian had a special gift for making her words provocative but appealing. "*Indeed, for with the* Equity *one lives, with the* Equity *one breathes, with the* Equity *one loves, with the Equity . . . One* Us *. . .* "

"What is that symbol on her forehead?" Erina asked.

"That's the emblem of the Equity," Duncan said, staring at it. It had a triangular layout with symmetrical marks on its sides. "She herself designed it and genetically imprinted it into her own skin."

"*—the Freedom of peace and tranquility, the Freedom of our beloved mother* Equity, *the Freedom of . . . the* Our Freedom."

"So here is where you loafers hide!"

Startled, both Erina and Duncan turned their attention from the monitor.

"What do you know? If it isn't Captain Foxso'l himself." Duncan stood up to exchange a clasp of forearms, as customary among friends. "Hey, have a seat, have a drink with us."

"With the lady's permission."

"You are most welcome," Erina said.

"Thank you."

A glamorous female, with features similar to Foxso'l's, passed by their table. Foxso'l grasped her gently by one arm. "Honey, when you have a break, can you bring me the same silver stuff my friend is drinking here? And, please, put a couple of ice cubes in it."

The waitress turned back with a pleasing look. "Schooner or regular?"

"Make it a schooner, honey."

"Okay," she sighed still smiling.

Foxso'l kept staring at her as she left.

"So, what a coincidence to see you here," Duncan commented.

"This ain't no coincidence, soldier-boy. We are leaving in less than an hour."

"Leaving?" Erina inquired.

"Yep. I've been asked to provide transportation to the *Intrepid* for you two guys."

"We understood the *Intrepid* was going to stop by here," Duncan said.

"Change of plans. She's been reassigned to a new mission, and SOC[139] prefers to keep its position as classified."

"So, you're taking us back to the *Intrepid*?" Erina asked.

"You've got it."

Duncan's brow furrowed. "Kind of strange that I haven't received any communication about this from Space Operations Command myself."

Foxso'l glanced at Erina with a jerk of his head. "It seems the boy needs a seven-star admiral to tell him what to do."

Erina smiled.

"No, no." Duncan grinned. "It's just that it's somewhat . . . unconventional?"

"That's the way things are. Every time your Royal Navy needs to have something done *unconventionally*, they resort to good old Foxso'l."

As he said that, the attractive dark-red waitress was back with the skipper's order.

"Here you are."

"You're very kind, sweetheart," Foxso'l said, and turned back to Duncan. "Say, I didn't expect to find such beauties that far from the center of the galaxy."

The waitress rolled her eyes with a slight smile and turned to attend to another table.

"So we are leaving in the *Angel Spark*, I guess."

---

139 Space Operations Command.

"Are you kidding me? I wouldn't dream of getting my ship closer than one *klawn*[140] to this station. It's not very safe goofing around these places."

"How are you planning to take us to the *Intrepid*, then?" Erina asked.

"I have a small shuttlecraft docked in here. We will use it to get to the *Angel Spark*. She's waiting for us somewhere in deep space."

"Back to your ship, Erina and I can give you a hand with the navigation."

Foxso'l glared at Duncan with unconvinced eyes. "Well . . . we'll see about that." He looked at the time readings on a monitor in the bar area, and then back to his friends.

"Are you ready, guys?"

Duncan turned to Erina; she nodded back. "I guess we are," Duncan said.

"Good." Foxso'l took the silver beverage, and poured it down his throat. "Ah . . . this stuff of yours is surprisingly good, kid."

"Why not another drink before leaving?" Duncan asked.

"Uh-uh, I'm driving tonight." Foxso'l got up briskly. "I gotta leave now. See you guys at pier two-forty-six, in, let's say . . . half an hour?"

Duncan turned to Erina again.

"It's fine with me," she said.

Foxso'l left a coin on the table. "I'll see you guys there, then."

73.

One hour after leaving Nereida, the *Blue Hawk* stopped its engines and started adjusting its course stealthily, by interacting with the gravitational fields of a star ahead and its planets. Foxso'l was an expert at *star-slinging* by the seat of his pants. The navigation had been uneventful until an alarm went off on the main control panel.

---

140 Analogous to 1.3 light years of our universe. The units, which dated back to the first days of interstellar travel in Foxso'l's world, and which had at one point become popular in many worlds, were rarely used in those days.

"What's that?" Duncan asked.

"I don't know," Foxso'l said, as he tried to make some sense out of the flood of bizarre readings his sensors were suddenly pouring forth. The anomaly seemed to be related to an unusual highly energized sub-particle field present in the area. Suddenly, the navigational display flashed white. A burst of radiation emitted by the star ahead had hit the vessel, disabling many of its systems.

Erina held on to the arms of her chair. "I don't like this."

"What is going on?" Duncan asked.

"Some funny activity from the local star." Foxso'l pointed angrily at the screen and checked his instruments again. "Hold on, everybody, a radiation shockwave is on our way."

"Let's start the main engines and get out of here," said Erina.

Before Foxso'l could take any action, the vessel was hit by a highly energized wave of particles. The ship cracked violently as a mirage of short-circuited beams of energy popped up all over the control panel. The gravitational system had been unable to compensate for the shock, and all the occupants on board were now semi-unconscious, strapped to their seats.

Duncan was the first one to recover consciousness. "Foxso'l, hey." He shook the skipper, who rapidly came around and checked his panel trying to assess the situation. Everything seemed to be very far from normal.

"Another wave on the way," warned Foxso'l with a slight grimace.

Duncan partially stood up, being restrained by the straps of his seat. "Let's blast the main engines out of here!"

"The main engines are dead, son. I'll try to find some shelter behind that planet," Foxso'l added, referring to a very close-by planet on the port side.

Using auxiliary propulsion, the ship veered quickly onto a parabolic trajectory. Five minutes later, when Foxso'l was about ready to have the ship skim over the upper layers of the planet's atmosphere, a strong energy vortex hurled the shuttle down towards the planet. Most systems onboard were not working any more.

Foxso'l spun the ship around using emergency rockets, in a desperate attempt to decrease the atmospheric penetration angle. A new energy shockwave now passed them by, but this time the *Blue Hawk* barely felt it. The planet seemed to have a narrow but powerful magnetic field enveloping it, capable of deflecting highly energized particles.

The shuttle began to pierce through the upper atmospheric layers at a speed considerably higher than what Foxso'l himself would have considered safe. "Hold on, everybody! I'll start the main emergency rocket."

A violent increment in the deceleration rate hit the ship like a brick. The internal gravitic system was definitively out of line. The quasi-parabolic trajectory the vessel was following produced additional Gs, which were now literally threatening to squash its occupants. Duncan started to come to the grim realization that neither he nor his companions were going to come out of the situation alive.

The surface of the planet was approaching fast. However, the rocket engine was starting to deliver more and more thrust as the vehicle got closer to the ground. It seemed that the lower atmosphere was very rich in some oxidizing gas, and the environmentally interactive rocket engine was making good use of that.

"Hold on, everybody!" Foxso'l howled.

As the remaining fuel was dumped, a parachute opened. The shuttle hit the ground safely—though not softly—shortly after that.

74.

Today: Time to be grateful; time to hope.

"There it is, behind those trees." Maliri pointed ahead and turned to her brother.

"Now I see it!" Agashu yelled.

"Let's take a look." Maliri ran off towards the intriguing object, followed by Agashu. As they got closer, they slowed down, finally stopping about thirty feet from . . . well, what was that?

"Wow, see the trail it left across the woods." A clear path had been blazed by the smoking contraption. The children stood there for a moment, gazing and wondering. There was no movement, no sound, nor was there anything special that seemed to pose any immediate threat. Slowly, Agashu approached the perfectly smooth polished surface in front of him. He finally extended a hand, bashfully.

"Don't touch it!"

"Why not?" Agashu frowned as he retracted his fingers with apprehension.

"I don't know, it's just that it looks like . . . it looks like the Star Carousel of the Prophecy," said Maliri, with a sense of respect and fear.

Agashu stepped back and took a walk around the object. "I don't know," he said, reappearing from the other side. "If it were the Star Carousel, it would have to have some door somewhere. But I don't see any door, or window. How could the *Ashuraii*[141] get in or out of it?"

"Maybe there is a door and we can't see it," said Maliri. "It *does* look like the Star Carousel. And these wiggling rainbows in the sky . . . "

Agashu looked up at the heavens. A splendid aurora borealis extended all over the firmament towards the horizon. It was impressive and remarkably beautiful, something nobody there had ever seen or heard of.

"Perhaps they expect us to open the Carousel for them, like a *yem*," he said. "Since they have no windows, they could be short of air."

Maliri nodded. "Why don't we try to open a hole in it?"

"Yeah." Agashu took a knife and began to apply its blade to the hull in front of him. "Good Ess,[142] this stuff is mighty hard."

"Let me try," said Maliri, taking the knife from her brother's hand. She pushed with all her strength against the surface without making a scratch.

---

141 The wise warriors.
142 Essray was the native word for God.

"Stop it." Agashu grabbed the knife from his sister. "See what you've done to my knife."

Maliri stared at the chewed blade in her brother's hand. "We couldn't even make a scratch on it." She gently touched the area she had been working on. Squatting down, she unearthed a medium-sized granite rock that was in front of her.

"What are you doing now?"

Using the stone, Maliri was now knocking on the silver-like shell. "If there are people inside, they could knock back at us and let us know they are in there." She stopped for a moment, putting her forehead ear—her singular ear—against the hull, but she could not hear anything. Unperturbed, Maliri resumed her knocking.

"Stop it! There is nobody inside. Stop it!" Agashu demanded, covering his ear against the racket.

"At least I'm doing something to get it open," Maliri snapped back.

Agashu stared at her impatiently. "I know," he added, softening his stance. "The whole mighty thing looks metallic. Why don't we melt a hole in it?"

"We'd have to go back to the Citadel for fire," Maliri said.

Agashu opened the purse he carried on one shoulder and took out two yellow stones.

"Fire-stones!" said Maliri.

"Yep, let's find a big log so we can start a fire underneath."

"One log won't be enough. We'll have to make a big fire to melt a hole. Let's gather lots of dry leaves and sticks and branches under the Carousel, right here, and then we'll set fire to them."

"But we may start a wood-fire," Agashu said with apprehension. "This is not the rain season."

"We'll put stones around it, like in the campfire of last summer," Maliri said. "There are lots of stones around."

"All right."

Soon, they had piled a heap of firewood on one side of the Carousel, carefully isolated from the grass by a circle of rocks. Kneeling down, Agashu started scraping his fire-stones against each other, until a small twig began to smoke. Agashu pulled back, and the whole pile was up in flames.

75.

A persistent noise finally made Duncan open his eyes. Foxso'l's image, banging on the control panel in frustration, pricked his disoriented senses. Slowly lifting his head, Duncan turned around to see Erina in her seat, still groggy. He unstrapped himself and approached her. "Erina . . . Erina . . . "

"What happened?" she muttered, her eyes still closed.

"Foxso'l managed to land. Everything's fine."

"Well, well, well, it was about time the kids woke up," Foxso'l interjected, intensely focused on his work.

"Where are we?" Erina asked.

"Somewhere on the surface of the second planet of this system." The instrument panel flickered on. "Yes!" Foxso'l blurted out.

Duncan pointed at a small screen. "What are those readings?"

"Atmospheric data and some other stuff," Foxso'l said, as he adjusted the intensity of one of the luminous displays. "So . . . let's see what we've got here: *bioxyn* twenty-seven percent, *catalyon* sixty-eight, *chrysosterion* about one percent . . . "

"*Chrysossetherion* . . . " Duncan corrected under his breath.

"And . . . well, a whole bunch of other gases we don't need to worry about."

"It sounds breathable to me," Erina said.

"Yeah, as long as we can get used to being in a ten-atmosphere environment."

"Ten atmospheres?" Duncan strained his eyes.

"I will pressurize the cabin gradually, so that our bodies can adapt to it."

"How long will that take?" Erina asked.

"Not to make it tough on us . . . one standard day."

"Why don't we just stay here until someone comes and rescues us?" Erina asked.

"It'd take a great deal of luck for anybody to find us here," Foxso'l said.

"What about the natives?" Duncan asked.

"We don't know if there are any natives," Foxso'l replied.

"But if there are, they would not necessarily be friendly. Even the Establishment might already have some presence in this place."

As they talked, Foxso'l's attention was growing ever more riveted on the control panel. There was a moment of silence.

"What's wrong?" Duncan finally asked.

"Something funny is going on out there. The external sensors show a sudden temperature rise." The external cameras were not working.

"What do you mean?"

"I mean a moment ago, the temperature gauge read sixty-five degrees, but now it shows two hundred and fifteen, and rising."

"There may be something wrong with it," Duncan said.

"I doubt it."

"Most systems on board weren't working well," Erina pointed out.

Foxso'l kept looking at the luminous dial, which was already up to two hundred and twenty. "Wait a minute," he said. "This is happening only on one side of the ship." A second indicator was showing only sixty-five degrees. Foxso'l tapped on it, not that the display could be influenced by the action of his finger.

"It's out of order, all right," Duncan said, pointing loosely at the instruments dashboard.

"Which of the two?" Foxso'l replied.

"Why don't we start equalizing pressures?" Erina asked, looking at Foxso'l. "You said you'd do it slowly. If the external temperature turns out to be too high, we'll soon find out, and then we would just dismiss our plans of leaving the vessel, at least for now."

"Officer's thinking, Ensign," Foxso'l declared with a satisfied expression.

"Yeah, the question is, what are we gonna do if the temperature *does* rise?" asked Duncan.

Foxso'l shook his head and moved to the rear of the cabin. There, he removed a panel and began opening the security valve, manually.

"What if . . . " Duncan insisted, as Foxso'l kept working on the pressurization sequence.

As a tenuous hiss began blowing inside the cabin, Foxso'l eased himself into the comfortably padded commanding seat. "We'll think about *what ifs* when we have a real one."

76.

"*Gureezai!*[143] What do you think you're doing?" said a soldier in silver armor. He had suddenly appeared from the woods, followed by two others, riding on some big animals.

"We are trying to melt open a hole to let out the people inside, Captain," Agashu said with child-like determination.

"Put that fire out on the double. You'll cook the people inside alive."

"I told you it wouldn't work," Agashu protested, turning to his sister.

"Tully, Maru, help the *gureezai* put this fire out," the captain commanded.

Leaving their saddles, the soldiers picked up some leafy branches and started raking dirt and dust on the fire. It took some effort, but eventually a smoky blotch of ashes was the only thing left.

Captain Ziku rode his *annay* around the intriguing artifact. Its surface looked unscathed. "Why do you say there is anybody inside?" he asked, turning to the children. "Did you find any door or window?"

"Don't you see, Captain? This is the Star Carousel, the Star

---

143 *Gureezai* is the plural of *gureez* and / or *gureeza*, the latter being equivalent to boy and girl, respectively, among the native inhabitants.

Carousel we've been waiting for."

The captain looked at Maliri gravely.

"The *gureeza* is perceptive, with my captain's permission," Tully interjected. "It does look like the Star Carousel of the Prophecy. And the mighty signs in the sky . . . " He gazed upwards with apprehension.

"We must go back to the Citadel at once and inform the Wise Elders about this," said Ziku, moving his *annay* away from the large flattened circular object.

"Yeah!" said Maliri. "Agashu and I will stay here guarding the Carousel."

"You *gureezai* are coming back to the Citadel with us."

"Oh, no, no, we don't wanna go back. The sun is still high," said Maliri, pouting her lips.

"You'll do as I say, *gureezai. Gureez* . . . " The captain pointed at Agashu. "You'll mount with Sergeant Maru, and the *gureeza*, with Private Tully."

77.

"Maybe it's too soon to say," Erina said, a few minutes after the pressurization of the cabin had begun. "But I don't feel any temperature increase." She was sitting close to the main air inlet, where she could feel a gentle stream of fresh air coming in from the outside.

"Hey, Foxso'l," Duncan called out. He was sitting by the control panel board. "Take a look at this."

The skipper stepped closer and gazed at the two temperature displays, now showing nearly the same readings, in the middle sixties. Foxso'l scratched his head. "Well, that's more like it," he said, shrugging his shoulders.

"Why don't we have some dinner?" Erina held out three food rations. "Afterwards we could try getting some sleep. I guess tomorrow will be a busy day."

Foxso'l sat down on the deck and leaned back on his hands in a relaxed manner, grinning at Duncan. "I'll never regret rescuing her from space."

"Want some juice?" Erina offered Foxso'l an already hydrated sachet.

"Sure do. Say," Foxso'l glanced at Duncan. "Are all earthly females as *nixy*[144] as your girlfriend?"

78.

The bodies of annays, *more specifically their torsos, are shaped like those of rhinos'. Their legs, four in all, are as long as horses' legs. Annays have flat large tails with long, skinny scales protruding from them, which resemble feathers. Wide necks emerge from their torsos. On top of them, large heads complete their bodies. The backs of their heads are similar to deer, with small horns on top with no spikes. These protrusions are slender and simple, with openings on their ends that function as nostrils. The faces of these animals end in a flat, horizontal snout, with a relatively small mouth beneath. A yellow ring that encircles three-quarters of their necks connects their multiple eardrums with the external world. [. . .]*

Annays are not rational creatures, but they are smart beasts. Their heads and necks are covered with a short feathery hide of different colors. Their torsos and legs are protected by shiny scales, which produce a wide variety of hues, as if they had been smeared with a thin film of oil. They are relatively light animals, by Realitas' standards. This fact, along with the low gravity of the planet, which is about one third of that on Realitas, allows annays to move with a graceful agility.

From Lieutenant Dahncion's tactical log.

---

144 *Nixy* conveyed the idea of nice, pretty, and bright, all together. Only applied to females, it was a trendy term in many worlds of the Realdom at that time, especially among young adults. Although that was not the case with Foxso'l anymore, the term had first surfaced on his home planet during his adolescent years.

Today: May it be them.

"Is everybody ready?"

Erina rubbed her head. "Except for this headache."

"You'll get used to these ten atmospheres," said Foxso'l, as he typed some instructions on his panel.

The main hatchway suddenly opened, and a fan of sunbeams darted inside the cabin. As the heavy gate slowly moved upwards, the scene ahead was gradually revealed. First they saw a green mantle with long and narrow shallow leaves, sprinkled with a morning dew. Behind it, they spotted bushes, also sprinkled with dew, and with winged tiny insects on their leaves, sipping the water droplets. Finally, an unexpected gathering appeared behind it all, backed by a forest, with soldiers riding on large animals, evocative of battle-ready knights.

"Interesting crowd," Erina muttered.

"Quite," Duncan added tensely. The pitches of their voices sounded different under the new environmental conditions.

"I sure hope these guys have nothing to do with the Establishment," Foxso'l said.

About five hundred individuals were gathered around the shuttle. The assembly looked more like an army than a welcome committee. Ahead of the ranks, here and there, some were mounted on large animals, which had metallic plates covering most of their bodies and embellished helmets topping their heads. Two riders, holding military standards, were very close to the ship's gate.

"Look at the sky," Duncan said as the hatch was still opening.

"It seems that the solar storm that brought us here is still pretty active," Erina commented.

Duncan took the initiative and stepped down from the vessel, immediately followed by Foxso'l and Erina. They were armed, but they kept their guns on their belts.

One of the riders approached them. His armor looked different from the others': it had a copper shine, unlike the silvery plates the rest were wearing. He stopped in front of the three visitors and took off his helmet, holding it under one arm. "Are ye from the stars?"

"We are," answered Duncan.

"Our humble welcome to the *Ashuraii*," the rider said with a respectful reverence.

Duncan did not understand the meaning of the last word. "We're most honored to be received by this mighty army," he stated confidently. "My name is Dahncion, and these," Duncan moved aside, "are Erina and Foxso'l."

"We are most honored to learn the names of the *Ashuraii*," said the same soldier.

"And, what's the name of he who welcomes us?" Duncan asked.

"I'm General Xanada. We've been assigned by the High Council to escort ye to the Citadel, if this pleaseth thee—and ye," he added, addressing Foxso'l and Erina.

"It pleases us, greatly," Duncan asserted.

General Xanada made a very respectful bow. "Three *annays* will take ye to the village along with us."

Duncan looked at his two companions.

"That's fine with us," Foxso'l said, nervously tensing his jaw as he nodded.

Xanada bowed again and ordered the three *annays* to be brought forward. Leather-like ladders hung from their saddles halfway to the ground. Duncan was the first to mount; Foxso'l and Erina followed.

Crossing amidst the ranks, General Xanada moved back. The three *annays* carrying the *Ashuraii* followed the general mechanically. It seemed that the Realitian guests would not have much to worry about during the ride. The animals knew what they had to do.

The general raised an arm, and one soldier sounded a horn. All *annays* lifted their forelegs, standing on their rear legs. From the

An unexpected gathering appeared behind it all, with soldiers riding
on large animals, evocative of battle-ready knights.

sides of all their saddles, long wide sails were deployed.[145] The dense morning breeze filled the sails swiftly.

Putting their forelegs back on the ground, the *annays* started to ride, carried by the wind across the steep northern grasslands. None of the animals was truly flying, although each gallop was about one hundred feet long. Xanada's cavalry quickly achieved a considerable speed. The surrounding vegetation was a bright—nearly metallic— light blue and green; it was very different from any flora of Earth or any other planet Duncan had already visited. Duncan's initial tension was relaxing with the beauty of the forest, and with the way they had been treated so far. But he did not have much time to think; after a five-minute ride, a colossal stone fortification, crowned by three needle-like towers, appeared behind a hill.

79.

Today: Faith.

"It's happening again." Duncan sunk his elbows in the muggy grass and rested his eyes on the mountains behind the lake. Only their peaks were snowy; their bases shone blue with the midday sun of an early autumn. Beyond the lake, the walls of the fortified city loomed over the foliage, following the wavy terrain of the surrounding hills.

"What do you mean?" asked Erina.

"First Dahncion, now the *Ashuraii* . . . " Duncan tossed a flat pebble, which skipped three times along the surface before sinking into the lake.

"Our arrival in a shuttle from space is something they don't quite see every day," Erina said.

"Yes, I suppose that's true. But once more, I'm about to get involved in a local conflict—that is, all of us. What gives us the

---

145 They hung on poles also deployed from the sides of the saddles, perpendicular to the bodies of the animals and at a small angle with respect to a horizontal plane.

right to meddle in such matters? Once more, people could get hurt, some may even die . . ."

"Well." Erina sighed. "You didn't promise we would accompany them on their expedition. You told them that perhaps we were not the *Ashuraii* they were waiting for. 'We are people of good will who have come to watch your progress.' That was a wise statement—they seemed to have taken it pretty well. And it gives us enough leeway to do whatever we consider best."

Duncan slid his hands on the blue grass behind his back.

"The barbecue is almost ready!"

Erina and Duncan turned around. Juicy *litics* were roasting over a few stones surrounded by red embers, all under the master supervision of Captain Foxso'l.

Duncan stood up and reached one hand towards Erina. "Let's have some lunch."

"How do you like it?" Foxso'l pinched one of the roasting *litics*, now dripping its reddish-blue *blavia*.

"How about well done?" Duncan asked as he got closer.

"You'll have to wait for that. What about the lady?"

"Medium rare."

Foxso'l pinched one of the fleshy roots with a sharpened stick. Nodding, he cut the *litic* in two halves with his jack-knife. "Here you are," he said, extending a greasy piece of meat in his bare hands.

Erina responded with a hesitant smile.

"Come on, grab it," Foxso'l added.

Erina grinned, trying to find some way to hold the meat without getting too soiled.

"Did you kids fill the canteens at the lake?" Foxso'l asked.

"Here they are." Duncan unhitched them from his belt and placed them on the grass.

"Good." Bending over the fire, Foxso'l cut another roasting root. "I guess this one might be ready for you." He pinched the piece of meat with his jack-knife and tossed it over to Duncan, who caught it in the air. "Is it burnt enough?"

"It's fine," Duncan said, shifting the hot piece of meat from one hand to the other.

Picking a medium-rare root for himself, Foxso'l continued, "So, when are we leaving?"

"Where?" Duncan inquired.

"You know, on that expedition." Foxso'l waved his jack-knife.

Duncan looked at Erina. "We don't have to go."

"What do you mean?" Foxso'l seasoned his meat with some spices he had gotten in the marketplace at the Citadel.

"For one thing, we might find some trouble in that city they talked about."

"So?"

"So, we shouldn't mess with other people's affairs."

"What's gotten into the soldier-boy?" Foxso'l said, looking at Erina, his mouth full of food. "These guys are good fellows. They are treating us pretty well. They could be good allies of the Realdom, you know."

"Precisely because they *are* a good people, they will understand if we just stay right here, out of trouble."

With a big chunk of *litic* sticking out of opposite sides of a clenched fist, Foxso'l grabbed one end of the meat with his front teeth. Gaucho-like, he spun the blade of the jack-knife he held in his other hand, slicing off a succulent piece. "Let me tell you somethin': I wouldn't stay in this same spot much longer. The entire quadrant is under Establishment surveillance, and we—at least I—don't want to make it too easy for them to find us. That Citadel," Foxso'l waved his jackknife towards the castle, "is too close to the crash site, and it's the first place an enemy patrol would search."

"What if our people were to find us first?" Duncan replied. "I'm sure they're looking for us."

Foxso'l stuffed his mouth with more *litic* and continued. "I don't think they could find us unless they—and we—are extremely lucky. Besides, we have short-range comm equipment if they came within range."

"If it is so difficult for the Realdom to find us, why wouldn't it be the same for the Establishment?" Duncan asked.

"Are you implying we're stranded here for good?" asked Erina.

"Not at all." Foxso'l grinned unconvincingly. "I'm sure somebody will find us pretty soon. But we don't know who's gonna find us first. And if we wanna keep outta the Establishment's prying eyes, the first thing we oughta do is get us outta here."

"This is not the *Angel Spark* that you can go hiding from asteroid to asteroid," Duncan pointed out acidly. "Besides, Erina and I are part of Realitas' Navy, and we're supposed to follow certain procedures in situations like this. In a crash event, we should stay as close as possible to the crash site."

"Have those stripes numbed your wits, son?" Foxso'l waved at Duncan's new lieutenant insignias. "I've told you already: our Establishment friends might find us first, and none of your regulations will help us then."

"Same regulations that apply to you for this operation." Duncan paused, realizing the argument was taking him down a confrontational path he did not want to follow. "This crash-landing of ours does not change anything."

"Sure, and that's why I'm telling you that we should get outta here—I can make it an order if it fits you better."

"You don't have the authority," Duncan muttered with a smirk.

Foxso'l looked straight at him. "According to your regulations, I was in charge. And our crash-landing doesn't change anything, as you just said." He picked up a wildflower and quickly threw it away with frustration. "Why don't we just sit down for a moment while we finish this gourmet barbecue nobody has thanked me for yet?"

"It was fantastic, Fox'," added Erina.

"Thank you." Foxso'l rested a friendly hand on Duncan's shoulder. "Listen, these people have been very good to us. Sure, they also have ideas about us, but should we be a bunch of spoilers? Let's go with them on their expedition. Everything will turn out right, you'll see, and we'll win them over to our side."

"I'm sorry, Fox'," Duncan responded, "but you've heard them. They are expecting to engage in battle with the people of that Holy City they mentioned, and if we happen to be with them, we may get involved in something we shouldn't."

"Don't you see? The Holy City, the would-be battle, the expedition itself: they are all part of their dreams, their legends. Let's give 'em the chance to live their dreams. They've just asked us to accompany them—that's all they've asked from us."

Duncan stood up, his eyes fixed on the lake. He shook his head and clicked his tongue. "Give me a couple of days to think it over," he added, turning around.

"Sure. Say, another juicy piece of meat?"

80.

Today: Optimism.

"How is Heaven?" asked Maliri, as she picked up a flower from one side of the trail.

Duncan smiled: "I don't know. I'm not from Heaven."

"But you came down from the sky, in the Star Carousel," replied his little companion.

"That's true, but Heaven is far beyond the stars."

"And beyond the moon?"[146]

"Yes."

"And beyond the sun too?"

"Yep."

The little *gureeza* kept staring at Duncan in awe. Running ahead, she started walking backwards in front of Duncan. "How can Essray see us all from that far off?"

"Well, I guess He knows everything," Duncan said.

"Of course He does," Agashu said. "He's everywhere."

For a moment, Maliri pondered the meaning of that, but she

---

146 The planet had one satellite, relatively large compared to the planet.

quickly came down to a more tangible question. "How far away are the stars?"

"Far, far away," said Duncan.

"But *how* far?"

"Very far."

"Like twice the height of the lake mountains?" Maliri asked.

"Much more than that."

"But how much?"

"Well, let's say that the closest star is up in the sky by more than one million, million times the height of the tallest mountain in the world."

The *gureeza* did not understand the meaning of *million*, so she readily accepted the distance to be beyond her grasping.

"The Star Carousel must fly very fast, then," Agashu concluded.

"It sure does." And before waiting for the next question, Duncan completed the idea. "It could go from here to the Citadel faster than lightning."

"Hey!" Maliri yelled. "There is the Star Carousel."

Beyond the thick foliage, the circular shape of the spacecraft was now visible. Both *gureezai* ran towards it. Duncan soon caught up with them.

After walking around the vessel checking that everything was unchanged, Duncan activated the opening sequence on a built-in panel in the front of the craft. The children watched as the main gate opened, mouths agape.

"You, kids, stay here." Duncan stepped into the vessel. He was there to pick up a few small instruments that might turn out to be helpful if they had to stay on the planet for a while. An emergency short-range communicator and a distress signal emitter would be particularly useful in case they picked up some friendly vessel traveling near the system.

He soon located the distress-signal device, which was in seemingly good working condition. But finding the emergency communicator was not as easy. Duncan searched all over the vessel, especially around the area where Foxso'l had been making repairs. While he was doing that, he checked a spare-parts compartment.

There he found a box filled with weapons that looked like hand grenades. He wavered for a moment, but finally grabbed the box. In doing that, an instrument fell from the bottom of the compartment: it was the emergency communicator. Duncan picked it up and turned back to the box. Hesitantly, he took a few grenades from inside and put them in a backpack he had grabbed from under his seat. He tried to turn on the emergency communicator, but it seemed to have some malfunction.

As he struggled to get it to work, Duncan caught a glimpse of the two *gureezai*, beyond the open hatchway, staring enthralled at what they could see of the ship's cabin.

"Okay, pop on in. But don't touch anything."

Agashu leapt inside first, and then helped his sister to come onboard. At first, they kept staring at everything at a prudent distance, but after a few minutes, the temptation to start fiddling with the instruments became too strong to resist. Duncan decided that it was time to return to the Citadel, where he could take a better look at the communicator.

"All right, time to go back home."

"Are we coming back tomorrow?" asked Maliri.

"Maybe."

"Please?" the children begged.

Duncan smiled and jumped off the vessel. "We gotta go home."

"Can we help you carry those gizmos?" asked Agashu, looking at the equipment that stuck out of Duncan's backpack.

"I can handle them, thank you."

"But they look very heavy," the *gureez* pointed out.

"That's why you can't carry them. They're too heavy for you."

After walking through the woods on rather flat terrain, they began to climb a hill. At the top, the Citadel appeared ahead, behind another elevation they still had to contend with.

"There's the Citadel!" Maliri yelled, and the two *gureezai* started running downhill.

"Hey! Kids—*gureezai*—come back here, right now."

They both stopped and turned around. "But we can run down the hill and wait for you in the glen," Maliri explained.

"No, no, no. You stay beside me; that was the agreement with your mom, remember?"

They waited, with the predictable protesting grimaces.

As soon as they started down the slope together, a warm thin fog began sweeping above their heads.

"Can we go with you on the Big Expedition?" asked Maliri.

"I think you are still too young for that."

"We're not," replied Agashu. "Last summer we climbed the big mountain of the lake—and we did it alone."

"Yes, but going on this expedition is much, much harder than climbing any mountain—and far more dangerous."

"But we want to go with you," Maliri said. "We want to fight alongside the *Ashuraii*."

Duncan smiled. "And who are the *Ashuraii*?"

"You are the *Ashuraii*."

"Do you mean . . . me?" asked Duncan.

"Yes, and the others who came in the Star Carousel."

"I see."

"So, will you let us go with you?" insisted Maliri. "I know how to cook very well. I could cook for you—and Agashu: he can fight."

"Yeah," added the *gureez*, with an aggressive look that inspired no fear.

"So you can," said Duncan with a forced frown and a brief smile. Maliri was staring at him with wonder. Looking at those eyes, Duncan decided not to foster false expectations. "You two are very good *gureezai*, and d'you know something? The three passengers of the Star Carousel will stay in the Citadel, guarding and helping you all the time, while the rest go on the Big Expedition."

"Why?" asked Maliri, indignant. "You are an *Ashury*, you ought to go."

"Well, maybe we're not the *Ashuraii* you are waiting for. They will surely come after us."

"No," said Agashu, "because the seven-day sign in the sky has already come and gone. And you are the only ones who came in the Star Carousel. So, you *are* the *Ashuraii*."

Duncan began to find the stubborn children's logic a bit troublesome.

"Yes, and you are the ones who will save us all, so you must go," Maliri added in a firm tone.

"So we will save you all," said Duncan rather casually. Even if he did not take it too seriously, the comment did cause him *déjà vu*.

"Didn't the angels of the stars tell you that you were to save the entire world?" Agashu asked.

Duncan smiled with a shake of his head. "Oh, yes, this, they did tell me . . . "

"You see, you see? You are an *Ashury*."

Duncan chortled.

"Don't you believe in the words of the angels?" Maliri asked, with a look of concern in her eyes.

"Of course I do. I do believe in them."

"So if they've told you that *you* are an *Ashury*, why aren't you going on the Big Expedition?"

"I believe in the angels of the sky, but you don't have to believe I'm an *Ashury*," Duncan replied.

"But I do. The Prophecy says so. . . " Suddenly, Maliri widened her eyes with a gaze of terrible suspicion. "Don't you believe in the Prophecy?" she asked, almost in a whisper.

The conversation was taking too many undesirable twists, and Duncan was now wondering how he could have let it go that far. "The Prophecy is a very serious matter, Maliri. Like you, I do believe in the *Ashuraii* who will save you all. And I believe they are strong, wise people who are coming from beyond the stars. They will surely fight bravely, and—"

"But you've just said the angels of the stars already told you that *you* were to save the world," interrupted Maliri, pointing at him.

"True, but it could have been a dream. Don't you ever dream?"

"Yeah," Maliri grumbled, and walked away noticeably disappointed.

Duncan's effort to avoid giving the *gureezai* false expectations had caused many unintended side effects. In particular, Agashu resented the "dream" comment, and both *gureezai* were clearly disillusioned, and even angry, with the reluctant "*Ashury.*"

"Hmm, this fog is getting very thick. I'd better check my compass." Once more, Duncan tried to change the subject, at least, with the remaining child.

"What's a compass?" asked Agashu.

"It's a magic box that tells you where to find the direction to the Citadel."

"We don't need a compass for that," the *gureez* replied. "We already know the Citadel is right beyond the hill."

"With all this fog, we can't be sure of anything," Duncan commented.

"Yes, we can," Agashu said. "We have seen the Citadel beyond this hill once. It was there, and that was not a dream. No doubt it's still there, waiting for us, right on the other side."

The *gureez* broke off running ahead and met with his sister. They briefly looked back at Duncan, disapprovingly, but this time he did not call them back.

Duncan was left alone, pondering. That last remark from a little gureez had struck some slumbering nerve within himself. True, he had many doubts, but it was also true that right before leaving Earth on the day he had accepted his mission—even if for an instant—he had seen his future so clearly. Had he not had, at that crucial moment, a special insight into his destiny, his life, his vocation?

What if now he were to say "yes" to all that again? What if he would dare move forward and put away—once and for all—the fog of his fickleness, the darkness of his fears?

"Not at all easy . . . " Duncan thought. Yet his tension had been replaced by a dawning peace. For, while he pondered, his personal doubts had weakened and dissipated.

81.

Today: Be helpful.

"Company, halt." Riding on his *annay*, General Xanada detached from the formation and stopped in front of the *Ashuraii*. "Aytana's dwelling is within those woods. You must follow the trail that starts beyond that rock." Xanada pointed towards the forest with his sword. "I will detail three warriors to escort you to her place."

"Thanks, General," Foxso'l said, as Duncan saluted.

Three Zureedaii stepped forward. "My name is Captain Ziku," one said, "and these are Sergeant Maru and Private Tully."

"Captain Foxso'l, Ensign Erina," Duncan introduced his friends.

"Nice to see you again, Tully," said Erina to the soldier, recognizing him as the same that had escorted them to the Citadel the day they had first made contact with the Zureeday people.

"I'm honored, ma'am."

"Are you ready?" asked Ziku.

"Yes, Captain," Duncan said.

As three troopers held the reins of their *annays*, the three Realitians dismounted, and followed Ziku's detail into the woods. It was a lush forest, but passable. Very tall trees, similar to conifers, rose over five hundred feet high. The locals called them *zungais*. Their leaves were bright blue, like their stems and branches, and their trunks displayed long bright yellow crevices. Their golden beauty had a strong connection to the *chrysossetherion*[147] present in the atmosphere.

---

147 Through a dynamical process that involves weak magnetic links, *zungais* incorporate atoms of *chrysossetherion* in their own molecular structure, even when

The forest sounded full of life, although it was hard to spot any particular creature. Captain Ziku and Sergeant Maru were walking ahead, followed by Foxso'l, Erina, Duncan, and Private Tully. The narrow trail kept the group in a single row.

"Why does this Aytana live here?" asked Duncan, turning around. "I mean, away from the Citadel."

"She's not of our people," answered Tully. "She is the last of the Ancient Ones."

"Ancient Ones?"

Tully nodded. "The Old Sages that ruled the world before Essray made us."

"Do you mean that some other people, different from you, also live here?"

"In the ancient times, yes. Very different people. They had three eyes—one of them in their foreheads, where we have our ear. Their legs were different and stronger than ours, and they had wings. You'll see Aytana when we get to her cottage."

"What happened to them?"

"Essray took them to Heaven because they were very good. They were the builders of the Holy City."

"So one day they flew up into the sky in big flying houses like the Star Carousel?" Erina inquired with condescending interest.

"Oh, no. I've told you: Essray took them up right into Heaven." Erina nodded.

"Why did Aytana stay here?" Duncan asked.

"To speak with the *Ashuraii*, to give them the key to the entire Holy City."

"It will be quite interesting to talk to her," Erina said.

After a one-hour walk, they found themselves at a wide, shallow stream. According to Captain Ziku, the stream meant they were very close to their destination.

---

chrysossetherion is largely an inert gas. The process has a connection to the extreme longevity of these trees, which can live up to more than one hundred thousand years.

Shortly after that, Maru noticed something ahead. "My captain, over there."

Captain Ziku raised his head. A structure could be spotted in the midst of the vegetation.

"Is that what we are looking for?" Foxso'l asked.

"Yes, Captain," answered Ziku. "It's the only dwelling place in this forest."

A few yards ahead, they came to a brown[148] *zungai* cottage. It was small and rustic. A dense white smoke was coming from a chimney on top of its slanted roof. The only other distinctive features were two small windows hung with colorful drapes, and a small door on one side.

"Excuse me." Tully turned to Duncan. "I must get to the captain."

"Certainly."

Private Tully hurried to join Ziku and Maru.

"What do you think of this story?" Duncan asked Erina, in a discreet tone.

"I don't know. It's mixed up with legend."

"So it would seem, but what if an advanced civilization *did* thrive here? This Aytana might be the key to help us find some way off this planet."

Erina pointed at the cottage. "That certainly does not look like any advanced space vehicle to me."

According to the custom of his people, Captain Ziku clapped his hands repeatedly to call the attention of whoever dwelt in the cottage.

"Maybe nobody is at home," said Foxso'l.

Ziku shook his head and pointed at the chimney, which was belching thick smoke.

---

148 Most (not all) of the *chrysossetherion* present in *zungai* wood is released shortly after a tree dies. Dry *zungai* timber usually adopts a brown tone, with a peculiar brilliance due to the residual *chrysossetherion* left in the wood.

The group had been waiting for about fifteen minutes when the captain clapped his hands once more. "*Donya*[149] Aytana, *Donya* Aytana."

"Excuse me, my Captain."

Ziku turned around.

"I couldn't find any footprints or trails," Tully said.

"Strange." Ziku rubbed both the top of his ear and his forehead. "We'll enter the cottage," he decided and unsheathed his sword.

Maru and Tully checked their weapons. Captain Ziku tried to see through one of the windows, but the drapes were too thick. The door had no lock or knob. Approaching it, he slowly opened it with the tip of his sword.

A small living room appeared, rustic and rather dark. Followed by the scouting party, Ziku walked in. In one corner, some embers were glowing in a hearth. To one side of the fireplace, an old copper pot hung from a hook. Next to a window, a door, barely ajar, connected to another room.

"Hey, there is someone inside there," Foxso'l whispered, the tips of his fingers clinging to the rim of the cracked door.

Ziku approached him and glanced respectfully through the narrow opening. He knocked on the door. "*Donya* Aytana, may we come in?"

"Yes," an elderly female voice replied. "Come on in, come on in." The six visitors stepped into the room, one after the other.

"My, my, my. Good morning, good morning." The female was lying on a wooden couch, her body covered with many blankets.

"*Donya* Aytana," Ziku said and waved a hand to his right. "With us are Captain Foxso'l . . . "

"*Donya*."

"Lieutenant Dahncion, Ensign Erina . . . " They bowed their heads slightly.

" . . . and your servant, Captain Ziku, with my soldiers Sergeant

---

149 A courteous title commonly used when referring to prestigious elderly females.

Maru and Private Tully." The three Zureedaii stood at attention, deferentially.

A few tears fell from Aytana's eyes.

Ziku bowed reverently. "We are under your roof with the *Ashur-aii, Donya* Aytana."

"I know, I know."

"How do you know?" Duncan asked with annoyance, though he softened his tone as he spoke.

"It's not too hard to tell you apart from the Zureedaii, even for my old weary eyes." Aytana wiped her tears away using the edges of her sheets.

"Captain Ziku said perhaps you wanted to talk to us," Foxso'l added.

Aytana remained silent for a moment. She looked deeply moved by what was transpiring in her house. "Yes, yes, so many things to speak, so many . . . "

No one spoke for about a minute.

"Yes, yes," Aytana resumed, composing her voice. "But first things first. I have something for you, something I kept for so many centuries, so many . . . " She sighed. "But I don't feel very strong today. So if I'd ask you to pick it up for yourselves . . . "

"Certainly," Duncan said.

"Please, in the other room, to the left of the fireplace. There you'll see a red stone, amidst the stones of the hearth arch. Pull it out, and you will find something for yourselves."

Duncan raised his eyes. "You may want to converse with *Donya* Aytana." Erina nodded.

Foxso'l and Duncan immediately left the room.

82.

"How long have you lived here?" Erina asked, kneeling down by the bed.

Aytana's eyes showed deep emotion. "All my life, almost."

"We heard you belong to an ancient civilization that lived in this world before the Zureedaii."

"Yes, yes, young lady, but that was a long, long time ago."

"It is said that your people were very advanced, as well as wise."

"Not all of us." Aytana gave a candid giggle.

Erina paused and began arranging the rim of the blankets in front of her. Then Foxso'l appeared from the living room. He caught Erina's eye, summoning her to the other room with a jerk of his head.

Erina nodded. "Excuse me, *Donya* Aytana, I'll be back in a moment."

The venerable female remained silent, looking at the ceiling with a face full of joy.

Stepping into the living room, Erina found Duncan holding a small, intriguing device. It was difficult to tell what kind of material it was made of. It was smooth, barely translucent, and it had the shape of two pyramids joined by their bases. Erina approached it with a scanner.

A blipping came from the object, followed by a pulsating red radiance emitting from all its faces. A fan of light flashed along the plane that joined the two pyramids. The light fan split up into two luminous cones that moved away from each other, until collapsing into two laser-like beams on the top and bottom apexes of the pyramids.

The device went inert again.

"Wow," muttered Duncan, looking in awe at the object. He had laid it on a table when it became active.

"What the heck is this?" Foxso'l asked.

"This is precisely what we are going to ask Aytana right now," Erina said excitedly.

But no sooner she had said that, another voice, grave and reverential, came from behind them.

"My regrets, *Ashuraii*." The three Realitians turned around. Tully was standing solemnly at the door to Aytana's room, holding one hand to his chest. "*Donya* Aytana is no longer amongst us."

"What?" Erina exclaimed in frustration.

"She has just passed away."

83.

Today: Never complain.

"Do you want some water?"

Duncan looked hesitantly at the soldier who was offering him his canteen. "I can't accept your share." By now, water ratios had grown low for everybody.

"Don't you worry about me," Tully asserted. "We Zureedaii need less water than you *Ashuraii*. I'd be very glad to share mine with you."

Duncan stared pointedly at Tully and reluctantly took the canteen.

"Have some more," Tully invited.

"That's enough for now, thank you."

"Do you want some, Miss Erina?"

"No, thank you, Tully."

"You look tired."

"I'm tired." She nodded. "But not thirsty."

Tully put his canteen in his backpack again.

They had already spent five days in the desert, and there were no signs of any change in the landscape—or of any clouds in the sky. Wearied and not very talkative, Foxso'l was riding alongside Duncan on his *annay*.

"I spent some time last night playing with that thing we got in the cottage," he eventually said, switching reins from one hand to the other.

Duncan moved an arm back to his backpack, reaching for the pyramidal device. "So you did?"

"Did you find out anything new?" asked Erina.

"Nope. I couldn't even get the darn thing to turn on again, like at the cottage. We may find out more about it when we get to that Holy City."

"If we don't find water soon, we won't get anywhere," Duncan remarked.

"Just a couple of days and we'll be out of this wilderness." Foxso'l shrugged his shoulders.

"Sure." Duncan glanced at Erina. She looked lost in thought, with her eyes roving over the horizon. "Anything new?"

Erina did not answer.

"Erina?"

"Birds," she finally said, "far above the skyline. And where there are birds, there might be water."

Duncan focused his eyes ahead, moving up slightly on his *annay*. "Yeah, I can see them too."

"Well, don't just stay there," Foxso'l said. "Let's go tell Xanada."

"Excuse us, General." To his right, Xanada found the three Ashuraii ridding alongside.

"Dahncion-*Ashury*."

"Sir, Erina has spotted birds hovering above the horizon, over there." Duncan pointed towards his left. "There may be water nearby."

"The *Ashury* is wise," Colonel Azatu, Xanada's second-in-command, remarked.

"How long until sunset?" Xanada asked.

"Less than two hours, my General."

"Very well. We will spend the night there, whether there is water or not. Pass on the command."

"Yes, my General."

The command was passed, and the whole army started heading towards the chosen ground. After an hour of marching, they encountered a stony landscape. The terrain was mostly flat and gritty, and yet large flocks of birds were soaring above for no apparent reason.

As the army marched on, a scouting patrol found a natural trail cut in the stone, with a small downward slope. Captain Mitzibu, the leader of the scouting patrol, was soon reporting his findings.

"Take ten of our soldiers and check what is up that trail," Colonel Azatu instructed him. Riding their *annays* around a corner, the party headed down the rocky trail.

"Halt," Xanada commanded. A horn was blown with the corresponding signal, and the voices of all captains began to echo back discordantly with the same command repeated to their divisions.

"It looks like the bed of an ancient river," Erina commented.

"The stony trail?" Duncan said.

"Uh-huh."

"That would not be good news," Duncan pointed out.

Erina turned around.

"It would mean there is no water down there," Duncan explained.

"Not necessarily."

"Hey, they're back already," said Foxso'l. The scouting party was approaching, riding very fast.

"Captain Mitzibu reporting, my General."

"Report."

"There is plenty of water below, my General sir. It's like a big pond in a rocky den."

Erina looked pointedly at Duncan with a raised eyebrow.

Moving in a single column, the army proceeded down the trail. It grew steeper as it progressed downward. On either side, barriers of stone rose to the sky, where countless birds kept soaring quietly. As the three Realitians rode on, the walls of rock on their right sloped down until a large pond, surrounded by thick vegetation, appeared before them. A lush waterfall was pouring down with a refreshing sound, its water seemingly flowing right out of the rock.

"Most likely a subterranean river," Erina remarked.

"Wow," uttered Duncan, overcome by the beauty of the view, which seemed magnified by the hardships of the past week.

"Don't you think we should go ahead and take a better look at the area?" Erina asked.

Duncan blinked, reluctantly looking away from the comforting sight. Holding onto the reins of his *annay*, he turned to Foxso'l.

The skipper was riding casually, his hat covering his eyes. "I'm officially on vacation."

84.

Today: Time to ponder.

Though the planet's atmosphere was too dense to have a sky packed with stars, the limpid skies of the Iazyrra Desert made for the starriest scene possible on the planet, each star twinkling intensely with a singular beauty. The waxing moon was beginning to rise behind some stony hills, dimming the humble glamour of the stars. Its relative size was three to four times larger than a rising moon on Earth, and its color was a mixture of red and magenta.[150] Tully was watching it all from his post, warming himself by the fire he was keeping—one of the main duties of his watch.

In about one hour, the bugler would call reveille, and Tully's watch, the last of the night, would be over. It had been a pleasant night for him, despite having been on duty.

Turning away from the fire, Tully looked to his right. A human silhouette was approaching in his direction from the encampment.

"Morning."

"Good morning. Up early today."

"Sort of," Duncan said, with his eyes barely open. "How's your watch going?"

"Good."

Duncan nodded and yawned, making some lazy effort to cover his mouth. On reaching the pond, he touched the surface rather

---

150 Although it looked bigger than our Moon, the dense atmosphere dimmed its luminescence. Still, it was brighter than our satellite.

apprehensively. The water was rather cold, but still a luxury, after nearly a week of exposure to the hot dry dessert. Duncan's skin was deeply tanned with a soft golden-blue hue bestowed by the peculiar composition of the atmosphere.

Duncan strolled around the crystalline pond towards the waterfall, and started washing his face in the spray. As the chill of the water woke him up, a strange glimmer caught his attention. He first thought it was a reflection from the campfire on the cascade, but as he continued to look, he noticed something shining behind the liquid curtain in front of him.

After some hesitation, Duncan stepped into the fresh stream, which glimmered with the intense moonlight. Moving from one slippery rock to the next, it took him five frigid seconds to cross the lush waterfall. Once he was on the other side, the sound of the water turned hollow.

The spot where Duncan was now standing was deeply carved into the rock. A green luminescence was coming forth from a small hole in the back of the hollow space. The glimmering was steady and soft. It did not look like fire; neither smoke nor heat seemed to be emanating from the opening. Duncan knelt on the ground, and started looking down through the opening on the rock. A narrow tunnel appeared to be going down at a steep angle. Its polished granite walls emanated a gentle phosphorescence generated by billions of microscopic lichens adhered to it.

Unexpectedly, the ground yielded, and Duncan was falling down the slippery, stony shaft. He screamed, to no avail, as he slid down faster and faster. In an instant, all had become completely dark. Duncan tried pressing his forearms against the slick walls in a useless attempt to break the fall.

The shaft suddenly ended, and Duncan found himself airborne. The unsettling sensation of being in the air for too long a time to hope for a safe landing struck him. Once again in less than a month, he experienced the sensation of being about to die. Many things crossed his mind in the never-ending moments he spent in the dark vacuum.

Splashing backside-down into what appeared to be a subterranean pond, Duncan plunged down deep, but soon he was back to the surface gasping for air. Stunned by the fall and surrounded by total darkness, he started swimming, panicked, without going in any particular direction.

As he moved his arms, Duncan felt the rim of the flashlight he carried on his belt. He immediately unhooked it and turned it on. He was inside a large rocky chamber. The pond spanned wall to wall. However, a small beach was discernible a few yards ahead. Duncan began swimming towards it.

No sooner had he started than a strong current took hold of his legs, pulling him down. He was now fighting desperately trying to reach back to the surface, but kept going relentlessly down.

As he ran out of hope, Duncan was suddenly jettisoned out into a very high waterfall flowing from the cave. As he fell, his eyes caught a glimpse of the moon shining on another small lake that appeared at a disturbing distance below. He screamed—again in vain—until splashing into the pond.

Fortunately, the lake was deep enough to break his fall safely. The dense and heavy atmosphere had helped slow down his falling rate, saving him from a mortal splash. Now Duncan was back up at the surface. He looked around, gasping for air, and then started swimming towards one side.

Nervously, Duncan jumped out of the water and dropped flat on the ground. He lay there for about five minutes. Kneeling down on the grass, he finally began looking at the waterfall from where he had just fallen. He remained staring at it for a while, trying to make some sense out of what had just happened. The sound of the falls was very loud, and the fresh smell of beating water, pervasive. High above the scene, a tenuous reflection of the campfire glowed dimly on top of the cliff.

Xanada's camp was more than five hundred feet above the lake.

"Hey, up there!" Duncan yelled. "Tully!" The cliff in front of him was a vertical wall. To the right, a flat wilderness bathed by the moonlight extended towards the horizon.

It seemed that the best way to get back to the encampment was going uphill around the lake. Duncan had barely begun climbing the hill when he noticed some definite structures off to his left, in the desert, some two or three hundred yards away.

Walking down a trail of marble sand, Duncan suddenly realized he was in the midst of an old city. Large stones following definite patterns, pillars, worn-out monuments, silvery spikes jutting out of the ground: the constructions were all over the area.

As he walked through the ancient structures, Duncan saw an object gleaming in the twilight. He reached for the flashlight on his belt, but he could not find it: he had lost it in the subterranean pond.

He headed towards the object. He was soon standing in front of what appeared to be a large polished stone. It was colorless, translucent, about twelve feet across, and its top was like a hollow, circular basin carved in the rock. But the most remarkable feature was the crystalline sphere that was hovering above it. The object was about six feet in diameter. However simple in shape, to Duncan the sphere looked utterly different from anything he had ever seen. It seemed as if it was made out of energy, but its glowing surface looked solid. He gazed at it for a couple of minutes, and then approached it, very carefully.

It was exactly when his fingers made contact with the pristine surface that a burst of blue light erupted in all directions. Duncan fell to the ground, covering his eyes. It was an intense, even painful, flash, which rapidly subsided into a mild blue glow.

"What . . . what is this?" Duncan uttered nervously, getting back on his feet.

"Who is what I am."

Disturbed, Duncan stepped back. He looked at the sphere again and noticed that it was actually spinning at an incredible rate. When he had touched it, he had felt a slight magnetic-like pull on his fingers, although he had not felt any current of air or any friction.

"So, *who* are you?" Duncan asked.

"I'm not a someone you can call *who*, as you call yourself *who*."

"Are you matter, energy . . . "

"I exhaust the potentiality of my substance. But my substance is of a different nature than yours."

"Do you have a name?"

"There is no point in naming my name."

"How so?"

"You would not understand it."

"I see. Incidentally, my name is Dahncion."

There was a pause in the exchange. "Yes, I have seen you within me, wherefore I do know your name," the sphere explained.

Duncan did not feel impressed by the statement. "Are you the being the natives call Essray?"

"I'm not he who they also call *Am*."

"You talk in riddles."

"It is you who understands in riddles."

Duncan stared at the entity as he sat on a short pillar, about five yards from it. "Since it seems that I understand you in riddles, let me talk about myself."

The sphere remained unchanged.

"As I've mentioned—and as you seem to know—my name is Dahncion, and I don't belong to this planet, in case you didn't know that already."

"Indeed, neither to this universe, since you are Duncan from Earth."

Duncan stood up, disturbed. "Who are you?"

"It matters not who I am. What matters is that you are here to ensure the continuity and ultimate destiny of the last civilization of this world."

Uncomfortable, Duncan nodded. "People keep telling me these sort of things, you know?"

"The device that was given to you . . . " The sphere paused, leaving the sentence unfinished.

"What about it?"

"You must take it to the city that is called Holy. There you will nurture the Yellow Pyramid with its power."

"So the device is a power source of some kind."

"It was crafted before the ancient races that inhabited this world were born; later, much later, it was entrusted to the Almiris."

"Donya Aytana . . . " Duncan muttered. "What happened to the Almiris?" His sullen attitude had turned into a keen interest. "It was a sophisticated and advanced civilization, wasn't it?"

A full minute passed until the sphere spoke again. "The night of emptiness is de-realizing the *Duhn-zaeon*. His purpose is drifting away; his life, dissipating."

Duncan stood up in silence as the sphere quietly began to rise.

Hovering in its position for a few more seconds, the sphere became very bright, radiating a dense blue energy. Under its influence, Duncan began to experience a heavy lethargy. Exhausted, he sat down on the ground, his back resting on a low wall. The sphere was now moving very fast towards the morning twilight, above the horizon. The first lights of a new day were starting to glow.

Duncan would not wake up until well into the morning.[151]

85.

Today: Hope and rejoice.

---

151 Duncan managed easily to find his way back to encampment, after his intense experience.

"Simply beautiful," Erina said, and smiled. Though erected in remote times and uninhabited for millennia, the city appeared as new.

"Just like the Zureedaii described it," Duncan added, putting an arm around her shoulders.

The city, which went beyond the horizon, glimmered gracefully with the last rays of the setting sun. Its buildings, some of which rose through the clouds, sparkled rainbows from their crystalline walls.

The streets, the squares, everything was covered by a gleaming, seemingly metallic bluish sheath.

"That construction, over there." Erina pointed at a yellow pyramid, as she leaned forward, standing close to the edge of the cliff. The shiny hue of her snug suit—gleaming in the twilight of a new evening—emphasized her female features. None of that passed unnoticed to Duncan. His growing physical desire for Erina was sufficiently evident to her. And though she had not directly returned his feelings yet, she was not making any effort to conceal her beauty either.

"I suppose this is the target of the Zureedaii," Erina added.

Duncan nodded. "It is consistent with what the sphere said we would find, last week."

Erina's silence was telling.

"Hey, I saw that thing," Duncan complained.

"I know you did."

"So you do." Duncan turned his eyes back to the city. It had no link with the ruins he had found a few days before, which were about eighty miles to the north.

"You do realize you had just gone through a very traumatic experience," Erina said, making reference to the drop down the subterranean river and the waterfalls. "The experience may have existed largely in your mind."

"Maybe," Duncan stated quietly. "But I kind of find it hard to believe that my mind could come up with something like that. I am not that sophisticated."

Erina put a thumb through her belt. "If there is any possibility that the pyramid is some type of communication station, as you think it is, the least we can do is check it out.

"I wouldn't dismiss any chance that could lead to our rescue."

Duncan stroked Erina's hair gently. "But not today, not now."

Erina looked into his eyes as he moved closer. Rather sharply, however, she pushed him away. Duncan scowled with frustration.

"The sky . . . " Erina gasped as she moved aside.

In the growing dusk of the evening, first a few, soon hundreds, finally thousands of white specks started springing up and spreading over the quiet evening heavens.

86.

Today: Faith and strength.

Having reached its final destination, Xanada's army was resting on a plateau, about one mile above the Holy City of the Zureedaii. The ancient buildings looked quiet and peaceful, but the heavens had been disturbed by an unexpected presence, though this was not surprising to Duncan.

"Those evil stars are nothing but Establishment battleships in geosynchronous quasi-orbits[152] ready to wipe us out in a fraction of a second with plasma vectors—if that makes any sense to you," he explained.

The War Council had been gathered for three hours already, and the course of action that it was leaning towards had an unsettling resemblance to a suicide mission from Duncan's perspective.

"The Prophecy is clear. It cannot fail, like no other prophecy has ever failed," was Xanada's stolid reply. "And Colonel Azatu's plan seems wise and in consonance with the Prophecy."

---

152 The ships were stationary above the city, maintaining their positions with their engines in quasi-orbital planes normal to the axis of rotation of the planet. Such planes did not include the center of the planet, and therefore were not coincident with the equatorial plane, far from that place, since the city was located at a latitude equivalent to about thirty-five degrees latitude on Earth.

Duncan frowned disapprovingly.

"May I, General?" Foxso'l asked.

"Please, Captain."

"I'm afraid what *Ashury* Dahncion has just said is one hundred percent true. But as long as those troops down there stay where they are," Foxso'l explained, referring to the Establishment forces that had occupied the city the previous night, "the evil stars up in the sky won't do nothing to us. I'm pretty positive Colonel Azatu's plan will surely work fine."

To Duncan, that had been an absurd comment, and he was not about to let it stand. However, to Xanada, the debate was exhausted. "When do you suggest to attack, Colonel?"

"The sooner the better, my General. If the enemy is as powerful as the *Ashuraii* say, we ought to attack by surprise."

"We will attack at dawn," Xanada confirmed. "Captain Mushido."

"My General?"

"You will lead the east wing." Mushido bowed.

"Captain Kamoto, you will command the west wing."

"My General!"

"Captain Ziku, you will lead the front wing with the *Ashuraii* in your ranks. I want your best warriors fighting alongside."

Ziku bowed respectfully. "My General honors my warriors and myself."

Xanada looked around. "The council is dismissed. I'll be in my tent making further preparations." He saluted his staff and left.

Breaking ranks, everybody hurried to get everything ready for battle. Soon only the three Realitians remained.

It was dark already, and the night dome was dangerously populated by many extra stars that did not belong to that sky.

"I hope you're satisfied," Duncan growled through clenched teeth.

Foxso'l turned his head to one side. "I ain't glad with what is goin' on here, son, but it is what it is."

"Even if they succeeded in reaching some secret spot they may know," Erina speculated, referring to the Zureedaii, "most of them will surely die."

"If *they* succeeded?" Duncan asked. "Make it *we*, since we're part of *them*, already."

"So, you'd rather have this people be equalized with the Establishment?" Foxso'l asked.

"No, but I think this is a foolish attempt. Nobody will remain alive one minute after our romantic attack starts tomorrow."

"Maybe it's gonna be so," Foxso'l said calmly. "But I don't think this is any more foolishly romantic than the Realdom's attempt to win a war over an overpowering enemy just for the sake of freedom. Maybe all of us are gonna die tomorrow, yeah, maybe so; but let me tell you somethin': this army is the last and only chance these guys have. Nobody will help them here. The Realdom is too busy already just struggling to survive. And it may well have no clue of what is going on down here. It's all up to this army—and to ourselves."

Duncan sighed. "The odds of taking the city are, are . . . one in a billion!"

"And even if we did succeed," added Erina, "what then? An entire enemy fleet would be right above our heads all the time."

"You forget something, sweetheart: that fancy gizmo we found at the cottage. I don't know how many *breps*[153] the soldier-boy had had last week when he saw that hovering sphere of his. But we don't need no fancy laboratory to tell us that this little baby of ours has a heck of an energy supply inside it. All the tests we've run on it tell us that. Besides, the kid's story about the sphere . . ." Foxso'l shrugged. "It makes some sense to me.

"What if there is some long-range communication system somewhere over there?" Foxso'l waved towards the city. "What if we

---

153 Native beverage with intoxicating powers when taken in excess.

find a spaceship, a weapon, or something? Who knows, maybe all this prophecy-stuff is not make-believe nonsense; there may be some truth in it."

Erina smiled with a touch of cynicism.

"What's so funny?" Foxso'l grunted.

"Nothing, it's that you just sounded a little bit like a good *sooggee*." That was the term the Zureedaii used for those with a strong commitment to the Prophecy.

"Well, why not, sister? I'd rather be a good *sooggee* tomorrow who happily happens to be in the right. Because if this prophecy buzz is just a myth, we may all be goners already. But if it happens to be true—just a little bit true—whatever is gonna happen down there might well save our skins."

87.

Behold the sign in the sky. The heavens shine with radiant colors, as in the days of Kaleb, as when the light was born to its glory. The day arrays itself in gold, and the moon gleams with glamourous joy. From midday to the Main Sea, from sunset to sunrise, all the heavens explode in mighty splendor. For the days of salvation are now at a close, the time of bliss is finally at hand.

[. . .] And on that day, the forces of darkness will grind their teeth and groan with horror, since what is to come grows insufferable in their eyes, a bitter gall too harsh to swallow.

But lo, from the gates of Abyss a terrible army awakes. The wrath of the Evil One commissions its hosts girding their loins for a new battle. From the blackness of the heavens they are gathered together, from the depths of the netherworld they heed the trumpets of war. On that night, the dome of the skies will pour forth the evil stars of oppression. The firmament will retch, and the moon will wail. Like furious wasps, the evil stars buzz over the entire land until at last they send forth their envoys. The lurking vultures hold their breath as they stalk in silent assault. The commissioners of darkness break forth against the beloved city, the city of emerald, of turquoise, of chrysolite, and of pearl. They spread over her holy palaces, like the locusts of summer, they plunder and prey, like the black ashes of the Mountain of Fire, they defile the white abodes of her beauty.

But behold, the army of the saints surrounds the encampment of the enemy. Blood and fire and brimstone and lightning are spit over the knights of all justice. The Ashuraii *are fighting amongst them, wielding the mighty sword of reality and the unbending shield of rectitude. And all the servants of Essray rejoice, yea, they all praise His almighty strength that stands forever. For the armies of the Evil One are wiped out like the sands of Iazyrra, and the sky is cleansed of the foul abomination, and the beloved city is purified of its lice, and the Seeker of Naked Nothingness mourns, and staggers, and cries, for once more the strength of* sternessence *has conquered in glory.*

From the *Zureeday* "Chronicles of Victory," *The Book of Prophecy.*

The Establishment fleet was still discernible in the sky, although the clarity of a new day was starting to dim its presence. The night had passed by calmly, with an occasional mild breeze lingering from the south. But the weather was not going to stay quiet for the rest of the morning. A windstorm coming from the desert was closing in on the area.

An Establishment soldier, leaning on a crystal column, turned his gaze towards the approaching storm. It did not bother him very much. His environment-proof battle suit would effectively keep him from experiencing most of the inconveniences of the incoming gales and dust.

The soldier kept his gaze on the northern hills. There was nothing unusual. Although he was aware of the nearby gathering of natives, it was considered an unlikely threat. A thick cloud of sand and leaves now started rising above the forest on the hills beyond the city. As the wind gained strength, swarms of glimmering specks began to shine forth within the clouds with the first lights of the dawning day.

88.

Today: All things with everything![154]

"Rig!"

From both sides of every *annay*, long poles with white sturdy sheets were hoisted. The sails readily caught the impetus of the strong Zonda[155] that had started blowing a few minutes before.

"Charge!"

Unable to withstand the force of the sails, the *annays* were swept along before Captain Ziku's command could reach his ranks. The strength of the wind, combined with the steep downhill slope, had put Ziku's company literally in the air, which, though unusual, was quite possible. *Annays* were related to flying species, and though they themselves were not endowed with flying abilities, they seemed to possess an excellent instinct for strolling across the air.

"Yeeha!" Foxso'l, along with his Realitian companions, were skimming along towards the target at a fabulous speed. A fluttering blue banner was now deployed from the tip of Ziku's right pole. All soldiers unhitched their crossbows in response, waiting for the ensuing command.

The army was soon flying over the city. Down on the streets, it was easy to recognize the alien equipment brought by the invading forces: it simply lacked the crystalline texture naturally embedded

---

154 It is not easy to translate this phrase into English. In a more colloquial form (wordier and still restricted in meaning), it could be rendered as *Today: all that you've got with all that you've got.* Nevertheless, *Today: All things with everything,* is not a mere literal rendition; in its original language, it strongly conveys this meaning.

155 Native name given to the polar wind, which after crossing the desert, becomes warm and dry, strengthening in speed.

The Zureeday army, and the Ashuraii, were skimming along toward the
target at a fabulous speed.

in the ancient constructions. A red banner replaced Ziku's blue one, which passed by swiftly, raging, on Erina's right side. In response, a shower of metallic spears released by the Zureedaii riders began falling upon the city.

Hastily, the alien forces began repelling the incursion with some type of energy beams. However, the counterattack was proving widely ineffective: all shots were simply bouncing off their targets with reddish bursts of light. Zureeday armor was made of an alloy that was effectively shielding all who wore them from the lethal beams. But the enemy soon realized the *annays* were much more vulnerable[156] to their energy beams, so they began shooting the attackers down by targeting the animals.

The wind was not strong enough to hold the flying army in the air any longer, and most of Xanada's soldiers were already landing. Once on the streets, the Zureedaii began fighting with their swords and *zuroobies*, a sort of crossbow capable of shooting small nets with sticky cords attached to their edges, which ended in spherical stones. The Establishment troops were neither prepared nor trained for such primitive tactics. Any small rent opened on an environmental suit[157] rendered an Establishment soldier out of combat.

Xanada's army was fighting with order and courage. However, the Establishment was rapidly reorganizing and strengthening its position.

89.

Duncan was running along a street, trying to avoid any personal engagement. Foxso'l, Erina, and a small group of Zureedaii were with him. Their target: the yellow pyramid a few blocks ahead. Although from the air the edifice dominated the field of vision, this was not the case down in the city streets.

---

156 Even when *annays* had some armor protection, their shields left wide areas of their bodies exposed.

157 The suits were not battle suits, but uniforms with functional environmental features.

"What's going on?" Duncan said, looking up at the darkening sky.

"It's the Prophecy," asserted one of the Zureedaii.

"What a time for a solar eclipse," Erina complained, raising her eyes.

"Can you see the target?" Duncan asked.

"What do you mean?" Foxso'l replied. "I'm following you."

"Don't worry, *Ashuraii*, we see it," Tully said. The Zureedaii were gifted with superb night vision.

Abruptly, enemy fire hit Duncan in one shoulder through a joint in his armor. He fell to the polished marble street. Running to his aid, three Zureedaii carried him behind a pillar, dodging the enemy fire.

"It's okay," Duncan stammered, as Erina began to unstrap the armor over his wound.

"It's not okay. Let me finish removing these plates."

"The enemy is coming, *Ashuraii*!" Tully's brother warned.

"Run to that corner!" Duncan yelled at Erina, who was working on his still-hot armor. "I'll cover you."

"You can't . . . "

"Do as I say, Ensign."

Erina yielded, moving behind as Duncan opened fire, covering her retreat. Immediately, Duncan realized he was dangerously isolated in his position. The enemy was closing distances very fast. Hastily, Duncan unhitched a hand grenade from his belt and threw it in the direction of the voices.

"Take cover, everybody!" he cried out.

Almost instantly, the device exploded. For a fraction of a second, all the surrounding edifices flashed back with a dazzling white. Duncan had been dangerously close to the detonation. The explosives were not intended as anti-personnel devices: they had been designed to inflict damage to military installations, never to be dropped manually.

Still not recovered from the blast, Duncan had already removed the safety catch of another grenade. He was about to activate it, when

Tully began yelling from behind: "The area is clear! The devils are dead. The area is clear!"

Duncan put back the explosive on his belt. Turning on a flashlight, he waved at the group to follow him. As he ran, he sporadically flashed the light on to minimize the chances of detection while trying to catch a glimpse of what was ahead.

Finally, behind a wide tall tower, the silhouette of a large pyramid became visible against the dark sky spangled with the alien "stars." As the team got closer, Duncan began to notice an almost imperceptible phosphorescence emanating from the pyramid's walls.

"We're almost there," said Erina, turning to Duncan.

The eclipse was making the enemy fleet very discernible, with patterns of lights developing quickly in the sky. Duncan watched it all with anxiety and despair in his expression.

The armada was patently getting ready to repel the Zureedaii incursion.

Duncan and his companions were standing in front of a huge wall. It had a forty-five-degree slope, and its edges met at a point at the top. With their arms hanging and their heads up, all looked stunned at their mission objective.

"So, how do we get inside?" Foxso'l said, his outline barely visible against the glowing wall behind him.

Duncan waved his flashlight. "Let's go around and check for some door, hatch—any possible access."

"With your flashlight?" Foxso'l chuckled.

"We Zureedaii can see in the dark," Tully pointed out.

Duncan hesitated. "All right, we'll be waiting for you right here."

"Follow me," Tully commanded. The Zureedaii vanished in the dark, reappearing quickly on the other side.

"We couldn't find any entrance to the pyramid, *Ashuraii*."

"We'd better think of something fast," said Erina.

"You must use the *toorin*, as the Prophecy says," Tully said, looking at Duncan.

Some muffled voices, not from friendly forces, were becoming louder.

"The what?" asked Duncan, agitated.

Foxso'l nodded. "Hand me *Aytana's* contraption." Duncan passed him the device.

The edifice in front of them was surrounded by a ring of small, hollow pyramidal carvings on its walls. Foxso'l took the pyramidal device and put one end in one of the carvings. It matched perfectly.

Like a reflex, a triangular aperture opened right in front of them. The Zureedaii gasped with wonder.

At that moment, shrapnel from a nearby explosion began raining down. A member of the team was hit and fell into the pyramid, and the rest rushed into it for cover. Without leaving any trace, the opening on the wall immediately closed behind them.

Tully knelt down before the motionless Zureeday lying on the floor. There was a deep silence; the team's spirit had abruptly fallen. Duncan laid a hand on Tully's right shoulder, but the soldier reacted immediately, overcoming the strong feelings he had now to contend with.

"There is work to do, *Ashuraii*," Tully pointed out, as he stood up with determination.

Duncan looked at him, uncertain. The dead soldier lying on the floor was Tully's brother.

The pyramid harbored another pyramid inside, like a smaller replica of the external one, although its walls were steeper.[158] A space, less than ten feet wide, separated the inner and outer walls. A ramp surrounding the internal pyramid led up to the top.

With no further delay, the Realitians and the Zureedaii started to climb the ramp. It was not steep but was very smooth, forcing them to walk carefully and close to the walls to avoid slipping. A dim luminescence was radiating from both the internal and external walls; the phosphorescence, barely noticeable from the outside, was significantly more intense in the inside.

Symbols carved on the walls could be spotted as the incline went up. The symbols, resembling hieroglyphics, shimmered with a gentle gleam that emanated from inside the walls. The ramp grew narrower as the team approached the top, finally reaching a point where it became impossible to advance any further. For a moment, everybody stood idle, looking at each other.

"Here," Tully said from the rearguard.

Everybody turned back. A hollow pyramidal carving, similar to the one that had let the group inside, marked the end of a long row of hieroglyphics. Right before it, one last sketch of an individual holding a triangular object was carved on the walls. Foxso'l placed Aytana's device on that mark, and an aperture opened before him.

He stepped in cautiously, followed by the rest of the group. After a few seconds, the wall closed back, leaving the platoon inside a pyramidal chamber that crowned the internal edifice. In its center, there was an elongated slender four-sided colonnade, with long trapezoidal faces. A red hologram of a tetrad crowned its top. The holographic image looked exactly like Aytana's device, or more precisely, like half of it.

Foxso'l immediately passed the device to Duncan, who was much taller than him. Standing in front of the colonnade, Duncan raised his arms, trying to place the device right where the hologram was, but it

---

158 As a consequence, the top of the internal pyramid did not end in a point since its walls intersected the outer pyramid before they could meet at a peak.

was beyond his reach.

"Let Aimeeru and me be the footstool of your victory, *Ashury.*"

Duncan stared at Tully as he and Aimeeru approached him. Putting their hands together, they invited Duncan to climb on their shoulders.

Foxso'l immediately took the device from Duncan, who started climbing on the hands of the two Zureedaii. Once in position, he looked at the hologram; it was right above his eyes. He turned around, and Foxso'l handed back Aytana's device. Holding it carefully, Duncan leaned towards the top of the colonnade. He was about to place the object on the spot, when Aimeeru slipped to one side. Both Duncan and Tully fell to the floor.

The *toorin* slipped from Duncan's hands, sliding across the chamber. Very close to the artifact, the grenade Duncan had refrained from using outside the pyramid was spinning loose. The explosive had accidentally unhitched from Duncan's belt, its safety catch still removed.

Rolling as it spun, the grenade hit Aytana's device and the explosive was activated. Nothing could now halt the imminent outcome.

"Take cover, everybody!" Duncan yelled desperately, knowing there was no place to find shelter.

Foxso'l ran towards Aytana's device and picked it up. He quickly applied it to one of the triangular holes carved on one wall, expecting an opening to materialize in response. Nothing happened.

There seemed to be no way out, but Tully found a way. He struggled with the idea for a moment, he hesitated, faltered and even shuddered, but beyond his weakness he found the courage he needed and opened himself to its strength.

"Get the hell out of there!" Duncan yelled from behind the

elongated colonnade, where he had taken Erina seeking a feeble shelter.

Tully was completely exposed standing in the center of the chamber. He suddenly leaped forward and fell on top of the grenade. Keeping the explosive between his body and the cold glimmering surface below, Tully held onto it tightly and started dragging himself to one corner, far away from everyone else.

"No!" Duncan cried out, but his cry was silenced by a strong detonation.

For a few seconds, there were only coughs and moans. Then, through the thick smoke, Duncan began searching for his Zureeday friend. But he could not find him anymore.

Everybody was dazed and not fully aware of what had just happened. Duncan crawled over to sit where Tully had been lying only a moment before. His head was bowed down, his face, stunned.

He raised his eyes. The elongated pillar was still standing in the center of the chamber. Undisturbed, the red hologram remained shining on top. Lying intact in one corner was Aytana's device.

Duncan picked it up and dragged himself towards the base of the colonnade. Leaning carefully on it, he began to stretch up his body, with his arms raised. The top of the pillar continued to prove beyond his reach.

With a painful cry (the wound on his right shoulder, though not serious, was very sensitive), Duncan jumped up with all his strength, swinging the device over his head.

This time, he reached the top of the colonnade. The *toorin* had finally reached its destination.

A dense energy surge flashed from the *toorin* towards the hollow apex of the roof above. A thunderous sound came along with a searing light, as the top of the pyramid became perfectly translucent. From the colonnade, a narrow beam shot to the transparent apex of the pyramid. A myriad of high-energy vectors instantly shot out towards the sky in all directions, each one of them winding up in a noiseless ball of plasma deep inside the firmament.

As quickly as it had begun, all became extremely quiet in a moment.

Recovering from the grenade blast, Erina looked at the sky through the external walls, which remained translucent. She could make out only a few static stars, whereas mere seconds before, it had been populated by a sheet of small yellowish moving specks—the Establishment fleet.

With a beaming smile on his face, Foxso'l kept his eyes fixed on the sky for a while. Aimeeru was standing by him, looking in the same direction, wondering if something else was still about to happen.

But Erina turned her eyes immediately towards Duncan. He lay still on the floor, exhausted. He seemed all right, but an intense blue luminescence was emanating from him. It was similar to the gleam she had seen in his eyes and around his body after the environmental restoration in Aquaelight, but much more intense.

The sight lasted perhaps five seconds, but it made a profound impression on Erina. She never confided what she saw to anybody else, not even to Duncan. Although the phenomenon could have been attributed to different causes, to Erina it was the confirmation of a long-held intuition.

90.

Duncan was sitting on a cliff, facing the ancient city. It was hard to believe that, that very morning, a battle had taken place in the crystalline streets shining below. As the last rays of the setting sun shone through the walls of the newly translucent pyramid, Duncan took a small charred notebook from one of his pockets. He had found it lying in a corner before leaving the colonnade chamber.

He opened it to its last page. A single sentence was written on top. The native alphabet, though simple and phonetic, was not easy for him, but he could read it with some effort. Flipping through the pages, he noticed that each one had a heading-like motto. There was a connection between headings, like an ethereal link that grew stronger towards the end of the notebook. Slowly, Duncan read one paragraph, *"Today: May it be them,"* and then another, *"Today: Faith,"* and another, *"Today: Optimism"*. The ideas grew ever more definite and concrete.

The last heading on the last page, jotted down at the beginning of a day that was destined to be the last, stood alone with simplicity and completeness.

Duncan rested his eyes on it for a moment. Looking at the sky, he then put the notebook away.

The last thought was something he would always remember. It was written with a few words, by a faithful friend he now regretted having not known well enough.

It was not a vague idea, a lofty wish that was not meant to be. For on that day, on that luminous day, Tully had truly given everything he had with everything he had. And in so doing, he had gone beyond himself—he had overcome death.

CHAPTER 14

One Last Day's Run

91.

"Up there," Foxso'l said, pointing at a small speck in the hazy, yet cloudless, sky.

The small speck soon acquired a flattened ovoid shape. It was unmistakably a Realitian shuttlecraft, and it was approaching rapidly.

The vessel halted very close to where Foxso'l and the others stood, hovering quietly above the surface. Crowds of natives gathered to watch the event, although at a prudent distance.

A sense of regret was soon replacing the initial excitement, since the hour for the *Ashuraii* to leave the world had finally come. But that was the way things ought to be. "The *Ashuraii* would fly into the sky, in a white bright star-carousel," the Prophecy foretold.

After a few seconds of hovering in its position, the shuttle landed. A woman, with *tori* features, stepped forward from an open doorway on the gleaming hull, followed by two crewmembers. Their willingness to cope with the planet's ten atmospheres without wearing environmental suits caught Duncan's attention. However, what most surprised him was seeing Clara again, standing on the top of the shuttle's ramp, her blond hair wafting gently in the morning wind.

As Clara stepped down the ramp, the three Realitians moved to meet the party.

"Lieutenant Dahncion reporting, Captain. The detail is ready to embark."

"Nice to see you again, girl," added Foxso'l. "As always, beautiful."

Clara smiled. "Time to go home."

Duncan looked at the captain, somewhat taken aback.

"Duncan," Erina interjected, as she handed him a beautifully carved box.

Nodding, he presented the box to Clara. "This is the way the Zureeday want to welcome the angels of the stars."

Clara received the gift and smiled mildly, but her eyes did not. A recurring thought had been afflicting her over the past few months. Now the intimacy of that name—*Duncan*—had strengthened the shadows of her fears. For while recovering from her wounds and even struggling to stay alive, another name—Dahncion—had been her silent but constant companion.

92.

"Lieutenant Dahncion reporting, Captain."

A virtual window materialized in the door to O'sihn's quarters. "Come on in, please."

Stepping inside, Duncan found the captain working at his desk.

"Please, take a seat." O'sihn raised his eyes. "So, how are things going today?"

"Fine, Captain."

There was anxiety in Duncan's face. "We can make this informal, Dahncion."

Duncan reclined in his chair. "Sorry if I get straight to the point, but my next watch is in thirty minutes."

"Of course."

"It's about what we discussed last week," Duncan added.

Duncan's subtle fiddling with his fingers did not pass unnoticed to O'sihn. The captain seemed to understand what was in his mind.

"So, you've been giving it some thought."

Duncan nodded. "I'm afraid I still feel the same." He paused, inviting O'sihn to add something, but he didn't. "I'm not sure I should be doing this anymore."

"What is it that makes you doubt?" O'sihn asked.

Duncan grimaced with discomfort. "Through my actions, many things have happened, many people have died—and that's not the only thing."

Duncan paused again, and again O'sihn remained silent.

"What gives me the right to engage in a fight in a universe that isn't even mine?"

"*Right.*" O'sihn tapped a finger on his desk three or four times. "How about duty? Duty to stand for what is right, regardless of any universe."

"*Right* can have many meanings," Duncan said. "What is right in one universe might not be right in another."

O'sihn took a *twees* from a small box on his desk and sniffed its sugary top, his eyes focused on Duncan. "The very fact that *right*, as in what is good and fair, has a common meaning for you and me, though we were born and grew up in different universes, shows that goodness itself pervades reality, and therefore any universe. It touches all, creating a common bond, a common good, and a common right to defend what is good."

Duncan shook his head. "I still don't think I should be involved in this any longer."

O'sihn kept his eyes on Duncan for a moment, with a grave, though gentle, look. "You're absolutely free, Dahncion, to resign your commission whenever you desire. Nobody will question your reasons, especially after all you have done."

"I've discussed the matter with Erina," Duncan continued. "We do agree on keeping our commissions with the Navy, as long as some serious consideration is given to getting us back home."

O'sihn nodded, putting aside the official notebook he was working on. "You have every right to ask this. We are the ones who brought you here in the first place. And it's also fair for Erina, who has served with us and risked her life for us on more than one occasion."

"I know these things take time and resources," added Duncan, "and the Realdom is at war. But we think it's something we should at least ask for."

O'sihn's serious expression was replaced by a warm smile. "And what you're asking for is at hand."

"The answer to your request may well lie in our current destination," O'sihn pointed out.

"It's a classified mission," Duncan said.

"Indeed, it is. We're on our way to pay a new visit to our old Veridiawan friends. We're heading back to the Althean system."

Duncan smiled politely, not yet seeing the connection between Veridiawa and his potential trip back home.

"Your presence here, in this universe, is closely linked to Althea 8," O'sihn continued. "Two years before your journey to Reality, Realdom archaeologists had discovered the ruins of an ancient city not too far from the Veridiawan village. Very little remained of it, but it had clearly been built upon a much older complex. In the beginning, the discovery seemed related to a non-technological civilization, until a *technon*[159] was found inside one of the buildings." O'sihn tapped his *twees* on his desk. "The *technon* was not operational, but it was found to be a trans-universal connector tuned into Earth, your Earth. It was this discovery—Doctor Oyhtter's discovery—that enabled the expedition to your world."

Duncan was distressed to learn that. He had never doubted that the technology that had brought him from Earth was the exclusive product of Realitian science. The assumption had always given him reassurance: even if the Establishment was a formidable enemy, the

---

159 Compact technological system of a size comparable to that of a building or a small complex.

apparently superior technology of the Realdom would eventually have the power to turn the course of the war around.

"This information is highly classified," O'sihn continued. "Until recently, we had managed to keep it from Establishment intelligence." O'sihn paused and fixed his eyes on Duncan. "Your next and last mission, Lieutenant Dahncion: to plant a localized T.A.T.[160] adjusted to disintegrate the entire trans-universal complex—right after you and Erina have abandoned this universe."

"You said the *technon* was not operational," Duncan pointed out.

"A team from SERI has been working on it for a long time, and they have finally succeeded in rendering it partially operational. However, it can't be used unless at least one living being from the target universe is present in the *technon*."

"But my body has been bio-assimilated."

"That should not be a problem. The information required by the *technon* is still in your body. Nevertheless, Erina has not been exposed to the RIBA device. Although we don't fully understand many aspects of her *transuniversal* organism, her partially assimilated body will guarantee the success of the process, even if you were not there."

"We would be safe, then."

"Though very small, there is a risk involved in the procedure." O'sihn paused. "Erina and you will always have the choice to blow up the site while remaining in this universe."

Duncan nodded.

"However, if you are positive about returning home, I would not miss this ticket. The risk involved is minimal, and it's unlikely that the Realdom could allocate the effort and resources for an alternative procedure under the current situation. Frankly, things have not been getting any better for the Realdom either. The First-Equitarian's strategic skills are proving exceedingly brilliant. If we lose this war, this opportunity at Althea 8 might be your last and only chance to get back home."

---

160 Time Anti-Time explosive device.

"Why blow up the *technon*? Why not move it somewhere else?"

"Such an effort would be very difficult to hide. Most of the structure lies underground. It's solid, compact, and it can't be dismantled. Its volume would require a major operation. Unfortunately, under the present circumstances, we have no other choice but to destroy it as soon as possible."

93.

"Althean system by the low port, sir." Lupain transferred the star readings to the captain's console.

"Copied. Down-starboard standard rudder, bearing one seven-zero dash zero-six-zero; regular orbital-adjustment speed to the eighth planet."

"Down-starboard standard one-seven-zero dash zero-six-zero; eight regular orbital, aye captain."

"Final average orbit, twenty thousand kilometers[161], regular," O'sihn added.

"Final ten thousand reg, aye, sir."

"Why that high?" Laida asked, keeping her attention on her scanner scope.

"I want to take a wide-angular scan before getting any closer." The captain checked the chart on his screen. "Tactical situation, T.O.?"

"All clear, Captain." Tygrum was on the bridge today at his console, near O'sihn.

O'sihn nodded and turned to his intercom. "C.I.C./conn?"

"Lieutenant Deehra, sir." The C.I.C. holographic virtual console materialized to the left and in front of the main screen.

"Stand by for tactical scanning."

"Aye-aye, captain."

"Constant distance readings, Lupain."

"Aye, Captain—present range: four hundred thousand kilometers."

---

161 Measured from the mean planet surface.

"Cilia?"

The virtual console of the communications officer of the watch came on. She had shared that duty with McAwian during the past two years. "Yes, Captain?"

"Call Ensign Erina to the bridge."

"She must be in her resting period," Laida pointed out. "She covered the last watch of the night. I'd rather have her wide awake later on the planet."

O'sihn nodded. "Order canceled, Cilia."

"Aye, Captain."

"One hundred and forty thousand kilometers," Lupain noted.

"C.I.C./conn?"

Deehra's console came on.

"Situation?"

"Fifty thousand kilometers, and scans read all clear, Captain," Lupain said.

"Copied."

"Orbital deceleration engaged."

O'sihn turned to Laida. "Once we achieve first orbital perigee—"

But the command was never completed.

94.

Everything was gray, with a sundry variety of hues, and yet nothing but gray. It looked like an endless, uniform jungle. But in one particular spot, an ashen, worn-out construction stood out from the foliage, disrupting the surrounding monotony. It was not easy to tell its purpose, although it resembled an ancient temple. A two-paneled door seemed to be the only connection between the edifice and the jungle. Carved on its gritty walls, long rows of hieroglyphics and other obscure symbols remained visible despite centuries of erosion. Standing at the entrance, Duncan was apprehensive—yet he had to get inside. He checked the doors: they were unlocked.

Very carefully, he cracked one pane, but its noisy hinges gave away the uninvited presence. A gray powder sprinkled down from

They started wailing morbid melodies.

the tall lintels as the door gradually opened. Duncan glanced around and stepped in, leaving the door ajar. Nobody seemed to be inside.

Although everything looked quiet, there were some disquieting clues on the walls. A few lit candles were casting shadows into a large semicircular amphitheater dug in the ground under a dome-like ceiling. There was a big basin in the middle of the chamber. To one side, a large, flat stone resembled a sacrificial altar. Behind it, a wide, polished black wall, with a texture like gelatin, went all the way up from the ground to the ceiling. This wall was totally unmarked, contrasting with the loaded symbolic scripture and ornamentation everywhere else inside the building. The big basin, placed before the black wall, contained a tar-like fluid. Viscous bubbles occasionally popped up from the sticky broth, impregnating the air with a rancid, acrid smell.

Suddenly, the sound of many voices began echoing from the jungle. Heavy steps could now be heard approaching very fast.

In the back of the amphitheater, ragged curtains hung shabbily to the floor from rusty hooks nailed on the wall, close to the ceiling. Hiding behind them seemed to be Duncan's only option. Through the curtains' dusty fabric, Duncan watched an uncanny assembly quickly gather around the altar.

The humanoid figures were clad in odd vestments—like ritual habits—that bore a resemblance to military costumes. The expressions on their faces were cracked and emaciated; their empty eyes gave forth a sense of hate and desolation. Once they had occupied the places that belonged to each, they started wailing morbid melodies. Their voices were dark and deep.

Standing between the altar and the basin, a faceless creature ministered the ritual. At one point, it lifted up its arms, and a dense silence followed. It immediately dissolved the quiet with the violent yelling of three names. Stepping towards the altar, three individuals came forward with three black phials, which they filled with the viscous content of the basin.

The faceless character displayed an anguished smile of wrath, invisible and yet perceptible. Turning to the black wall, it started whispering murky sounds. It was subtle, patient, and perseverant. It did not take long for the wall's dark texture to yield its blackness, exposing a glassy-brilliant screen to which it was attached.

A whole variety of shapes became visible. Everything beyond the screen was seen as through a clear, blue brightness.

The crystal shield started moving upwards, exposing all the treasures that lay behind it. As the three creatures, armed with their bottles, went through the doughy gelatinous wall, the gathering cried out, intoxicated with hate and unbearable pleasure.

The landscape beyond the curtain had a remarkable beauty. It was like a vast garden planted with precious stones, with a sea of liquid crystal to one side. Amethysts, diamonds, rubies, emeralds, agates, sapphires, pearls mounted on topaz, opal: they were all crystallized in a sundry variety of refined geometrical forms. But nobody was keeping guard of the treasures, as if its keeper had been bribed.

The three operatives moved quickly and determinedly. They seemed to know their jobs very well. Without wasting time, they started smudging and splattering the impeccable scene with the sticky black broth they carried in their phials, which seemed never to go empty. The garden of clean, radiant colors was rapidly turning into a murky, loathsome pigsty.

The ground, made out of mother-of-pearl inlaid in marble, was quickly losing its splendor. One of the creatures headed straight to the sea of liquid crystal, and once in front of it, started pouring out its phial. The wraithlike character was very meticulous at its job; it certainly did not want to get splashed by any crystal drop that might stain its clothes with persistent blotches of beauty. It took only a moment to turn the sea into an oily quagmire.

Inside the temple, everybody rejoiced with mystifying misery.

The three creatures soon completed their assignments. As each one now came out through the gelatinous wall, an oppressive expression of pleasure darkened the contorted shadows of their faces.

The wall resumed its black texture, but the crystal screen behind it did not come back to protect its ravaged gardens again.

The foul ritual had concluded. Clad in bitter silence, the attendants began to leave the building. They had managed to spend an agreeable, acrid evening, but now, despair was resuming its ruthless yoke. They were alone with their incurable, inscrutable pains, carved deep within themselves, upon their very names.

The last one to leave slammed the doors behind it. Inside, a few candles remained glowing.

Duncan was standing alone in the midst of a desolate silence, soaked with a cold sweat. He attempted to take a step, but he fell on his knees. He strove to get up, but he could not. Helpless, and trembling, he looked at his hands: from beneath his nails, he saw a dark, thick fluid dripping slowly onto his fingers. He pressed his eyes shut and closed his hands tight against his chest, but in doing so, his clothes pasted onto his flesh with something thicker than sweat.

In the center of the chamber, a lightning bolt burst. The walls began to melt; the altar, the basin, and the gelatinous wall imploded. A cloud of shadows was left, but it gradually dissipated. Only Duncan remained, floating in a deep blue sky, too bright for his eyes to stare at.

In front of him, a human figure began to take shape. Duncan suddenly recognized him: it was the same who had once disclosed to him the meaning of *sternessence*. Duncan tried to remember his name, but he couldn't. Well, that had been a dream . . .

"I must be dreaming," Duncan concluded in a whisper.

With a somber look, Lan Leakim fixed his eyes on him. "Your childhood, your childhood, your childhood . . . "

The quiet words resounded intensely in Duncan's mind. He did not understand this; it was as if he were blind, and now he did become blind. He could not see any more, only a black, sticky darkness.

And then, the dreadful explosion . . .

Duncan woke up, startled. The emergency panels of his quarters were on, their intermittent red lights blinking on and off in frantic desperation.

95.

A convulsive cracking rocked the entire ship. Only the lights of some instruments remained visible on the bridge. Both the main and emergency gravitational compensation units had been overridden, unable to cancel out the large accelerations induced by the explosion. The first thing O'sihn saw when the lights came back on was Laida lying on the floor, with one of her elbows dislocated from its natural position. She also seemed to have received a severe blow on her head. The X.O. had been momentarily knocked out, and now she was fighting to regain consciousness.

"Don't move." O'sihn got up from his seat with some difficulty and knelt down by Laida. She kept trying to get up, until the pain from her dislocated elbow rendered her totally motionless. "T.O., assume X.O. Get the bridge reorganized."

"Aye-aye, Captain," Tygrum acknowledged.

A flood of intercom traffic was coming from the commanding console. Still kneeling beside Laida, O'sihn pushed a button on his console. "Damage control/conn, overall damage report."

Lieutenant Baboorez's virtual console flickered on with distortion. "Still working on it, Captain. We have a very dense traffic of data coming from all sections."

"I need a rough estimate."

"Captain!" Lupain cut in. His virtual console remained intact and bright in the twilight of the bridge. "We're falling off from orbit. I have neither drive nor rudder control."

O'sihn raised his eyes. "Time for reentry?"

"Forty-three minutes, captain."

O'sihn nodded. "Damage control." Baboorez's console was a blurry noisy screen, totally disconnected from its source.

"Damage control/conn?" O'sihn insisted, using an intercom channel.

"Damage control, Capt—" a voice came through with distortion.

"I reach you, DC. Give me whatever you've got."

After a short pause, Baboorez proceeded. "Captain, we have at least ten pressure failures;[162] main life support system virtually inoperative; auxiliary life support system operative at sixty-five percent; sixty percent hull and structure permanent deformations; main power system, eight percent operational—"

"I've got the picture," O'sihn interrupted. "Transfer all the information you have to my console. I'll come back to you as soon as I can."

"Acknowledged, Captain."

"Tactical situation?" O'sihn asked, turning to the virtual console of the officer of the watch.

"I don't detect anything unusual, sir," Leepardian answered.

"How about an attack from the surface?"

"I don't know, Captain."

"I suggest checking with the C.I.C.," Tygrum interjected.

O'sihn nodded and turned back to his console. "C.I.C./conn."

"Lieutenant Deehra speaking, Captain." No VC (or virtual console) came on, only audio. "It seems we ran over a micro-mine g-cluster. Tango[163] is recreating a virtual scenario of over three thousand gravitational singularities whose effects seem to match the damage pattern we've suffered."

"Keep working on it, but check for other hostiles in the area, including—especially—from the planet."

"Aye-aye, Captain."

"Conn/damage control."

"Yes, damage control."

"Sir," Baboorez continued, "the main gravitational system is

---

162 In order to maximize environmental efficiency, a relatively small percentage of the ship was pressurized, mainly in the crew operational areas.

163 Ship's tactical computer.

out of line, and all life support systems have collapsed. I've already activated the photosynthetic chemical recycler."

"How long are repairs gonna take on the life support system?"

"Frankly, I'm not sure we *can* repair it. The photosynthetic recycler will keep us alive, but not for long."

"Try whatever's necessary to get any of the support subsystems operational. It doesn't matter how partially you get them to work."

"We're on it right now, Captain, but I don't think there is much we can do."

At that point, the engine-room virtual console went blank. Lin Beaver's voice came immediately through O'sihn's intercom. "Engine room, conn."

"Chief."

"Preliminary prop status report, sir: main engine energy *singularizer*[164] is seriously damaged—we may be able to get it operational at minimum efficiency in about two hours, but only for a limited time. Main power system has collapsed—time for repairs still undetermined. Auxiliary system is showing clear signs of severe stress—likely overall power failure, though we're working to prevent this. These are the critical items, sir."

"Concise, Chief. Keep me posted."

"Aye, Captain."

"Status on the emergency rockets, Lupain."

"They were automatically jettisoned by the damage control supervisor, sir. They exploded in space."

"How about trying an atmospheric bounce?"

"At our incidence angle?"

O'sihn raised his eyebrows.

"Impossible, sir."

"So it is, Lieutenant?" O'sihn's inflection was growing sharp and rigid.

---

164 A system that makes particles collapse into a so-called *dimensionless state*. More accurately, particle dimensions are pushed to a size smaller than what could be measured through any physical means, according to the physical models in use at that time.

"Our terminal incidence angle is close to forty-five degrees—and the ship has a 0.89 RPM residual spin, sir."

O'sihn rubbed his forehead and sighed. "Engine room/conn."

"Chief Beaver, Captain."

"Lin, in about half an hour we're gonna hit the atmosphere with an incidence of forty-five, at a 0.89 RPM spin."

"We have no control at all, Captain," Beaver said hurriedly, anticipating any instruction from the captain.

"I am aware of the situation. Now, what if we rigged some chemical device—even explosives—to help us gain some momentum, reduce the incidence angle, and perhaps eliminate some of the spin?"

"I . . . I don't know, sir; I'd need a detailed report from damage control. The structure has suffered compromising damage and—"

"The time for reports is up, Chief."

There was a brief hush, partially filled in with the background voices from the congested open channel.

"I'd be working in the dark, Captain. We would most likely worsen our present situation rather than helping it."

"We have no choice. Put all hands on this, Lin. Do whatever you can, and call me back when—"

"Sir, with all this lack of information, it will be a shot in the dark that could likely leave us with a pronounced angular momentum, which we may not be able to compensate at all."

"Your experience and expedience are our last hope, Chief. We still have a little over thirty-five minutes."

A gentle touch on one of his ankles made O'sihn look down.

"It's useless." Laida coughed, staring at her husband. "It's useless, O."

O'sihn shook his head and stepped back.

"Abandon ship while you still can," Laida continued. "She is dying, but her crew is still alive."

Leaning back on his seat, O'sihn stared at the planet surface peacefully displayed on the main TD. Laida's words had sapped his energy and strength, dragging him down to almost depression levels.

The X.O. was right; there was no way out of the situation. After half a minute of silence, he finally activated the console intercom. "Engine room/conn."

"Chief Beaver speaking, Captain."

"Last directive canceled. Start making preparations to abandon ship."

There was a delay in Lin Beaver's reply. "Sir, we can still try a bounce on the atmosphere using gravitational flaps. Some of them are still operational. They may give us up to thirty extra minutes to work on something else, including reducing incidence angle and spin."

"Negative, use gravitational flaps to tweak the ship's trajectory to effect reentry close to Veridiawa."

"Aye, Captain," Beaver muttered as the captain closed the channel.

O'sihn leaned back in his seat. The atmosphere of the planet, speckled with clouds, appeared serene and gentle on the main tactical display.

"O'sihn?" Tygrum said, turning to the captain.

As if disconnected, his friend was focused on the planet, deep in silence.

96.

"To all personnel of cruiser *Intrepid*, this is the captain."

With all intercom channels open, O'sihn's voice reached every corner of the cruiser. "As a result of the last attack, the ship is starting to sink into the atmosphere of Althea 8. We have half an hour left—perhaps a few more minutes." Distorted, the captain's image now materialized on several virtual displays in all departments. "Our ship has been our post and our home for the last four years. But this last day's run of hers is not the last of our team. We will overcome this crisis, and soon we will be back serving the Realdom again, with the best of who we are, to the last drop of who we are. We will meet back down on the planet's surface."

The captain paused and met the gazes of his officers on the virtual consoles. "You can close all channels, Cilia."

With an awkward movement of her hands, Cilia complied. All virtual consoles, including hers, went down.

"All personnel implement plan two of emergency abandonment procedure. All personnel implement plan two of emergency abandonment procedure . . . "

O'sihn opened a new channel, but nobody responded. "Lieutenant Commander Clara to the bridge," he said, using 1-MC. "Lieutenant Commander Clara to the bridge."

"Conn/sickbay, Doctor Raikun reporting."

"Yes, Rai."

"Sixteen people dead or missing, Captain; five seriously wounded; forty-seven injured. I'm still receiving updates on the medical situation."

"Can those who are impaired be taken to jettison stations?"

"We're working on that at the moment, sir."

"This is our first priority now."

"Certainly, Captain."

O'sihn nodded and turned back. Clara was already waiting at the entrance to the bridge. "Keep me posted, Rai."

"Aye."

"Come on in, Clara."

"Sir."

"You are currently assigned to raft two, aren't you?"

"Yes."

"The X.O. is the senior-most officer of your raft." O'sihn glanced down. His wife was still lying on the deck, semi-unconscious.

"She'll be all right, Captain," Clara knelt to help Laida up. The X.O. did not respond.

"Let me help you, Sub Commander," said Tygrum. Together, he and Clara were able to carry Laida off the bridge.

"Sickbay/conn." ·

"Raikun, Captain."

"Once the evacuation of the wounded is completed, you and all your personnel will abandon ship."

The doctor delayed his acknowledgment. "Sir, request permission to stay on board along with the M.P.S."[165]

"Request denied. Everybody—including all search parties—is to abandon this vessel immediately."

"Captain—"

"You have your orders, Doc."

"Sir."

"T.O.," O'sihn added, addressing Tygrum, who had returned to the bridge. "You will take charge of raft number one. But first, make sure we launch the pod[166] with the material we need to execute our mission down on the planet."

"By the time the captain gets to the raft, everything will be ready," Tygrum said.

"Negative," O'sihn replied. "As soon as you have everything ready, you will jettison your capsule at once."

Tygrum remained silent.

"Standard procedure, T.O. I'll be searching for survivors until the last minute, and then I'll jettison myself in an escape pod."

"With all due respect, sir, I think there is nothing left to be done here. And I'd rather have the captain as the commanding officer of raft number one."

O'sihn nodded. "You will be in charge of raft number one today."

Tygrum knew that arguing with his old friend would be useless. He limited himself to the salute of protocol. "I hope everything goes well with you, Captain."

O'sihn did not respond. He was holding onto a picture of Aleia, his eldest daughter. She had given her life, not long ago, to save the same ship that, today, he could not save.

---

165 Missing Personnel Search team.

166 The pod was a rather large unmanned capsule packed with instruments and other items needed for the mission still to be accomplished on the planet.

Strands and stripes of smoke furrowed the air of the bridge. Intercom traffic was rapidly dwindling. The background noise of a few still-operating instruments was becoming the dominant sound remaining in the commanding room.

"Damage control/conn," O'sihn said, turning to his console. "Damage control/conn?" He switched over to another station. "Engine room/conn. Come in, engine room."

O'sihn kept trying all departments, no one replying in each case. "Attention, all decks," he finally said through 1-MC. "This is the captain. Whoever may still be onboard must contact the bridge immediately. I repeat, whoever may still be onboard must contact the bridge at once."

"There is no one left onboard, Captain."

O'sihn turned back. Duncan was standing at the entrance to the bridge. He was wearing the space suit required for abandoning procedures. Folded over one arm, he was holding another.

"I stopped by your quarters and I brought you this."

"You should be onboard raft number one, Lieutenant."

"Raft number one is still waiting for her captain."

O'sihn glanced at Duncan; he looked determined to get him out of the ship. Not in a mood for confrontation, the captain merely got up from his seat and moved towards the X.O.'s console.

"You must proceed to your raft immediately, Dahncion." O'sihn started typing some instructions on a luminous virtual panel. "And that's an order, Lieutenant," he added sharply, turning around.

O'sihn completed some computations, after which he stepped towards the exit of the bridge.

"Where are you going?" Duncan inquired.

"There could be survivors trapped in—"

But at that point, O'sihn fell to the floor. The metallic cup of an E.C.F.E.[167] had blown off, hitting the back of O'sihn's head.

The sound of the captain's massive body hitting the deck did not

---

167 Emergency Chemical Fire Extinguisher.

pass unnoticed by the T.O., who was still waiting at the entrance of the bridge.

"I guess you need some help," said Tygrum, standing at the doorway.

"You bet."

97.

While struggling to lift the captain up, Duncan and Tygrum stumbled and fell slowly to the deck.

"What was that?" Tygrum said, coughing heavily from the effect of the E.C.F.E. gases.

The weight they had been trying to lift had suddenly lightened. A major gravitational system failure was propagating throughout the ship. Duncan and Tygrum discovered they were now able to carry the captain's massive body with no major difficulty. However, they had to adjust their movements to the new low-gravity environment, a situation for which they were well trained.

Soon they reached a major corridor. The raft pier was not far away.

"Are you sure she is okay?" Duncan asked Tygrum, the same question he had asked twice, at the raft launching station, prior to returning to the bridge to look for O'sihn.[168]

"As I said before, raft number two lifted off with a cut and clean *nothing to report.*"

Duncan winced with anxiety.

"Will you stop worrying about Erina? She's fine."

98.

Already in space, Laida started recovering consciousness.

"Jettison effected as programmed; nothing to report, Commander," Clara said, levitating in the absence of any net acceleration. "We

---

168 Duncan had asked his questions while still waiting at the launching bay for all the assigned personnel to reach their raft.

are about one kilometer from the *Intrepid*, now. Twenty minutes to reentry."

Laida moaned and nodded. On her ocher eyes, barely open, the shape of a woman was clearly drawn. "Is everybody all right?"

"Yes, Commander."

The raft was similar to a piercing capsule, though wider and furnished with many instruments, along with water, provisions, and other survival items. Like a piercing capsule, its hull was made of a transparent metallic material.

"Erina, where is Erina?" Laida inquired.

Clara glanced back. She knew each of the crewmembers assigned to her raft, a basic item any officer first ascertained when assigned to a ship. "All personnel assigned to raft two are on board, Commander. Ensign Erina is assigned to raft four."

"*Ensign* Erina was assigned to raft four," Laida corrected. "But *Lieutenant* Erina was reassigned to raft two upon promotion."

Clara's eyes changed perceptibly.

"It's not your fault, Clara," Laida stressed, noticing her alarm and sense of guilt. "O'sihn made the change late yesterday. You had no chance to check your daily instructions." Clara had been on duty that morning. "Surely she is on another raft, most likely raft four."

As Laida talked, Clara tried to make contact with raft four, and other rafts, with no success. They were most likely going through their reentry phase. She also tried calling Erina on her personal communicator, but had no response.

Laida showed Erina's communicator to Clara. "She forgot it on the bridge last night."

"What if she is inside the ship? We may be able to reach her through—"

"The ship's network is out of line,"[169] Laida interrupted.

---

169 The hull would not allow standard communications with any terminal of any sort inside the ship. However, there was a communications interface, now out of line, that under normal circumstances would enable linking with the ship's internal network, and through it, with any communications terminal.

Clara shook her head with distress.

"She *is* on raft four," Laida asserted.

"We can't be certain," Clara objected. "She was on duty last night.[170] She may be unconscious or injured in her cabin."

"The Captain will never leave the *Intrepid* until he is certain that everybody still alive is off his ship," Laida replied.

"I was still on the virtual bridge when Captain O'sihn asked Doctor Raikun to check for all wounded personnel," Lieutenant Cilia put in. *"Check for all wounded and evacuate them in any available raft,* were the captain's words."

Clara stared at the *Intrepid*, gleaming in the distance, slightly disfigured. Occasional tongues of flames were bursting from its hull.

"We're still too close to the ship, Captain Clara. We must gain more altitude."[171]

"Request permission to check status on Lieutenant Er—"

"Request absolutely denied," Laida interrupted briskly. "You forget you are in charge here, *Captain*."

Clara evaded Laida's gaze, her eyes drifting towards the *Intrepid* again. Laida started issuing some technical instructions to a young crewmember, who was staring back with a confused expression. Struggling with her pain, Laida strove to make her point more clear. In the meantime, Clara began drifting towards the control panel. Reaching the tactical display, she set on the raft opening sequence and blocked the command with a password to prevent anybody from interrupting the procedure.

A synthesized voice was immediately heard on the raft. *"Zero-atmosphere opening procedure in progress. Fifteen seconds to execute."* A countdown started flashing on several displays, seamlessly built in in the hull of the raft.

At once, all space suits were automatically sealed and activated

---

170 This implied that she would have had an extended sleeping period in the morning.

171 A common Realitian expression used when speaking in relation to a large body, like a large vessel.

by the safety system. A luminous red band lit up along the path where the raft was about to open.

"Seize Lieutenant Commander Clara!" Laida shouted through her speaker. In calling Clara *Lieutenant Commander* instead of *Captain*, Laida had expressly taken charge of the raft.

The personnel onboard tried to get hold of her, but the Veritian Marine was too much for them. The weightless conditions on the raft were not helping either. In the meantime, Laida was struggling, in vain, to unlock the opening system. "Give me the damned password, Clara. Do it!"

The internal bulkheads were already taking in the capsule's atmosphere. The hissing of the reabsorbed air quickly ceased, and the hull opened up in two halves.

With the capsule open, Clara jumped off into the vacuum. Abandon procedure suits, or A.P.S.s, had a limited ability to travel in space, and she was now using hers to its maximum capacity.

The members of the raft tried to catch up with her, but they quickly realized that was not going to work.[172] They soon reconvened in one of the raft halves. The other half automatically re-joined with theirs, and the raft closed. A.P.S.s were capable of performing very short-range maneuvers. Aware of that, and before starting the opening sequence, Clara had grabbed an air tank and an emergency flare gun with the intent of using them as rudimentary propulsion devices. She had hitched them onto her belt along with a C.T.C. (contact tape cartridge), which was similar to a roll of adhesive tape, but with electro-magnetic attaching properties.

Immersed in space, Clara aimed the flare gun in the direction opposite to the *Intrepid*. She immediately shot the five cartridges her

---

172 Even if they could catch up with her, they might not be able to get back to the raft in time for a safe reentry.

flare gun carried, rapidly gaining significant momentum towards the ship.

"Come back. Don't be a foo—"

Clara disconnected the communication channel. Right after that, the raft's safety system automatically resumed control and the vehicle continued its trip down to the planet.

Releasing the valve of the extra air tank, Clara began to gain additional speed. The small propulsive mechanism of her A.P.S. helped her correct the trajectory back to the ship.

Very rapidly, the impressive view of the *Intrepid*—almost a quarter of a mile in length—started taking up a wide angular scope.

A cloud of incandescent gas erupted from the hull near the center of the ship. An ignited jet immediately followed, streaming out of the vessel with a soundless power. Clara was clear of the trajectory of the gases, but the proximity to the event made her become more aware of her relative speed. She immediately shut off the valve to the air tank, halting her accelerating rate. As she got closer to the vessel, she realized that her terminal speed was dangerously high. With the intent of reducing it, she aimed the air-tank she held under an arm towards the ship and opened its valve.

The pressure was already low. Clara reacted quickly by reorienting the modest propulsive thrust of her space suit in a new attempt to break off her speed. It had a limited effect. When she was about to hit the hull, Clara threw the empty tank against it in a last effort to decrease her relative momentum. The tank bounced off, and right behind it, Clara bumped onto the hull at a still dangerous rate. She was only stunned by the impact. Reorienting the propulsive system of her suit, she began to move slowly over the smooth surface.

Clara knew the ship very well, so it did not take her long to reach one of the emergency bays. She quickly found what she was looking for: a small rectangular glowing mark—one of the external digital opening terminals. She activated it and typed in the corresponding password, fearing it had been locked. But an opening immediately materialized in front of her.

Clara slid through into a narrow chamber. The hatch above her head suddenly shut, and a hazy cold air flowing from the entire floor panel began flooding the chamber. When the ship's internal pressure was reached, a hatch swung open. The light on top of Clara's helmet cast shadows inside a dark corridor that lay ahead.

What to do next? Where to start a search for anybody in a quarter-mile-long ship? Clara knew that Erina, together with Duncan, had been covering the third night watch that week. That meant she would have had a special resting period during the morning. She would start by checking her cabin.

Clara began moving towards the hatch to an internal emergency corridor. She did not dare check how much time she had left. Fortunately, the hatch yielded at her first try. A shaft appeared, connecting to the officer's quarters a few decks below and several sections ahead. Clara dragged herself through it as fast as she could. The gravitational system was not working anymore, and the ship retained a residual spin. The resulting centripetal acceleration was small in that area, due to the proximity to the ship's center of gravity. But as Clara began to move faster, using the propulsion system of her A.P.S., she literally started walking on one of the bulkheads.[173]

On reaching the officer's quarters deck, some disturbing data appeared on a small infrared window on Clara's visor: the floor was dangerously hot, a clear sign that a fire was raging on the deck below. Objects of all sizes were floating everywhere, along with debris and smoke.

---

173 A Coriolis acceleration was induced by the rotational spin of the ship combined with the speed Clara was gathering as she moved down the shaft. This acceleration worked in a similar manner to a gravitational pull against the surface along which Clara was moving, enabling her to walk and even run along the shaft without the assistance of her A.P.S.

Very rapidly, the impressive view of the Intrepid—almost quarter of a mile
in length—started taking up a wide, angular scope.

Clara moved carefully down the corridor until she finally found a door with the yet unchanged inscription *Ensign Erina* on it. The corridor's overhead had suffered severe deformations, which had firmly compressed the door onto the bulkheads. As Clara struggled to get the door open, an explosion, coming from somewhere inside the ship, shook it violently, causing her to slam backwards into a bulkhead.

Taking her gun, Clara hurried back to the door and started melting an opening; she quickly realized that was going to take too much time. Taking some tape from the C.T.C. on her belt, she fixed her gun against the door and activated its self-destruction system.[174] As quickly as she could, Clara now struggled to get away from the spot—not an easy endeavor in a micro-gravity environment.

The gun exploded, thrusting Clara forward violently. She cried out with fear, remaining momentarily still, shuddering against a bulkhead. A splinter had reached her suit above her right knee, opening a rent on it. The memory of what had happened to her in Aquaelight had imprinted a mark in her psyche.

Clara's A.P.S. quickly took on the same atmosphere of the ship. Due to the gases released by the explosions and many fires on board, the ship's air was difficult to breathe, but all in all, the environment was still capable of sustaining life. The corridor was filled with a cloud of smoke, and it was hard to see. She had to feel her way back to Erina's quarters.

By the time she had reached the spot, the air was becoming clearer. The door to Erina's cabin was partially torn off, with one side virtually welded onto the bulkhead, and the other twisted back inside the cabin. Curled up in a back corner, a motionless human shape was discernible. Clara stepped inside at once.

---

174 The system allowed for different modes of self-destruction. The most violent would have caused serious damage and would have killed anybody in the vicinity. Thus Clara set her gun to a mild self-explosive mode, hoping this would release enough energy to force the door open.

"It's all right, Erina, it's all right." Clara stooped down beside her. She was in some kind of a shock. Her face had a vacant expression. "I'll get you out of here in no time," Clara added softly, as if talking to a child. "You'll be fine."

Erina was wearing her everyday uniform. The first thing Clara had to do was to get a space suit for her. After a brief struggle with a stuck drawer, its damaged front broke off. Handle in hand, Clara hit the bulkhead behind her and bounced off towards the cabin's overhead. Quickly checking her watch, she realized there was no time to try to get Erina to put the suit on.

"It's okay, I'll get you out of here," Clara muttered, agitated, as she hastily stuck the suit around Erina's hips using more of her C.T.C. tape. She intended to put it on Erina once they were safely inside a raft or an escape capsule. "Everything is going to be all right now."

Putting one arm around Erina's back, Clara began to move through the ship's dark corridors. Erina was in a deep trance. Most likely, after the *Intrepid* had been hit, she would have heard all the abandoning instructions coming through 1-MC. Having accidentally left her communicator on the bridge, and with her comm. terminal out of order, Erina would have tried in vain to report her position and status. As time went by and everybody abandoned ship, desperation would have finally set in. The increasing *bioxyn* depletion would have contributed to the condition in which she was found.

At the end of the corridor, there was an emergency escape bay. Dragging Erina along, Clara quickly reached the spot. She tried to operate the hatch to the bay manually, but it would not respond.

Recalling the twin abandoning bay at the other end of the same corridor, she immediately grabbed Erina and started moving on again. The corridor seemed as if it had no end. Clara began coughing and moaning miserably, and her vision began to blur. As she stopped to catch some air, another explosion rocked the ship.

Almost instantly, Clara found herself right in front of the opposite bay, along with Erina. Immediately, she tried to open the hatch. At first, it would not respond, but with some persistence, its emergency handle loosened and the hatch opened up. An escape capsule was stowed to one side.

Clara moved towards the pod and activated its opening system. The first thing she did was to set the landing coordinates on the navigational display. Waiting until after launch could be very risky; she could fail to do that in time, or worse, lose consciousness before doing it. Once done, she dragged Erina inside.

There was no time for a safe by-the-rules launch, so Clara set on the jettison procedure without further consideration. The bay hatch was blasted into space, and so was the capsule. The pod's automatic propulsion system responded immediately, not just trying to get the vehicle away from the ship, but mostly struggling to gain some altitude to avoid hitting the dangerously close upper atmospheric layers at the capsule's ejection incidence angle. For a disturbing moment, a tenuous luminescence glowed on the pod's hull as it scraped the silent surface of the gaseous fathoms below.

The *Intrepid* was swiftly becoming another star on the horizon. Clara looked at it with a mixture of sadness and nostalgia, as the sunlight reflected on her hull slowly faded out. After a minute or so, the weak white star turned into a bright red sphere.

The Realitarian battleship had begun her last journey, carving a furrow of fire in the higher atmospheric layers of Althea 8.[175] As it slowly submerged herself into the vast oceans of the Veridiawan heavens, Clara stood salute (as it were), her sight fixed on the blazing trail. Her hair was levitating gently around her face. Above her now peaceful eyes, tears were left to float immersed in a resigned silence.

---

175 The ship would automatically disintegrate soon after hitting the atmosphere to minimize any damage it could cause to the planet's surface.

CHAPTER 15

A Short Rest

99.

A new day was dawning on the warm Taicidias steppes of the north. Above the horizon, to the west, a growing red sunrise was relieving each star, one by one, from its ancient task of sprinkling beauty on the Althean sky.

With sleepy red eyes and without much haste, two characters—rather different—were crossing the dewy fields. They had always liked taking that cross-country walk back to the village without following any particular trail.

The calm air and the hazy horizon were heralding a warm, muggy day. But, for the time being, one of the travelers was enjoying the cool wet vegetation of the early morning, as he pondered the celestial sight he had just witnessed.

"What a sky-light shower," the *keiro* said in his distinctive sluggish cadence.

"Yep," Seidy agreed while riding on his friend's back. "That sure was a good one."

"And that red little ball of fire falling all the way down from the sky . . . " Boldowa continued.

"Little? It was like a sun," Seidy remarked. "And the trail of fire it left over the clouds . . . "

Boldowa frowned. "Why do sky-lights fall down from the sky, Seidy?"

"Simple: sky-lights are tiny, all made out of light—that's why they float in the sky. But when dust gets into a star, even the weight of a tiny grain can make it fall all the way down to the ground. You know, last night being so windy and dusty and all . . . "

"Oh." Boldowa frowned again, not understanding much of his friend's explanation. "Seidy?"

"Yes?"

"I had never seen a sky-light before—that red sun we saw, that is."

"So?"

"Sky-lights *are* beautiful."

"Hm," Seidy muttered absentmindedly.

The *keiro* kept on strolling for a while, his mind still wondering about the star shower. "You're very lucky, having been born a *wuol*, and being so smart."

"You are absolutely right," Seidy confirmed with his usual lack of modesty. His next comment was not as predictable, though. "But you are a very big strong fellow. Your hide is like copper, and your horns are like swords. You're a pretty impressive guy too, Boldo."

"Oh, please, don't call me Boldo."

"*My name is Boldowa,*" both spoke in unison.

The landscape was slowly switching to a multicolored grassland full of flowers as the first mild rays of the local sun began to loom on the horizon.

"You are so good, Seidy, you being my friend."

The comment surprised Seidy. Boldowa's friendship had never been a particular subject of his considerations. He thought of saying something, but the few words that popped up in his mind were just not the sorts of things he was comfortable saying.

"Hey, down there!"

Seidy looked up. A tight formation of *golloondias* was flying fast towards the north. Seidy took off and approached the leader. "Hey, what's going on?"

"Haven't you seen the lights in the sky?" Inury said.

"Yeah, the falling sun, and the shower of sky-lights. Man!" Duncan's passage through the village had left unmistakable marks on the Veridiawan vocabulary.

"But that's not all," Inury commented. "A moment ago, Daih-youleeby got back from his post, and guess what? Dozens of *newones* have arrived with the lights."

Seidy frowned, amazed.

"And that's still not all! Guess who's among them?"

The *wuol* raised one eyebrow. "Girl-Captain Clara?"

"Exactly, and the Boy-Dahncion, and—"

"See ya later," Seidy said, and dived down sharply. "Hey, Boldo, we gotta go back!" he yelled from the air.

Bemused, Boldowa remarked, "But, but, we're going back, already."

"No, dummy, we gotta go back to the north, to the place where the lights have fallen."

Boldowa's confusion turned into apprehension. "What do you mean, Seidy? You know: 'Tis not good to go where sky-lights fall from the sky'."

"Those were no sky-lights from the sky: they were sky-lights from the Realitas village. Girl-Captain Clara has come back—as she promised."

Boldowa's expression was transformed, his eyes fixed on the air. Everything seemed too good for one single day. And it had barely begun.

"Hey, what are you looking at, you, you . . . ?"

Boldowa flashed a grin. "Hold on."

"Aaah!" Seidy yelled, as he flapped his wings trying to compensate for the *keiro*'s swift acceleration.

A new trail sliced across the thick Taicidias grasslands as the thunder of Boldowa's heavy gallop slowly faded to the rustle of the mild morning breeze.

100.

The first thing Patriarch Coelious did the day after the arrival of the Realitian forces was to add the newcomers as official new *newones* Veridiawa. An entire expedition was being rapidly put together to accompany the girl-Captain and her friends to the distant ruins of the south. The furthest thought from Coelious' mind was to let it depart with *outlanders*[176] in its ranks.

The initiation ritual had been lengthy and ceremonious, as Veridiawan rituals went, but once it was over and all Realitians had been incorporated as *newones* Veridiawa, the packed Ivory Chamber was expeditiously cleared up. Veridiawans knew how to leave a place immediately when there is no more to be done. In any case, everything had happened faster than usual that day, since a great festivity was ready to take place in the village.

The total dependency upon the natives had given the Realitians an unexpected much-needed rest. Even Captain O'sihn, having lost his ship along with ten of his crewmembers (the original figure of sixteen personnel dead or missing had gone down) was starting to find peace and comfort, overwhelmed by the Veridiawan hospitality.

Music and laughter started to animate the occasion. A huge variety of foods and beverages were served, specially prepared by each family. It had not taken long for Duncan to finish his first barbecued *wedia*. As he got ready for his second, he spotted Erina walking by. She was wearing a dress that had been adapted from a Veridiawan costume. The way it fitted her body emphasized her feminine qualities.

From a distance, Clara was discreetly aware of her. Duncan was soon talking to Erina quite animatedly. She could not hear what Duncan was saying, but at some point, Clara heard Erina laugh noisily, as she swished her hair from side to side.

Clara decided to distance herself from the crowd. As she walked away, it crossed her mind that perhaps this would be a good time to start overcoming her feelings. "Really," she thought, "whatever is best for Dahncion is best for me." Seeking refuge in lofty ideals is often easy, expecting comfort from them, vain.

---

176 General term applied to individuals that did not belong to Veridiawa.

Far from the festivities, Clara could not hear any other sound than the constant singing of the summer cicadas. As she walked through a field, she turned around absentmindedly, and stopped. A threatening cloud of black smoke was emerging from the center of the village.

101.

Behind the first wave of enemy fliers carrying impact projectiles (mostly sharpened pieces of stone), a squadron of forty-seven *jarrons*[177] rushed through with incendiary torches, at a low altitude, dropping them on the straw roofs of the houses they flew over.

The Veridiawan intercepting[178] air battalions did not have enough time to get organized. Though all of them had been set airborne immediately, they were rapidly repelled and neutralized.

The Creptions had apparently planned their incursion quite thoroughly. The initial assault had followed a pattern that efficiently prevented the Veridiawans from reaching their weapons. The impeccable element of surprise and the fierceness of the attackers triggered a state of confusion and chaos that was making any counterattack difficult.

Nevertheless, the Realitians had promptly united under their captain, and the second enemy air strike was effectively neutralized by weapons that astonished the Veridiawans. But then it was the Realitians' turn for surprise, for a third enemy wave broke through with modern Establishment weaponry.

The situation had turned grim. Enemy platoons were breaking in from different spots on the village borders. They were small units— four to five soldiers in number—but there were many of them. Yet the worst was yet to come: platoons with Kervian commandos in their ranks began to attack the village, causing panic among the Veridiawan people.

Debris mixed up with scattered food, streams of blood, the

---

177 *Jarrons*: intelligent flying species with strong predatory features.
178 Veridiawa had intercepting air battalions and attack air battalions.

increasing number of casualties, the moans and crying of children, were all contributing to the dreadful scene. Nevertheless, an improvised Veridiawan company had started to offer a strong resistance, along with O'sihn's people.

Amidst the havoc, a humanoid figure made its appearance, riding on a Creption *whymeenidy*. He did not seem interested in the battle; he acted as if searching for something. At first, nobody paid much attention to him. The humanoid began to ride into the mob, wielding his sword from side to side, efficiently eliminating anything or anybody in his way.

Realizing his intentions, Antares—the Veridiawan who had fought alongside Duncan in the Battle of the Glen, as the Veridiawans came to call it—ran towards the rider and pounced, intending to pull him from his *whymeenidy*. As he attacked, a Creption arrow struck his right thigh, rendering Antares out of combat.

Duncan, who was trying to help Erina up from a minor blow, froze upon hearing Antares' yell. Immediately after that, he found himself in front of a gray sturdy *whymeenidy* standing on his back feet, neighing savagely.

Before Duncan could do anything, the Kervian riding on the Creption *whymeenidy* aimed an odd long weapon at him and shot. A sticky net wrapped around Duncan, completely immobilizing his body. Leaning to one side, the soldier snatched the net with one hand, lifted Duncan between his chest and the *whymeenidy*'s mane, and rapidly merged back into the mob. Some Realitians, along with several Veridiawan warriors, tried to stop the Kervian, but they were repelled one by one. The enemy's focus had suddenly shifted to protecting the Kervian rider as he strove to leave the area with his human captive. Trying to reach Duncan had become impossible. It quickly dawned on O'sihn that the whole objective of the attack had been to capture Duncan.

Piercing through the crowd, the captain, followed by Lieutenant Bueyington, began to run, struggling not to lose sight of the captor.

Ivorai, the same Veridiawan who had been part of the mission to rescue Doctor Oyhtter, was right behind them.

Upon reaching the village borders, the Kervian began riding away into the northeast steppes, following a seemingly erratic trail. When he had reached sufficient distance from the village—about half a mile—the soldier turned to his left and adopted a straightforward path.

Yet the so-far-flawless enemy plan was about to suffer a glitch. Tripping on a hole hidden by the grass, the Creption *whymeenidy* broke one leg and fell to the ground. Both rider and captive were cast over the *whymeenidy*'s head, falling a few yards ahead.

The Kervian got up on the spot. Running towards Duncan (who remained completely immobilized), the alien soldier picked up the net with one hand and placed it over a shoulder. He looked around hastily and immediately resumed his getaway on foot with a remarkable display of speed and strength.

102.

O'sihn, Ivorai, and Bueyington had finally reached the village borders. They had not witnessed the *whymeenidy*'s accident, but they did spot the Kervian running away with Duncan on his back. Being faster than O'sihn, Ivorai and Bueyington dashed onto the steppes ahead of the captain, only to collapse to the ground when two mechanical devices—similar to bear traps—clenched their ankles.

O'sihn rushed in intending to release Ivorai.

"Forget about us, bear-Captain! The boy, run after the boy," Ivorai gasped.

O'sihn stopped and looked intently ahead.

"Look out, Captain!" Bueyington yelled. "The whole field may be rigged with traps."

O'sihn picked up a stone and hurled it into the grassland. A trap snapped cleanly from the scrub. Lifting another stone, he repeated the same action, with the same results. Still refusing to give up, he threw two more rocks. In both cases, he could even spot the traps leaping up as they sprung shut. The captain was left standing frustrated and inert, watching the captor and his hostage disappear rapidly into the steppe. Although a free-trap corridor had obviously provided a safe pass-way for the Kervian, it was very well concealed by the tall grassland.

The entire field had effectively been blocked off by the enemy.

103.

Deadly skillful with his weapons, keen and sharp in his movements, incredibly strong: the Kervian was the embodiment of the perfect warrior. As he proceeded with his getaway, his heartbeat was almost pounding on Duncan's head. The more he ran, the faster he got, as if efficiency and power increased with his speed and exertion.

Abruptly, a dried-up *seawidee*[179] branch crashed against the Kervian's legs, and the alien stumbled to a stop. A marine had sprung from nowhere to block his way.

With clutched fists and a grim expression, Clara stood defiant, gripping a broken branch in her hands. "You must release your hostage—if you want to live."

The soldier went through the motions of complying with her demand, until he suddenly slung the net—with Duncan inside—at her. Though taken by surprise, Clara moved aside in time to evade the human projectile. As part of her complex movement, she launched a kick at her opponent. Duncan clearly heard Clara's boots impacting on the back of the alien's head and the soldier's subsequent heavy fall.

"The sword . . . on my back!" Duncan yelled.

Clara ran towards him and gripped his Veridiawan sword. In seconds, Duncan was free, but only for a moment.

---

179 *Seawidees* are very tall trees with thick foliage and long branches. They are well known for their bright yellow flowers.

A sticky net wrapped around Duncan, completely immobilizing his body. O'sihn and his crew followed Duncan's captor.

Eight Kervian soldiers emerged from the forest, taking the two Realitians by surprise. Clara and Duncan looked around for some way to escape, but they were surrounded. The Kervians immediately took hold of them.

The commanding officer of the platoon approached the knocked-out Kervian on the grass. As he did so, Duncan pushed the soldier who was trying to handcuff him, and taking advantage of the split-second confusion, ran off into the woods.

The platoon shot at Duncan with weapons similar to the one used to capture him in the village. The jettisoned nets clumsily wrapped each other and the bushes lying along their trajectory.

The aliens rushed after Duncan, as their leader turned impassively towards Clara. Both her legs and hands were handcuffed. The Kervian glanced at Clara for a moment, and then forced her to the ground, putting a foot on her neck. Efficient and businesslike, he held an instrument to her right ear. Immediately, the device began buzzing until it flashed white.

The officer nodded and recalled his personnel. Back from their failed pursuit, the soldiers found their leader still holding the instrument he had just used on Clara.

"Never mind the boy," he said, pointing to the woman with reassurance. "Here is all we need; she's a *quickener*, all right."

104.

The grass was soft and dense, gracefully covering the silky soil where it spread. *Weamooses* stood tall here and there. These leafy bushes did not bear flowers, yet needed none for beauty. *Swiniadas* further enhanced the greenish-blue scenery with yellow, indigo, and purple three-clustered flowers. Each flower of every cluster had a distinct aroma, which when blended produced an exquisite fragrance.

But all the surrounding beauty was imperceptible to Duncan.

After running for a couple of minutes into the thicket, he threw himself to the ground, exhausted. Pulling himself together, he quickly decided to return to try to help Clara.

Locating the spot was not difficult, but no one was there anymore. After aimlessly searching for clues, he glimpsed a shadow slithering through the foliage, not very far away. Having no gun or any means of communication, the best he could do was to keep track of whatever signs the captors might have left, and try to follow them.

Two shots came from the forest, and immediately, Duncan threw himself to the ground. He tried to locate the attacker, but the thick vegetation made it very difficult. Resuming his chase, Duncan was now looking around, trying to find any trace of Clara or her captors.

Eventually he stumbled upon the small ribbon of a blue lace, from Clara's hair. A few yards ahead, a smashed *swiniada* three-flower was lying on the ground. Trying to visualize a straight line between the ribbon and the tattered three-flower, Duncan started moving in that direction, helped by his compass. But soon he was out of clues again. Tired, he picked up a small stick, and started fiddling with it.

As he thought of what to do next, he heard a metallic and recognizable buzzing sound. He stood up immediately and began moving towards it as rapidly as he could. All of a sudden, he found himself in an open area that had been wiped clear of vegetation in a crude manner. Duncan looked up above the treetops and was struck by what he saw. An unmistakable assault vessel was lifting off the ground, gaining altitude very rapidly. He kept staring at the craft until he lost sight of it behind the surrounding treetops.

Disturbed by the implications and overwhelmed by how quickly everything had happened, Duncan knelt down, beating his forehead in frustration and despair against the singed smoky grass.

As he lay there, Laida arrived. She paused for a moment and gently approached Duncan. Kneeling down beside him, she placed a hand on one of his shoulders.

"They've taken Clara away," Duncan said in a low tone.

Duncan knelt down, staring at the craft until he lost sight of it behind the
surrounding treetops.

Laida gripped him tightly with tears in her eyes. Getting back on her feet, she gently extended one arm. Duncan glanced back at her with a strong manly expression, finally forged by war.

"We're gonna get her back, Dahncion." Laida nodded. "We will get her back."

CHAPTER 16

Sternessence

105.

"Somebody is coming," Seidy said, walking to the top of Boldowa's head to try to get a better look.

"It's very, very night. I can't see anything, Seidy."

"It's too dark all right, even for me. Go ahead, Boldo; ask them, ask them."

Boldowa cleared his throat, finally inquiring in a loud languid tone: "Who is living in the darkness?"

"Warrior Engadye, leader of the expedition to the Ruins of the South."

"Countersign," Boldowa challenged.

"Light shower!" replied Engadye. "Counter-countersign."

Boldowa kept standing at a loss, until Seidy discreetly added, "*Swiniada* of the sky-lights."[180]

"Oh, yes, *swiniada* of the sky-lights," repeated Boldowa to himself. "*Swiniada* of the sky-lights!" he howled, looking ahead.

Four *keiros* carrying O'sihn, Laida, Duncan, and Erina emerged from the tenuous fog, followed by six other *keiros*, three *whymeenidies*, two *jarrons*, and five *wuols*.

"Please, *newones*," Boldowa said as Laida passed by. "Please, rescue the girl-Captain, please?"

Laida patted Boldowa's back. "Will do, Boldo."

---

180 *Swiniada* of the sky-lights: in some rare instances, *swiniadas* bloomed in monochromatic white. The natives regarded this as a good omen.

The *keiro* stared at Laida, as if wanting to add something.

"He doesn't like people calling him Boldo," Seidy explained, rolling his eyes and shaking his head.

Boldowa stepped back slowly. Engadye's voice was heard again, ordering the group to speed up the march. They had a long trip ahead, and they intended to cover it in half the time it would normally take.

"How can they find their way to the Ruins of the South, Seidy?" Boldowa asked. "This is the northern post."

"They have to get around the Creption fortress, silly."

"Oh, yes, yes, the Creption fortress. But it's very dark. How will they find their way to the Ruins of the South, Seidy? It's badly dark."

Seidy flashed one of his self-confident smiles. "There are five *wuols* following the formation. For us *wuols*, darkness is not a problem. Besides, turn around." Seidy walked across his friend's neck towards his back. "Do you see that sky-light with the long white tail in the sky casting faint shadows on the field?"

Boldowa raised his head over the foggy layer, which lay above the ground no more than three feet. "I see a thin white cloud up in the sky, Seidy."

"That's it. The sky-light with the tail will show them the way."

106.

It was the last night of the expedition, and the last night of a long journey. If everything went according to plan, tomorrow Duncan would step on the trans-universal chamber at the center of the *technon*, and a moment later, he would be back to Earth. The thought gave him a measure of relief, but for some reason, he did not find the peace he expected from it.

Perhaps it was about Clara. She had fallen prisoner to the Establishment while trying to rescue him; the idea of leaving her behind was not pleasant. He felt he had to stay, at least, until her situation was clear. But that would mean staying in that universe for who knew how much longer. It could be years, if ever, until he could get back to Earth. Even as he considered this possibility, he knew

Erina would not share it, although he had not discussed the subject with her. His attachment to her was intense, and he could not find the strength to let her go back to Earth alone, perhaps forever.

On the other hand, even if it had not been easy for him, he had somehow grown accustomed to the life he was leading. Meeting new races, being exposed to amazing technologies, making contact with very different and intriguing cultures, contemplating the beauty of a sunset on one planet, and then on another, and another, witnessing the magnificence of space—and all in a different universe. Wasn't all that much more than what he had always dreamed of? Hadn't such impossible dreams come true, far beyond any expectations?

Back on Earth, he would certainly have the great benefit of his incredible experience, which could open many doors for him. And he could not wait to share all this with his family and his closest friends.

But now, Duncan had to contend with an unexpected grief. He realized he had developed a strong affection for those close to him, to the Realdom, and even to the Royal Navy, things he had never thought would happen, at least not to that degree. He had made excellent friends, like he had never had on Earth. They felt like family to him. He already had a life in Reality.

However, the unresolved *sternessence* issue, combined with the anxiety caused by the high (though silent) expectations that many in the Realdom had about him, Duncan felt, produced in him a strong desire to go back home where he belonged.

Duncan was sitting on the ground, somewhere in the Pampwinian steppes. As he thought, he stared at what he recognized as the Milky Way. It was not a faint belt in the sky, as he would expect to see on Earth, but two vivid crossed bands, one with stars shining in pure white, and the other, with dots of light that radiated yellow and blue. Glimmering here and there, red and crimson stars completed the scene. Yet all the beauty was beginning to dim with the light of a new large moon rising above the horizon.[181]

---

181 Althea 8 had several satellites, although only one was big enough to have a

With the tall grass looming above his head, Duncan was out of sight but not *out of smell*, and *ossians* have a keen sense of smell.

"Enjoying a pleasant evening . . . I hope I don't disrupt."

Duncan had already identified his friend by the characteristic sound of his stride. "No, not at all."

O'sihn sat down beside him, leaning on his hands, which he stretched backwards onto the grass. "This is our last night together, Dahncion. I would like to discuss a few things before you leave us."

"Sure, O'sihn."

"First of all, I want to emphasize that you don't have to leave. Both the Realdom and the Royal Navy would be more than happy to have you among us. And you don't have to stay in the Navy either. The royal couple has made it very clear to me[182] that they would be very happy with your living among us outside the armed forces. You have already given a very valuable service to the Realdom, service that was very generous on your part."

"I've been thinking a lot about these things," Duncan answered. "I appreciate your words very much—and the kind offering from their royal majesties—but I think I do have to leave tomorrow. I have no words to describe my experience in this universe. I have had the privilege of doing something unique and so very special. You can bet it won't be easy for me to step on that *technon* tomorrow, not at all."

O'sihn closed his eyes, showing respect for Duncan's decision. "So, what are you planning to do back on Earth?"

"Well, for one thing, I'll resume my college studies, and then, well, I don't know yet."

"You realize that, although you will remember all that happened

---

discernible disk. Its apparent diameter would vary between one and twenty minutes of arc, depending on the distance to the planet, its orbit being highly elliptical and having a large precession of its perihelion.

182 Not in person, but through classified correspondence.

here, you will not have a way to prove your ever having been here."

Duncan nodded. The particulars of the *transreal* reentry had already been explained to him. The *transrealization* would affect the bodies of those going through it and anything under their bodies' vital influence. This would include elements like hair, body fluids and food being processed. However, other objects, including clothes, would stay in that universe.

"I know, but Erina will be able to prove it. Her country sent her, and she will be back with her people. Even if she will have no way to take any evidence from here, her story, which will agree with mine, will carry enough weight."

"You both will be reinserted onto the space reality from where you departed. Therefore, you will be thousands of miles away from each other, probably entering your universe at different times," O'sihn explained. "Besides, you two will be speaking different languages. Erina will not understand your native tongue, nor you hers."

"We both speak Realitian."

O'sihn shook his head. "I'm afraid Realitian will be completely gone from your brains."

"I will find a way to contact her."

"She belongs to a highly classified project of a country that, for you, will be a foreign nation. She might not be able to get in contact with you, even if she wanted." O'sihn noticed the discomfort these comments caused Duncan. "I apologize for my frankness, Dahncion. I'm just trying to have you realize that things may just not work out the way you are thinking right now. We don't even know the process through which Erina was sent here, to this universe. Although there are sufficient reasons to believe that her trip will be a safe one, her experiential life may not remain as crisp as yours for her."

"What do you mean, her *experiential* life?"

"To put it in rough terms, she lacks some of the psychophysical conditions that the RIBA body-reconfiguration bestowed on you. After her body—and therefore her brain—goes through the Realitic reinsertion tomorrow, her life in this universe, although still real for her, may likely remain as an *oniric* experience—a dream-like experience. As a consequence, her feelings, her life-experiences, could remain in a weak and fuzzy form. If that were the case, she may not recognize you as Dahncion, a name that will be gone from your and her vocabulary, anyway.

"The possibility that you will continue your life on Earth as if you had never been here is not at all unlikely. This is not necessarily wrong." O'sihn stood up and straightened the back of his uniform, making ready to leave. "But I think it's important that when you step in that *technon* tomorrow, you will be doing it having considered all factors."

Duncan fixed his eyes on the captain. "Before you leave, I have one question, O'sihn, a very personal question."

O'sihn nodded and motioned to Duncan to go ahead.

"I know you believe my destiny lies here, that I am a key element to win this war," Duncan stated.

O'sihn looked at him, neither assenting nor dissenting.

"Why do you believe that so strongly?" Duncan asked.

O'sihn shook his head. "I don't think we should discuss this."

"Why not? If you really want to help me make the right decision, wouldn't your opinion—the opinion of a good friend who knows me quite well—be important to me?"

O'sihn pressed his lips together and squatted in front of Duncan. "You are the one to build your own destiny. You must be the *realizator* of your own reality."

"My own reality . . . how could my reality be to fight and conquer a . . . galactic empire out there in a foreign universe, to stop its Equity, to confront someone like the First Equitarian—in short, to help the Realdom be real when I am not even from its reality?"

O'sihn squinted. "In the same way that Ms. Paulina's house was Mars for you, while still being your next-door neighbor's house. In the same way that the enemies of those little animal action figures you played with and knew by their names—Oseén, Blankita, Teegrom, Rogelio . . . [183] you called us, if I remember well—had to fight their mortal enemies the Keerwians, who lived on planet Keer, which was also your other next-door house. In the same way that the playground close to your house was the Moon, while still being the playground. In the same way your living-room tile floor was the ocean on which your interlocking-block aircraft carriers sailed to the islands of your mats, while still being mats. In the same way your interlocking-block spaceships traveled to your distant Venus, which was still your grandpa's house. In the same way O'sihn, Laida, and the rest would explore your universe as you took them in your secret little cases, which were actually spaceships, while still also being little cases. In them, they would travel to the house that your grandparents had by the sea, which of course was a distant planet, or to this hotel with a large sand playground, which was another distant planet. In the same way so many other great stories that you and I know so very well . . . "

O'sihn stopped, and Duncan stepped back almost in fear. "How do you know all that?"

"We saw those things in our dreams. We lived them in our dreams —many of us in Realitas: the same dreams, on the same nights, for quite some years—dreams of a growing child, for whom his games were both truly dreams and truly reality."

"Are you suggesting all this . . . reality has been but a dream?"

"No, not at all. Reality, this universe, is no dream, no, sir. Its existence does not depend on yours. But your existence and ours, and that of many on your Earth, are intimately interwoven. The point of contact is our souls."

"I don't understand. How does this whole thing work?"

O'sihn shook his head. "Have you ever wondered why you, in this universe, look *rilitian* like I do, and all those from Realitas do?"

183 O'sihn, Laida, Tygrum, Leonidas, respectively.

"Yes, many times."

"That was the way you conceived us in your childhood games, which happened to be how we really are in this universe. Your perception and your conception are mutually inclusive. It's a gift, an extremely rare and very subtle gift. What the RIBA device basically did was to capture the image of the reality of this universe in your mind and project your entire self into your own image of how you would be in this reality. Your body may look different, but its substance is the same."

"But I didn't appear in this universe. I was miniaturized in my room, still in my universe."

"Technically, you were already in our universe. The only thing our trans-universal ships did and could do was to project their reality into yours, by focusing into the mind of a *child-quickener*. Our ships— Laida and I, when we talked to you—were literally in a *transuniversal* bubble materialized in your room, and furthermore, we were communicating with you directly in your mind. It was your love for us, from your childhood games, that provided the link between your reality and ours, which made it possible for us to lock on onto your reality, while we were still in our own.

"You didn't notice that, but although you kept using your native language, you were communicating with us in your mind. When your body was reconfigured into a *realitic* form, your brain acquired a *realitic* morphology. At that point,[184] our Realitarian language was infused as a surrogate language.[185] To you, Realitarian seems like

---

184 The procedure was part of Duncan's *transrealization* carried out by the RIBA device

185 There is much more than what O'sihn had succinctly explained here. Most races of the *Realitic* universe have the mutual ability to link in with the brains of people with whom they talk, being able to speak spontaneously the language of their interlocutor, while having the perception of speaking their own native languages, even if with a minimum effort they could notice the difference. When Duncan's body acquired its Realitic nature, his transformed Realitic brain was "upgraded," so to speak, with this ability. Therefore, Duncan could speak the language of any individual that had the same ability, as we have seen from the accounts related in this book. Since the Realitarian language was the first he was exposed to when traveling to the Realitic universe, it crystallized in his consciousness as a kind of a second native language.

your native tongue, though they are completely different."

"Will I remember anything of this Realitian language, or at the very least, the name of Dahncion?" Duncan refused to accept what he had heard a moment before about this.

O'sihn shook his head. "Once you go back to Earth, you will be part of its reality again. Your body will take back its earthly human traits, and your tongue will be the one you learned from your mother's lips. Nothing will remain as evidence of your ever having been here, except for your experiences, which are already deeply imprinted within yourself. Even the images associated with those experiences will be different from the ones you have right now, reconfigured—translated so to speak—to the physical reality of your universe."

"But why hasn't anybody told me about all this before, especially all these things regarding my childhood games . . . your awareness of them?"

"To preserve your freedom," O'sihn stressed.

"My freedom?" Duncan sighed. "Knowing what you've just told me was much more important than my freedom."

"Reality is stronger, the stronger the freedom of those who make it real," O'sihn replied. "And to defeat the enemy we are fighting against, we needed a strong reality, a very strong reality."

107.

"Let me take a look," Duncan said with anxiety.

"Stop it." Laida put down her binocular-looking visor, and the only visor they had brought along. "This is an operation like any other, Lieutenant." The X.O. had a cast on her right arm.

Through another opening in the wall, Erina was trying to gather more information from the target. Laida passed the visor to her.

"I visualize a small tetrahedral construction right at the center of the triangles," Erina said. "It has a close resemblance to the description of the trans-universal chamber."

"And it's surrounded by heavily equipped military forces,"

O'sihn put in, coming down from a flight of stairs.

"We haven't detected any activity from here," Laida said.

"From the roof of this building, you wouldn't need any visor to see an entire Kervian army assembled inside the triangular grooves."

"Grooves?" Erina asked.

"Yes. They may look like flat concentric triangles from here, but they are actually deep narrow grooves with thick walls that end up at the same level. Let's go upstairs and take a better look."

They were in the twentieth level of the ancient construction, and they had to go up thirty more levels to reach its top. Once there, they tried to pick up more details of what was transpiring below, but except for a significant number of troopers, nothing else could be seen.

"Quite an assembly," Erina said, handing the visor to Duncan.

Duncan adjusted the focal range to the maximum, but he could not pick up much else. "It looks like some kind of ritual."

"Not quite," O'sihn said, as Laida took back the visor.

"Not, indeed," Laida concurred.

Duncan glanced at them. "So?"

O'sihn leaned on the back of the wide balcony-like area.

"It looks like an invasion force," Laida said, and passed the visor to O'sihn.

"Those troops are loaded with full gear—including sophisticated equipment and supplies," O'sihn added. "And the booth at the center of the emplacement closely matches the trans-universal chamber we are looking for."

"Even if they were to enter the chamber one at a time," Duncan objected, "they could never get through most of their bulky equipment."

"Unless the whole triangular construction is part of the trans-universal complex," Laida pointed out.

Laida leaned forward. "Check for activity at three o'clock."

O'sihn aimed the visor to his right. Three individuals appeared in sight approaching the triangular constructions. From each corner of the outermost triangle, three ramps led to the center, where an elongated pyramidal structure, about nine feet tall, stood, shining with a crystal-blue hue

"The one in the middle: he, or rather, she, isn't wearing any military suit." O'sihn passed the visor to Laida.

It took her little effort to recognize the person. "It is Clara, all right."

Clara had a suit on that seemed to keep her arms immobilized. Her legs were restrained with some kind of a short cord around her ankles.

The group soon reached the central structure—a tetrahedral chamber with crystal-clear stony walls, which resembled quartz. One of the walls opened up from the floor to a horizontal lintel located one third of the way down from the pyramidal apex. Clara was compelled to step inside. Immediately, a trapezoidal panel started rising up from the floor.

"What's going on?" Duncan said.

Laida shook her head. "It's as if they are planning to take Clara along with them."

"It doesn't make sense," Erina said.

"They need a human being from my universe," Duncan added.

O'sihn stood up to get a better view over the rim of the walls that crowned the building. He remained silent for a moment. "Maybe they think they *do* have a human being from your universe," he said, turning up the collar of his uniform. "Perhaps they have mistaken Clara for Erina."

Duncan grabbed his weapon. "We oughta stop 'em."

O'sihn strained his eyes and stepped back, while Duncan and Laida began brainstorming about how to get to the chamber. But O'sihn was not paying attention. His thoughts were following a very different path.

"Lieutenant."

"Captain?" Erina looked up.

"Rig your howitzer with plasma ammunition."

"Aye, Captain."

Laida and Duncan turned back at once. There was a moment of uncertainty.

"What are you planning to do?" Laida whispered, stepping towards O'sihn.

"Complete our mission and get us out of here."

Duncan stayed still, stunned by the captain's decision.

"O'sihn," Laida said.

"Yes, X.O."

"Maybe, if we waited till dark . . . " She put a hand on her husband's forearm. "Evening is close."

"I don't think this army will give us that much time, X.O."

"Plasma ammunition will not be enough to destroy the complex," Duncan objected. "That's why we brought this little baby along," he added, patting his backpack with the T.A.T. device[186] inside.

"The T.A.T. is much more powerful, indeed," O'sihn said. "But the plasma ammunition will destroy the enemy forces and will quite likely destroy the complex as well, sparing us from having to use the precautionary extra energy of the T.A.T."

"Aren't we too close to the target for plasma ammunition?" Laida asked.

O'sihn shook his head. "We are a mile away, and the lethal range of the ammunition is about a kilometer."

"We can't just blow Clara up," Duncan interjected. "There oughta be some other way!"

"That's enough, Lieutenant." The captain's tone sounded definitive.

"Listen, O," Laida said, still thinking she could influence the decision.

---

186 Time Anti-Time explosive device.

"No, you listen to me—both of you. Those guys are about to engage that *technon* any minute now. If they are wrong—as we think they are—and they are trying to use Clara to configure, somehow, the machine to get themselves to Earth, all of them will die—including Clara. But if we try to blow the complex up, at least Clara, being inside the chamber, will have some chance of survival—very slim, yes, but at least some chance."

The discussion appeared to be over, though not for Erina. "Excuse me, captain."

"Lieutenant?" O'sihn said, still staring at Laida.

"Maybe they have found a way around the problem. Maybe they don't need a human from my universe. If that were the case, they might be holding Clara in the chamber for some other purpose."

"If that's the case, Erina, it becomes imperative that we destroy those installations at once in order to prevent an imminent invasion and control of your planet—and subsequent control of your universe."

"Not necessarily, Captain," Erina said smoothly. "I don't think this relatively small army—even with all its technology—has the necessary power to override Earth's defenses. Its success may well rest on ensuring a constant connection between universes." Erina glanced in the direction of the trans-universal complex. "Even if that force were able to succeed in its trip, we could still neutralize it by destroying its logistic chain. Blowing up the whole complex right after the army has left could both spare Clara's life—on Earth—and alert the people of Earth of the potential threat from this universe."

O'sihn looked at Erina. As usual, her analysis was sharp. Laida was about to pick up that line of thought, but O'sihn immediately rejected the alternative. "I don't think that's an option. Besides the fact that there is no guarantee they would keep Clara alive if they reached their objective, Earth's defenses could lack the power to stop this invasion. Even if the defending forces were to prevail, it could be at the expense of large amounts of casualties and resources from your people. And we don't know what the Establishment could achieve if it managed to secure a position on your planet." O'sihn shook his head. "I'm sorry, Erina. I'd certainly like to do more for Clara. And I am also aware that this course of action will deprive you and Dahncion of—"

O'sihn was still speaking when the natural light of the mild afternoon was abruptly multiplied by a factor of ten. An instant later, a strong shock wave blasted the four Realitians against a wall.

Unexpectedly, a series of energy vectors had broken through a thin layer of clouds, reaching the trans-universal complex below.

108.

"Ninety-five percent direct hits, Captain."

"Very good." O'sirof checked the information his T.O. had just passed on his console. The actual effectiveness of the attack was still not clear. "C.I.C./conn."

A VC popped up on the bridge. "Yes, Captain."

"Kanovan, what are we picking up from the surface?"

"Hard to tell," Lieutenant Kanovan said. "We have a confirmed ninety-four point six percent direct hit, but we are still too far away to assess effectiveness."

O'sirof nodded. "Keep working on it."

"Aye, Captain."

"Near-target evaluation, X.O."

Commander Ossihanna looked up from her tactical display. "I'd strongly advise against any near target evaluation. We still have three destroyers searching for us."

"Enemy torpedo signature! Bearing one-three-two dash two-nine-zero, dist. twenty-five," Lieutenant Stripen, the Tactical Officer, interjected from his virtual console.

"Starboard chaff," the captain directed, his eyes focused into the scope on his left.

"Intelligent debris in the ether," Stripen confirmed, referring to the *chaff*.[187]

"Full up-starboard rudder, escape acceleration."

"Full up-starboard, escape 'A', sir," Lieutenant Pumway acknowledged.

"Dist. nineteen point three," Ossihanna said, "point two, point one, point zero. Eighteen point eight . . . "

"The torpedo is gaining on us," the X.O. warned.

"Amid-ship rudder."

"Amid rud., aye, Captain," Pumway echoed.

The new course was taking the ship directly towards the local sun.

"T.O., rig three plasma missiles to follow our present trajectory matching our kinematic pattern."

"Acknowledged."

"Local star radiation levels too high already," Stripen alerted. "We're getting saturation on most sensors." The dazzling image of Althea 8 on the tactical screen was rapidly losing its shape with digital distortion.

"Missiles ready and standing-by, Captain," the T.O. reported.

On O'sirof's display, a yellow marker signaled the missiles-ready-to-launch status. "Stand by to engage rudder with Tango. Set helm for a sharp down-port turn towards the destroyer on bearing three-three-zero dash three-one-zero upon missiles launch."

"Aye, Captain," Pumway acknowledged, passing the procedure on to the tactical computer. "Programmed maneuver on stand-by, Captain."

O'sirof waited a few more seconds. The tactical screen had become a digitalized mess. Noise saturation was almost complete. For a moment, the projection of the surrounding space from the 3D (which

---

187 Chaff consisted of particles spread out as a cloud designed to simulate the presence of a real ship in order to lure enemy weapons to move onto them. They were called "intelligent debris" since all particles interacted in a communications network that enabled them to move in a coordinated manner mimicking a ship.

enveloped the bridge) got momentarily disconnected, but soon it came back again.

"Release missiles."

"Plasma missiles in the ether, Captain," the T.O. confirmed. The ship automatically responded with a sharp turn to one side. The gravitational system could not perfectly compensate for the maneuver, which caused many of the crew to be dragged off their posts.

"Enemy torpedo on route onto local star, Captain," Stripen reported with excitement.

"Open fire on target: bearing, zero-three-zero dash zero-one-zero."

"Fire on target zero-three-zero dash zero-one-zero, aye, Captain," the T.O. acknowledged.

The surrounding holographic image of the local space went off momentarily as the bow battery discharged all its energy vectors onto the enemy vessel ahead.

"Full, up-port rudder; steady as she goes, Pumway."

"Full up-port, steady aye, Captain."

"Conn / C.I.C."

"Sir, seventy percent direct hits on target."

O'sirof smiled cautiously. The situation had swiftly changed from a precarious condition into a promising one. "Copied, Kanovan. Anything new on our primary target?"

"We are not picking up any more omega radiation from the planet surface, Captain." That was a clear sign that the mission target, the destruction of the trans-universal complex down on Althea 8, had been achieved.

"Excellent."

"So, what's next?" asked Ossihanna, the X.O.

O'sirof turned around and smiled, nudging her with one elbow.[188] "What you have in mind, of course."

---

188 Like O'sihn and Laida, Ossihanna and O'sirof were a married commanding head.

"Pumway."

"X.O.?"

"Plot a straight course towards the nucleus of the battle, close to Althea 8."

Lieutenant Pumway turned around with apprehension. The command was definitely not in line with headquarters' directives.

"Carry on, Lieutenant," O'sirof confirmed.

109.

The shockwaves released by the energy vectors that had hit the trans-universal complex had propelled Laida against a wall, causing further damage to her already injured arm. She was lying on the floor in great pain, though out of danger for now. The rest of the team had not suffered major harm. After checking on Laida's condition, they were all now trying to assess the situation.

"Confirmed, Captain. The trans-universal chamber is still standing," Erina said, turning around. "It seems to be operative."

"Any signs of enemy activity?"

"Negative. The field around the chamber has been completely leveled."

O'sihn nodded. "If the chamber still works, you and Dahncion will program the T.A.T. device to detonate after you have left the universe, as planned." O'sihn looked at his watch and turned to Duncan. "Set the device with a thirty-minute delay. Zeenthy and his flyers will be picking us up before that, as you recall."

"What if the chamber is not operational?" Erina asked.

"You will still install the T.A.T. with a thirty-minute delay, and then reconvene here."

"You will follow the events through the visor . . ."[189]

"Negative," O'sihn replied. "You and Duncan will take the visor and the biosensor. I may be able to follow the trans-universal opera-

---

189 They had not brought the standard communicators they had available, since they would have been easily detected by Establishment forces.

tion from here, if it still works. But I will not leave this place until the last minute. We will be waiting for you, just in case something goes wrong."

"What if Clara is still alive? What if she is injured?" Duncan asked.

O'sihn looked at Erina.

"I don't detect any signs of life," she said, showing her biosensor. "Though we are too far away."

"Try to see inside the chamber," O'sihn said.

"The chamber looks empty." Erina adjusted a few settings on the visor and looked again. "I don't see anything at all inside— no objects, no remains—nothing. Wait . . . visor sensor reports—" Erina turned around with a quizzical expression. "*Perfect vacuum inside?*"

O'sihn remained pensive for a moment. "The chamber works under the premise of preserving the reality behind its walls, either within this universe or an alternative one."

"An alternative universe?" Erina frowned. "Clara . . . sent to a different universe?"

O'sihn shook his head. "We don't know much about the chamber. We don't know what may have happened to it, or what it may have done when it was bathed in radiation."

Laida started crying. Kneeling down by her, Duncan placed a compassionate hand on one of her shoulders. He looked disturbed.

"Dahncion."

Duncan did not answer.

"Lieutenant Dahncion."

"Yes, Captain," Duncan asked, still kneeling by Laida.

"I'm sorry. We don't have much time."

Duncan stood up slowly, staring at O'sihn in silence.

The captain perceived the great sorrow Duncan was going through, for both Clara and Laida, and for being about to leave everything behind. O'sihn embraced him warmly. "Stern strength, my friend. Stern strength . . . " That was something Clara might have said; they both knew it. As they looked at each other, Laida nodded as if bidding *goodbye*, while still crying.

Duncan was overcome with grief and could not talk anymore.

"We will never forget you—all of you," Erina said, taking Duncan by the hand.

They left the building at once.

110.

Duncan and Erina were running towards the leveled area ahead. The small trans-universal chamber was standing right at its center, pristinely intact. Behind the chamber, a few rosy clouds blurred the splendid comet that hovered above the horizon. As he ran, Duncan repeatedly checked for signs of enemy activity, but did not detect any. Followed by Erina, Duncan started walking on a vitreous field. They had to walk slowly, the ground being so smooth that it offered little traction for their boots. As they approached the chamber, Duncan tried to pick up anything behind its walls. It was not easy: the quartz-like panels were now reflecting most of the reddish light coming from the setting sun.

After a few minutes and several falls, Erina and Duncan finally made it almost to the center of the vitreous field. They were now in front of a mound, on top of which stood the crystalline chamber.[190] Almost at once, a human form began to materialize inside.

Clara had suddenly appeared, sitting on the floor. She looked disoriented, but unharmed.[191]

---

190 The attack had leveled the triangular constructions to their bases, leaving a flat vitreous field all the way up to about thirty feet from the trans-universal chamber. In being bathed with radiation, the energy deflection from the chamber's walls had generated a mound of crystallized debris with a uniform slope all around the chamber.

191 When bathed with radiation, the chamber had automatically created a singularity in its own reality in order to shelter its content. The purpose of the singularity was to generate a mini parallel universe of the same kind outside its parent universe. It could only be maintained for a few minutes, but it was more than what Clara needed to be isolated from the high radiation levels of the attack.

"Hang on, Clara! We'll get you out of there in no time," Duncan yelled, but she could not hear him.

He and Erina climbed the mound[192] and stood on a flat platform, about three feet wide, which extended all around the chamber. As they searched for a control panel that would allow them to open it, Clara began to move her head vividly in a given direction, as if trying to indicate a certain spot. She was still wearing the captors' straitjacket, plus the cord around her ankles.

Following the direction hinted by Clara, Erina hovered a hand over the platform. "Here!" A circle materialized right there. A few seconds later, other circles began to appear around the first.

Erina put one palm over the first circle. In response, one of the walls began to recede into the floor until the chamber was fully open. Clara tried to move, but tripped and fell to the floor.

As Erina helped her up, Duncan unsheathed his Veridiawan sword and cut open the straitjacket that kept Clara immobilized. Her arms were released. With a clean stroke of his blade, he severed the cord around her ankles.

Duncan stared at Clara, but she fixed her eyes in the sky. His eyes followed hers to a dazzling and brilliant star that had suddenly appeared, and which rapidly faded away. The light had been so intense that all three of them had covered their eyes. A battle was clearly raging not far from the planet.

Erina pressed Clara's hands. "I must check if the chamber is still operational."[193] Several circles were now present on the platform. When touched according to a certain sequence, the chamber would

---

192 The surface of the mound was not as smooth as the rest of the field, since it had crystallized with a corrugated pattern due to eddies produced by the energy deflection from the chamber. This enabled Erina and Duncan to climb the mound, with some effort.

193 Erina and Duncan had been instructed how to operate the system on board the *Intrepid*.

establish a trans-universal connection with the universe of the person inside who met certain conditions.[194]

Duncan took Clara's hands and pressed them tightly against his chest. He then looked deeply into her eyes.

Suddenly, a yellow luminescence began flowing from the chamber walls.

"Done," Erina said and got back up.

Both Clara and Duncan turned around.

"No time to lose," Erina added, looking at Duncan.

Duncan nodded and passed the T.A.T. device to Clara. "You will meet with O'sihn and Laida in that structure." Duncan pointed at it. "It's about one mile away. Veridiawan flyers will pick all of you up there."

"Timer setting?" Clara asked, looking at the T.A.T.

"It has already been set to thirty minutes."

"Copied." Clara placed the device on the floor, by the chamber.

Soon everything was ready.

Duncan entered a password on the T.A.T., and a light began to flash. Immediately, Clara checked the readings on its display. As she bent down, the back of her neck, beneath her hair, was exposed. Her *tori* features were very strong in that area. Duncan noticed that, but let his eyes wander towards the sky. It was dark red, with the bright comet spreading its white tail close to the horizon.

With departure imminent, Duncan experienced again his attachment to a universe that was not his. He began to wonder about many things. What would await him back home? How would his life be after all he had experienced over almost two years? Would no

---

194 In order to establish a connection between universes, the system would search for transuniversal brain activity. Such activity was strong in Duncan due to his extremely rare *quickener* attributes. This alone might have been sufficient to operate the chamber, regardless of which universe was his native universe.

evidence truly remain of his ever having been in another universe? In a way, Duncan felt as if he already were part of that reality. The fear of not being able to take even his memories haunted him.

"It's time to leave," Erina said, taking hold of Duncan's right hand. "I feel the same."

Duncan looked at her and nodded. They quickly stepped into the chamber.

Following Erina's instructions, Clara began to complete the activation sequence. The yellow luminescence engulfing the structure was suddenly replaced by a blue, gleaming light. A series of hollow sounds followed, riding on the echoes of an eerie tune. They impressed Duncan as a cold and mathematically perfect procedure, insensitive and oblivious to the decisive moment in his life. Its pitch turned metallic, and at that point, a blue halo enveloped Erina's and Duncan's bodies.

Very slowly, a trapezoidal door started to come up quietly from the floor. Delicately, Clara saluted, weeping in silence, her long blond hair, slightly wet by her tears, waving in the mild wind. Above the horizon, next to the chamber, a mild explosion of light softly brightened the sky.

Duncan stood still, staring at Clara. As he did, he absentmindedly raised his right hand to his chest. The medallion Clara had once given him was still hanging there, along with his Royal Navy military credentials, both of which would necessarily stay behind. He had grown accustomed to the medallion's presence, becoming unaware of it. The day Clara had given it to him, after she had been seriously injured on Aquaelight, he had not been certain if he would ever see her again.

His memory flashed back to the morning of her transfer to the YSF *Temperance*. The sadness and sense of loss he had experienced on that occasion became as fresh and painful as if it had happened the day before. And with it came a sense of failure—total failure—of having accomplished nothing but finally managing to get back from where he had come. But why did he have to experience all that? What would it take to change all that?

Duncan let go of Erina's hand. He looked at Clara and thought of her as the woman that she was. But when he got close to grasping her female beauty, once more the *tori* features of her body—her drawing-looking features that made him perceive her as something not fully real, not fully woman—dissuaded his spirit from advancing any further. However, this time his heart fought back.

Duncan looked at her again, and then at his own *rilitian* skin. As he did that, he thought about his native earthly appearance. Although it was not there, he made it be there. Looking at Clara again, he focused his mind on her femininity, and in doing that, a vision of her emerged juxtaposed with herself. In his vision, she was all woman in her strength and in her softness, in her intelligence, and in her power of love.

Although Clara herself still had her *tori* features, it was possible to imagine her with the appearance of a woman of Earth, and so Duncan made her be with the appearance of a woman of Earth, even when she was still fully *tori*. From the deepest layers of Clara's own femininity, the *child quickener* was now bringing forth Clara's full womanly beauty, both external and internal. And that was no vision or imagination: it was a solid, quickened, perfectly inclusive reality that even Erina could see[195] now. Clara was becoming blazingly and visibly beautiful, both with her *tori* features and with the perfect appearance of a woman from Duncan's world.

Still her external beauty was nothing but a freezing shadow in the light of her woman's heart, which Duncan could finally see—and in the furnace of her female *sternessential* love, which Duncan could finally feel. He had overcome the obstacles that had prevented him from reaching true reality and making it be. Duncan was reaching Clara's hidden and visible realities, making them one, for there was

---

195 Erina noticed the vision but, from her reaction, it seems it did not make a big impression on her. She probably took it as an illusion produced by the active chamber.

nothing incompatible in them.[196]

As he beheld Clara's full reality, Duncan saw the fullness of his own, even if far, very far, from comprehending it all.

Duncan could never fully understand—much less explain—what made him do what he did next.

When the door was already up to his chest, he jumped upwards with all his strength. In doing so, he hit his head on the lintel of the chamber. That left him in bad shape for a moment. In any case, he was already halfway out, with his chest lying on the rising door.

"No!" Erina cried out, pulling on Duncan's leg. Clara also tried to get him back into the chamber, pushing her arms against his shoulders. The situation had rapidly become critical: the slow-rising door was starting to press on Duncan's chest, as his back pressed against the chamber lintel.

"Not this way . . . help me ou—"

Recognizing the seriousness of the situation, Clara grabbed Duncan's hands and transferred all her weight onto them. The moment she touched Duncan, a strong energy surge burst into her body, and the bluish luminescence that enveloped Erina and Duncan flashed all around her. Clara felt a strong compulsion to let go, but the stronger the urge, the harder she grasped Duncan's hands. Abruptly, one of her hands slipped, and her arm slashed the air like a whip.

Bouncing on the ground with one foot and using her free hand, Clara managed to grab the grip of the sword that Duncan was carrying on his back. After pulling it out of its sheath and casting it to the ground, Clara immediately seized his wrists with both hands. Caught between Duncan's back and the lintel, the empty sheath

---

196 *Child-quickening inclusive realization* has its antithesis in the *either-orness* of a grown-up mind.

collapsed due to the pressure caused by the rising door. In that split moment, Duncan's body was released, and both Clara and Duncan fell immediately to thè ground.

The door was soon completely closed. The chamber was sealed. The diamond-shaped booth glowed with an intense blue, screening out the inside from their view. For an instant, it seemed to Clara as if Erina were hitting her hands violently against the walls. All activity quickly ceased, and the chamber soon recovered its pristine transparency.

Erina was not there anymore.

111.

Outside the window, the moon was rising gently over a lonely silo. To the left, a pair of shoes lay one on top of the other, just as they had been left minutes before. Behind the door, the lights from the small corridor that connected to the living room were shimmering again, tenuously but irregularly. Low-pitched noises could be heard coming from there.

For a while, the living room remained still, but then the lights began flickering with an irregular pattern once more. Strange noises followed, apparently coming from every place in the room. Soon, the noises were pounding with deafening strength, until they ceased brusquely, giving way to a high-pitched rasping beat.

A blast of light flashed from a dimensionless dot in the center of the room. A glassy tongue of surreal luminescence followed, emanating from the incandescent ignition point. It was not an empty drop of light. As the glaring tongue gradually took shape—over a period that spanned several minutes—its content grew increasingly definite.

A living entity was moving inside it. It had a female appearance, but it was not moving quite like a woman, and much less like a man. The face, desolate, was filled with anger and frustration. In desperation, she finally drew her nails onto the inner membrane of light. The tips of her fingers protruded through the glassy *realitic* membrane, but there was no way they could pierce their own reality. For something to transcend its reality, it needs to be pulled, in some way, by a different reality.

The boundary of the *realitic* protuberance began to wobble. The expansion process had reached its limit. For a minute or so, the bubble struggled to keep its volume and its existence. However, the quickening that was keeping it alive was rapidly being reabsorbed, and without it, the trans-universal globule could not be sustained for much longer.

Abruptly, the protrusion collapsed back into its ignition point. Before it disappeared, a cry of defiance pierced the bubble's own vanishing reality as it went to naught.

112.

"She's gone," Duncan whispered, staring at the silent crystal chamber. Although he had a heavy sense of loss, his pain was shallow, like a very sensitive superficial wound. In experiencing the reality of Clara's beauty, his physical attachment to Erina had been severed. Although he was not aware of it, his feelings towards her were fading quickly. Clara could see his eyes reflected on the walls of the chamber. They looked different from the ones she knew. They were calm and composed. But the peaceful moment was very short.

"We've got thirty minutes to get ourselves out of range," Duncan said, looking at the active T.A.T. by the chamber. "We must reconvene with O'sihn and Laida," he added, pointing at the structure where they were to be picked up by the Veridiawan flyers.

Clara grabbed him by the hand, but no sooner had she taken the first step than she slipped to the floor, and Duncan with her.

"Clara?"

"I'm fine, I'm fine."

Clara stood up with a muffled groan, enough for Duncan to realize she was not fine. Indeed, she had injured a shoulder. He helped her up and led the way, only to fall again at the first step. They tried again three more times, falling down each time.

"This is crazy," Duncan said.

"It's called creep crystallization," Clara explained. "It happens to *psamosites*[197] when they are bathed in plasma. It will get only worse, more and more slippery."

Duncan frowned. "Let's try crawling."

Crawling seemed to work, but they moved very slowly. Ten minutes later, Duncan sat up and took a distance fix to the chamber using his visor. They had only covered fifty yards, and they still had more than one hundred to reach the edge of the crystallized field. Duncan sighed and grabbed Clara by a hand, pushing himself forward, but she held him back. "We will not reach the boundary of this field before the T.A.T. explodes," she said. "And by then, we should be at least four miles away from here, anyway."

"We can't just give up," Duncan replied.

Clara shook her head. "I will crawl back and try to deactivate the T.A.T. You just keep crawling forward. I will catch up with you."

"It took us more than ten minutes to reach this spot. It will not take you less to get back to the chamber. The math doesn't add up."

Clara shook her head.

"Besides, deactivating the system will not be straightforward, assuming it can be done."

"I can handle it!" Clara said with frustration.

Duncan grasped her hand. "And I won't part from you either."

"Don't—" Clara could not end the sentence.

"Our orders are to destroy the complex, not to stay alive," Duncan added, with a resigned smile.

"I want you to live." Clara started sobbing.

"And I *will* live, holding you, and loving you, right here. Nothing else matters now."

---

197 *Psamosites* are minerals similar to what in our universe would be classified as silicates. The high energy levels of the plasma attack had crystallized the *psamosite*-rich surface around the chamber. The crystallization process continued beyond the energy irradiation event. Gradually, the surface was getting smoother and more slippery.

Clara moved her head down. Her blond hair, covering her eyes, brushed the diamond-like floor. Her tears fell delicately on the pristine surface.

Duncan embraced her tenderly and kissed her head. His decision of staying in Reality had sealed his fate. And yet, perhaps for the first time in his life, Duncan was happy, truly very happy. For what was left of his life had more meaning than a thousand years. Loving Clara, and holding her, had become more precious than his own life.

It had been a long and difficult journey, but in the end, *sternessence* had seared its mark through his heart.

As they held each other, Duncan stroked Clara's hair, moving it to one side. In doing so, he discovered something remarkable: Clara's skin was rapidly losing its *tori* features.

"The chamber," Duncan muttered, enthralled by the warm feminine appearance quickly materializing right before his eyes— perfectly earthly, beautifully human.

Clara raised her eyebrows. "The chamber?"

And at that point, they were snatched up into the air.

113.

The chamber began to glow yellow again. Its brilliance was mild but steady, until a burst of light flashed from it with all the colors of the rainbow. Spectral fans stayed on its surface for a few seconds, radiating in all directions. When all the luminescence had faded, one of the three triangular walls began to melt down, turning into a stream of fluid that soon crystallized into a thick tongue of phosphorescent ice-like material that refused to melt.

A soundless energy surge was ebbing back and forth with a regular beat between the sides of the opening, veiling the interior of the crystal chamber. To one side, the setting Althean sun was exposing the silhouette of a distant mount far on the horizon. Above it, the tail of the comet remained steady.

As the sunny rays softly warmed a passing gentle breeze, a shivering limb reached violently through the chamber's energy screen. An entity began to emerge with slow and heavy movements. As it crawled out, it looked into the sun, but its eyes did not blink. A moment later, the creature began to regurgitate and agitate violently. A wiry device was expelled convulsively out of its mouth, along with white oily fluids that rapidly turned brittle.

The individual was breathing with difficulty. Its complexion gleamed with an earthly human likeness. There was a womanly resemblance in her.

Digging her nails into one of her arms, she ripped off a shred of what appeared to be her human skin, all the way down to one wrist. The true appearance of her real skin underneath was revealed. It was rugged and brittle, and it looked like an old hide that had been burnt by time. Not being able to withstand it any longer, she tore away the deteriorated genetic mask that covered her face. For a long time, the device had allowed her to breathe and pretend to eat[198] in an environment alien to her physiology. Together with her synthetic skin, they had effectively masked her true nature, even from the piercing scrutiny of medical and scanning instruments.[199] A brilliant greenish skin was exposed on her forehead. The female's head was covered with seemingly blue hair roots, with pronounced receding temples exposing the scalp all the way up to the crown.

The female knelt, managed to get on her feet, and even to walk a few steps.

"My never-ending-naked-nothingness," she uttered, turning to the remnants of her mask and her synthetic skin, which she could

---

198 The device was used for eating as well, although in rare occasions.

199 The synthetic skin could generate an "ontological image" of the interior of a human body, perfectly mimicking all human organs and their functions. The female wearing the synthetic skin had always refused invasive medical tests that could have risked exposing her true identity, her decision having always been respected.

not see. The parts that had been in contact with her body were still emitting an intense white luminescence, like the interior of an active optical fiber.

The female the Realitians had known as Erina was in agonizing pain. Her long life was now passing in front of her like a series of movies all played at the same time: each episode, each word she had said, each act she had performed became as clear as the reality of her agony. But suddenly, the flow of time stopped. One experience from a very recent event stood out as a final trial, invoking a final realization, a crucial choice.

Clara had always been an enigma to her. As much as Erina had tried to understand her feelings, her motivations, and ultimately her ideals, Erina had not succeeded in reconciling her personal view of reality with Clara's actions. Trying to decipher why Clara had risked her life to save hers before the *sinking* of the *Intrepid* had become a recurring riddle for Erina. What was Clara trying to achieve, what was she trying to prove? What had been her true purpose, her ulterior motives, perhaps, or real gain in doing what she had done? All these questions, which now appeared as one, had surfaced several times since the forced landing on Veridiawa. Nothing seemed to explain those actions, except for one reason. But Erina despised that reason, and so she had rejected it every time.

For only love, *sternessential* love, seemed to be the basis of Clara's actions and motivations. Em-Rasinka, the female behind Erina, had fought most of her life against such a *culturally imposed degrading notion*, which bluntly contradicted her own inspired Equity principles. For if everybody could eventually *sternessentially* love each other, the unity that would ensue would be absolutely inclusive with the diversity of each individual, challenging the perfect uniformity the Equitarian philosophy of life stood for. Perfect love would foster and mutually strengthen the non-repeatable, unique, and irreplaceable qualities of each person. Only in this way, the seamless fabric of the multifaceted unity of love would be maintained.

And yet, no matter how much Erina felt repulsed by that, it would seem that this Realitian love had saved her life a week prior. So what? Wouldn't it have been better dying rather than going through the current torment and defeat? What could possibly be the torturous purpose of this extra week?

Her thoughts were silent for a moment, gradually and unexpectedly being filled in by the notion of a last choice she could still make, a final surrender she could still afford.

Had she been wrong for most, if not the whole, of a very long life? Erina shook her head. *Too late* is always punctual, and the time for change was over for her. Yet, such surrender would have enabled reality to quicken the fabric of her being with one last drop of a *sternessence* more stubborn than death.

As long as we live, we will not know if, at the last moment, Em-Rasinka opened her heart to that ultimate reality. I, as a witness, would only like to add that the last expression I saw in her face suggested that she did.

114.

As the defoliation process progressed rapidly inside the inert body—induced by the *realitic* insufficiency and subsequent catastrophic failure of the chamber's procedure[200]—the two-hundred-and-fifty-six-year-old *tilian* now rested motionless on the glassy ground. Off the forehead, the genetically imprinted emblem of the Equity began to defoliate in thin scales, swiftly carried away by a light breeze.

---

200 The chamber had attempted to project Erina's, or rather Em-Rasinka's, reality into Earth's reality. But it had been disconnected from Duncan's influence, after he had abandoned the chamber. The anomalous process that ensued resulted in a lack of cohesion of the molecular structure in Em-Rasinka's body, which started a slow disintegration process or *defoliation.*

115.

Zeenthy, Zainy, Jasiris, and Jasindon were flying in a tight V formation led by Daihyouleeby. They were flying fast, very fast, gaining some altitude but mostly concerned with covering as much distance as they could. How far did they have to go to be safe? It was hard to tell, but they knew that if the Mahyoudee river was not behind them before the sun had set, "the mighty" light would swallow them, as O'sihn had warned them. Daihyouleeby constantly turned back to check on the sun: it was more than halfway below the horizon already. Ahead, the waters of the Mahyoudee shone red as if with blood. But it was a thin red line; the river was still too far away.

"We must fly much faster!" Daihyouleeby cried out, turning his head. The other four fliers behind him knew that, but they were exhausted. Each one was carrying a Realitian solider, and despite his superior physical strength, Jasindon, who was carrying O'sihn, was lagging behind.

"Free formation!" Daihyouleeby shouted and soared up into the sky, looping down rapidly. He was the only flier who was not carrying a solider. Soon, he was approaching Jasindon from behind.

Laida, carried by Jasiris, turned back and saw O'sihn being dropped into a free fall, to be immediately caught midair by Daihyouleeby. It was a well-practiced Veridiawan maneuver.

"Don't you worry, bear-Commander," Jasiris said, looking down. "Daihyouleeby is almost as strong as Jasindon."

Laida nodded slowly with resignation as to the outcome of their desperate escape. She looked down and let her eyes wander over the giant fern forest below, not daring to look ahead, lest she would find the Mahyoudee river still too far ahead.

A moment later, the soft reddish twilight of the new evening, along with the deep green of the giant ferns, turned into a blinding white blue. The Realitians covered their faces, as the Veridiawan fliers shut their eyes tight.

116.

After the explosion, a column of blue energy surged from what was left of the *trans-universal* complex. The peculiar energy jet pierced the atmosphere and burst into deep space. As it fluxed, the ionosphere was highly energized, producing an extraordinary display of blue lights.

Jasindon was the first one to open his eyes. He saw the Mahyoudee river right below him. But the Veridiawan did not pay any attention to it. His sight was transfixed on the sky.

"Girl-Captain, what is this stern blue essence washing the sky with light?" asked Zainy, his eyes fixed on the heavens.

Long tongues of blue shining clouds were spreading from the epicenter of the phenomenon all the way to the horizon. They were slender and straight, with gushes of bluish rivulets of light flowing to the sides here and there. The twilight of the new evening had become as bright as a splendid noon, but without a sun.

"*Sternessence*, Zainy," Clara said with joy. "Beautiful *sternessence*."

A formation of Realitian interceptors appeared, flying below the tongues of light. The circular insignias of the Realdom, painted on their fuselages and small winglets, glistened bright with their cyan and yellow colors, with red marks. All the positioning and navigational lights were flashing randomly. That was the custom of the Realitarian Navy after winning a battle.

The battle was over, and indeed it had been victory for the Realdom. However, there was still a war to fight, and a peace to win.

The Veridiawan fliers began to resume their original *V* formation.

For a few seconds, Duncan could see Clara hanging from
Zainy beside him.

As they did, Zainy and Zeenthy flew very close to each other. For a few seconds, Duncan could see Clara hanging from Zainy beside him. She smiled radiantly pointing at the interceptors. Turning to Duncan, she made the Realdom's sign of victory.[201]

He smiled back, placing a fist over his chest, the Veritian way of saying *I love you*. He stared at her as Zeenthy positioned himself behind Zainy. Clara looked so beautifully human.

'The chamber,' Duncan said to himself once more. He had correctly surmised that when Clara was trying to pull him out, the energy discharge from the trans-universal chamber had set off the process of transformation of her *tori* features through his hands. What Duncan did not know yet was that, although Clara's complexion was truly acquiring a warm earthly trait, neither the chamber nor his own quickening powers could have ever switched any born-genetic microstructure into another.

While immersed in the *realitic* field of the trans-universal chamber, Clara and Duncan had made *realitic* contact. They had met in their one humanity; they had found their common origin, and as it happened, Clara's true appearance had begun to emerge.

---

201 The Realdom's sign of victory consisted of putting both forearms arms on one's chest in the shape of an X, fists closed.

About the Author

Author Daniel Liut is an aeronautical engineer with a PhD in engineering mechanics from Virginia Tech. He has always had an interest in science, languages, and philosophy, as well as a passion for fantasy and science fiction. His love for nature occasionally takes him skiing, or surfing the mild waves of the Delaware beaches. But it is at home, by the Chesapeake Bay, where both family and nature merge as a quiet source of inspiration.